WITH
IMMEDIATE EFFECT...

A Satire on Office Life and Business

Philip Algar

TRAFFORD

Printed in Victoria, BC, Canada

Note for Librarians: a cataloguing record for this book that includes Dewey Decimal Classification and US Library of Congress numbers is available from the Library and Archives of Canada. The complete cataloguing record can be obtained from their online database at:
www.collectionscanada.ca/amicus/index-e.html
ISBN 1-4120-2937-6

TRAFFORD

This book was published *on-demand* in cooperation with Trafford Publishing. On-demand publishing is a unique process and service of making a book available for retail sale to the public taking advantage of on-demand manufacturing and Internet marketing. On-demand publishing includes promotions, retail sales, manufacturing, order fulfilment, accounting and collecting royalties on behalf of the author.

Offices in Canada, USA, UK, Ireland, and Spain
book sales for North America and international:
Trafford Publishing, 6E–2333 Government St.
Victoria, BC V8T 4P4 CANADA
phone 250 383 6864   toll-free 1 888 232 4444
fax 250 383 6804   email to orders@trafford.com
book sales in Europe:
Trafford Publishing (UK) Ltd., Enterprise House, Wistaston Road Business Centre
Crewe, Cheshire CW2 7RP UNITED KINGDOM
phone 01270 251 396   local rate 0845 230 9601
facsimile 01270 254 983   orders.uk@trafford.com
order online at:
www.trafford.com/robots/04-0765.html

10   9   8   7   6   5   4   3   2

Chapter 1

It was an unexpectedly sunny and hot Sunday in mid April 2002, the sort of day when even the most dedicated of kamikaze pilots would have had second thoughts about flying a mission. The cloudless sky was deep blue, the birds were twittering approvingly, butterflies fluttered silently but purposefully and Henry's Copsewold home was being demolished.

He stood impotently in the lounge, staring at a recently-cut lawn, wondering why this should be happening. Henry Perkins, introvert and innocent, had just passed his 55th birthday and was beginning to realise that his life was lacking, well, life. More immediately, he must do something to stop the damage. What? As usual, when lacking the spirit to respond to troubling circumstances, he rationalised his inaction. It would all be over soon so why exacerbate a potentially difficult situation?

Mrs Jill Perkins, eight years younger than Henry, brown-eyed, auburn haired and slim, still attractive despite her addiction to clothes favoured by ethnically-minded octogenarians, emerged from the kitchen to ask Henry to tell the tribe that lunch was nearly ready. He nodded.

"Why should I have to pretend that our home is not under attack? We must say something about it."

"Just tell them that lunch is ready, then they'll come in. Really, Henry, I've told you thousands of times not to exaggerate..." Her words were interrupted by the sound of breaking glass.

They rushed into the garden and were met by Henry's brother, Peter. He and his family were paying their spring visit. Until recently, Sheila, an attractive red-haired 14 year old, had helped her brother, Jeffrey, an impish-looking 10 year old, to create havoc. Today she merely urged her brother to greater excesses, hoping that his activities would promote an interesting row between their father and kindly but weak uncle.

Peter, younger and brighter than Henry, had been to university. Indeed, although their parents had saved hard to send Henry to a minor public school, Peter, who had secured a scholarship, was their mother's obvious favourite. His shameless exploitation of this had always irked Henry. After Oxford, Peter, six foot tall, distinguished and looking successful long before he was, embarked on a profitable career, buying and renovating old houses. Henry mused that Jeffrey would soon be able to knock down even the most resolute building, thus saving his father the bother of hiring contractors. The tribe lived some 50 miles away and this prevented more frequent meetings and thus helped to preserve a reasonable friendship.

Life had been hard for the young Henry. The family had lived in an early 20th century terraced house which lacked adequate heating and, in the winter, the inside of the bedroom windows frequently became severely frosted. Henry never asked why, unlike his friends' families, they lacked a car or television set. He knew that the answer was the expenditure on his schooling as he was frequently urged to "show some gratitude" but, only a child, he did not know how to react to this. Later, as his father was promoted and as Henry's years at public school ended, money became easier: central heating was installed and a modest television set, black and white, and a small car, black, joined the family. Peter took this for granted and Henry remained mildly resentful that his brother had enjoyed a more lax upbringing amid greater comfort.

"That greenhouse of yours isn't safe" barked Peter. "Poor little Jeffrey's just fallen off the roof and it's a wonder that he hasn't been cut to ribbons." Peter's wife, Carol, nodded agreement, aping a puppet politician alongside a minister during a televised parliamentary question time. She was austere-looking and had a pinched face. That is not to suggest that it had been stolen: few would have wanted it as a gift. It just seemed that she lacked sufficient skin to fully cover her mean-looking features.

Sheila, exuding innocence, giggled infectiously. She always enjoyed these visits to uncle Henry because he was so tolerant. Jeffrey wouldn't be allowed to behave like this at home so he indulged himself, confident that his father would always defend him. It would be fun if her father and uncle had a row but it seemed that today was not to be the day, although Uncle Henry, who did seem very cross, was becoming more

6

assertive. Although she was already a teenager, she would visit for as long as possible as she sensed that, one day, there could be a seriously interesting encounter between her father and uncle, assuming that Jeffrey remained boisterous. She would ensure that he did.

Peter asked Jeffrey if he was all right. He was but confessed to being a little sore. "That's hardly surprising. You should have realised that Uncle Henry's old greenhouse had seen better days and couldn't support your weight."

Henry opted for the least hostile of potential responses. He didn't want to antagonise his brother who had always bettered him in any quarrels and Henry hated arguments and bad feelings. He was close to being a coward but he knew the value of saying little, even whilst being condemned for having a greenhouse which mysteriously fell apart when a heavily-booted and well-built young boy jumped up and down on the roof, understandably believing that it was a trampoline. Clearly, Henry should have erected a notice, saying that "this edifice, despite any appearance to the contrary, is not a trampoline but a greenhouse, the main constituent of which is glass".

A more tactful person than Peter might have refrained from subsequently noting that by demolishing the roof, "clearly in need of replacement", albeit a little sooner than Henry might have wished, Jeffrey had actually saved him some work. Surprisingly, there was no demand for compensation for services rendered in removing the roof or for counselling fees to assist Jeffrey to overcome his undoubted trauma.

Instead, Henry was denounced by his brother for "allowing" Jeffrey to risk such serious injury. The diffident Henry, seizing on a pause in the indictment, began what passed for his defence.

"No, I'm sorry, I'm sorry, oh no, no. Me allow him? No, I'm sorry, I can't accept that. I was in the lounge at the time and, unless I've missed something, I thought that you were his father. It's a bit of a clue that Jeffrey has lived with you all his life. A pretty generous gesture, if you ask me, if he's not your son. If I'm wrong, and we're responsible for Jeffrey, I should be told. I really believed that we didn't have a family but I suppose that we can all make mistakes. I just think that I'd have known about it. No, sorry, I know it's old-fashioned, but I thought that parents should still accept some responsibility for their offspring."

Sheila looked at him encouragingly. Emboldened because Peter had not reacted, and surprised at the unaccustomed vigour of his own response, Henry continued "anyway, he shouldn't have been up there and he should know better at his age. Look at the damage that he has caused. It won't be cheap having that lot repaired". He didn't expect any cash from his brother and no offer was made. All that came was some kind of grudging apology which, in any other relationship, would have been deemed totally inadequate.

Jill looked inquisitively at her spouse, surprised at the vigour of his defence, half-expecting more but the matter seemed closed. At least Henry had not suggested that the roof was in need of repair anyway and that it was good that children today still had some spirit. A few years ago, that would have been his reaction. Was he becoming just a mite more assertive? Jill tolerated the annual spring visit with commendable but polite silence, conversing only when necessary to avoid seeming impolite. Her main regret was that when she and Henry visited Peter's house, usually just before Christmas, lacking offspring, they could hardly wreak the physical havoc inflicted on their home. She had to confine herself to re-assuring Peter and Carol, in response to the unasked question, that the required repairs, "after your spring visit" had been made "although they were a lot more expensive than we feared". The most that she had ever done was to pretend to wipe her muddy shoes before walking into the lounge and she felt guilty for the rest of the visit.

Jill had met Henry when she was working, as a temp, in his department in Broadoak Oil during a summer break from university. After a few years of steady but unspectacular friendship, they married in 1976. Her father, a successful senior manager in an engineering company, had retired very early but both her parents had been killed in a car crash just after her wedding to Henry. Jill, the only child, had expected to receive the bulk of her parents' assets, but was dumbfounded when she discovered that a large sum had been left to the local zoo. According to her father's will, he had enjoyed many happy hours at the zoo after decades of dealing with people. He was particularly complimentary about the hippopotamuses, which reminded him of one of his (unidentified) relatives, and the monkeys, more intelligent than most of his erstwhile colleagues.

Jeffrey, although not cut, had been sufficiently shaken to remain relatively peaceful for the rest of the visit, apart from kicking Henry on the ankle during the delayed lunch. Retaliating for once, Henry was agreeably surprised at the apparent impact that an elderly slipper could make on a youthful and grazed shin. However, a careless lunge by Jeffrey resulted in his tomato juice being spilled on a white rug and Carol's cavalier comment that it now looked like an Arsenal footballer's shirt did little to calm Henry or Jill, struggling to say nothing. Jeffrey disagreed, pointing out that the rug lacked any advertisements.

Some adverse thoughts from Jeffrey about the implications for his long-term health, caused by eating beef, did not influence his short-term appetite. Indeed, apart from scoffing his generous portion he also finished what Sheila could not manage.

The usual lunchtime conversational topics were covered. Henry confirmed that their annual holidays, once again, would be taken in Westhaven, on the south coast, which provoked Peter to ask why they always went there. "Perhaps you like being the youngest male in the town? How many times have you been there?" Jill, heartily bored by the resort, said "too damned often". Peter and Carol were planning a motoring holiday in New England in the fall. "That's autumn, you know." "Yes, we do know" mumbled Henry.

The weather then came in for typically British scrutiny before Carol, feeling obliged to speak, revealed that she had recently read an article on population trends which said that the UK population will fall which would be bad for the economy and that we'll all probably be much poorer.

Carol's education was confined to what she had gleaned whilst serving behind a Boots counter and she had then assumed the views that she felt should accompany wealth. "I think it's because too many married couples decide not to have families. It's everyone's duty to have children. Some selfish people don't have children because they know that it's so expensive. Apparently, the cost of bringing up a child is now at least £100,000. Knowing what it would cost didn't stop us, did it darling? Childless couples ought to be more severely taxed and the money should go to families who want more children but can't afford them."

Carol often embarrassed her husband by unthinkingly opening her mouth which was so small that it seemed to be the result of an afterthought, despite the frequent insertion of a foot. Visibly embarrassed, Peter struggled for something to say.

A silent Henry, studying the carpet, felt Jill bristle. Many years ago, they had decided that they could not afford children immediately but a few months later they learned that they could not have their own family. They both rationalised it at the time but never discussed it after the initial shock. Even now, Henry felt almost a physical pain whenever recalling that he would never be called "daddy", would never feel an infant's clammy hand seeking his for reassurance and would never see a child, his child, their child, grow up.

Jill reacted fiercely. "Has it ever occurred to you that there might be other reasons, that some couples who want children can't have them? The trouble with you is that money is everything. You forget that much of our taxes goes to finance education, or what passes for education these days under that spineless party of yours which is more interested in looking trendy and finding jobs for its cronies than doing anything positive. Education these days is a waste of money. Many children are ignorant and ill-mannered and for years parents haven't bothered to exercise any kind of control. They think that their main responsibility is to put a colour television in their children's bedrooms."

Henry noticed that the reference to the provision of televisions in children's bedrooms provoked a meaningful look from Sheila who was enjoying the unexpected exchange.

Perkins, the potential peacemaker, said that he didn't think, that, like all generalisations, Jill's comments were entirely fair but, seeing his wife's expression, hastily added that many people would agree with what she had said. His well-intentioned intervention forced Peter to disagree with what his wife had said but, lamely, he noted that "we all live in a free country, so Carol can say what she likes and, frequently, when she opens her mouth, it's only to change feet." This apparent

10

joke eased the atmosphere and the incident passed without further acrimony.

The occasional post-prandial incident, the noise and the unaccustomed heat meant that by 7 o'clock Henry and Jill were not sorry when Peter and Carol announced that they really ought to be going. However, the usual ritual was initiated with the routine round of falsely sincere requests to stay a little longer. "Have another cup of tea and give the roads time to clear." Peter then outlined various routes home and he generously included all the relevant road numbers, junctions and pub names. Henry, who only knew about the M25, suffered in silence. Eventually, it was agreed that Henry and Jill "must come and see us before the bad weather sets in again".

The family retreated, leaving a tired and angry Henry to contemplate the mess and to take a pill or two to alleviate what was his biggest headache since their last visit. Although the tribe always visited on a Sunday, the saga began on Saturday and normality was only restored by Monday evening.

Henry enjoyed Saturdays. He did nothing but did it well and with commendable spirit. Yesterday morning, the temperature had soared to record highs, persuading today's tabloids to employ the word "phew" some three months ahead of schedule. The broadsheets took the temperature as yet more evidence that global warming was already present and offered articles on how nasty foreign insects could change our way of life whilst the nation sipped good quality wine produced in the Highlands of Scotland.

Henry and Jill had sacrificed Saturday morning to shopping. His protests, that sufficient food was being bought to feed the Chinese army on prolonged manoeuvres, the duration of which might even suggest an excursion into North Korea, were ignored. Routine weekly shopping excursions were bad enough because Mrs Perkins, on being confronted with a shop, viewed it as an intellectual challenge to think of something that she needed "desperately". Henry had become accustomed to this and had even contemplated taking her to a shop dedicated exclusively to the sale of bagpipes, the noise from which they both loathed. However, some sixth sense had induced caution and the trip never took place.

After shopping, the remainder of the day was given to "cleaning and tidying up". Apart from applying the vacuum cleaner to carpets that were already clean and dusting furniture on which no dust had landed, the operation involved moving frequently-used and favourite objects from where they were traditionally kept to apparently safe hiding places. Subsequently, many hours were wasted, hunting for them. Henry always complained about the cleaning and tidying, arguing that the family made such a mess that their work would be undone in minutes. Jill, inwardly acknowledging the logic of this argument, nevertheless maintained that was no reason for their not bothering. The house must start the day clean and tidy. Furthermore, as Mrs Perkins always observed, never having seen a porcine quadruped's domicile, except at a range of 100 metres from the A303, "just because they make the place look like a pig sty, that's no excuse for not tidying up before they come". Henry grunted as befitted someone who would soon be inhabiting a sty.

Mr and Mrs Perkins were sitting in the conservatory, relaxing with a drink. They were not sharing it: life was not yet that difficult. Jill opened the debate and began by accepting that it was only an annual visitation. "I know the children are trying and, frankly, Carol was as bad but I'm not going to let it upset me any more. Although the greenhouse looks as if it's has been the victim of collateral damage, inflicted by the highly skilled and internationally-respected US military, I think that we can fix it ourselves."

Henry smiled wanly. His wife of 26 years, whom he still occasionally introduced as his first wife, "to keep her alert", was trying to calm him. However, it was not just the damaged greenhouse, or even the soiled dining room rug that upset him. Yes, the children, especially Jeffrey, were very trying. Indeed, he would love to see the brutes tried and then locked up because of the damage to the house. What really riled him was that their visit made him so tired.

When hopes of having a family vanished, Jill had joined a local company with interests in conferences and publishing. The firm had grown and Jill's role had expanded. She now had a senior position but she played it down because she never wanted her husband to feel intellectually or financially inferior.

Jill then offered a few barbed comments on the number of repeats on television, the meaning of life and the difficulties of gardening on clay. In some ways, Henry was not too displeased at these periods of silence, for, apart from his work at Broadoak Oil, and the delays occasioned to his trains, he contributed little to routine conversation. He would never have won any competitions for small talk, and, as the years passed, his ability at big talk was exposed as similarly feeble. Only weather forecasters, cricket, the blathering of ignorant politicians and flagrant injustice really aroused him. Being British, he seldom had to practice the art of small talk on most of his fellow commuters because they had not been introduced.

He was irked by the fact that the fine weekend, the first for weeks, and doubtless the last for months, as the cricket season had just begun, had been wasted. When young, he had enjoyed some success in club cricket, reaching the second eleven at a time when his club fielded five teams. Now he was just a spectator. The rest of his spare time was taken up with photography, gardening and watching television which enabled him to participate in discussions in the office. He did not have many friends outside work but counted on a few acquaintances locally and at the cricket club for social intercourse.

Henry had worked hard at school, with little encouragement, and left with six "O" levels in 1964, when he was just 17. He had no idea on careers and, on his father's recommendation, sought opportunities in big companies. Apparently they offered more job security and the best in that and other respects, according to Perkins senior, was the oil industry. Henry, if accepted, had a job for life, providing he behaved himself. After a few abortive interviews for really interesting jobs, Henry accepted a junior clerical position with Broadoak Oil in London. Following weeks of relentless tedium, doing work that only an imaginative devil could have invented, Perkins decided to study. Working in his spare time, and shunning parental advice to "go out and enjoy yourself", which always prompted the question of where, how and with whom, he secured four more "O" levels and three "A" levels. Thus encouraged, he studied for an economics degree but, having failed in part one, he abandoned his efforts and remained bitter at what he frequently called the Wasted Years. When Henry was still young, the emphasis in business was on experience: now that he was experienced, the emphasis was on youth.

When he admitted defeat, he was only 24 but, even then, he seemed chastened and resigned to a life of steady mediocrity. One colleague called him one of nature's clerks which did not seem unfair. Nature had blessed him in one respect: he was moderately handsome. His hairline was receding slowly and his long nose was designed for wearing authoritative glasses, which he used for close reading. When enclosed in a business suit, he looked more managerial than most directors.

Henry's acquiescent approach to life and people, determined in childhood, had been maintained through his school years. Regularly reminded of his parents' financial sacrifice, he had taken great care to avoid upsetting them, even when being falsely accused of errant behaviour by his favoured brother. There was much to be said for the quiet life, even now, if the price was submission. His one indulgence was a dry sense of humour but he kept it under control, lest he upset anyone. Having been told by his father that he was lucky to have a job with a very large oil company, as he had no "real" qualifications, he tried to work hard without upsetting anyone. His failure to finish his degree was the last blow to his pride and the modest ambition that remained soon evaporated as did his self-confidence and self-esteem.

In his early days, the company had regularly promoted allegedly bright young Oxbridge graduates ahead of Perkins. His pay had risen encouragingly at that time, and ahead of inflation more recently, but, although his job title changed occasionally, Henry had never been promoted. What mattered now, however, was that he still had a job, however boring, and a regular income that enabled him to look after Jill, his home and his few inexpensive hobbies. That might be an appalling waste of life but Henry had long since accepted that his lot was destined to be modest. Whatever the frustrations, he would not follow the example of an Egyptian lawyer who protested against his company's failure to promote him by removing and igniting his clothes.

The unhappy Henry had to retain his job for another five years, after which he would collect a reasonable pension at the age of 60. It was imperative that he stayed because no other company would want a single-company man in his fifties. This meant adopting an even lower profile in order to survive but this was difficult because oil companies, like big companies in many industries, obsessed by short-term thinking and in thrall to the accountants, were shedding thousands of people. The last few years of work were crucially important to his longer-term finances. The trouble was that his excuse about staying for a "decent pension" was one that he had used to himself for at least 15 years. The longer he stayed with Broadoak, the more logical the excuse seemed. Henry had worked for the one firm since leaving school, and apart from the pensions issue, he was frightened about working elsewhere. He felt that he knew nothing except how his company operated and this was hardly a commercial asset on the open market, especially as everything, except him, was changing. As usual, his powers of rationalisation came to the rescue.

What particularly riled Henry, although he would never say so out loud, was that these unthinking, financially comfortable and tactless chief executives would always describe their staff as their greatest asset before disposing of another few thousand. This was dangerous. He was beginning to think for himself. Years of compliance must be maintained if the pension target was to be achieved. Henry knew that Jill was doing well but they had always assumed that he alone was the provider. That concept was so deeply rooted that Henry always overlooked his wife's possible contribution to their retirement funds.

Now, things were becoming worse and his stance of silence was under threat. He was thinking more objectively than in his earlier career and was critical of the few companies which worked in countries where human rights were not only being ignored but were being suppressed by the military with the help of oil revenue which was based on western investment. Henry felt strongly about injustice, suppression and intolerance and it seemed to him that some industrialists were indifferent to human rights as they rationalised their presence where they thought they could make money for their shareholders. Although loath to admit it, he abhorred his boring job and company more with each passing week so he really appreciated weekends. The only mitigating factor was that he had a few friends at work with whom he enjoyed an undemanding but agreeable relationship.

Henry and Jill had cautiously moved up the housing ladder, although his prudence on matters financial, occasionally and unkindly labelled as stinginess by his next of kin, had resulted in a relatively low mortgage. Henry had failed to take advantage of inflation so their homes, over the years, although most desirable, as estate agents would have averred, were smaller than those of his contemporaries. However, an elderly aunt of Jill's had died, leaving the Perkins a large sum which allowed them to pay off their remaining mortgage and to buy a larger house. They lacked the money for an ostentatious lifestyle but liked their large and comfortable house and garden which they had never expected to be able to afford. The real joy was the garden. In the front, a row of trees hid the house from the semi-rural road and reduced the noise from the modest amount of traffic. Henry enjoyed pottering in the back garden which was dominated by oak trees which provided shelter when the sun was a problem and were themselves a problem when Henry and Jill wanted to sit in the sun. Jill was the expert, planting, cutting and generally encouraging long-named but short-of-stature plants to thrive.

Henry sat back in the conservatory, sighed wistfully as he cradled a Bloody Mary, and glanced at the Sunday paper. Apparently, some 20,000 different kinds of bugs now lived in our homes, including blood-sucking bed bugs. Henry wondered who counted them and suddenly his own job seemed less boring. Another article claimed that work was the best part of our lives. Perkins sneered and braced himself for another truly mind-numbing week of unmitigated boredom. After all, he thought, all weeks are the same, aren't they?

Chapter 2

Henry was shaving before returning to jail after his weekend parole. He used an electric razor because it provided a safe and efficient shave whilst allowing him to think. Today's topic was his future. Seeing his wealthier brother had, once again, confirmed his own failure. Unlike Peter, he had no pride in achievement: all he had achieved was corporate longevity.

Now 55, and a hard worker over many decades, his remaining ambition was to survive the corporate lunacies which deemed that men of his age were no longer relevant. Henry feared redundancy. What could he do but was he prepared to remain the docile schoolboy in long trousers? He glanced at the mirror to confirm that he had done a reasonable job and saw a pleasant, agreeable face, dominated by large brown eyes which conveyed a sense of innocence. He had avoided putting on much weight and, being about five foot ten, looked younger than his years. He always tried to dress well, having been brought up in the belief that it was important to look smart for work and, in order to do your best, to have a cooked breakfast before going out. However, this latter injunction had long since been ignored and, if the price of suits continued to soar, his appearance would succumb to economic reality.

Henry pondered the question he feared most. "On your last day of work will you be able to look yourself in the mirror and say that you did what you really wanted?" He sighed, pursed his lips and shook his head. He had known the answer for many years. Having failed to secure his degree, he was angry that he had gambled his early adult life and lost. There could be no more gambles. He must not speculate, masochistically, on what might have happened if he had persevered. He was also dogged by the persistently-haunting experience of failure. The anguish was becoming ever sharper and he could do nothing to lessen it.

Jill, using the en-suite, was also deep in thought. Organising successful business conferences was becoming increasingly difficult as most industries were either in or feared recession. Was the heyday of conferences over? Why should expensive executives pay large sums of money to sit in a darkened room, listening to an incompetent speaker droning on about something on which the audience was often better informed? Interesting speakers were now rare because employers insisted that they spent their time exclusively at work. She was also worried about Henry. Although he seldom discussed it, she knew that he hated his job. It was better than unemployment but how long would he survive as industry was shovelling all those aged 55 or more on to the scrap heap? Then what would he do? In the last two years, her own salary had exceeded Henry's although Jill had not told him this, to avoid embarrassment, and she had invested in some medium-term bonds but it would have been unwise to cash them in prematurely.

It was time for breakfast, or, more accurately, coffee. Henry, already in the kitchen, poured out her traditional black beverage and turned on the television. They sipped steadfastly and silently. The weather forecaster thanked the programme anchorman excessively for his simple introduction before beginning his patter.

"Good morning folks, I hope that you all had a good weekend." Henry snorted. He was not a folk. "The day will be mostly quiet and cloudy although we expect the sun to break through from time to time, but only if the cloud cover is dispersed."

Henry asked if a noisy weather day was when it thundered.

"Most of the country will enjoy some dry spells. Temperatures will be below normal, so take a coat when you go out, but spits and spots of rain could break out anywhere, especially during daylight hours or early in the evening and they might later be intermingled with longer periods of wet weather, especially in the south and west. The north will see organised showers, except in those areas that will remain dry. In the east of the country, unlike the west, which might just escape with only an occasional pulse, the showers may merge to give longer periods of rain, followed by accumulations of wet weather. So, remember folks, take your umbrella, especially in the south east, where our radar shows that it is already drizzling."

Henry, living in the south east, growled, moved the television set 90 degrees as the sun was now shining brightly on the screen, and asked who organises the showers.

"Quiet Henry, I want to listen."

"The outlook for tomorrow is for the weather to remain much as we expect it today although there could be a radical change if different conditions prevail."

Henry exploded. "Just what did the moron say and how dare the patronising oaf tell us what clothes to wear? Why didn't he recommend the weight of our underwear?"

Jill, ignoring Henry's outburst, which was more predictable than the weather, asked if he wanted a lift to the station.

"No thanks, I think I'll walk today. The exercise will keep me slim, young and desirable."

She smiled, patted him on the head, thus reinforcing his view that he was still not really perceived as an adult, and brushed his cheek with hers in what passed for a kiss in a 26 year old marriage. "See you tonight." "Yes, have a good day." "You too."

A few minutes later, Henry put his cup and saucer on the drainer, picked up his brief case, inserted a novel and the newspaper, shut the front door and marched out to waste another day of his remaining life doing unnecessary and boring things for irritating and self-important people who regarded their colleagues as human resources.

On a fine day, Henry enjoyed the short walk to the station. As he walked to the gate, some squirrels, which Henry regarded as up-market rats, bounded across his path. Manfully, he ignored them, turned left and strolled down the lane to the station. Some sheep were strolling round in the field opposite chez-Perkins and the remaining clouds were beginning to fade, allowing the early morning sun to illuminate the more distant woods and hills. In the foreground, the cows were already out, grazing contentedly. Henry wondered how anyone could know they were contented? How would cows show bad temper or even a mild irritation? By behaving like bulls in a china shop?

Few of the houses on his walk to the station were visible from the lane as they hid behind tall fir trees and rampant laurel bushes. This was to protect the gardens from the wind, (Mrs Perkins) or to hide the house and occupants from view. (Mr Perkins).

Henry and Jill were fortunate to live in such an attractive area. The railway station, being one of the few in the area, was well-patronised but most passengers, or customers as they were now called, drove to the station and left their cars in the car park, which, astonishingly, was still free. Henry attributed this to bureaucratic incompetence, rather than generosity or an example of an integrated transport policy.

Usually, Henry would have been irritated at having to go to work on a fine day after a wasted weekend. He had to serve another five days, without remission for supine behaviour, before becoming a human being again. However, Henry accepted that he was physically tired, so, for once, going to the office was almost tolerable because he could remain sedentary for most of the day.

A car passed and Henry noticed that it carried a notice indicating that caution was required as the vehicle had show dogs on board. Given this information, what, precisely, should he do? As a pedestrian, should he leap into the hedge, doff his hat or lower his head in respect? If driving, was he supposed to give way or be prepared lest the highly-strung dogs suddenly attacked the driver? He must make a notice for his own car, saying "Caution: human beings on board". It was as silly as those local government vehicles which bore signs saying that they were "working for you, working for your community", implying that their motivation was solely altruistic. Perkins' council tax demand implied otherwise.

As usual, the walk to the station passed uneventfully. Nothing much ever happened locally although the headline in a recent edition of the village newspaper, in what was doubtless a world exclusive although, modestly, it was not so claimed, was that nine pigs had escaped in the village centre but that the "errant porkers" were eventually rounded up by the driver of a passing Volvo and the town clerk. Henry wondered if it was a saloon or an estate car and he also speculated on the role of the town clerk. Was he charged with rounding up stray porcine quadrupeds, or indeed, other animals, or was he merely in the area at the time and had proved to be a kindly cove? Another favourite edition was the page one APOLOGY to a woman whose name and age were both revealed. The paper wished to express its regret for incorrectly giving her age as 35, not 34, in the report on how some vital elastic failed at a crucial moment during her wedding.

The local railway station was a tribute to Victorian architecture. Although repaired and altered occasionally, the basic design would have been recognised by travellers, sorry customers, from many decades ago. Henry bought his weekly season ticket, made his usual joke about wanting to buy a ticket, not the entire network, and joined his intending fellow passengers.

A new notice dominated the end of the platform. It just said **Pickpockets Operate at this Station.** It was presented in the same boastful way as information on cheap day returns. Not every station has pickpockets! We do! Henry, irritated by the indiscriminate use of upper case letters, was beginning to escape from the real world and was sliding into the comfortable refuge offered by his immature but seldom articulated humour. Then he noticed that last week's new sign, indicating that **Busking is not Allowed at this Station**, had been changed to read **Bonking is Allowed at this Station.** He was also intrigued by the notice that told passengers not to leave unattended luggage alone. If.. no, never mind.

Oddly, the sign showing the station name, Greenreed, had been replaced. An even larger sign bore the legend: **Welcome to Greenreed**. Henry, anxious to seek assurance for his views and shunning the necessity of a formal introduction, such was the seriousness of the change, spoke to an elderly man standing close by.

"I see that we've a new sign but it's wrong."

"How? It looks all right to me. What do you mean?"

"Well, I think that they, the railway authorities, speaking on behalf of their employees working here, are issuing the welcome to you and me. In other words, it originates from them and is intended for us."

The elderly man looked blankly at Henry. This was not a good way to start the week. "Of course, that's what they mean" he replied, burying himself inside his *Financial Times*.

Henry persisted. "Yes, but they don't say 'from', they say 'to'. My point is that nobody is called Greenreed and I'm sure that even if a few people are called that, and I trust you're not, sir, it must be intended that the welcome is not confined to those afflicted with such an odd name. After all, I assume that the same applies to Paddington. Apart from a bear from Peru, I imagine that there aren't too many people lumbered with such a moniker. Let's think of other examples. It would be very silly to welcome people called Manchester Piccadilly, wouldn't it? Whoever heard of someone called Bristol Temple Meads? Nobody would endorse any discrimination by surnames, would we, so the welcome should be from, not to, Greenreed to all passengers."

The FT shuffled away, and, convinced that he had unwittingly participated in a new and sadistic television programme, looked for the hidden cameras. Henry glanced at his erstwhile companion who so resembled a fox that walking in the countryside when hounds were being exercised could have been dangerous.

Having enjoyed this banter, Perkins toyed with the idea of asking the ticket inspector, whenever the train eventually arrived, what the train opposed. This insane concept was promoted by having heard numerous claims to the effect that "this train is for…" What Henry wanted to know was what was it against?

Recalling the very old joke, he thought that he might even ask anyone working on the London underground system where he could find a dog. Assuming that the victim would then ask why he was making such a request, Henry would say that he wanted to ascend on the escalator but could not as it said that "dogs must be carried on the escalator" and, sadly, he didn't seem to have one with him. Such puerile but controlled lunacy, seldom revealed to his colleagues or even to Jill, kept Henry alive.

Bert, the garrulous and elderly local stationmaster, dispenser of tickets and in charge of just himself after another painful bout of redundancies, enjoyed talking. He had attempted to ensnare Henry in a conversation but Mr Perkins neither heard nor saw him as he approached. There were two big advantages of being cloaked in *The Times*. You could hide behind it whilst simultaneously impressing those fellow passengers who still perceived it to be the country's leading paper. Bert often started a chat by raising an interesting comment on when the world was likely to end or the future of the UK rail network, which, for him, was the same issue. Then, when the trap was sprung, the hapless victim was treated to a detailed dissertation on the difficulty of collecting the litter that always swirled around the station.

When the train failed to arrive on time, Henry's fellow passengers decided that the presence of an alien leaf, probably in Scotland, was responsible. Then Bert's voice crackled out a virtually inaudible message over the loudspeaker system. Only the last sentence was clear. It seemed that apologies were being offered for a delay and that the train would arrive in 15 minutes, "that is one five minutes".

Henry believed that incomprehensible announcements were intended to hide the latest disaster from the passengers and to encourage strangers to speak to each other. After the last metallic noises had faded, there was always an instant discussion amongst the travellers, to determine if anyone had actually understood the message. Perkins maintained that those who made such incomprehensible announcements had been trained to make noises that sounded like words but which were just noises. As, generously, he was wont to explain to fellow customers, he could not believe that an organisation, responsible for millions of lives each year, was so technically retarded that it could not convey messages clearly over a public address system if it really so wished.

Another theory was that when the metallic voice apologised for a delay, and was intelligible, the train would be at the platform, not in one five minutes, but in three, repeat three. Henry was pleased to note, that, at least this time, he was proved correct. The intending passengers, braced for a long wait, were soon gratified by the train's unexpectedly early arrival and thus decided against writing angry letters about frequent delays.

Because it was a Monday morning, and some week-enders were travelling back to town, from their rural retreats further down the line, the usual six coach train had been reduced to three. The train was nearly full but Henry managed to secure one of the few remaining empty seats. The journey to London took the passengers through lush and varied countryside, characterised by occasional farms, rivers, fields and woods. Sometimes, the trundling train would stop at those little stations that stupid politicians, decades before, had carelessly overlooked in their zeal to rob the country of a reasonable system. Lanes meandered lazily over the hills on both sides of the track and the train, seldom exceeding 30 miles an hour, seemed determined that the passengers should enjoy the scenery and the names of some of the small stations, long since abandoned but still wearing proud but mildly eccentric names, the origin of which had been forgotten years ago. Henry particularly liked Blaircumbrown, Widdy Howard, Hague Major and Thatcher's Halt, which was closed only in November 1990.

Henry wondered what the week would bring. He had said nothing to Jill but rumours suggested that Human Resources planned another cull. Henry feared the worst but hoped for the best. His reverie was disturbed by an unruly young child of the male persuasion, dressed entirely in yellow, looking like a bad-tempered banana, running up and down the crowded coach and shouting support for something called man u. He was followed at a sedate pace by a young man, whose badge on his dark blue uniform suggested he was purveying comestibles of the very highest quality. Instead, he was pushing a trolley, loaded with elderly sandwiches and refreshments at very contemporary prices. His plaintive cry suggested that he was accustomed to failure. "Anyone want any refreshments, at all, at all?"

The ticket inspector approached. "Any tickets to be checked since Greenreed, please?" Henry had long since thought that the man was a frustrated school teacher. He examined each ticket carefully, commenting "excellent, well done, fine, thanks very much, good, well done..."

Before he could begin reading his newspaper, Mr Perkins was induced into conversation by a scarf and anorak, combined in one anonymous but perspiring male, the shape of whose head resembled a badly baked Hovis loaf. After the exchange of some frank comments on the weather, it was soon agreed that it was likely to stay fine as everyone was back at work. There was also unanimity on the proposition that last weekend had been very hot and that the very mild winter in the nearby village of Tuckers Treat, apparently favoured as a residence by the anorak, proved that global warming had, indeed, arrived.

Turning to economic matters, the anorak wanted to know if Perkins was aware of the causes of high unemployment? Henry sometimes called himself an economist, although like some hospital carpenters and porters, who, according to the tabloid newspapers, were now undertaking operations, because they needed the money, he was unqualified. Although he had failed part one of the economics degree, he contended this was "a darn sight further than most people". When asked at which university he had studied, Perkins was wont to tap his nose grotesquely, in conspiratorial and confidential fashion, before replying "the university of life". This immediately ingratiated himself with the unqualified but alienated him from those who, having studied the subject for some years, deeply resented the implication that such endeavour was unnecessary, as, of course, their consistently inaccurate predictions confirmed.

Before Perkins could reply, the anorak had launched forth afresh. "Money is the cause of all the trouble and people's concern with money starts when a commuter is put on their desks." Henry thought rapidly about some of his fellow commuters and who he would like to put on his desk. His choice would be the blonde whom he had seen almost daily for six months. Recently, notwithstanding the lack of an introduction, he had smiled at her and said "good morning". Encouragingly, although Henry, of course, lacked any motives beyond the desire to be courteous, she had replied, using precisely the words that Henry himself had employed, thus demonstrating beyond reasonable doubt that they had something in common. Perkins wondered why having a commuter on your desk promoted a desire for money and then realised that the anorak meant computer. Henry asked the anorak for more details of this interesting thesis, lest he had overlooked something rather important.

"Money leads to prostitution." Henry, now concerned that a computer could play havoc with his morals, and still vaguely intrigued at the thought of having the blonde perched on his desk, responded. It was unfortunate that, at precisely the point when the train emerged from a tunnel, his volume was so high that the entire county must have heard him ask "why does having a computer lead to prostitution"? Papers were lowered to half-mast as fellow commuters felt that this was something that merited their attention.

"No, not prostitution, destitution. How could having a computer lead to doing naughty things with girls for money?" Heads that had appeared above the parapets of the country's leading newspapers sank back and their owners resumed reading about more interesting matters such as the compensation paid to incompetent managers who had ruined their companies. Mercifully, the anorak left at the next station, Botham-cum-Willis.

As Mr Perkins opened his paper, it fell open on the page where birthdays and obituaries appeared. Some people, whose age used to be the same as his, were now younger and few of those whose obituaries appeared were older. That was not a good start to the week.

One tabloid, now being waved in his face, had two stories on the front page. Apparently, a man had killed his wife but the judge, having heard that he had been called a fat slob by his erstwhile next of kin, said that no point would be served by jailing this man. He had been provoked and killed his wife. Now he had no wife so nobody was in danger. Consequently, he ordered the man to undertake 50 hours of community service. A motorist, detected eating a sandwich at traffic lights, was less fortunate. A local magistrate, sentencing the hapless woman to three months incarceration, argued that if this habit was extended, motoring accidents could proliferate with a severe loss of life.

Mr Perkins studied his fellow passengers. As usual in April, some men remained huddled in overcoats and scarves, clearly following the dictum that it was inadvisable to cast a clout before May had yielded to June. Others had shed a few clouts and had placed overcoats and even jackets, somewhat precariously, in the overhead racks. One man, either lacking confidence in his memory or determined to become better known, had his name on his shirt pocket and on one cuff. Henry assumed that he must be an American. Many girls had reasonably assumed that the day's weather would probably be like yesterday and were dressed in a manner destined to make life hotter for their male colleagues, most of whom were imprisoned in striped suits.

Henry tired of waiting for a clout to fall from the overhead luggage shelf despite a very sharp stop at Dogfoot Mallet. He began re-folding his own paper but gave up after accidentally wrapping it around an elderly female passenger sitting on his left. Henry looked at the papers favoured by those around him. He noticed a particularly interesting article on the very page in *The Times* that he had been reading whilst waiting for the train. Why was it that even when other people were reading the same paper, they always were on a more fascinating page than he was or had been? The mystery was on a par with the fact that however many pairs of socks were inserted into a washing machine, an odd number, always below the numbers entrusted to the machine, emerged.

Most people were engrossed in the world as reflected by the so-called quality papers which dominated the reading of those on the train each day at this time of day. Henry wondered how many of his fellow passengers would even acknowledge a life outside that portrayed by their favourite newspapers.

His attention was caught by a photograph in a tabloid. The ambiguous caption was simply "April showers". It certainly seemed accurate, assuming that the young lady was really called April. Inexplicably Henry started to read the accompanying text. April, aged just 19, was a dentist's assistant and at the end of each demanding day, apparently, there was nothing that she liked more than to take a shower, seemingly whilst still wearing thigh-high boots. She intended to study in her spare time to become a barrister and she hoped one day to work for the United Nations in Africa. Perkins smiled, as much at himself for reading the text as for the banal aspirations attributed to the young lady.

The refreshment trolley had returned. Henry asked for a "white coffee with sugar, please". "With milk?" "Yes, that what makes it white." "Sorry, it's so automatic sir, here's your £2 change."

A young girl, seeing one man answer his mobile phone, said in a loud voice "look, daddy, there's a lout. You said that all people who use mobiles on trains were louts". She was shushed but later enquired whether another fellow passenger who had used the toilet twice since the last station was ill.

After a few more abortive attempts to read his paper on the swaying train, now approaching maximum speed, judging by the way in which it was keeping up with cars on a parallel road subject to a 40 miles an hour limit, Perkins finally folded his paper and put it in his brief case. He couldn't miss some of the stories that were shouting at him from other newspapers. A middle page spread in one tabloid was devoted to a court case about an individual who had stolen four locomotives and 27 coaches. The judge had told him that he had betrayed his employer's trust and that society had to be protected from people like him. Henry sided with the judge. It was important to crack down on this kind of thing now as otherwise everyone would be stealing trains and the nation would be left with an inadequate network. Thank god for someone with common sense.

A broadsheet carried a scientist's claim that some man-made fibre, if in regular contact with the skin, could cause men to become impotent. In the US, one individual, aged 70, now unable to contribute towards creating a family, had successfully sued a shirt manufacturer for $105 million. The decision was warmly welcomed by his five sons and two daughters. Some students who had flown the Union Jack from their college rooms, to celebrate an England triumph at dominoes, had been told to stop mafficking as such celebrations would upset foreign students living in the block.

Another tabloid revealed that a vicar campaigning for the restoration of family life had followed his own advice by creating families in Wales, Scotland and just outside Croydon. Several papers reported that killer bees, encouraged by the warm spring weather, another aspect of global warming, would soon land at Dover before moving, remorselessly, to the capital. They tended to attack red-haired people. A former UK foreign secretary was not worried but close friends were quoted as saying that he was taking basic, but unspecified precautions. Perkins wondered it he might become a Whig.

The government was planning to give away free toothbrushes to fight tooth decay in deprived areas, which Henry assumed to be the mouth. Another paper reported that a leading scientist wanted volunteers to help him determine whether there was such a thing as genetic laziness. Henry thought of co-operating but then decided he could not be bothered.

Two elderly ladies near Perkins were talking. Apart from a few girls, whom Henry assumed were keen secretaries, women were seldom seen on the early trains. The chatterbox and her victim, attired in a dress seemingly made from rejected wartime black-out cloth, were both probably in their seventies.

"I can't play bridge, now, not with my leg."

What did this mean? Was it because the lady was immobile, in which case why was she now on the train? Alternatively, was it because she had a secret code, involving kicking her partner to stop him or her bidding? The owner of the inadequate leg was determined to secure maximum publicity for the hapless limb. "I took it to hospital", she said, in a loud voice, as if it were some distant relative for whom she was doing a favour, "but they said there was nothing that they could do for me".

Perkins, expecting further dramatic news, following this appalling revelation, was disappointed when the victim of the monologue took advantage of the leg-owner's need to breathe and injected a medical report of her own. She, too, had been in hospital last week and she had been "as ill as she could have been". Henry marvelled that she had apparently been so close to death so recently and now, only days later, she could challenge the early part of the rush hour. What a wonderful national health service we have!

Curiosity overcame her friend.

"What was wrong?"

The response did not impress the leg. "Food poisoning?" she intoned, as if she could hardly believe her ears. "Food poisoning? What did you eat, then?"

The junior hypochondriac said that cod had caused all the trouble. The leg was not impressed.

"I've had cod many times and it's never given me any adverse affects." For some reason, she stressed the adjective, causing Henry to wonder what obvious and beneficial affects could be gleaned from the consumption of cod.

Elsewhere, one elderly man told a friend that "I spoke to him before he died". Henry admired his timing: leaving it any later could have been difficult.

A familiar platform came into view but the train came to a stuttering halt just outside the station, apparently reluctant to admit that the journey was over. The usual message was being conveyed to the customers. "This is your SENIOR train manager speaking. Welcome to Waterloo, which is our next and final station stop, repeat our next and final station stop, where the train will terminate, so will no longer be available for customer use, having terminated. Please ensure that when you leave the train you take everything, everything, with you. We are sorry that we have arrived 45, four five minutes late and apologise for any inconvenience that this might cause. The reason for the late arrival was an unscheduled union at speed between two trains ahead of us, proceeding in opposite directions and operated by another company. On behalf of myself, the customer service host and the manager, mobile comestibles, we thank you for travelling with us and hope that you all have good day. Do take care when alighting from the train on to the platform."

Because it was the rush hour, only one escalator was working and, naturally, it was the one devoted to the few passengers who wished to catch a train, rather than leave the station.

The office was only a few minutes' stroll from the station but Henry was soon enveloped in noise and the smell of diesel as he walked past the ungainly and unappealing mixture of 19th and 20th century buildings. He stopped at a cafe to buy a sandwich for breakfast. There were vast grey plastic containers, full of the things.

"Ham please, with white bread." "No problem." Henry handed over the necessary coins. "Why did you assure me so promptly after my request that there would be no difficulty in affecting the transaction? When you said that there would be no problem, I had not tendered the necessary money so, in retrospect, you may feel that your assurance was premature."

His humour, as dry as Saturday's sandwich, vanished in the smell and bustle of the English fried breakfast served by the Indian elder who at least had demonstrated an understanding of the vernacular.

Chapter 3

Keenly anticipating a rest, Henry Perkins glanced at the sun for the last time for a few hours and headed for his cell in Broadoak House.

BH was an uninspiring and ugly nine-storey building, constructed in the late fifties. If located in Eastern Europe, it would have compared unfavourably with state prisons. Listeners to a London radio programme had voted it as the office building that they would most like to see razed to the ground. Henry agreed which was why he had voted 32 times.

Hubert Bennett, the chief executive, known as HB because he was seldom sufficiently sharp, pleased with his company's newly-acquired fame, maintained that all publicity was good publicity. Indeed, he had only been narrowly dissuaded from trying to persuade a travel company from including the office on its tour of famous London landmarks. Initially, this idea had been attributed to HB's sense of humour but it was later realised that this was one of those rare occasions when he was simultaneously serious and sober. A leading designer wrote that architecture should bring a smile to peoples' faces. Henry had sent him an anonymous letter saying that Broadoak House made him laugh. The building was fusty. Elderly and smelly linoleum covered the corridors, the lifts seldom worked and the heating, lighting and ventilation systems were totally inadequate. Henry recalled the time, some 45 years ago, when his appendix had been removed in a Victorian-built hospital. All that was missing in Broadoak House was the smell of disinfectant and chloroform and starched and bustling nurses.

After the radio-inspired publicity, some building experts had visited the office and later invented the concept of a sick building, the illness of which was caused by inadequate ventilating systems which re-circulated germs. Their report was described by HB as "a major scientific advance" when many hitherto healthy employees suddenly succumbed to colds and minor illnesses.

The depressing dark brown corridor walls, on every floor except that occupied by senior management, were lined with paintings of sombre, pompous, self-important former senior executives. They hung alongside several framed and elderly certificates, indicating that the company's safety record had won recognition from an unknown organisation many years ago. Company cynics maintained that if renovations were not undertaken soon, an offer from the National Trust would surely be forthcoming and one unidentified wag had suggested to a friend in the BBC that the office and its senior inmates should feature in a programme devoted to Britain's past.

The six members of general management, including the main board directors, who occupied the whole of the eighth floor, literally saw no cause for complaint. Their own accommodation matched anything in the capital but they seldom ventured forth to other, dilapidated floors. Their colleagues always visited them and the more important meetings were held at expensive rural hotels. Discussing serious matters in the office was impractical. Phones rang, middle management needed guidance and it always seemed to be time for lunch at which, naturally, crucial decisions were taken with industry friends.

Henry glanced at the ornate table in the reception area. It was adorned by Saturday's edition of *The Times*, a paperback, *Medicine for Beginners*, and a copy of the company's irregular newspaper, *The Broadoak Oil Group Courier*, previously known as *BOG News*, which was where it was usually read. The current issue, dated March, reflected the editor's bravery. Following some sarcastic comments from junior staff, he had only used five photographs of the chief executive. This edition featured photographs of staff allegedly enjoying themselves at the Christmas party. All wore silly hats, were holding glasses and were waving their limbs around grotesquely. HB, having read an article on the virtues of staff bonding, would have been pleased to learn just how seriously some personnel were taking this concept although those who had most lustily embraced the idea did not appear in the photographs, being occupied elsewhere at the time. There was also news about the safety manager. He had been taken to hospital after tripping over a sign warning colleagues to be careful because of a loose piece of linoleum. He had stumbled, banged his head on something electrical and plunged the building into darkness for some minutes but was now recovering at home.

Henry greeted the receptionist with his usual cheery "good morning" and an enquiry about his health, which was always answered literally. However, Henry seldom heard the full response because he was on his way to the lift and another boring day.

At about 10.30 am, by which time most senior managers had arrived, the "full-time" receptionist took over. Until then, Taffy, elderly, tall, grey-haired, pink-faced and dignified, formerly a policeman in Glasgow, was on duty. Later, he became the company's odd job man. He had many tales of life in the police and was always guaranteed the attention of young male employees. Whether he was recounting the details of a minor traffic offence or a major incident, the story always ended with his discovering a young lady, who, in his own words, "was naked of course". He breathed the words as if any other condition was unthinkable. When the young Perkins first heard some of these stories, he was almost tempted to join the police. It sounded exciting and the expression, "may the force be with you" took on a new meaning.

Predictably, the lift to the sixth floor, where Perkins shared an office with seven colleagues, was not functioning so he puffed his way, increasingly slowly, up the stairs. Henry, rationing his decreasing supplies of breath, nodded and grunted early morning greetings to colleagues. Eventually, breathing heavily, he reached his destination, sat down, unwrapped his sandwich which now looked as if it had been constructed at about the same time as his nine-year old chair, and stirred the free coffee that he had persuaded the machine by the inactive lifts to yield without, for once, burning his fingers.

Perkins and his colleagues in Management Analysis Division, (MAD), occupied one of the least desirable office areas in the building because management, fearing the consequences of bomb blast during a period of political disruption, had coated the windows with a heavy dark substance which supposedly prevented the glass from shattering. Consequently, this division's part of the floor was in relative gloom for most of the day, causing the lights to be left on. MAD people, usually those who had little prospect of promotion, were given the tasks that other divisions had rejected.

Most of the company's 300 inmates worked in open-plan spaces, hidden behind the dark walls of numerous corridors. These areas were punctuated by dark green, dusty plastic plants but Henry and his colleagues operated from a small partitioned area that offered marginally more privacy for their hutches.

Being second in command, although lacking a title to prove it, Henry's box backed on to a window. Two bureaucratic barriers, formed by filing cabinets and a tall bookcase which was home for all MAD's studies over the last 15 years, separated him from his neighbours. Henry's ancient desk, facing the open side of the box, was in front of the window. When involved in heavy thinking, or even day dreaming, Henry was able to turn round 180 degrees and study his fellow workers' reflections in the window.

He stretched across to pick up a fax that was on the machine. It said that "as per the voice mail, here is a fax of my most recent e-mail sent to the refinery". Henry read it, screwed it up and lobbed it into the waste paper bin.

The division head was Jim Holmes. He was single, 62 and probably the most humourless person in the company. His face bore an uncanny resemblance to that of a garden gnome that had consistently incurred the wrath of an angry cat. Although the official retirement age was 65, Holmes had long since been anticipating a silver handshake and consequently did as little work as possible, hiding his sloth by delegation. He had done little for about 20 years but curiously had escaped previous purges. He illuminated a room by his departure.

Jim believed that the country was trapped in a remorseless and irreversible spiritual, social and economic decline although, inconsistently, he admitted that this could change. He generously spent much of the company's time explaining his views which were based solely on his reading of a certain tabloid paper for the last 45 years. Today, for example, it carried a story suggesting that all school exams were to be eliminated. Pass rates had risen and, if the trend continued, nobody would fail, which is what political correctness required. Consequently, the government was to abolish all exams, saving the country many billions of pounds. Anyone who challenged his thinking was often confronted by a lengthy recitation from that day's edition, which, naturally, proved that Jim was right. This deterred discussion so Holmes believed that his colleagues' silence implied agreement.

34

He regarded this as his most impressive achievement since joining Broadoak as a raw teenager, direct from school. Occasionally, he would describe himself as a self-made man but he seldom heard the rejoinder. "That removes a great responsibility from the Almighty."

Today, Jim was, again, holding forth on declining morals. Reportedly, Chinese filling stations were offering the services of prostitutes to all male customers who spent more than the equivalent of a few pounds. Henry asked whether the company had any sites in the UK and his intended but clumsy joke, linking the provision of tumblers given with petrol in the UK, with tumbles of a different kind in China, drew an instant rebuke. There was more. An American airline was selling photographs of cabin crews, scantily clad, to subsidise low fares. The newspaper, thoughtfully, had printed no less than 12 photographs in its double-page colour spread diatribe against such a lewd concept.

Henry had long since given up any hopes of having a sensible conversation with Jim.

Another colleague was 35 year old Mike Horton, a blazer-wearing, pipe-smoking, intellectually empty, management-sucking-up graduate who prompted his colleagues to wonder how such an oaf could secure a degree, unless it was in toadyism. He was married to a wealthy but ugly girl and was always irritatingly cheerful, mainly because he lacked the wit to see things realistically. Unlike Henry, he believed that management was always right. "If they weren't right, they wouldn't be senior management, would they, and you're not senior management, are you?" Henry reeled in the face of such intellectual rigour. Horton was so immature that even his breath came in short pants and colleagues claimed that he had been obliged to stand on a chair to reach puberty.

He always did well on courses because he challenged nothing and the company, especially the human resources manager, liked acquiescence. Mike was a full-blooded slimy company creep. Some hostile comments on the quality of those who inhabited the eighth floor had reached that level because of Mike's "loyalty" so conversations with him were always short and innocent. When not praising management, Mike was droning boringly about buying a flat that he could not afford and going to the races. Oddly, he also liked cricket and this puzzled Henry who had always assumed that, by definition, such people were decent chaps. Once, when playing for another division, Mike's manager was struck by a bouncer. Horton, who was batting with him at the time, memorably ran down the wicket, crying out "speak to me, sir, speak to me, sir".

Last year, Mike had been sent on a tough outdoor course, which, naturally, had shown management's wisdom and, which was, for him, the "opportunity of a lifetime", although for what was never made clear. Henry had challenged the view that commercially worthwhile bonding could result by taking employees away from work, depositing them on a difficult landscape and then demanding that they do unusual, physically dangerous things for which they had received no training.

"Frankly, I wouldn't trust you lot to see me across a country lane on a quiet Sunday afternoon. Course organisers think that a group, some of whom cannot swim, working together on the problem of crossing a fast-flowing river, in a snow storm, and provided with just three match sticks, develops character and team spirit in solving the problem. An anxiety shared may be an anxiety reduced until you're the one who falls into the river. Then you have rather more than your share of worry. The intelligent thing would be to concede that such a challenge is dangerous, ill-advised and stupid and that the training and experience necessary to undertake such a mission is inadequate. The group should show initiative in hiking back to the nearest railway station and scan situations vacant columns on the way home. The whole basis of these courses is fallacious because they imply that an ability to make sensible judgements under pressure in this kind of context has some relevance to routine office life. It's a load of rubbish, patronised by the stupid and financed by the wealthy and gullible."

Mike seldom talked to Henry after that.

Stan Gray was the backbone of the division. He had been moved there some 10 years ago, after failing to run the company's UK filling stations successfully. He had worked for Broadoak since its inception, some 40 years ago, and probably knew more than anyone about the company. He never panicked, even when the division was under the most irrational pressure. Some years ago, for example, he had been asked a particularly stupid question by the particularly stupid chairman. His reply was typically honest. "I can spend two weeks in detailed research or I can give you a provisional response later this morning. Which would you like?" The chairman, showing the incisiveness associated with his job title, opted for detailed research and a response that morning. Stan retreated to the outer office, chatted to the secretary and then returned to offer his thoughts. The mighty man was impressed, not with Stan but with himself for demanding full and prompt research.

Henry enjoyed his conversations with Stan who shared his dry and, at times, almost puerile sense of humour. This Monday, he was chuckling quietly to himself as he read the latest demand for a study. It came from Bernard Fricker, head of human resources, appropriately known as BF. He wanted to know the pros and cons of a 360 degree feedback appraisal system. Stan and Henry agreed that the company had been going round in circles for years.

John Scanlon was a young, bright, amiable economics graduate who had joined under the company's graduate intake programme. HB referred to him as "the best of our graduate intake of recent years". That was true: he was also the worst, because he was the only graduate who had been taken on under the short-lived scheme. John was assiduous and brought an academic discipline to the team that was totally ignored by the majority of the division who knew that their grip on continued employment depended almost entirely on the chief executive.

Simon Plummer, approaching retirement age, was short and amazingly boring. He was incapable of sustaining silence for more than a few minutes. It was not that he had anything to say: his conversation, or, more accurately, monologues, because nobody was allowed to interrupt, consisted almost entirely of prejudice and ignorance. Somehow, he seemed to have overcome the need to breathe whilst talking. Like Jim Holmes, he was always right. Some perceived Plummer as kind but Perkins saw him as someone who could never mind his own business which explained his apparent "interest" in others. He offered gratuitous advice, usually preceded by "we've known each other a long time, so I hope that you don't mind if I mention…". This, in his eyes, seemed to give him carte blanche to make comments that normal, mature, balanced people would not even contemplate. For example, Plummer had told Henry that his career might benefit if he wore white shirts, not the coloured ones that he had favoured in his younger days. Plummer, who always wore white shirts, had spent virtually his entire career in MAD and had failed to reach even the position of deputy division head, but Henry was too polite to mention it. More recently, Plummer had sought to deceive colleagues that he was in the office by leaving an old jacket on his chair, whilst he went shopping.

Simon, a specialist in useless information, had some particularly irritating and useless phrases in his collection and was always surprised at everything. Henry treasured one classic. "Surprisingly, very oddly, and this is surprising and strange because the television said that Poppleford St. John Major was the wettest seaside resort on the south coast. Surprising, that, because when I was there, last year, in real terms, technically speaking, it never rained all day. Odd that."

He was capable of arguing with a signpost and colleagues maintained that he had given his brain, unused, to medical research when young. Irritatingly, he completed other people's sentences. Once, Henry had composed a few remarks with which he would begin an apparently benign conversation. "I was sitting the other day in." Plummer suggested the office, home, car and garden. Henry ignored all these and said "a mood of deep contemplation when I thought how much fun it would be to walk". In came some suggestions. "In the country, to the shops with my wife, to the cricket club". Henry continued "backwards, very fast, on one leg".

Henry had long since given up any hopes of enjoying Simon's monologues.

The oldest man in the company was Arthur Williams, who was retiring in the autumn. He had never recovered from learning of the death of Grace Fields and lived in fear of hearing of the demise of Vera Lynn. He was a sharp-nosed, short-sighted timid man whose few remaining wisps of hair were combed forward to reveal a near triangular face which, correctly, gave the impression that he was sly. He had the maturity of youth and the impetuosity of old age and retained an interest in females that a frustrated 17-year-old would have regarded as excessive. This happened to be the age that Arthur seemed to think he was. He was disliked by his colleagues, male and female, and irritated Henry by wearing blue suits with brown shoes. Arthur and Simon, in particular, were scarcely on speaking terms, following a "helpful piece of friendly advice" from the latter on how sordid it was to see a man of Arthur's years lusting after females. Not being on speaking terms with Simon was a position that induced widespread envy. Few had reached this halcyon position. Arthur was one of nature's leading grumblers and whenever he attacked a new target, that victim immediately was guaranteed support from those who heard the moans.

Jane Lewis, an attractive, vivacious, shapely and popular brunette in her early twenties, had joined the division last autumn direct from secretarial college and was proving to be a very competent colleague. She was responsible for everything but undertaking research. This included filing, making travel arrangements, organising meetings, typing letters from the crude efforts of the males and keeping all the necessary records. She always treated everyone in the same friendly way: HB, apparently, had even been addressed on one occasion as "love" and, it was rumoured, had blushed although how anyone could detect a change in his complexion, which reflected years of hard drinking, was a mystery. Her single status provided a challenge to the division's deep thinkers, or would have done if there were any, and her taste in fashion, already revealed on a few hot days last September, boded well for the summer. Jane always seemed to be brown, although whether this was because of expensive holidays or an addiction to a sun lamp nobody knew or cared. Lengthy speculation on how she might dress when it became really hot was being answered today. She was nearly wearing a short pleated tartan skirt, a white tee shirt and white high heel sandals. The tee shirt, with a deep neckline, was obviously one of her favourites as it had shrunk so much that it failed to reach her waist whilst simultaneously exposing her to draughts higher up.

Henry enjoyed looking at her during conversations.

The division had no clearly defined and regular duties. It had been created many years ago when senior management realised that there was no capacity within the organisation to undertake important *ad hoc* studies. Consequently, Henry and his colleagues had no work at all occasionally whilst at other times they were rushed off their feet. Currently, there was little to do. They had just concluded a study on whether Broadoak should diversify into men's haircutting. HB, having no local barber and not wishing to patronise one in London, favoured providing such a facility on most of the company's 300 gasoline outlets around the country, one of which, fortuitously, was close to his home. MAD, convinced that it was a silly suggestion, naturally endorsed the idea and prepared a tome supporting the concept which, initially, they suggested could be called "Something for the week-end, sir?" This was thought to be too long and they eventually settled on "Premium cut". By supporting the chief executive's idea, they retained his goodwill, essential in the troubled times now facing the industry, whilst knowing that the rest of general management would reject the concept because MAD had supported it.

Henry's job, like the work of the division, was ill-defined and he had never adequately conveyed to Jill what he did. Her suspicions that his work was undemanding had been fuelled by a friend's young son, who had accompanied Henry to work one day, as part of a school project, and had written a very unflattering essay on Perkins' work, headed "And what else do you do?" This had been heralded as a satirical masterpiece by his English master, who could not believe that anyone could do so little as Henry for what he imagined was so big a salary. Indeed, he so enjoyed the piece he took it home with him to read and re-read during his eight-week summer holiday, before sending it to Rory Bremner. Although the piece had prompted a courteous acknowledgement of "an imaginative piece of work", it had not been used on the talented satirist's television programme as it was "too far-fetched".

Predictably, now that all the workers were in their offices, shops and the few remaining British factories, the early morning cloud had yielded to hot sunshine and the high temperature had already persuaded even the more conservative men to undo the top button on their shirts and to loosen their ties. It was curious, mused Henry, leaning back in his chair, that, when the forecasters predicted good weather during the week, and rain over weekends, they were usually right. Today was Monday and a heat wave was imminent. Nevertheless, the central heating was still on and the windows could not be opened, as this would have upset the allegedly sophisticated heating system and the very unsophisticated boiler man. The heating season was from the middle of October to mid May, and irrelevant factors, such as the temperatures experienced in a hot spring and a cold autumn, could not intrude on the programme agreed by management, which, naturally, knew best. Henry, aware that the central heating system used oil supplied by his company, which only occupied five of the nine floors, suspected that the inability to turn off the boiler reflected a desire to sustain sales figures.

The sun was trying to illuminate the corner of Henry's office but was thwarted by a dusty collection of files, perched precariously on the window ledge. Even without them, it would have failed because of the dark windows but Perkins had bravely removed a few square inches of the dark protective coating which allowed him to peer at the traffic and Lowry-like people below.

Henry reflected on his lost weekend and consoled himself with the thought that at least one in the near future would be hot and sunny. Whatever used to be called the FA Cup final still had to be played. The English game was booming, to judge by the saturation coverage on television, despite the fact that the national team had not won a match for five years, since they crushed the Cayman Islands 2-0, but the players were worshipped as gods. What particularly amused Henry and the other two other people in the United Kingdom who disliked the grip of professional football on national life, was that some leading sides were composed entirely of foreigners: vocal support for home teams had diminished considerably in recent months, because the local fans could not pronounce the names of most of the individuals in their teams. This had prompted the introduction of grunts, rather than words, thus confirming the massive benefits of decades of free education.

With the first plastic container of company coffee already consumed and the dry sandwich but a distant memory, Henry Perkins relaxed in the relative peace of his hutch and read some elderly circulars. The first, five weeks old, told staff to pass on such missives more quickly in future. Recipients must read, sign and date circulars quickly and then pass them on. There were no signatures or dates and Henry was the last on the list. He was reminded of the occasion, some years ago, when there was a train strike every Tuesday evening and members of what was then Staff Department ran around an empty office, looking for long-since departed employees to tell them that they could go home early. The reverie was interrupted by a familiar voice.

"Perky, BF of HR wants to see you as soon as possible." Henry Perkins flung a hand in the air to acknowledge Jane's message.

Henry Perkins had mixed feeling about being addressed as Perky. Part of him thought that he merited rather more respect from a junior member of staff, although he admitted that his work was seldom more demanding than that undertaken by his younger colleagues. That was not his fault: he had always done what he had been asked and he was conscientious. He thought that one reason for his failure to progress was that he never carried a clip board, when they were fashionable, or, now that the culture had changed, a large, ruled and stiff-covered notebook. Similarly, he never rushed anywhere nor did he shout and he never parked a pen or pencil behind an ear. Those who followed these fads exuded a sense of urgency that attracted attention and even promotion but Henry always seemed to be cruising at the one pace.

Did his age alone entitle him to some respect? No. Somehow that reinforced his own intense and deep sense of failure and frustration. It also reminded him that one day, possibly sooner rather than later, he would be following Holmes, Plummer and Williams into retirement for which he was not ready. Despite being worn down over the years, he still believed that he could do so much more. What was it and how he could attain it? There was also a part of him, buried deep in his imagination, that relished being called Perky by a young and undeniably attractive girl. It reminded him of the youth, always coveted and never enjoyed because of his shyness and the Wasted Years. He was convinced that he was born at the age of 25 and immediately became an office worker and commuter. Finally, he reasoned, whether he liked the appellation or not, there was nothing that he could do about it, so he might as well enjoy it. That, in a sentence, was the overall philosophy of Henry Perkins.

Perky, "BF wants to see you now". The repeated message, with the emphasis on the last word, woke him from his reverie.

"Why does BF want to see me?"

"I don't know but he emphasised now because he said he has to attend a government task force meeting later this morning."

Perky had occasional informal meetings with BF, for no apparent reason, so there was not necessarily any significance in the early morning summons. Both men had joined Broadoak on the same day, and, despite BF's progress up the corporate ladder, he still liked to have the occasional chat with Henry. He knew that Mr Perkins, wiser than he, unwittingly provided him with some useful ideas, which, of course, were presented to senior management as BF's own work. Poor Henry had never noted how some changes, over the years, had reflected his own thinking.

Chapter 4

Henry pushed his chair back, marched towards the lift, pushed the button for the eighth floor and, when nothing happened, puffed up the stairs.

Access to the leaders' floor, through heavy glass doors, installed to deter the most determined of unwelcome intruders, was only granted after he had bent down to the microphone in the wall, some two feet, sorry, Brussels, 600 millimetres, off the floor. Suitably positioned, he announced his identity and the name of the person who had summoned him. He felt ridiculous as he crouched to reveal his name to a girl, the other side of the door, whom he had known for about five years and who could see him clearly. She dutifully wrote the details in a large book, pressed a button and beckoned Henry to push on the now unlocked door.

This was a different world. Secretaries, mainly young and attractive, rushed around, seemingly bent on urgent and important missions, but, actually, visiting one another to discuss last night's television, boy-friends and, probably, the relative merits of open outcry and electronic trading of currency futures. They knew how to play the secretarial game which was why they had risen above their contemporaries, both literally and financially. The floor was heavily carpeted and Henry noticed, with his usual internal grin, that his ankles had almost vanished. Strolling towards BF's office, he thought about the senior executives who inhabited this strange land.

Hubert Bennett, chief executive, was dedicated to ensuring the prosperity of the local pub, The Thirsty ox, or The Thirsty Fox, depending on the direction from which its patrons approached, obligingly located next to Broadoak House. Hubert's unselfish action had resulted in his acquiring a purple complexion and incurring substantial expenditure. It also meant that his colleagues had to discuss business with him between 10.15, when he usually arrived at the office, and 12.15, when he was preparing to resume his crusade. He tackled this task with such relish that in the afternoons he was usually tired and emotional.

That said, he was a kindly, well-meaning man whose rise to the top had surprised everyone including him. His knowledge of business, despite working for the company since his youth, was surprisingly inadequate. This was not evident because most of his colleagues were marginally less bright than Hubert who showed the occasional flash of acumen. He treated jargon and obfuscation with contempt and employed his sense of humour to good effect in the boardroom. He was very fond of striped clothing as his suits, which looked more like old-fashioned pyjamas, and shirts testified. Thus attired, he looked like a mobile road map. Another characteristic was his fondness for plain, single-colour, knitted ties. His dark hair was always plastered with what seemed like heavy-duty oil and he seldom wore glasses, despite being 63. HB was a thoughtful man. When flying, he insisted on holding his heavy briefcase on his lap, to minimise the weight on the plane's fuselage, "to stop the damned thing from falling out of the sky".

Lance Boyle, the managing director, in name only, as HB wielded all the power, had worked in several industries before coming to rest in Broadoak, some five years ago. Stunningly garrulous, he enjoyed disseminating his usually totally uninformed views on everything. Colleagues, before entering his office, were wont to ensure that their house insurance was paid up, any pets had been fed and summer holidays booked. Unthinkingly, he lectured overseas visitors on their own cultures, totally undeterred by the fact that he had never even visited their region. Once, according to his erstwhile secretary, Lillian Pond, he was talking to a visitor from Syria. "Lance went to the large map of the world that covered a single wall of his office and then said that we in the UK should be more interested in the fascinating developments now occurring in your country. Here, having helpfully pointed out the location of the UK to his Ph.D. guest, he felt he ought to be consistent and indicate just where Syria was. His executive finger came to rest on Saudi Arabia."

Alan Stewart, the company treasurer and finance director, was a mild-mannered man. He would have regarded clapping hands to discourage birds from eating prize garden plants as the act of a bully. His reputation in the City was high and many analysts wondered why he remained with Broadoak where the scope was so limited. Cartoonists, cruelly noting his large ears and propensity for wearing old and crumpled suits, portrayed him as a down-at-heel mouse.

Shirley Church was the company secretary and the only female manager in the company. Allegedly, she had been appointed because HB thought that she was a good typist. Aware that she had to be more able than the men, not very difficult in Broadoak, she always did her homework and was a very competent and kindly woman.

Dick Wood was director and general manager, operations. Balding and moustached, he looked like a military man which he was when recruited about 25 years ago. He still used military expressions and his brisk, no nonsense demeanour was ill-suited to what he called civvy street. He always wore the same suit but they never betrayed such apparent regular use because he had two new identical ones made each year. Apparently he maintained a chart in his home office, showing when each suit had been worn and the cumulative total days of wear it had endured.

Bernard Fricker, general manager, Human Resources, was a conceited, intense, humourless and justifiably hated man for whom "advancing the company's fortunes" was synonymous with dismissing employees. The company was his entire life and BF, who only spoke in management jargon in the office, was always busy, but it was not entirely clear what occupied him. Because human resources was the current management fad, he had inveigled himself on many external committees whose work was being delayed whilst the members plotted to find a way of removing him. Henry, like his colleagues, nevertheless had to appear friendly towards Fricker as he was so powerful.

Several rooms were reserved for the non-executive directors who used the facilities to pursue their well-paid activities for other companies. Peter Nascott was a former Conservative Member of Parliament who had fathered children with three different partners in a short time. He had eventually resigned, to spend more time with his families, according to some columnists. Nobody knew why he was appointed to the board because his energetic and enterprising style was seldom associated with Broadoak. Other non-executive directors included Sir Willerby Wistleton-Nugget, who was as daft as his name, and Alex Gardener, an economist and wit who enjoyed a big reputation.

Henry was in BF's secretary's room. The unfortunately named Rose Bush was a phlegmatic lady, in her mid fifties, who bore her humourless parents no ill will. She was very plain which was partly responsible for her remaining a Bush. That was sad because she was sensitive, intelligent and always helpful and she dressed very smartly. Rose came from an age when it was considered normal to look clean and well-dressed in an office.

"Good morning Henry. "Mr Fricker is on the phone at the moment, but he will finish soon. Please go in." She ushered Henry into his presence, mouthing unnecessarily "Mr Perkins to see you".

"My own view is that modern blue skies out-of-the-box fast-track management theory, even if backed by phased functionality, is frequently complicated by a fractured set of seemingly cohesive imperative drivers which, inherently, not only disrupt value chain analysis but undermine total quality management procedures whilst remaining distant from eternal verities. Ephemeral pragmatism must encourage us to reject simplistic paradigms and we must not concentrate on such transitional incongruence. Forgive me, but I had to over-simplify that because I have a visitor. We'll finish this later. Bye."

"Good morning, Perkins, come in."

Although Fricker maintained that "ambiguity is the enemy of clear communications" HB was often heard to mutter "I don't know what the hell that man is talking about". BF, although not very bright, nevertheless realised that, providing colleagues never asked him what he meant, obfuscation and long monologues allowed him to secure what he wanted. Their silence was guaranteed because they did not wish to expose their ignorance. Addressing Perkins, whom he knew appreciated straight talking, would be easier than trying to communicate with other colleagues. Although he had known Henry for some years, it would be appropriate to address him today as Perkins. It was, after all, a serious meeting. Henry would not mind: it seemed to reflect the different levels that the two had reached. Good old Henry, he seldom minded anything.

"Thanks for coming up." Henry, who did not know that he had a choice, smiled.

"Sit down Perkins. I thought that we should spend some quality time in a face-to-face session but I've got to attend a meeting soon, so forgive me for being brief." Henry nodded sympathetically and vanished involuntarily into the further recesses of the comfortable leather armchair, the quality of which immediately set the manager apart from ordinary mortals. Struggling to sit further forward, he looked around the room which was adorned with all the usual meaningless impedimenta that managers collect to impress the gullible. Despite Henry's efforts to sit higher, the low chair meant that, like all BF's visitors, he had to look up to conduct any form of conversation. This, of course, was to put the visitor at an immediate disadvantage.

The room was littered with photographs of BF with people whom Henry assumed to be important executives and politicians but he didn't recognise any of them so felt guilty and ignorant. It did not occur to the innocent Henry that the people in the photographs were nonentities, who, like BF, richly deserved their status. On a table by the far wall, models of company road tankers mingled with business magazines and cubes of North Sea oil much favoured in the early days. A smart bookcase contained volumes with titles such as *Employment law in the 14ᵗʰ century*, *Human resources management-the supreme science* and *Julius Caesar-a failed HR manager* and, oddly, *Pekinese as Pets*. Henry wondered what other roles these odd little dogs might play. Could they seek lost human resources on mountains or skilfully guide blind human resources around busy shopping centres? Surely, the dogs were so small they would sink into the snow or people would stand on them, unwittingly? Society was becoming increasingly unfair to dogs. Only last week, the local paper had carried a piece headed "Local dog trials results". Perhaps some guard dogs had teamed up with some criminals and provided inside information on a robbery?

The paintings on the walls were incomprehensible but there was one that Henry had not seen before. It consisted of violently coloured-arrows, solid and broken lines, swirling and inter-connected concentric circles and triangles which merged into an orgasmic mess. Was this the doodling of a drunken and talentless artist who was enriched by the spending and fawning of the gullible? Was it the effort of a small child, given some coloured pens whilst father was on the phone? A closer look revealed that this was the latest representation of management's organisational thinking, compiled by an expensive information consultant. The title of the work, which clarified everything, was "the new holistic conceptual image, recalibrated to reveal re-engineered competence and the release of renewed leverage in the context of human resources".

BF helped. "PACT's impressive, isn't it? It's a fascinating new diagnostic tool which will help us to redesign corporate architecture and articulate a new sourcing strategy for key skills whilst simultaneously prioritising expectations in core communities and rationalising corporate visibility."

"PACT?"

"Yes, it stands for Personal Action Catalyst Plan."

The senior executive's desk was bare: no paper sullied its purity. Was this because BF had no work to do or because he delegated satisfactorily? Some years ago, Henry's annual assessment criticised him for failing to delegate. Jill advised him to protest, which he did on the grounds that he had nobody to whom he could delegate. The adverse comment on delegation was removed but his report was annotated to the effect that he was unable to take management criticism and was a potentially disruptive force in the office. That, unknown to Henry, was one of many reasons why he had never been formally promoted. Another reason was that years before data protection acts, a clerk had told Staff Department, subsequently Personnel Department, Employee Relations Division and now Human Resources Division, that Perkins had a damaged ankle which impeded his mobility. This was wrong. However, the records were confidential so Henry had not seen them and therefore never knew of his corporate-imposed disability, which, fortunately, had not prevented him from playing cricket for the company with some success.

Rose Bush, elegant but, like so many of her kind, almost assuming the rank of the man she served, returned. Would Mr Perkins like tea or coffee? He took the proffered coffee, in a china cup, decorated with the company logo.

Why had he been summoned? He was always amused by BF's bizarre management language so was pleased to add to his collection of phrases with which he entertained Jill sometimes. Occasionally, to impress BF, Henry employed some of the words used in management articles although he did not understand their meaning which was, of course, the best part.

Senior management was about to speak. Henry put his coffee carefully on the executive glass table alongside his chair. Once, he had spilled a cup of tea on the white, shaggy carpet and was now so keen to avoid a repetition that, being nervous, he dropped a plate of biscuits on the floor. As if to assure his host that he had a sensitive stance on company costs, he blew the whiskers off a custard cream and consumed it.

BF was short of stature and, liked so many of his limitations, tried to offset this by being officious, imperious, bumptious and totally pompous or pumptious for short. He was overweight and his smug, round, fat and well-creased face gave the impression that he was smiling. This had caused problems for some of the company's new employees, who, seeking to please, had laughed at the wrong time in their first interview. Fricker no longer had much hair but had camouflaged this by being one of the first in the country to have a shaven head. He had few friends, even within his family. His taste in clothes had always reflected what fashion pundits maintained was the most appropriate for senior management. Today he was wearing a double-breasted, grey pin-striped suit, a maroon striped shirt with a stiff white collar and a gaudy but obviously expensive tie that clashed horribly with the shirt and suit. A red and white spotted handkerchief, that matched nothing else and which was hanging foppishly, seemed to be trying to escape from his top pocket. All this, of course, conveyed management status, for only those with the confidence borne of apparent achievement would have dared to look so unco-ordinated and silly.

The unseasonal heat had prompted BF to push his jacket back, revealing a pair of red braces. BF, like the portraits of railway navvies, was also wearing a belt. Henry resisted the temptation to see if string was bound around the lower part of his trousers to keep them clear of his boots. What deep-seated lack of confidence prompted the use of braces and a belt? Henry looked up and thought that BF's head, which appeared to grow out of his collar, looked as if it should have been re-potted some time ago. Although it was early in the morning, his neck already bore a thin red line where he had turned his head. Now, addressing Perkins, he swivelled the whole of his body round, to avoid the possibility that the cautious head of Human Resources could lose his head.

Having discovered that Henry was in good health, BF asked about his "lady wife". Was he planning any holiday this year and how were his rhododendrons looking?

"All right, thank you, Westhaven and very good, respectively."

"How are things with you?"

"Well, I'm looking forward to our month's holiday in the States. We'll be driving from coast to coast and it's taken a lot of organising. I think that when it's over, I'll need another holiday." Henry smiled dutifully.

"I've been very busy with our new system of internal mentoring and devising a competence framework so that we can diagnose our cultural norms and then draw up a flexible template that we can incorporate into our company architecture. It's important that we roll out an infrastructure that captures value before moving to the next platform. I've also been pretty pre-occupied with our new decision trees because I think that this can revitalise and re-engineer the whole company providing that we take into account the comprehension shortfall anxiety of those people out of the loop. After all, there's no point in taking a helicopter view unless we adopt a blue skies approach."

Henry, who had no idea what BF was talking about, nevertheless enjoyed employing his sense of humour tacitly in what, clearly, could be a light-hearted start to the week. He nodded knowingly and wondered whether tending decision trees was more difficult in hot weather.

"I welcome this opportunity to interface with you, for, as you know, I'm very much a bottom-up, rather than a top-down man." Perkins unsure whether to smile, wince or seek clarification of his superior's physical predilections, opted for silence.

"I believe in bonding."

Perkins, shaken, did not stir at the manager's confession, even in the context of his previous admission that he was a bottom-up man. Clearly, BF just wanted to talk out loud about his habits in front of an old colleague. Henry's role was to listen and look sympathetic.

"That's why I wanted to walk through some ball park concepts, which could represent a step change and to indicate our overall game plan so that there's no comprehension shortfall. I've always believed in the upward feedback process but sometimes this must be subordinated to the imperative need for senior management to articulate the corporate core message. We must not peal the banana prematurely. As you know, we all promise that, each day, each hour, we shall review our own contribution to the corporate effort, to use our imagination and resources to be a force for good in everything we do, balancing and meeting the needs of our shareholders, the communities in which we operate, our own human resources and society and the environment in general."

Perkins had often wondered why the company appeared to be indifferent to the needs of the unborn which was surely a glaring omission. He tried to look pensive but realising that he looked silly, nodded in agreement.

"I also have to fill you in on the corporate landscape, during this window of opportunity which we have created together at this moment in time."

Perkins, pleased to be identified with the creation of a window of opportunity, although he was unaware of the nature of his contribution, was curiously uneasy at such a straightforward exposition of the reason why he had been summoned. He struggled to stay awake.

"How do you see our mission statement and the best way it could be rolled out in relation to existing human resources? For example, do you favour modular strategies, heeding multiple performance measures, leading to balanced scorecards?"

Perkins, oddly, had never considered such matters but it did not seem the right time to confess to such neglect. He attempted to articulate his asymmetric bilateralism theory of management but, feeling out of the loop, gave up. He tried, once again, to look intelligent. A mission statement? Did one of the many unread circulars explain all about mission statements? Perkins always regarded mission statements as nonsense prepared by the intellectually challenged to impress the gullible. He attempted to wear an expression that conveyed passionate interest in everything that BF was saying.

Sensing that Perkins was uneasy, the manager generously tried to put it into a fuller context. "What I really want to talk about, and let's remember that my priorities relate to the human resources in this age of corporate information democracies, is our mission statement in the context of downsizing at a time of negative operating profits. Manifestly, we must optimise our resources, and apply leverage to our products and services. One way to do that is to retreat to our core profile, whilst avoiding the most serious implications that could be caused for the company by a knock-on effect on the portfolio careers owned by our co-workers. Above all, I don't want to become involved in turf wars. I imagine that would also be the view of most of the staff."

A blinded Henry nodded sagely on behalf of the staff.

"Equally, we must initiate new concepts leading to sensible and relevant inter-locking modular concepts that enable us to take advantage of a win-win situation."

Perkins, feeling that he really ought to contribute, muttered that this was, indeed, a big issue that all staff must consider. Somehow, he implied that, whilst he had thought about little else in his waking hours recently, curiously he had not come up with a satisfactory response. Henry knew that BF was spouting nonsense but he envied him his confidence and authority. That said, was BF showing off or was he, in his tortured way, trying to tell him something? Henry decided that the former was the right answer.

"We have taken on board, at the end of the day, if you like, the need for a level playing field between the different divisions of the company so changes can now be made, without prejudicing customer awareness or the supply chain relationship. We must optimise the benefits of implementing top-down feeds, whilst overcoming overhanging regulatory impacts as we unbundle services. Consequently, we must re-define the limits of empowerment and organise ownership of key issues as we progressively de-layer the organisation. We must ensure that we have the right combination of assets and resources, however painful it might be to align specific goals with diminished resources caused by the Parton-Briggs-Barton impact."

Perkins, fatigued by the heat and the gibberish, wondered if he was in a foreign country, asleep or drunk. He seemed to be awake, sober and in England so some action was required. He suddenly agreed with such enthusiasm that BF, pleasantly surprised, looked at him. Perhaps this was not going to be such a difficult chat. Henry had been around for many years and was well aware of the challenges faced by management. Sensing that his colleague now clearly understood the point of this disciplined and analytical approach, BF resumed.

"Given the relative possibilities of either downside or upside potential, we have decided to accept that our best option, providing that we do not lose our view of the importance of customer awareness, is to downsize."

Perkins nodded. He added that he too, was considering downsizing, as was Mrs Perkins. "She has a good figure but she insists on hiding it in full-length dresses."

BF, pleased that he seemed to be communicating with Perkins, despite the latter's rather laboured effort at humour, resumed. "In a carefully co-ordinated step change function, we must move towards a result-targeted series of objectives, to eliminate under-performers, which realise a synergy."

Perkins, still failing to follow the monologue, thought that it was time to agree again, grunted approval.

"In our right-sizing plans, we must now consider a major policy of de-layering at the individual and corporate level."

A sleepy Perkins indicated that this had long been an essential pillar of his own philosophy.

It seemed to BF that his colleague understood what was necessary which was gratifying because he had really feared this interview. What he had to say was not easy which was why he was choosing his words with such care.

Seeing that his superior was slightly surprised, Henry continued. "Mrs Perkins and I have long held the view that, in a downsizing situation, the key is to have a mission statement, or preferably a core message, which can be discussed freely, between a man and wife, in a bottom-up or even top-down situation, if you like." He then implied that this kind of discussion had in fact dominated his married life and had given both he and Mrs Perkins much mutual satisfaction.

BF, like Henry, totally unaware of the meaning of what had just been said, attributed the bizarre outburst to his colleague's nerves.

"We have spent many hours devising the big picture scenario, and, as you know, we have sent some staff on multiple-day events to discuss it and establish appropriate attitudes on environmental orientation, the overall concept of de-layering and downsizing and the potential for introducing this concept at an early stage. The resulting statements of attainment suggest that these courses have been very useful. One of the main features has been the high quality feed-back from the break-outs."

Perkins immediately sympathised and nodded. If he had been on one, breaking out would have been one of his first objectives. Then, struggling to recall a single management phrase that he had read recently, he gave forth. "It's important to ensure that empowerment is properly delegated to de-layered management lest peer support be lacking, particularly if the company is thinking of abandoning its matrix structure. After all", he added triumphantly, having driven BF to an unusual if temporary silence, "facilitators must adopt a modular approach, at the front end of the corporate process, especially during the re-engineering process, if difficulties are to be avoided". Seeing that, unusually, he had the attention of BF, he concluded "if we don't succeed, we run the risk of failure".

This most enjoyable game would have to end soon but it made a change from listening to his sixth floor colleagues.

BF stared. The man was ignorant. How could senior managers like BF communicate with people who probably did not even understand simple routine phrases like "environmentally-motivated value judgements"?

"I know that you, Perkins, are keen to see the company in a win-win situation and that we avoid a doomsday scenario, or a double whammy and I take on board your comment on the need for peer support."

Henry, unaware that he had said anything about this, looked both gratified and surprised.

"Consequently, we must free up some HR human resources, ASAP."

Perkins, nearly asleep again, happened to look at his watch and BF noted the gesture, which he took to indicate his subordinate's understandable nervousness.

"Perkins, I'm going to have to let you go now."

Perkins made no effort to leave as he thought that it was rather rude to go without any further comment, after such an interesting chat. Besides, there was one biscuit left. He really enjoyed being on the fringes of management. Perhaps if only he had learned the language of monumental bluff earlier, he might ....His musing on the influence and material gains that might have come from a life in management was interrupted by BF who was now showing some signs of impatience at his continued presence. This was really confusing.

"I must let you go."

Rose had appeared, summoned by a secret bell under her boss's desk. She was holding the door open although the thick carpet would have ensured that the door stayed open unaided. BF added, with unmistakable emphasis, as if to encourage Henry's departure, "with immediate effect".

Perkins, ever the agreeable, struggled out of the managerial chair, helped himself to the remaining biscuit and said cheerfully, "yes, I must go, I've things to do. Thanks for your time, the coffee, biscuits and the chat. I enjoyed it and I hope that your next meeting goes well."

BF smiled and said "I wish you well and remember me to Gillian".

Henry said nothing, temporarily unaware of whom he meant.

Rose, looking surprisingly sad for no apparent reason, thought Henry, as she showed him out and said "good bye" more positively than she had said it on previous visits. She even shook his hand, placing her left hand over their temporarily joined manual parts. She had never done this before and Henry noticed that she appeared to be suffering from hay fever, for she was rubbing her right eye.

Perkins returned to his office. For once, the lift was working and the mechanical voice warned him "doors opening, doors closing". Because this was a slack time in MAD, his colleagues were involved in earnest discussions and hardly saw Henry return. Jim Holmes was chatting to a visitor and Simon Plummer was revealing that recent growth in his garden had been "absolutely astonishing, quite surprising, very odd, really, and everything's gone mad." He then told his Accounts colleague that the trouble with the world was that two thirds did not understand how the other half lived. His friend, looking increasingly old, and apropos nothing, said that shrinking in old age was getting him down.

Only Jane was curious to know what happened but refrained from asking directly. Instead, smiling, she looked up and said "everything all right?"

Henry seldom told anyone to mind their own business and he had no reason to start now, especially to a young friendly colleague. "I think he just wanted a chat. You know he's not the swine that everybody thinks. I feel sorry for him. I think he's lonely."

Henry gave no more thought to the chat and read the evening paper, as usual, on his way home. Apparently, a parrot was to appear in a divorce case because the wife maintained that, after she had been away for a weekend, the bird's vocabulary had been considerably extended. Now it favoured the use of the word "darling" and the phrase "let's go to bed now" had become its favourite, displacing the question of who was a pretty boy.

Later, at home, Perkins was being debriefed by his wife, although not in a way that, if the scene had been televised, it would have had to appear after the so-called watershed at nine pm. "Anything interesting happen in the office today?"

"I spent some time first thing this morning with BF."

"What did he want?"

"I really don't know. You know how he talks in riddles. I tried to follow it all but it was hot and I'm not sure that I didn't drop off at one stage. He stared out of the window all the time so I don't think he noticed. He made a few jokes and I think, but I'm not sure, he may be planning another reorganisation."

Jill Perkins distrusted BF. She had met him at several Christmas parties, before he had introduced admission charges, and always said that he was duplicitous. Henry would doubtless have agreed if he knew what the word meant. She disliked BF for being so besotted with the company but, above all, despised him for not promoting Henry despite their apparent friendship and her husband's talents. She also hated him for growing a moustache within weeks of Hubert sprouting whiskers and, according to her revered spouse, the twerp, Jill liked old-fashioned terms of abuse, in another pathetic attempt to impress, had started to buy suits like those worn by HB.

" He must have said something."

"No, as I said, it was all very vague and I was so confused that I didn't realise that the conversation was over until he told me that he had to let me go, with immediate effect. He had to go to another meeting and it suited me because I was becoming very sleepy."

Jill paled "How did the conversation end?"

"That did puzzle me. He wished me well and asked to be remembered to Gillian, who, I presume is you. Earlier he had told me that he was off on holiday to the US soon, so I imagine that he realised that he would not be seeing me for a little while."

Jill gulped. Aware that she had probably gone white, she covered her face with her hand and hardly dared to look at her feet which were turning into boiling water. Hoping for the best, she said nothing.

Chapter 5

Bernard Fricker left Broadoak House promptly to attend a meeting of the government-industry task force, SONS (Save our North Sea). He was sitting on a standing committee charged with determining how the work of study groups, peer panels, review groups, focus groups, a cross-industry forum, five task forces and a working committee could be improved. The new committee had been formed to challenge the views of some oil and gas experts who believed that there were too many such organisations which only created work for those who merited unemployment. BF, totally unbiased, because he knew nothing about exploration and production, maintained that all that was required to sustain indigenous oil production was improved communication. He was, therefore, a natural for the position of deputy leader of this team.

The meetings were going well. BF believed that this was because committee members were progressive civil servants and plain-speaking individuals from industry, just like him. Indeed, by only their fourth meeting, they had agreed on the shape of the table at which they met, oval, whether tea or coffee would be served in the afternoon, both, and whether biscuits should be made available, yes. Potentially more divisive was how the leader would be addressed during debate. After intensive argument, and the subject was so complex that it took nearly a complete meeting to resolve, it was decided that whether the most senior male or the only female on the committee were presiding, the correct term of address would be chairman or chair.

Today had seen a spectacular advance. It had been agreed that the minutes would be mailed within two months of each quarterly meeting and, after only minimal debate, it was decided that they would be printed on yellow, blue, green and red paper, one colour for each quarter, respectively, to allow immediate recognition. BF, however, asked what colour should be used for the minutes of any *ad hoc* meeting. The use of white paper was nominated, seconded and agreed. The sheets would not be punched before being circulated. BF had astutely pointed out that some companies favoured files with four holes whilst others opted for two which might not overlap the four holes.

Fricker had condemned the proposal to distribute the minutes by email on security grounds. This topic, too, had been carried over, unresolved, from the previous session, so BF was pleased that an accord had been reached. It demonstrated how goodwill could solve even the most complex problem when senior people were involved. The session ended just after the debate had been prolonged sufficiently to allow a free lunch to be delivered.

Mr Fricker then hurried to address a conference attended by young management consultants and industry "high flyers" from around the world. The organisers had stressed that they wanted a challenging and intellectual paper, acknowledging the different levels, cultures and, particularly, the nationalities of the well-educated delegates. They should be stretched. If any stretching was to be done, BF felt that he was just the man. The organisers had never heard Fricker speak but, unlike their first five choices, he was available.

BF was determined that his paper, on MMTAPACITMW, as he liked to think of it, for short, management method, theory and practice, and communication in the modern world, for long, would be memorable. Formal introductions were made by the chairman and the room darkened even although Fricker had told the organisers that he had no visual aids.

Fricker stumbled towards the podium, found it without mishap and placed his notes carefully on the poorly illuminated surface. They would not be needed. Not only was he word-perfect but the flow of the analysis, once he had commenced, was so logical and compelling that it would be impossible to lose his place. He was greeted with only restrained applause which he attributed to the fact that he was speaking in the graveyard slot. They would soon be aroused because what he had to say was fundamentally important to their profession and their careers.

"Can you hear me at the back?" There was no answer and he did not hear someone's comment that he could but was willing to swap with anyone who could not. Undeterred by the lack of a response, BF grasped the sides of the lectern, cleared his throat, looked fiercely into a darkened auditorium and began.

"Good afternoon, ladies and gentlemen. I hope that there are some ladies out there, but it is difficult to see in this Stygian gloom."

The organisers immediately turned on all the lights, thus waking some participants who had enjoyed a very good lunch and who were disappointed to realise that they had missed nothing.

"I look forward to addressing you, the future management consultants, inter-cultural impediment removal executives, business resiliency coaches, information architectural planners, personal action catalyst analysts and corporate re-engineering specialists without whom, dare I say it, industry could not and should not survive.

"Thank you for the invitation to address you. It's an honour for me and for my company, Broadoak, where I'm a very senior executive with responsibilities for human resources."

He smirked in what was supposed to be a self-deprecating way but which was widely interpreted as a full-blooded arrogant sneer.

"I intend to touch base, during the available time frame, on what is fast becoming a new mind set. It is truly exciting to see so much young management talent in one room."

One of the young girls in the audience, encased provocatively in tight-fitting black trousers and wearing a white open-necked blouse, sitting with her knees coyly positioned just under her chin in a pose that might be found in fashion magazines, looked angrily at him. When he uttered the word talent, he just happened to be staring at her. She left the hall.

"We, on the senior management side, say 'chapeaux bas' to you all and wish you well in your burgeoning careers. I am impressed by the IQ symbolism present and the consequent potential for a cohesive yet oriented transformational osmosis, especially during the coffee breaks.

"Although we face increased demands at work, we must retain a sense of savoir-faire, even if occasionally, we do enjoy la dolce vita, as I'm sure that we shall after this session. I know that I shall. Let's hope that even a faux pas, committed in a moment of joie de vivre, will always be met, faute de mieux, by some understanding, not a coup de grâce. After all, errare est humanum and we must ignore cries of proh pudor, as I know you would. That is not the sort of comment that we want to hear. I know that I don't and I'm sure that I speak for you all in saying that you don't.

"As something of a rare avis in what I suppose we must now regard as the ancien regime in management terms, I want to speak to you, inter alia, about the present situation, per se. But, ab initio, I want to remind you that, in all industries, il faut d'argent! That is a sine qua non, and we forget that at our peril, as I'm sure you agree."

The nodding heads indicated not agreement but the onset of slumber.

"I speak to you as someone whose personal organisational and aspirational pendulum is moving in favour of a new game plan which, ceteris paribus, pushes back the envelope and kicks some old concepts into the grass. Even those of you from the undeveloped, third world, know precisely what I mean when I say that." Several young Asians left the hall.

"It's important that we assemble a cross-spectrum of multi-talented, multi-disciplined well-focused multinational analysts who can discourse to mutual benefit, whilst simultaneously leveraging their personal knowledge capital, both tacit and explicit, via the most appropriate modular approach. This will allow participants to synthesise with each other and to achieve mutually acceptable goals en route to self-actualisation and full integration.

"Increasingly, it will be necessary to architect and implement an enterprise-wide, value-added flexible template to enable us to secure a significant message for the environment, without, of course, losing sight of the need for a similarly clear and unified theme by which the industry can be identified, with a minimal adverse impact on cohesion. A totally integrated solution to our problems of communication should be properly engineered to take us into the next chapter."

Here, having delivered his own key message in Churchillian style, BF paused, expecting applause. None came. Somewhat nonplussed, Fricker resumed but was gratified to see that some listeners had placed their heads in their hands and were looking forwards, eyes shut, as if in a trance, clearly determined to exclude external factors lest they intruded on their understanding. This was most encouraging.

"It has been suggested to me that it might appear, prima facie, something of a non sequitur for me to address you this afternoon, in the light of recent events. Although we should not peal the banana prematurely, I believe that we must confront the issues and think out of the box in decentralised concentric synergistic circles of varying radius, even if this means re-engineering and recalibrating the game plan.

"I must confess to a certain élan in speaking to you about what is already being hailed as a détente, which has all the appearance of a fait accompli in what many critics regard as an anus I mean an annus mirabilis. You may feel a certain ennui or even a sense of déjà vu but I sincerely hope that I shall not be accused of adopting a position which might be crudely called post hoc ergo propter hoc, as I bat this around and indulge in some hard ball.

"Industry must face up to its challenges which constitute the essence of business thermionics, especially as global warming takes hold. It would be negligent of us to ignore the tertiary transfer implied by the warning not to dig too deeply into the cornflakes packet, particularly as we move to the cutting edge. Nor must we overlook the value of inter-locking modular units, especially as they interface with the basics of behavioural concept analysis.

"The raison d'être, quod erat demonstandum, to use le mot juste, is to carry out a post mortem on this de facto and now de jure magnum opus, the details of which, I know, I do not have to spell out to an audience of this calibre. We, on my side of the compound in the ball park, firmly believe that we must continue to drill down, through every window of opportunity, to seek out the most appropriate time frame but we must maintain our guard against our critics. It was Vergil, I think, or was it Horace, perhaps someone can tell me, who said, and how appropriate this is, procul este, profani. I know that there is not a person in this room who would dissent from this."

He paused to allow the hear-hears to develop. None came. Somewhat nonplussed, BF resumed.

"Nevertheless, it's clear to me, and, I know, to you, that we heed the suggestion not to brûler la chandelle par les deux bouts, notwithstanding the obvious lack of talent that I see every day."

Some more members of the audience left but BF, now firmly enmeshed in a cocoon of management madness, failed to see them. Belatedly realising that the audience could take offence at the comment on a lack of talent, he added "in my company" before sensing his new error and muttering "I mean in society at large".

"Yet, in today's circumstances it is difficult to avoid this as we strive to communicate our vision beyond the usual parameters of stakeholder focus. Paradigm shifts are must begin at the coal face. We must strive for a structural dynamism, popularly thought of as a circular cohesive rounded structure and you, of course, have a major role in the dialectic process of explaining this big picture to the world. The key, surely, is phased functionality carried out in asymmetric bilateralism.

"I can do no better than to remind you of the words of a high-ranking European politician who said that reform strategy proposals should identify ways to integrate resource assessments with decisions on positive and crucially negative priorities. He argued that a system of activity-based management, facilitated by strategic planning, should be introduced. I am overawed by such clarity and beauty of language and these words are as relevant today as when they were uttered last week.

"Before I close, I realise that an audience like you would expect a speaker to comment further on the evolving situation. However, I think that you will understand that, to say anything at all in this speech could create the impression that I had something to offer. Thus I am confident that in your wisdom, that innate wisdom that we have in our proud, value-adding, client-focused, result-driven industries, and how right we are to be proud of each man and, indeed, woman in these sectors, you, like me, will have forgotten how I started this sentence."

BF's only attempt at humour was totally ignored. Clearly, his intellectual tour de force, characterised by his breadth of vision and eloquence, had left them stunned.

"However, tempus fugit, so I must end, merely reminding you that the matter is effectively sub judice, c'est à dire. You will understand, therefore, that il n'y a pas à dire, n'est-ce pas? Could I just remind you that plus ça change, plus c'est la méme chose?

"Thank you for allowing me to touch base with you on the left field and I wish you well, particularly in your efforts to improve the bottom line in an ongoing, win-win, fast track, proactive strategic fit with your clients and colleagues. Au revoir and bientot and may you all prosper according to your merits."

He left the platform to minimal applause. In truth, it signalled relief from those who had managed to remain awake that the ordeal was over. In turn, their "appreciation" woke their colleagues, none of whom showed any regret at having missed the speech. The chairman, presumably sorry that the presentation was finished, sighed audibly and thanked BF for "a speech that those of us who heard it, will remember for a very, very long time".

Meanwhile, a director of another oil company was ringing Hubert Bennett to complain about the most outrageous and incomprehensible tosh that he'd ever heard. He would be demanding a refund for his five delegates and he strongly recommended HB to muzzle this idiot, "a total disgrace to the oil industry", before he further undermined the Broadoak reputation.

HB thanked his friend. Although it was late afternoon, when his fatigue and emotion usually peaked, the call, oddly, gave him some unaccustomed energy. He summoned Benita Harris, his secretary, and dictated a note which was then inserted in BF's file.

Chapter 6

Henry's week was proving unexceptional. He hadn't attributed any significance to the conversation with BF and Jill had said nothing about her fears for her husband's job. Demands on MAD remained minimal so Henry read a few more old circulars, did some filing and participated in the department's instant "slack season" debates.

A school in Grimeshire had been closed because the staff had struck in support of a female colleague. The 58 year old teacher had been sentenced to two years' imprisonment for defending herself with undue force when attacked by a 16 year old boy with a knife. The hooligan had twisted an ankle when trying to avoid her flailing arms. He intended suing the teacher for damages. The pimpled ringleader of the pressure group, students against teachers, SAT, described the closure as "a victory for common sense".

Crime rates in a small northern town had plunged after some local criminals had been taken to the West Indies, at the expense of the council, to show them a different way of life. They then employed their skills in a small and hitherto crime-free village. An official, one of nine travelling with the miscreants, said that his council's plans to pay local criminals to behave, as it was cheaper than locking them up, might have to be reconsidered.

According to a broadsheet newspaper survey, one in four respondents believed that they had lived before. A young waitress maintained that she had been a World War 1 German general and then a crocodile in an early James Bond film.

Bernard Fricker was pre-occupied with finalising details of his family's holiday. On Saturday, they would fly to Boston where they would spend a few days before driving a large camper van to San Francisco, via New York, for the return flight. BF's occasional visits to America had suddenly ceased after his US colleagues told London that he was "incomprehensible, patronising, ignorant and mannerless". BF never wondered why his US trips had suddenly ceased but HB had left a detailed note on the personal file retained in his office.

This year BF wanted what he called a "proper" holiday. His wife, Christine, who had pointed out that she had never accompanied him on an improper vacation, even before they married, had wanted a quiet time, sitting on a warm beach, with some friends close by to challenge his unremitting selfishness and to absorb some of the verbal torrent. At home, denied the chance to baffle with daft management phrases, BF tended instead to talk remorselessly. As his long-suffering wife was wont to say to Mary Lebone, her understanding neighbour, "it's not that he ever says anything. He just goes on and on with his dogmatic assertions, prejudice and ignorance in a non-stop torrent. He drains the energy out of me. I'm tired and I need a relaxing holiday, without him." Her pleas for such a vacation, even with him, had been abruptly dismissed with a curt reminder that they could all benefit from a visit to the United States, especially 11 year-old Horatio, and, lest there were any doubt, he added, "and that's where we're going".

BF had bought dollars some weeks ago, just before the pound rose to its highest level against the dollar for a decade. Now, on Thursday, despite being one of the most loyal of employees he was finding it hard to concentrate on office matters.

Rose Bush, his reliable secretary, had seemed more distant and formal since Monday. She was behaving like Mrs BF when he had supposedly done something wrong but had no idea of the nature of his alleged offence. He had not asked Rose what was wrong, half expecting that, if he did, he might hear the familiar words, "if you don't know, I'm not going to tell you". She had been away on Wednesday, with a heavy cold. The temp was dismissed that evening after a few hours of richly imaginative incompetence. Rose, back after one day, forecast that it could be "up to a week" before normality could be restored.

BF still had to work out the route for the holiday, where they would stop each night and the frequency of rest days when he could take Christine and Horatio to local events and sights. This was not just a family holiday: it was to be "a voyage of exploration and an education" which, hopefully, would improve his relationship with his son. The trouble was that he seldom understood what Horatio was saying. He seemed to speak entirely in jargon and apparently most things were measured in terms of temperature, being cool or uncool, or in relation to illumination, being brilliant or unworthy of the adjective. Despite his tender years, and presumably influenced by too much television watching, he already seemed interested in police work. Repeatedly he requested his father to "get off my case". He was an odd child and BF wondered where he had gone wrong.

Mrs BF also often wondered where she had gone wrong but the question related to her husband. Her mother had always said that he was a strange chap but she conceded that his shoes were always clean, which was a good sign, although of what she never revealed. His eyes were too close together, implying he was untrustworthy, and "people don't like that kind of thing". Her daughter should watch this, presumably to determine if the relative positions of the eyes changed for the worse.

Christine wondered why she tolerated her husband. When she had married him, 15 years ago, despite the precise location of his eyes, he was trusty, considerate, generous and even humorous. Now he was boring, self-opinionated, selfish and since his promotion, he had become besotted with Broadoak. The extra money was welcome but one major disadvantage was that his holiday entitlement increased. Christine hoped that he would not be promoted again, although, mercifully, since that promotion, he had been too busy to have his full holiday.

Mrs Fricker understood neither her husband nor her son and was dreading being cooped up with them both for so long, denied the traditional escape to the neighbour's for a coffee. As she put it, with cutting irony, her human resources were being drained away even before the holiday started. Fortunately, BF himself was responsible for all the planning, except selecting the clothes that she and Horatio would take.

In the office, Hubert Bennett, belatedly realising that the European Commission in Brussels was interested in personnel matters, had asked Fricker for an urgent brief on their role and how this could influence the company. He wanted it on one sheet of paper and although BF said that this was impossible, unless a particularly large sheet, about two metres square, was produced, HB had dismissed his protests immediately, pointing out that the company did not stock such a large size or, so he assumed, not understanding the metric system. "Please ensure that I can understand it easily, so I don't want any bureaucratic jargon and I want you to write it." Consequently, Fricker himself would have to select and summarise the key points whereas if he could write at length, that responsibility could be transferred to his chief executive. Furthermore, if something unexpected happened, BF could be accused of failing to highlight this. This request must be taken seriously.

The board had accepted Fricker's plan on personnel numbers so he had immediately issued a circular to all division heads, advising them that, with immediate effect, they could not replace staff who had left. By the time that the circulars had plodded their way to their intended recipients, some job offers had been made. Worse still, some new people had already arrived, just in time to read the circulars, saying, in effect, that they should not have been engaged.

Not for the first time, BF cursed the fact that the company shunned modern communication systems. Fricker had previously allowed himself to become irritated with HB, on the need for an Intranet and a comprehensive e-mail system but because the chief executive was frightened of anything modern, nothing had happened. Perhaps what had happened on staff recruitment would frighten the purple-faced little Luddite into accepting change. He must write a strong note to his chief executive. Fricker realised he was tired, but dare not delay the composition. He had reserved the afternoon and Friday morning for the report that HB wanted on the European Commission and employee relations. However, he dated the hand-written note for the following day.

Rose had been deeply moved by Henry's dismissal. She had known him for a long time and he had always been polite and friendly. Above all, he was normal and decent and she could understand everything that he said. She had never detected such qualities in senior management who often seemed pre-occupied with their own importance. Frankly, she regarded many of them as over-promoted clerks as lacking in courtesy as they were in competence. Henry's reaction to his cold-blooded dismissal worried her. Was he numbed by the news? He hadn't asked any questions and had even attempted a joke about their next meeting and the dear man thanked them for the coffee and biscuits. Suddenly, she realised that years of practice had enabled her to understand BF. An odd thought crossed her mind. She shivered. Did Henry realise that he had been fired? Was that really possible? She hadn't seen him today but that was not necessarily significant. She decided against making any enquiries.

Late on Friday afternoon, just before BF left the office, Rose found his note to the chief executive on communications, saw that it was not signed so thoughtfully initialled it on a pp basis, without reading it, put it into an envelope, sealed it and despatched it. HB would be at the pub for the rest of the day but he would see it first thing, well, second thing, on Monday. How could she have known that BF had decided against sending it but had forgotten to destroy it?

Rose realised that BF had still not completed all the paper work relating to Henry's enforced departure. As an efficient secretary, she knew that she ought to have reminded her boss, but she was also a sympathetic human being. After all, she said to herself, "I'm only a secretary, not a manager. I'm paid to do as I'm told by managers, not to remind others, the managers who are paid much more than me, to do what they should remember to do anyway without me having to tell them, earning less than them, to remind them of what they ought to do." She was unimpressed with the way in which she had expressed these thoughts, but, being an intelligent woman, she knew what she meant. Rose was always professional but what she was thinking was definitely unprofessional. She disliked BF and the way in which the company disposed of people abruptly as if they were old clothes. It could be her turn one day: it was time to look for a new job.

A few weeks ago, senior executives had spent a long weekend at an expensive hotel in Paris, drinking wine at £50 per bottle, deciding how many people would be jettisoned in the latest purge. The rejects, apart from any in MAD, for which BF had full responsibility, were to be told their fate by their managers, after HB had routinely agreed the usual details, at the end of the cowardly BF's first week in the US. Rose despised him for this. She decided. Company loyalty must be a two-way process. Currently it was not. She could not do much to help Henry but if the forms were not completed before BF left the country, that would give poor old Perkins at least another month's income. Rose knew that she would be blamed for forgetting to remind BF that he had forgotten to organise the necessary paper work but it was worth a few harsh words, followed by an insincere apology, to give Henry a few more weeks. She was always blamed if anything went wrong so this would be a neat way of achieving some justice for previous miscarriages.

By the following Monday, Fricker was in the United States. Fortunately for the future of Anglo-American relations, he was thought to be Australian.

Peace reigned in Broadoak House. Henry Perkins, unaware of what had happened, remained a member of staff. Jill assumed that her contempt for BF had clouded her judgement and she gradually forgot the conversation between Henry and the frightful Fricker.

Just after a decent liquid lunch, HB was reading the note from BF, complaining that the company should join the 21st century. HB understood this part which was written in normal English. He also understood that the main theme was that the company must invest in modern communications and that senior management had a duty to understand the value of computers. BF also argued that management "at the top level" had not made provision for training which was "a serious but typical oversight". Thereafter, the note became even less polite and the reference to the dark ages did not go down well with HB. The remark about managers who "palpably cannot manage" really irritated him, especially when he discovered what the adverb meant. When BF returned from his holiday, he would have a few straight words with him. He also recalled what the US had said about BF some time ago and the more recent comments provoked by Fricker's conference presentation.

HB was angry that, apparently, BF's unacceptable note was copied to all senior managers. BF was becoming too big for his boots. Some cutting down to size was required. He thought about this for a moment and, still basking in the afterglow of his time at the pub, was unsure if, worded like this, it was BF or his boots that had to be diminished. He smiled. BF had to be officially warned. After all, HB was chief executive and that surely entitled him to some respect, didn't it? After a moment's thought, he reached the unanimous decision that it did and anticipated what he would say to the smart alec.

As the days drifted on, and as HB was unable to speak to BF, still presumably undermining the relationship between the US and Australia and then Italy, such was the sophistication of middle America, the irritation festered. HB's anger rose when he realised that he himself would be away for a couple of days when BF returned, thus delaying the confrontation and denying him early satisfaction.

The hotel in Boston was built in 1929 and Christine Fricker opined that many of the staff were probably working there on the opening day and Horatio wondered if they had helped to tip that fateful cargo of tea into Boston harbour. After a walk around the block and a quick snack, the Frickers slumped into slumber.

The rooms were expensive, old and small but the real problem was the lack of restaurants. BF, performing in front of his family, discovered that the two mentioned in the brochure were being renovated and indicated that this reflected badly on management. The restaurant chosen that evening, opposite the hotel, was full. However, the intending diners were promised by the receptionist, who smelt of permed hair, that a table would be available soon. Horatio helpfully added that they would also need three chairs. BF was asked for his name, so that he could be called when the appropriate furniture was available. Being British, and not having heard that the majority of potential customers seemed to be called Chuck or Skip, he said "Fricker, Bernard" and then, trying to clarify matters added "Bernard Fricker".

During the wait, Horatio asked whether five towpaths made a footpath and why some children had four fathers. His parents tried to explain that this was impossible, without revealing any biological details, before their chuckling son said that he meant forefathers.

About 20 minutes later, the public address system boomed out that the table for Fricker-Bernard-Bernard-Fricker and his party of three was now ready. As they were led to their table, Horatio asked whether people with long names had to wait longer. Perhaps, after all, he might enjoy this holiday.

Every night during their stay in Boston, as an irate BF explained to hotel staff, the nearby streets were used by emergency vehicles, seemingly, to test their sirens, whistles, hooters and all the other bizarre noises that such fire tenders, police cars and ambulances emit. Horatio added that the noises indicated that they were also going backwards. BF told an apologetic duty manager that "I just cannot believe that so many accidents, crimes and fires occur in the early hours of the morning in this small area, night after night".

During the day, the city was much quieter. Horatio suggested that this was because all the crimes were committed in early morning. "Surely, the police cars, wailing in the night as their occupants drive through the empty echoing streets, warn criminals that they are coming. So it must be more sensible to commit crimes in Boston during the night as the police kindly tell the crooks they're coming." He finished this perceptive insight with the thought that the only criminals who were caught at night must be deaf.

After the emergency services had finished their nocturnal games, the local workmen arrived to tear up the sidewalk immediately alongside the hotel. Commendably, they did not leave the old paving stones by the side of the road because people could trip over them and then sue the local authority. Consequently, large cranes picked them up, the stones, not the people, and dropped them into an otherwise empty skip. The paving stones then bounced but their noise reverberated with diminishing effect, until the next stone was dropped, when the whole cycle began again.

After the first day in Boston the weather improved and the family followed the brochure's advice and walked and walked around the parks and historic sites. On the second day they took a trolley ride around the city and its environs. The driver, who announced that he used to be a banker, wanted to "share" everything with his passengers. Christine said that it was a pity he did not do that in his previous occupation. She also wondered if he was paid by the word but Bernard could hear nothing wrong in his comments which were "clear and concise". Even Horatio laughed at this.

"Ladies and gentlemen, boys and girls, guys, I should like to suggest to you, if I might share the idea, that you might like to consider looking out of the bus on the left hand side, which, if you do, and I recommend you to do, if you don't mind my mentioning it, but I think that you will find it interesting, if you would permit me to say that, because I do want to share with you…. " Unfortunately, it took him so long to go through this patter, that whatever was being described had already passed. He was later replaced by another driver, a youth whose commentary would not have taxed the understanding of a retarded parrot.

One restaurant offered "eat as much as you like for $6.95" but the smell emanating from the building had deterred any customers. Horatio, encouraged to use his eyes and ears, to "maximise the on-going benefits from visiting the New World" asked if his parents would mind if he exchanged his watch. A puzzled Christine asked what he meant. Triumphantly, he said that he'd seen a notice which said "Watch for cars". In the young Fricker's view, that represented good value. Later, Christine wondered why Americans, having asked a question, such as "what's your name?", and being told, said "ok" in a manner which implied approval of the answer.

On their last morning, they collected their camper van, dubbed Winifred Bago by Horatio. There were a few incidents during the rest of the holiday and Bernard, for example, was angry that, on their last day, a traffic policeman had abused him after what seemed to be a very minor traffic violation. The arrogant BF converted an ordinary misunderstanding into a fully-fledged crisis. The policeman, handicapped by being foreign, although BF only suppressed this observation at the last moment, had merely wanted to remind him that minimum speed limits applied. Common sense, courtesy, tact and intelligence were discarded as BF thought that it would be wise to retaliate first. It was not. Mrs Fricker's frequent warning tugs on his sleeve had been ignored prompting him to pause in his opening speech to say "for god's sake woman, stop that. I'm trying to explain to this, this man, here that I've done nothing wrong. I didn't know that there was a minimum speed, seems pretty silly if you ask me". Christine said that nobody was asking him.

He addressed the policeman again. "Let me make myself crystal clear, I was most certainly unaware that you, apparently a police officer as I now learn, were behind me and I certainly did not know that the ludicrous noise that you were emitting was designed to encourage me to stop. I accelerated so sharply because I thought that I was being chased by a lunatic." It was only a hissing "Bernard" from his knowing wife that saved BF from adding "and now I see that I was". "My instinct was to look for a policeman. Then I realised that you were. I mean, not a lunatic, but a policeman, so I stopped." This extraordinary outburst, promoted by the cocktail of arrogance and nerves, prompted a heated conversation. BF's ancestors, according to the enraged policeman, had been deported from Britain to the colonies and, in his considered opinion, if BF was an example, they certainly did the right thing. The only problem now was that occasionally, "some of you Australians escape over here".

Christine's calm intervention saved BF from serious trouble. After a final roasting, which HB would have enjoyed, BF was allowed to proceed. Christine, meanwhile, hid her head in her hands. Her mother had been right. He was a strange chap and as she stared at the floor of the camper van, she noticed that his shoes were dirty.

Horatio's desire to join the police force increased. It must be great fun to be so rude to an adult and to be paid for it. Because his recent negotiations for increased pocket money had ended in acrimony, he enjoyed his father's humiliation. His mother was not enjoying the holiday, even before she succumbed to food poisoning. She had been obliged to remind Bernard that she had not deliberately contracted her "problems" just to upset his plans, contrary to the impression that he conveyed to everyone they met.

Horatio had enjoyed parts of the holiday but not for the reasons his father would have predicted. Apart from the traffic incident, there had been some other highlights. One night, after Christine had insisted that they stayed in hotels and not in "that mobile box", BF and spouse were allocated a bedroom with a very high ceiling. Seeking to pull the curtains in their room, Bernard had ignored the cord and his wife's advice and had sought to unite the two very tall maroon curtains by hand. Because of their weight, nothing happened so more effort was applied. Suddenly, the curtain rail gave way under the strain. The elderly curtains and the rail fell to earth. BF was immediately trapped and as he tried to escape, Christine and Horatio, coming in from the room next door, on hearing the noise, were overcome with laughter. This did not please BF whose precise location could only be determined by the occasional bump in the heavy velvet and very dusty material sprawled all over the bedroom floor. When he was released, he looked as if spiders had been practising their web-making skills on him for several decades, which, in a sense, they had.

A shower was essential and, as if to prove that this was one of those days, as Bernard turned the bath control to shower, the device fell away from the wall, showering him not with water but brick dust. The following morning BF and the hotel came to an agreement that took into account the two incidents. Horatio, who had listened to the discussion with ill-disguised glee, told his mother that he had really enjoyed this overnight stay and that in future, he wanted to be called Chuck. Christine recalled that this happened to be the name of the manager who had been so critical of her husband.

Back in the office, an exhausted BF felt that a peaceful holiday sitting in the sun, doing nothing for a few days, would be very welcome. That, of course, was precisely what his wife had requested in the first place. What made it more irritating, was that today was the best so far that summer. Unfortunately, the end of the American holiday had been marred by some of the worst storms for several years. Flooding had forced BF to abandon his original route and the instant improvisation had created more problems with Christine and Horatio who seemed so ungrateful for what he was frequently told was "the trip of a lifetime". Nevertheless, BF immediately resumed work. Because he was unpopular and incomprehensible, nobody really wanted to hear about his vacation and, as he had frequently reminded colleagues, "we're here to output-optimise, not to verbalise".

Soon, he realised that the paper work necessary to achieve Henry's dismissal had not been done. This must be rectified immediately. Pausing only to berate Rose for not doing it herself and for not reminding him, he completed the paper work, signed the forms that she had eventually produced from his drafts, put some of the documents in an envelope marked Accounts and placed it in his outbox.

Broadoak still had a messenger system and used, or, rather, abused, the national youth training scheme. This allowed them to use low-cost labour for some routine jobs, under the pretence of training some well-intentioned young people. Nigel Smalljoy was no idiot. He had already obtained four "A" levels and had been offered a place at the Business School at Dartcaster University. Perhaps naively, he thought that working for a big company for a few weeks before he went north would give him some insight into how such a group operated. It did but not how he had expected. He was astonished, for example, at how some senior managers treated their junior colleagues and he could not understand how industry, if this company was representative, could ever expect to recruit new, young graduates if the way the group conducted itself were ever publicised. He and his contemporaries believed that this was a "hire and fire" industry which paid little regard to the impact of its operations on the environment and which was "managed" by some particularly stupid people who had inexplicably floated to the top.

Instead of doing something that would have helped him in later life, Nigel had been assigned to what was called the post room. He had become very friendly with Taffy and his chums and, taking an interest in the company's business, read much of the inter-office mail. He had particularly relished the note from BF to HN, which had mysteriously fallen out of the envelope that Rose had licked inadequately into submission. That said, he was concerned at its contents. What worried him was that when a new electronic system was introduced, as BF had noted, the company could dismiss all the members of the post room, thus making big financial savings, and it was clear from the way that note was written, BF had little regard for the messengers "who are more interested in the disgusting pin-ups on their walls than in distributing mail around the building efficiently". That was really unfair. Most of the girls in the pics were particularly attractive. Although he was not a permanent member of staff and would soon be at university, he felt for his new colleagues. They deserved better and, anyway, the remarkably pompous BF, addressing him as "Littlejoy", inaccurate and rude, had loftily shouted at him for failing to address him as "sir". He had apologised to "Sir Fricker" but this comment failed to reach managerial ears.

That afternoon, Nigel collected BF's latest mail which, unknown to him, included the note on Henry's dismissal, went to the toilets and stuffed the documents carefully into his now empty plastic lunch box. Later, the contents were taken home, torn up without being read and placed in the dustbin.

Even a few days later, BF was still exhausted. At least, he had sorted out the Perkins problem. Being a loyal employee and senior manager, he enjoyed making an impact on the company and if this meant making people redundant, so be it. There were too many parasites who thought that the world owed them a living and who did very little for their money. BF, seldom stirring from his office, knew very little about the company or the people for whom he had some kind of responsibility, but he just knew that there were too many slackers. It was good to be able to reduce their numbers from time to time. For example, almost every day, when he left about 80 minutes after the official closing time, the place was deserted. What had happened to company loyalty? Perhaps another round of meaningless redundancies would encourage the others? He knew that, financially, the money saved by these dismissals was marginal and that external factors seldom justified the cull but it was good to show them who was boss. Besides, the shareholders always reacted favourably when redundancies were announced and he had a large number of shares himself.

He never thought of his colleagues as people: they were, he said, in a moment of unambiguous clarity and candour, "factors of production and, as in any process, the combination of factors changes and economics demands that the unwanted factors be discarded".

His plans, that the dismissed should have been told their fate whilst he was away, had not happened because in his pre-holiday haste, he now discovered that he had not completed all the forms properly. He must make up for lost time. Despite being weary, he laboured late into the evening and was pleased to be able to add another six to the total number of redundancies already agreed. He drafted out all the documents and put them on Rose's desk, for processing and despatch to the chief executive.

The following morning, she looked at the routine papers relating to those whose working lives were about to be terminated. One name on the list screamed at her. Bernard Fricker had named himself as one of those whose career in Broadoak should be ended. After a little introspection, and because she usually did as she was told, she dutifully keyed in all the details for submission to BF. He was, if anything, even more tired because his slumber had been disrupted at 1.50 am. by a telephone caller, whose number had been withheld, who asked him to send a taxi to pick up a couple from a cottage in the neighbouring village. It was obviously an honest mistake because BF could not think of anyone who would play such a cruel trick. In his fatigue, he forgot that this was the third time that this had happened since last year's redundancies and there was still the mystery of why some un-ordered manure had been dropped by his front door.

Rose, regaining her professional stance, had decided that she should make some mention of BF's imminent "retirement". She had worked for him for years so she really had to say something. She tried to hand over the documents and started to make her prepared remark but was angrily interrupted. "Don't bother me with that lot. I've already counter-signed them all. I'm far too busy to discuss it. You know what to do, you've done it often enough for heaven's sake, then take them to HB. He wants to see them now and then the individuals can be notified as quickly as possible. Just get on with it."

Rose was happy to obey. She checked the forms, made a note of the names, sealed the envelope and headed for HB's secretary's room. She was away, using up the remainder of her sick leave, spending ten days walking round the Dorshire coast, so Ms. Bush placed the documents on the chief executive's desk. He grunted, looked up, saw Rose, for whom he had always had a soft spot, courteously asked her how she was, thanked her for the documents and requested her to please tell BF to come to see him in 20 minutes.

When Rose entered, he had had just re-read the BF note and had been working himself up into a controlled but modest rage. Now that he had been polite and friendly to Rose, he had to start again. Idly, still pondering what he would say, he flicked through the list of those who were to be "let go". Suddenly, he saw the name of Bernard Fricker. His possible departure had never been discussed, so HB concluded that he had decided to leave and this was his typical way of submitting his resignation. Without further ado, a stunned HB countersigned all the documents, summoned a temporary secretary and sent the documents on their way to Accounts and to the individual departmental managers to break news of their departures to the redundant.

A few minutes later, BF knocked on HB's door. The chief executive seemed to be in a most affable mood as he sang out "come in if you please". Uninvited, Fricker sat down. HB responded. "Take a chair my dear chap. I hope that you had a good holiday and that the locals were agreeable. I expect Christine and your son really enjoyed themselves, didn't they? What' his name, Nelson isn't it?"

"No, Horatio, actually."

Small talk always bothered BF and he wondered why he had been invited to see the chief executive. His unasked question was about to be answered.

"I had wanted to talk to you about your recent note." Fricker paled, did not notice the use of the pluperfect, and resisted the temptation to say, at this early stage, that he was sorry and that it had not been his intention to send such an abrasive communication. Perhaps it was not the rude note? No, it couldn't have been, he hadn't sent it. It must be another note on something else. Perhaps it was the one on Europe? It immediately became clear that it was not.

HB then made a few restrained comments about the intemperate note on computerisation but the prepared remarks and rebukes remained unspoken. Fricker was astounded. He had expected a very severe rebuke. Instead of that, the chief executive was virtually benign. Perhaps he realised that he, Fricker, had been right?

What happened next was the biggest surprise BF had ever received.

"Anyway, that's now academic. I see that you want to leave us."

"I'm sorry, I don't understand. I hope that I haven't done anything dreadful." Was this HB's way of saying that he was being dismissed, but for what? The human resources man began to compose an appeal against his sentence and decided that, for once, he must grovel and, worse still, it must be in plain English. Before he could speak, HB obligingly filled in the details, from which it was clear that the note played no part in the termination of his services.

"I've got a form here, countersigned by you, recommending redundancy. Look, here it is, it's not a forgery is it? Anyway, I assumed that it wasn't and that it was your way of saying that you wanted to leave us. I've counter-signed all the necessary documents relating to the next round of dismissals so all that remains to be agreed is the appropriate date of your departure."

BF had gone very pale as the enormity of what was being said sank in. Slowly, he recovered some of his composure, but not, as it transpired, his job. "I really have no idea how my name appeared on that list. It's a complete mystery to me. I think that I need a holiday. I've been working too hard lately."

That was too much for HB who was beginning to enjoy himself. "Good god, man, you've only just come back from umpteen weeks, swanning around the US. " Fricker came close to pointing out that this was the first year in which he had taken his full holiday but decided that this would not help his case. "I apologise for all this and I really don't know how it all happened but as you know, HB, I really have been under sustained pressure for some time now and, although I don't like to mention this, my wife has been ill. I really don't want to go, I enjoy my job too much and I don't think that I should ever find another company, and, I must say, a chief executive, for whom I have such respect."

HB was having more fun than he had experienced since he was last drunk, which, lets' think this through, was yesterday. A few grovels later Fricker begged "please, could you just tear up the forms and then forget it?"

The chief executive could not agree, and, with hands together and forming a triangle as if in prayer, said "I know that I'm regarded as a simple chap, but it seems wrong to me that anyone on the list of compulsory redundancies should have the opportunity of trying to persuade me to reverse the decision of a very senior manager", and here HB positively purred, "in this case that means you. Also, if one person were allowed to argue their case against dismissal with me, then everyone should have the right and that would be wrong. I imagine you would agree with that. Am I right? In this case, as I say, the senior manager is you." The chief executive delighted in reminding BF again that it was his own apparent decision. "I suggest that you have a word with yourself but I warn you, in such circumstances, I always support the original decisions of my senior colleagues otherwise we would have anarchy."

A flustered and bewildered BF, still unsure if this was a giant hoax, made another plea. "We both know that, however this happened, it was a mistake and that nobody ever intended that I should be made redundant. My name's never been on any list and I've always worked hard and it would be most unfair to penalise me in this way. Surely, even senior managers are allowed to make one mistake?"

HB said that many of the others that BF had recommended for dismissal had also worked hard for the company and, as far as he knew, had not made even one major mistake. Then, showing unaccustomed mental agility, he readily agreed that dismissal for one mistake would not be fair. BF sighed with relief but HB had not finished. "I won't argue with the view that nobody should be asked to leave for one mistake but your first mistake was to upset our American colleagues who asked me never to allow you to visit them again because you were so rude and arrogant. Your second mistake was to send me that hostile note about computerisation. Clearly, you think that I'm an idiot."

BF was not sure whether he was supposed to comment but, even although he had little to lose, decided against commenting on whether or not HB was an idiot and said that he had not signed the note and that the only it only carried the pp of Rose Bush. It was not his intention to send it to HB. "I wrote it when I was very tired and I know that I should have destroyed it but I didn't and I'm sorry because I know what I wrote was unfair and confrontational. It was also ill-advised."

HB was now really enjoying himself. "It certainly was that. As it happens, matey, you might like to know that I had made arrangements for staff training so that we could all use an Intranet and e-mails in our work. I was also about to ask you to devise an advertisement for a keen and knowledgeable young computer services manager."

"Your third mistake was to deliver an incomprehensible and apparently insulting speech to a conference in London recently. A friend of mine said that it brought this company into disrepute and having seen a transcript, I agree, in so far as I can understand a single word."

"Your fourth mistake was to advance yourself for early retirement. I'm not going to reverse that decision, which, if I may say so, is one of the best you have made for some years. We've all tolerated your use of pompous language and self-importance here in Head Office for too long and you've always implied that you're so superior. Perhaps it's because you use such silly management speak. Well, you're not superior to the rest of us. Frankly, you lack the human touch necessary in human resources work. Making staff pay for the use of coat hangers was a big mistake as was asking secretaries to clean their own offices. Without Rose's help, we could have had a strike and our US shareholders were not impressed with the adverse publicity we received here in the tabloids. In any event, I was considering moving you to our boiler maintenance division in Macgrimville in the north of Scotland. Now, please excuse me because I've work to do. I'm going to have to let you go, with immediate effect."

Back in his own office, BF sat down, sighed and stared at the wall. This was his life. What on earth would he do? What could he say to his wife? Above all, what about the financial arrangements? He looked at the file copy of the documents that had been passed to the chief executive. His compensation cheered him up. He had been generous and HB had said that he had approved all the documents. He would emphasise the size of his compensation when telling Christine that he would be at home for some time, whilst he looked for a "small, local job" because being a senior executive had been very stressful and he feared for his health.

Chapter 7

Mrs Christine Fricker was enjoying a few minutes' peace before Bernard returned home from the office to give her a generously detailed account of the day's activities in which he played the hero. He never asked about her day but as she was not an important executive, nothing interesting could have happened. Christine, still weary after her vacation, dreaded the sound of his key in the front door. She would take time to recover from their "holiday" which she had described to her friends as a sentence with no remission for tolerance. Horatio was playing in the garden with a friend, enjoying a new game which he called cop and motorist, which allowed him to be thoroughly offensive to his friend with total impunity.

A stunned Fricker did not know what to tell Christine. His human resources instincts, which had carried him to the highest levels of management, suggested that there could be some friction. Christine had not been a jovial companion for some time and he sensed that he should not expect sympathy and a shoulder he could use in lachrymose fashion. He opted for the truth. He would tell her that he was going to leave the company. Unfortunately, that was as far as his executive brain had taken him. He could claim that he couldn't stand the strain any more and had resigned but then Christine would have told him that he should have discussed it with her in advance. He also realised that any reference to his health would have invited the charge that he had said nothing about this before and, doubtless, "you were well enough to drive us across the US in that prison cell on wheels".

Should he say that he had been obliged to accept compulsory redundancy? No, this would have implied that the company felt that it could manage without him. Just briefly, in a moment of insanity, he had even contemplated admitting that he had accidentally fired himself but had laid down excellent terms. That would unwise but now he was going home without a plan.

BF, now on the train, turned to the business pages of his paper. The main feature argued that work should always be a joke as that improved productivity. A sneering Fricker turned to the situations vacant page. He ignored the numerous ads for chefs, headed "Pan European opportunities" and was pleased at the number of vacancies for serious people.

There were many organisations, including some whose function was impossible to discern because of the jargon, who wanted dynamic, thrusting market leaders, who could grow fast in a continually-changing environment, who were clearly focussed on customer relations, pre-occupied with strategically-selected core values and possessed of worthy cultures. Encouraged, BF knew that he could thrust with the best of them. He read a few more ads and became convinced that he was ideally qualified for many of these advertised positions. Companies wanted workaholics who could think strategically and clearly, with enquiring minds and an enjoyment of people, although BF was not sure what this sloppy liberal thinking meant. Successful candidates would relish the opportunity to make a significant impact on the business of their new employers, and have a high degree of intellectual curiosity and a persuasive, well-informed and "action-centred style".

BF turned to the local paper and the following ad immediately caught his eye.

We want a powerfully-motivated, dynamic well-rounded strong person who wants to make a real difference to society. You will enjoy the challenging and exacting work in a team-led environment, occupying a highly visible role which exposes you to the community. Significant communication skills are required as you and your colleagues prioritise and resolve problems. You will need resilience and tenacity to ensure that everyone involved in the project remains focused on collecting and then delivering results. You will also have a role in driving the team, at least once a week, towards its predicated goal and you will enjoy limited travel. We can promise you that each day will bring a fresh and sometimes not so fresh challenge.

BF particularly liked the wording of the ad. It was the sort of thing that he used to write himself. If he were selected for this obviously important job, he would save on the expensive fares to London and would be able to spend more time with his family. He read on. Applications should be sent to the Managing Co-ordinator, UDMCRS, (Unwanted domestic material community removal service), at the local council. Candidates should explain why they wanted to be associated with the reclamation scheme, RUBBISH. (The removal of unwanted bins and bags into selected holes.) Envelopes should be clearly marked: "Working for the local community".

Of course, most people know that honesty seldom dominates job advertisements. Umpteen decades ago, company personnel managers bleated boastfully that the sky was the limit. Apart from becoming a company pilot, the closest anyone came to that level was achieved by the lift attendant. An honest advertisement might have been written along these lines:

"Young single man, preferably a dullard, required for light but tedious work in an over-staffed department in a well-known major company. Duties will include the organisation of departmental Christmas parties and collections for colleagues who are doing something that merits a party. Work-related duties are too boring to mention but pay is good and lifetime employment is virtually guaranteed for the right sycophant. The department is well-known in the group for its cricketing skills so preference will be given to a fast bowler but prowess with the bat would be an added advantage. Free membership of a well-run sports club is available to all staff members who are automatically eligible to receive free railway tickets from London to the club. The post will not suit bright people who will become bored and thus disruptive."

BF returned to his broadsheet. It seemed that all the jobs were challenging or exacting and many were "fully in keeping with our culture that allows people to challenge the accepted and to think outside the box". BF knew precisely what that meant but lesser-educated people might have wondered if this meant that thinking ended when they were in their coffins?

He was just mildly concerned about the emphasis on being a good team player. He had always seen himself as above that kind of thing. It seemed that some companies wanted people with "hands-on experience" or "hands on" team players. Who, precisely, or what, could they expect to handle, especially those leaders with "high energy levels", which could indicate health problems? Most companies specified "self-starters" but what can be said of those who demanded "gregarious self-starters"? Didn't gregarious mean "living in flocks"? Some companies wanted gravitas, which, given the nature of their ads, would have amused readers with a sense of humour but BF was impressed. Orientation was also important. To be successful in any job application, it seemed that candidates should be oriented towards client services, profit and results, the nature of which was never specified. They should be prepared to "forge careers in a stimulatingly-oriented role".

Occasionally, applicants were told of the necessary posture that must be adopted on being selected for a post. Many had to be "client-facing" but that was difficult to reconcile with another group which wanted the new person to have an "on the desk role".

Roles to be played by successful candidates included being pivotal, diverse, key and of a nature that added value. Many roles were "highly visible" and "at the very heart of the organisation" and some successful candidates would be exposed to portals, senior management, risks, competition and new relevant regulations. Successful candidates would be enthusiastic, sometimes to the extent of "bubbling over" and energetic. They also had to be excellent communicators, dynamic and self-motivated. BF became even more confident.

A more objective observer might have noted that it was desirable for a candidate not to be bothered about split infinitives, the incorrect use of the apostrophe, the indiscriminate Use of Upper Case letters or total gobbledegook. One organisation confided that it had chosen "to grow it's own people" and another promised successful applicants that they would be able to "shape and develop this fairly greenfield stepping stone structure".

Mindsets and acumen were important. Candidates should have a "strong commercial mindset", or "strong commercial acumen", or "obviously commercial acumen". An ability to play cricket used to be one desirable characteristic but now it seemed that athletics would be favoured, given the number of times a good track record was cited. Driving was important, although few ads mentioned cars. Instead advertisers wanted successful applicants to drive the company's global presence, new ideas, systems and teams. Construction skills were also in demand. "Cross-functional relationships" must be built and one group wanted someone who enjoyed "building client relationships".

BF was much encouraged. He could help any of these companies. Although he still had to face Christine, he felt that the future was not as bleak as he had feared. As he walked down the path to his front door, Bernard was acutely aware that he had still not decided how to break the news to his wife so, seated in the lounge, he started with the headlines.

"I'm going to leave Broadoak Oil."

The announcement was greeted in total silence. Indeed, Christine's first reaction was that she was having an unpleasant nightmare. A shake of her head and a self-administered and unexpectedly painful pinch, confirmed, alas, that, quite definitely, she was awake. Apart from losing an income, it seemed that she was being sentenced to jail and gaining the most irritating man she knew as a cellmate. She was so startled and angry that the composition of her initial sentence took several seconds. Christine's opening attack, which could fairly be characterised as unfavourable, assumed that, because BF had said nothing about alternative employment, he had resigned to take early retirement. As her pithy comments were less than conciliatory and contained not a syllable of sympathy, he tried to say something. His chance came and went, even although Christine seemed to be taking in a large breath to allow her to express herself for longer and with greater force.

There was an impressive silence whilst she organised he next onslaught and a braced Bernard could say nothing. Unusually, he was speechless but he didn't have to wait long for the verbal hurricane.

"I don't suppose that you thought that you needed to discuss such an important matter with me, first, before applying for early retirement. Oh, no, after all, your son and wife count for nothing. You made that clear when you insisted on that terrible holiday. This is just typical of you. As always, you put yourself first. Bernard, you're selfish, egotistical and unthinking. How do you think we're going to pay Horatio's school fees? I suppose you've decided that I must go out to work and look after the house and garden as well? Is that what you want? Thanks for letting me know in advance. I'm really grateful.

"Only a fool would leave without having another job to go to or are you really going to retire completely, in which case where do you think the money's coming from? Why did you do it? At times like this, I must admit that I don't know why I married you. My mother was right. What do you think that we're going to do now?"

BF, never a quick thinker, nevertheless, realised that his wife had made the wrong assumption about the reasons for his departure from Broadoak. This made it even more difficult for him to explain. He had also noted the reference to Christine's mother's views but decided astutely that this was not the best time to open a new front. Anyway, he had never liked the old woman who looked like a bulldog and who always spoke in riddles. He couldn't tell Christine the full truth so his only option was to cite compulsory redundancy and the great difficulties that faced the industry. Just six months ago, multinational groups had been making record profits. In some cases, the figures dwarfed the national income of countries. Now, as the oil price had gone down by a few cents, thousands of redundancies had to be made as the supine companies sought to appease the immature and inexperienced braces-wearing analysts.

His pride would be severely damaged if he admitted compulsory redundancy but, if she persisted in her erroneous view that he had resigned voluntarily, it might be more than his pride that was damaged. He might even attract a scintilla of sympathy and avoid another highly critical torrent of words. Of course, he had been incompetent in including his name on the list, but HB could have deleted it. No, he was satisfied, it had clearly been a forced removal.

He stopped his wife's tirade by holding up his hand and saying "this was not" and he emphasised the negative, "voluntary, as you seem to think, and I certainly did not resign". He even sought to regain a little lost ground by adding "do you really think that I would let you and young Horatio down by leaving without having found another job? What kind of fool do you think I am?"

Christine decided that this was rhetorical.

"No, I have been made redundant by the company that I have given the best years of my life to. I've played a leading part in making that company what it is today and now they just tell me to leave. I've been discarded, like an old sock. Good god, woman, do you think I wanted to leave? I enjoyed working there and I like to think that I've helped by streamlining the workforce, for example. In the last three years, I've helped to get rid of nearly half of the staff and profitability is now much higher." BF had a vague feeling that something here did not strengthen his case nor endear him to his increasingly enraged spouse.

Mrs Fricker returned to the attack, seemingly no less angry than in her opening salvo. "Don't call me woman. I'm your wife, God help me."

"Sorry."

"You're supposed to be in charge of personnel or whatever fancy name you give it now. Doesn't that give you some influence? Anyway, how can you be made redundant? They'll still need someone to look after staff matters. You've always told me that you and that Bennett man are very close and that he relies on you and then, suddenly, without any warning, you're fired. Some friend. I just don't believe it. There must be more to it than this. I reckon you must have a legal case against the company. We must investigate." She paused for breath.

During the onslaught, BF, desperate for some peace and sensing that he was sinking in an ever-deepening hole, even re-considered the option of telling the whole truth. He tried another approach and even as he uttered the words, he knew how absurdly inadequate they sounded and awaited the new verbal blows. "As you know, I've always been a loyal company man but I just felt that I couldn't really fight this although I did have a word with HB."

Mrs Fricker snorted so loudly that a passer by might have been forgiven for thinking that some pigs had taken up residence chez Fricker. "You know, Bernard, you're even more stupid than I thought. Loyalty is a two way process. Let's face it. The company has just sacked you."

Bernard tried to interrupt but a wagging finger warned him to stay silent.

"You talk of your loyalty. Are you completely mad? Did it not occur to you, even although you're handicapped by having a brain smaller than a shrivelled garden pea, that you should have raised merry hell? You had a word with him. What, precisely, was the word? I think that on such a historic occasion the world has a right to know which word it was. Was it right-ho?"

BF thought that this was two words but remained dumb.

"What did he say? Did this word immediately silence him or persuade him to change his mind? I think not. Are you a man or a mouse?"

Bernard took advantage of the lull, induced by his wife's need to inhale, and took an instant decision not to pursue the seemingly irrelevant but interesting issue of whether he was a human being or a rodent. Apart from anything else, conceding that, in some ways the latter was accurate, there would be adverse implications for Horatio, to whom nature had given some large ears. He also admired the way in which his spouse had constructed her last paragraph, despite being very emotional. On balance, silence on this issue was advisable.

"When I say that I had a word that was just my way of saying that I let him know, in words of one syllable, what I thought about the whole appalling business. I also thought that if I raised hell, my compensation might be cut and, frankly, it's not bad and a darn sight more than we paid the last batch of losers, I mean redundant staff." Somehow, as he uttered the words, he realised that this was not a very powerful argument. Christine, well aware of her husband's penchant for using long meaningless words in the office, sensed that he could never use words of one syllable so, even if he had spoken out, it was unlikely that the chief executive would have understood what he was saying.

"HB told me that he had been thinking of transferring me to another job but nothing appropriate had cropped up. One suggestion was that I moved to Macgrimeville in the north of Scotland, to look after boiler maintenance. We agreed that was not a good career move, especially as I know nothing about boilers and hate the Scots. I can never understand what they're saying."

Mrs Fricker nodded assent. She was the one who always rectified a fault on their boiler, solved any other household problem or summoned expert assistance and then briefed the repairman very specifically with all the necessary details. She returned to the attack. "So, you decided that moving to Macgrimeville, wherever that is, was worse than being unemployed. I'm sure that other human resources managers, or whatever silly title you had" and she cruelly stressed the word 'had', "will immediately see that. Couldn't you even have said that you would think about it, to buy yourself some time"?

Untypically, BF used his imagination. He knew that Christine, like him, had never been to Macgrimeville, so he thought that it would help if he painted a dire picture of the place. He took a deep breath and, in the temporary silence, he heard Horatio shout out, "I don't care if you do come from Australia, any more of that talk and your holiday will come to a sudden end. Now, stand with your feet apart and put your hands on this car roof, I mean fence." Fricker resumed. "The place is barren, cold throughout the year because of howling gales, almost unpopulated except for thousands of noisy sheep and miles from anywhere and the people have funny accents and hate incomers. I know that you would never have liked it. It's almost impossible to garden there because of the wind and cold and most importantly, I know we'd agree that Horatio's education should not be interrupted at this crucial stage. I think that the nearest good school is miles away and he would probably have to have been a boarder."

This won a respite and a grudging comment from his wife that she understood all that "but it would have been nice to have been consulted and anyway, if there are no people, only sheep, why do they need a boiler maintenance service? Do the sheep feel the cold? Don't they have wool, or are they a superior kind of boiler-owning sheep?"

Bernard, sensing that the tide might be about to turn, ignored the caustic questions. "I was able to negotiate some fairly good financial terms". BF omitted to mention that the figures were standard and that no discussions had taken place between the human resources manager and the redundant worker. It was all laid down in the standard contract and BF had always insisted that no more was paid.

The rest of the evening was devoted to what BF would do in the future and his wife, calmer after the initial shock, kindly said that she would spare no effort to help him find another job as soon as possible. What she did not say was that it was in her interests to ensure that his seven day a week occupation of the house was terminated as rapidly as possible. Meanwhile, she would ease the pressures on the family budget by taking a part-time job with the local estate agent. What she did not say was that it was in her interests to be out of the house for as long as possible. "He's been pestering me for ages to work there for at least three days a week and this could help us if we have to 'move on' ourselves". BF shuddered. Life was not going to be very pleasant. Others whom he had callously and thoughtlessly dismissed could have told him that.

Chapter 8

After an early lunch, a pensive BF, with just a few more days of Broadoak employment remaining, approached the eighth floor lift. The man walking towards him looked like Henry Perkins but this was unlikely because most employees seldom worked out a period of notice. He looked more closely. It was Perkins. For once communicating unambiguously, he snarled "Why are you still here? I told you that you were redundant before I went on holiday. I distinctly remember saying that I was going to have to let you go, with immediate effect. Then I went to the US and the forms were completed when I got back. You shouldn't be here."

Shattered by these totally unexpected comments and angry with himself for not realising the fool's intentions, a pale Perkins muttered "well, I'm still here and nobody has sent me any papers". He managed to rally quickly enough to say that he gathered that BF had been made redundant but, assuming that HB, who had summoned him, was about to dismiss him "again", felt faint. One thing, he thought, if he does fire me, at least I'll know what he's talking about.

BF, astonished to see Henry, omitting to ask him how he knew about his own imminent departure, launched into his well-rehearsed interpretation of events. "Frankly, when I was in the US, I realised that there was more to life than working for Broadoak and trying to keep up with modern management techniques so I decided on early retirement. I may write a book or two on management and I expect to do some broadcasting. I've often been told that I'm a unique communicator. Actually, I'm waiting for a reply from the BBC to my letter telling them that I was available for management and business programmes."

"Forgive me for not stopping, BF, but I'm on my way to see HB." He headed for the chief executive's office, still dazed by what he had just heard about his own future but pleased that, for the first time, at the last opportunity, he had called his tormentor BF. Why was he still on the pay roll if he had been dismissed? BF was usually very efficient.

Benita Harris, HB's regular secretary, just back from using up her remaining sick leave and looking appropriately fit and brown, announced Perkins' arrival. A fearful Henry, invited to sit down, did so timidly, concerned that, if the chair were like that in BF's office, he would probably vanish. That seemed appropriate: he was just about to be dismissed. However, he could still see HB behind his impressive antique desk. Perkins sat expectantly, fearing the worst but hoping for a miracle. His legs turned to jelly. Was he about to receive his desert? He was too worried to glance at the usual management trophies littering the office but he could not avoid noticing incredibly ugly pink plastic models of a fox and an ox, newly presented by the grateful owner of the local pub. He was only interested in why he had been invited to see HB who was back from lunch suspiciously early.

"Henry, we've known each other a long time." This was an inauspicious start. Perkins was worried. HB, who had returned early from lunch, had addressed him by his first name. All this did not bode well. Another few sentences and he would know his fate. Hopefully, he could stay for another two months, when he would have completed 38 years of service and his pension would increase. HB was not a bad chap; he would understand and some of his outstanding holiday could be commuted. As far as Henry knew, Jill was doing well in her job and he might be able find some local work although it would probably not pay well. Typically, Perkins was already rationalising what might come.

His reverie ended.

"And I want to thank you for the consistently good work you've done in your department. That's why I'm sorry that you won't be working there in the future."

Henry gulped and knew that his face was ashen. The same could not be said of HBs' face which contained enough colour for both of them. The axe was poised above Henry's head.

Jill Perkins, usually charged with finding speakers and venues, was trying to stimulate attendance at an imminent conference to be held in Aberdeen, the home of the UK's offshore oil industry. All senior staff had been diverted to bolster the number of delegates for the event which was concerned with the impact of costly new environmental regulations, imposed by Brussels, on the oil refining industry. She had explained that Aberdeen personnel were involved in looking for oil, not refining it, but her protests had been ignored. So far, two people had signed on, both from Latvian Railways.

Mrs Perkins had not heard from her husband at lunchtime. Although they had been apart for only a few hours, it was traditional for her next of kin to call on most days, unless he was involved in a meeting. It was a pointless ritual but she appreciated it. Nothing much was said but it was just one of those odd traditions that had developed over the years, for no apparent reason. Henry would not have willingly broken it. Lunch had long since passed and tea was imminent. No call from Henry. Jill sensed that something was going on but one of the rules of this endearing and enduring game was that she would never call Henry, unless it was very important, such as asking him to bring home another white loaf. Her restless mind pondered possible reasons for his silence and more than once she nearly phoned him.

She was worried. He had not told her that he was going out or had any meetings, so why was there no call? Then she remembered that Henry's seemingly pointless conversation with that worm, BF, had ended with a chilling phrase. Her husband had been told that he was "to be let go with immediate effect". Jill had thought that this was an odd way to end an informal chat but Henry hadn't attached any significance to the words. She had accepted his view that BF was "barmy", but remained puzzled about the reason for the meeting. That said, she had been comforted by the fact that nothing had happened for more than a month.

Jill became convinced that her husband had been told the brutal truth and didn't want to convey news like that over the phone. Once again, she resisted the temptation to call. If the news were bad, Henry deserved a few hours to compose himself and tell her in his way.

Henry stared, almost lifeless, at HB's navy blue woollen tie, awaiting final confirmation of his delayed dismissal. The chief executive, pink of face in the mornings and now sporting a reddish after-lunch hue, was still speaking.

"As I'm sure you know, BF has accidentally made himself redundant". HB chuckled, prompting a judiciously cautious smile from Perkins, "and being a loyal company man, he wisely decided to implement his own decision. He will be leaving very soon because I decided not to stand in his way."

Henry, still bemused, wondered why he was being told this, especially as it did not correspond to what BF had told him in the corridor. More importantly, he wanted to know his own fate. Why was he there? HB stopped talking as coffee was being delivered and Henry croaked that milk and sugar would be fine. Tea and sympathy might have been more apt. HB, unaware of BF's bungled attempt to discard the hapless Henry, was ignorant of the need for prompt clarification. He graciously and meticulously poured the coffee into Henry's elegant executive cup. Henry took it in a trembling hand.

Would Henry like a biscuit?

"No thanks."

"Are you sure? These bourbons are really good." Henry remembered that the Bourbons used to cut off people's heads.

"I suppose I must eat at least 10 a day", he confided, whilst Henry was in mental torment. Eventually, HB resumed his pre-coffee patter. Henry, fully braced for the worst, was so taut that his leg had gone to sleep, his head hurt and he was not entirely sure where he was.

"So, following Fricker's decision to leave us, there's a vacancy. I want you to take it." Henry, astounded that he was not being discarded, smiled broadly, inanely and uncomprehendingly. After a few moments, during which time he tried to work out if he were asleep, he replied. "Thank you, but I have no relevant experience in human resources and, frankly, I don't speak the language."

HB groaned. "I don't want someone I can't understand. BF has scarred me for life. One of your virtues is that you are without guile and that you are totally honest, as you just showed. Unlike Fricker, you care about people. I've seen that in your reports and I always understand what you're talking about. Don't underestimate your experience. Anyway, I don't want you to replace him directly. We're going to have a re-organisation. I haven't decided on the final changes yet and that's something that we must discuss. I think that I'll promote Stan Gray to be head of a new planning group, reporting to you and bring in a new person to head personnel, I'm dropping that horrible phrase 'human resources. If you accept, and I hope that you will," at which point a much-relieved Henry nodded enthusiastically without knowing what he was to do. "As a general manager…"

Henry gasped. Not only was he being retained, but he was being promoted for the first time ever. What was more, he was missing out an entire layer of hierarchy to become a general manager. He refrained from pinching himself and concentrated hard. He also decided against asking about BF's attempts to dismiss him. It was obvious that HB did not know and it was probably best that he remained in ignorance. The offered promotion was real and was happening, to him, now.

HB realised that Henry was stunned by what had been said so he generously repeated "as a general manger, you'll be responsible for staff and training and a new division created by merging your current department with Planning and Economics and Investor Relations. I don't like our PR consultants so we'll recruit someone to work in-house, reporting to you, but the final structure still's to be decided. We'll probably call the new department corporate reputation, assets and planning. I don't think that any other company has used that label. You'll not only be our general manager, CRAP, but the first person in the world to wear such a hat." HB, hearing the new acronym out loud for the first time, then said that the name had not yet been finalised.

Henry didn't hear this bit. He was having difficulty concentrating. HB, assuming that Henry's nodding and gulping effectively implied that he was accepting the job, congratulated him. No other members of staff should know about the changes until a circular was, to quote HB's memorable verb, "circulated". "It's important for staff to have the full picture. I don't want them to be worried about the changes and I certainly don't want them to start speculating. Now, I suggest that you give yourself what's left of the afternoon off. I'm delighted for you, Henry, and I certainly wish you well. I'm really pleased that you have accepted this new challenge and by the way, as you haven't asked, I'd better tell you that your salary will go up by 70 per cent, you'll have an expenses account, Fricker's old office and a company car."

The stunned general manager designate of CRAP returned to his office. He had not had time to tell his colleagues that he had been summoned by HB and they were curious to know where he had been for the last hour.

"You really should always tell us, chided Simon Plummer "especially in case HB calls. We would look silly if we had to say we didn't know". Henry thought that Simon always looked silly but said nothing.

As if addressing a retarded child, the patronising Plummer continued. "All that's required is a comment to the effect that "I'm just going to see.. If we're on the phone, just write it down. Here, if you like, I'll devise a simple form and then you can fill it in as you leave for the meeting." Looking as if he had just discovered the secret of eternal life, Simon sat back in his chair, wearing a challengingly self-satisfied smirk. Perkins swallowed hard and repressed several instant remarks before saying "Simon, just, for once, shut up and go away and play marbles or something appropriate to your mental age". Everyone fell silent. It was as if the entire nation had been reduced to the kind of noiseless, disbelieving awe that accompanies England's latest exit from a major international football tournament. Only a distant squawk of an uninformed pigeon broke the peace. Henry resisted the temptation to apologise and noted the admiring looks of some of his colleagues. Although only just having been told about his new job, he was already beginning to feel that, in some circumstances, it might be easy to be more assertive, despite his conditioning over the years.

Jane approached him in his hutch and perched elegantly against a cabinet. "I don't want to pry but is everything all right Perky?" "Yes, Jane, thank you, I'm pleased to say that it is." Grinning, he asked her to tell Simon that he was going home shortly.

Henry rang Jill. With some difficulty, he conveyed that all was well but, and, lowering his voice he said "I do have some news". His astute wife, already denied an answer to her immediate query about why he hadn't called before, asked him to tell her the whole truth.

"Have you lost your job?" she demanded. "I suppose I have", the honest husband replied laconically. Jill paled. "Oh my god, I'm so so sorry, Henry, love, but don't worry, we'll be all right and I know that you'll find something else." Henry told her that she was right on that point but he couldn't discuss it now and that he would be home early tonight. Jill, aware that there was a vacancy in Macgrimeville, as it had become a company joke, worried afresh. Henry was being very secretive. "Have you been offered much compensation? Do you have a job with the company? I realise that you can't talk, so just say yes or no."

John Scanlon and Arthur Williams then showed some interest in Perkins', mainly because he seemed to be speaking into the inner recesses of his jacket, which was where he had placed the phone to avoid being overheard. "Don't worry. The answer is yes but I must go now." Jill, always more precise than her husband, but whose brain was being suffocated by concern, wondered if the affirmative response was in relation to compensation or a job. She would have to wait but at least Henry had sounded cheerful.

Henry was so excited on the way home that he almost forgot to read the early edition of the evening paper. The lead story was that an official survey, produced by a focus group, working closely with a panel of experts, had discovered that graduates enjoyed better health than those without degrees. In a revolutionary move, the government decreed that all those who had passed any recognised exams after the age of 14 would henceforth be regarded as graduates. The Health secretary hailed this as a most imaginative move which would take billions off the cost of running the National Health Service. A new survey showed that 75 per cent of people had gardens but that only 42 per cent had any garden tools and the American president was angry that millions of his countrymen had below national average intelligence.

One fellow passenger told his companion that, just as everyone could remember where they were when they heard of John Kennedy's death, he knew that everyone in the country would have their own personal recollections of the Queen Mother's 100th birthday.

Because it was only late afternoon, there were relatively fewer business people and more children travelling than on Henry's usual train. They smelt of crisps and were gratuitously advertising the manufacturers of their clothing whilst noisily engaged on their mobile phones. One mannerless child, seemingly of the male persuasion, asked Perkins if he had the right time. "I really don't know" he replied honestly.

Later, at Chez-Perkins, the new general manager was acquainting his overjoyed wife with as much detail as he had. Henry was not very clear on the nature of his new duties but all this would be discussed later with HB. "And then he mentioned a new salary. It's 70 per cent more than I am getting now. I'll have an office on the eighth floor and I can choose the paintings that I want on the wall. Will you help me to choose them, please? I'll have an entertainment and travel budget and a company car although it must be British and I can choose the colour."

She listened with pleasure and pride as he burbled on.

Jill had always known that her husband was capable of doing so much more with his life and job, but she did wonder how he would cope with such a post for which he had little knowledge or experience. Nevertheless, for now, with tears of unalloyed pleasure streaming down her cheeks, she hugged and congratulated him again. He was always totally honest and that would serve him well, wouldn't it?

Chapter 9

Henry was sitting in the garden one Sunday afternoon, a few weekends after SRUP (secret redundancy and unexpected promotion). Jill, who had warned him about following industry's obsession with acronyms, was pouring out a COT. Typically, more tea landed on the table than in the two cups astutely positioned in the target area, prompting her to ask why, if men can visit the moon, it was impossible to have teapots that did not spill. She offered her husband a bourbon biscuit and, grinning broadly, he took it with relish, although not of the pickle variety.

"Why are you laughing at a bourbon biscuit, dear?"

"HB offered me bourbon biscuits just before I thought that he was going to fire me."

"Well, you're still there, so they must like whatever you're doing. I still don't know what you do. Whenever I ask, you're too busy or too tired. Just what do you do?"

"We're forming a new division, Corporate reputation and planning. It's based on some existing departments and some new ones. It'll take time to finalise but, for example, I'm responsible for example, for R & R..."

"There you go again with your initials. You don't mean rest and recuperation?"

"No, it's recruitment and redundancies within a strengthened personnel and training division. I'm also supposed to be looking after investment divestment, that's getting rid of old and unwanted assets, resolving contractual problems, all external corporate relations with pressure groups, the media, environmentalists, customers, government and investors, and forward planning."

"Right now.."

"Henry, I hope that you're not going to speak American?"

"At the moment, I'm trying to learn as much as I can. Formulating new policy must wait but I'm getting a few ideas and I'll be making some changes." Jill had already noticed that Henry was acquiring more confidence but the idea that he could formulate policy was difficult to imagine. He had trouble deciding which flavour of ice cream to buy and if Jill had not bought socks for him occasionally he might well have gone barefoot to work.

"I still don't know why HB appointed me. I'm sure he didn't know that Fricker had tried to fire me. I don't care really but I would like to know what happened. Still, I have a job and, at last, a chance to make a mark on the company, after all these years. The other day, I overheard Justin Thyme of Stocks Control tell Ivor Ledger of Accounts that HB had said that I was honest and had a safe pair of hands. Tiny Kerr, you remember him, told me in the gents that he was pleased that a decent chap had been promoted. That made me feel good."

"I thought that you now had your own superior loos?"

"Yes, but I forgot and anyway, it seems disloyal to those I've used for so many years."

Jill winced. How could anyone feel loyalty towards a loo?

"All this is flattering and I'll do my best, but I'm worried because I know so little about the work of those I now have responsibility for."

Jill assured him and didn't correct his syntax. "I'm sure that, as you've been there so long and have so many friends, they'll help you, particularly as that frightful Fricker has gone."

Henry nodded. His new tasks included many that his fellow workers had loathed so it was unsurprising that his colleagues, who might otherwise have felt irked that he had overtaken them, were not jealous. HB had already acknowledged that some of these tasks might be "a little difficult". "In fact, Henry, you may wonder why I'm loading you up. Quite simply, I like your open and honest approach. That's rare in business. You're just the man for this job, but let me know if any problems crop up. Remember, you report just to me."

Jill pushed back her chair, cut off the head of a plant that, with heroic impudence for so small a growth, had exceeded its authorised height by a few millimetres, and busied herself around the garden. Henry glanced briefly at the local paper. The main feature, the first in a series, was how to introduce your horse to a pig. The new general manager, pondering the number of different animals still in the world, felt that this was a series that could last for some time.

He lapsed into a peaceful reverie. Henry had chosen Rose, BF's former secretary, to work with him. She might otherwise have been made redundant but Henry wanted her because she was a decent person and a conscientious and knowledgeable colleague. On their first day together, he had encouraged her to speak freely about company issues. She, in turn, had sought to increase Henry's confidence. "You've been with the company for many years and worked in many departments. You've also worked with HB and the board and you know how they operate. You under-estimate yourself. I've seen many general managers come and go and they knew far less about the company than you but their ignorance never deterred them. Incidentally, and I shouldn't pass on gossip but I heard that Christine Fricker and her son, now known as Chuck, have left Bernard to live with the estate agent in a desirable and deceptively spacious property. I don't know what happened to him."

A dozing Henry inadvertently leaned further back in the plastic garden chair than the manufacturers had intended. A terrible cracking sound rent the air as Perkins tumbled on to the ground.

"Henry, are you all right? I thought the tribe had returned."

"I'm ok, Jill, thanks."

Henry was happy and his pleasure was magnified by the rarity of the experience. Later, he went to his study to deal with some correspondence. He began with a letter to his gas supplier of many years.

Dear Sir or Madam,

Thank you for your kindly and personal interest in my welfare as manifested in your recent undated and unsigned letter. You point out that the evenings will be drawing in soon, that winter is coming and I shall need commercially-provided heat. How true! I really don't want to burn any more furniture.

Certainly, in making these assertions about the weather, history is on your side, even if the longer-term future may not support such forecasts. However, I really don't want to hear such facts until after my annual holiday, which I always take with my lady wife at Westhaven, which, incidentally, I recommend unreservedly, after the Wimbledon tennis championships. I really wonder when we are going to produce a champion? I digress.

You tell me that because my house is not connected to your gas mains, liquefied petroleum gas could be made available to me. I'm puzzled. For many years, and this implies no distaste for LPG, which I'm sure is a fine fuel, marketed by people whom I would be happy to have as friends, we have had gas central heating. Now, it seems that the gas did not originate from you as you tell me that I am not connected to your mains. How, I ask myself, did it enter the house without causing serious explosions? We don't have a cat flap, mainly because we lack a cat, so the only other obvious way is via the letter box and I can rule this out categorically. Clearly, the gas must have come through pipes which belong to another company. As Mrs Thatcher, as she then was, would have said, "there is no alternative". Incidentally, do you like her new statue and how do you feel about its beheading?

However, you have been billing me for gas supplied over many years, and I, for my part, have paid the bills with commendable celerity in the mistaken but understandable view that it was your gas that warmed Mrs Perkins and me and, indeed, any visitors that we had. Sadly, we have no children.

Now, as you are conceding that the gas was not supplied by you, notwithstanding your bills, I would appreciate your prompt assistance. Firstly, please send me a cheque, by first class post, so that I can cash it before the heating season starts, for the gas that I thought, wrongly, I had bought from you over the last four years. I think that a compound interest rate of six per cent would be fair. Secondly, any help you can offer in tracing the identity of my true supplier would be much appreciated, as I am anxious to pay them.

Next, he drafted a letter to a travel group that had booked him into a London hotel before a recent trip to the continent. Rose could tidy it up and send it tomorrow.

Thank you for organising my accommodation in London for what proved to be a memorable stay. You should know that the few staff were of unknown origin, and, in some cases, indeterminate gender. None spoke English, thus causing what can fairly be described as a major problem in communication. There was no restaurant, the bar only offered sparkling water and there was neither a mini-bar nor a packet of biscuits in my bedroom. Given the filthy state of my room, this was probably advantageous.

The bedroom was so small that swinging even a modestly-sized kitten would not have been possible and the décor resembled the before part of an advertisement showing how a room could be improved by new wallpaper and a pot of paint. The bedspread was marked by several severe stains, the nature of which I should not like to speculate upon, but its unique character was imparted by a large hole, caused, I suspect, by a blowlamp. Indeed, when I first noticed the hole, in the dim light, I mistook it for a large black insect or worse, and, after arming myself with an umbrella, only felt confident to approach it when it had remained stationary for some minutes.

During the night, I nearly fell down the ridge in the middle of the "double" bed, which had been created by putting two single beds together. My first reaction was that I had acquired a friend whilst I was asleep.

The ill-fitting window was single-glazed, thus allowing the noise and draughts of London to caress me whilst I sought slumber. I can understand that overseas visitors might enjoy being cosseted with the capital's scents and noises, but I had a different objective. I wanted to sleep. Another problem was that the low nocturnal temperature could not be offset by more heat from within: the radiator did not work although it thoughtfully reminded me of its presence by whining regularly.

The small black and white television set, which no self-respecting teenager would have allowed in their room, lacked a remote control and teletext facilities and it struggled to bring even the land-based free channels. Certainly, the room did have a telephone but, like the heating and the light over the bed, it did not work.

In the bathroom, a very loose toilet seat created unique and potentially dangerous problems, the nature of which I shall not discuss. Because of the positioning of the taps, taking a conventional shower without flooding the floor proved almost impossible, although, to give praise where it's due, the hot water arrived in only eight minutes. I wished to persist with personal hygiene whilst preserving the floor so was forced, for the most part, to shower in what I can only describe as an unnatural position but my doctor says that there should be no long-lasting effects.

You may decide that it would not be commercially wise to book your clients into this hole again.

Perkins was in the office early on the morrow, Monday and resumed the review of his new responsibilities. His job description was inadequate but, as he was enjoying learning how to be a manager, it didn't matter. That, at least, was what he assured Jill, night after night, having left the office only when the cleaners and security staff insisted that they had homes to go to and they assumed Perky did as well. Having been a nonentity for so long, Henry did not receive the

106

respect due to a general manager but he didn't mind that either: in a way, it was a compliment.

One of his objectives was to make the best use of the talent available, irrespective of age or sex, in the interests of the individuals and the company. When he could organise it, younger and competent people, like Jane, would be promoted to avoid the frustration he had felt for so long. He had also been angered by all the half-truths and lies dripping from management mouths over the years. He would tell the truth. Spin, pragmatism and self-interest would have no place in his philosophy. Why be in a position of authority if you could not change things for the better?

His accumulated frustration was oozing away and Henry even looked forward to Mondays. Now, he could make a difference and his brain, which previously closed down between 09.00 and 17.00 each weekday, was being exercised.

So much had changed. The Perkins now ate out once a week. Last week, the assertive Henry embarrassed Jill by asking whether the fish, that he had ordered some 45 minutes before, had reached the restaurant. Occasionally, neighbours Ian and Shirley were invited in for a meal but Henry had been obliged to work late so the last date had been postponed. Ironically, although the Perkins' income had risen, there was less time in which to spend it. Because of business commitments, they had cancelled their provisional booking for a fortnight in August in Westhaven. Jill had suggested somewhere warm, in the winter, for three weeks and Henry had readily agreed.

There were so many major changes in Henry's life that occasionally he found it difficult to adjust quickly without exposing his inexperience. Sometimes, when on work, he took a taxi. HB had stressed that if a company car and chauffeur were not available, taxis must be used, adding, jokingly, Henry assumed, "otherwise our expenses will be much higher than yours and that would never do".

Henry had to travel around the UK and he became accustomed to using the trains. Many years had passed since he patronised an inter-city train and the novelty was slow to wear off, despite late arrivals and the occasional infestation of unruly children when there was no first-class coach. At least, Henry thought that they were children but it was sometimes difficult to tell. They usually wore baseball caps, the wrong way around, jeans, trainers, anoraks and one earring, presumably because, having spent so much on designer clothes, their parents could only afford the one.

Henry also disapproved of the incessant bleating of the guards, many of whom were clearly frustrated broadcasters, judging by the frequency of their announcements. "Ladies and gentlemen, this is your senior guard speaking." The emphasis on the word "senior" had prompted Perkins on one occasion to ask how many guards were employed on the train.

"Just me, sir."

"Why, then, do you and all your colleagues stress the word senior, if it is not necessary to indicate who, out of all the guards, is addressing us? Would it not be equally meaningful to avoid the stress on the word 'senior' or even to omit the adjective entirely?"

"Er?"

"I presume, then, that you announce your job title and your name, to assure us that the vital system of communication on the train has not been taken over by enemies of the railway company? It's rather like reading the news during the war, isn't it? This is the BBC Home Service. Here is the news, read by Alvar Lidell. Thank god, we all cried, we recognise that voice. Broadcasting House has not fallen to the enemy unless poor old Alvar is being forced to read the news at gunpoint."

"You must excuse me sir. As the senior guard, I have some duties to perform."

Henry's pet hate was the indiscriminate use of mobile phones and the vapid bellowing of inanities favoured by their owners. Recently, on a trip to the Midlands, Henry had seen an avuncular, theatrical-looking gentleman sitting opposite a woman whose loud use of her mobile phone attracted the attention of all the residents of whichever county was being traversed at the time. Eventually, Drury Lane man could tolerate it no longer.

"Do you feel no embarrassment at letting the entire train know the contents of your conversation?"

Her response was deemed inadequate. In a voice that combined the strength, timbre resonance and authority of all the greats of the English theatre, and which would not have been out of place at Agincourt, let alone on a train from London, she was rebuked further.

"Nothing that you said was in the slightest way urgent. I know that because I and the rest of the train had to listen to you."

One traveller, with a face that looked like an inconsistently peeled potato, had sat staring, motionless, at his mobile phone for hours, clearly desolate that there was not a single individual, anywhere, who wanted to communicate with him. Others tapped furiously at their laptops, seemingly working but secretly playing card games. Another favourite pastime was to take the following week's television programmes and mark in yellow those that the sad person wanted to see.

The time Henry spent on trains allowed him to do some office work but he also tried to read more. One of his new magazines, circulated only on the 8th floor, contained a regular humorous column.

He glanced at the latest issue.

"Aware that the world is becoming more complicated, we asked Professor Ivan Inkling to explain a few phrases used in business.

Average: *A standard that few people reach so it's odd that the level is so high.*
Basket of currencies: *This was how, in the old days, unused foreign coins were taken to the bank to be exchanged for sterling. This was before airport shops selling junk were established to separate coins from travellers.*
Bear: *The opposite of a bull.*
Budget: *A sum of money allocated to a specific project which is often increased as costs rise, so that businessmen can claim that the budget has not been exceeded.*
Bull: *The opposite of a bear.*
Business cycle: *An environmentally friendly mode of transport, favoured by managers at "photo opportunities".*
Capital intensive: *A company based in London.*
Cash flow: *Money spent on a wet holiday.*

Contango: *I don't know why this is included as it is the Spanish for "with orange" or, alternatively, a dance programme that includes the tango.*

Credit squeeze: *Too many plastic cards in a thin wallet.*

Demand: *A perceived need, frequently prompted by advertising, backed by cash.*

Deflation: *A short-term reaction to a smaller pay rise than expected.*

Depression: *A longer-term reaction to a smaller pay rise than expected.*

Disinvestment: *The process of selling assets, often because of a management blunder, whilst implying that the sale is part of a deliberate and carefully-planned policy.*

Diversification: *The policy of companies to move into areas in which they have little or no experience. They do this either because they have failed in their main line of business or they have been so successful that they think that they can do anything.*

Durable goods: *Those expensive household items, such as television sets, fridges and camcorders, which go wrong just after the guarantee has expired.*

Exchange rate: *The mechanism by which the value of sterling goes down just before a foreign trip and up again before you convert foreign currency back into pounds.*

Forecast: *An estimate that will be altered immediately there is any change in the circumstances in which it was made.*

Glossary: *A subjective selection of terms with equally subjective definitions, designed to fill editorial space when holidays and business trips preclude the writing of anything more sensible.*

Hot money: *Cash used on a continental holiday.*

Imperfect market: *A shop that does not have what you want to buy.*

Inflation: *The phenomenon that makes individuals believe that their income is always falling, irrespective of any rises in salaries etc.*

Interest rate determination: *The mechanism that ensures that the cost of borrowing falls within weeks of your completing a 40 year mortgage on a fixed and higher rate.*

Inventories: *The application of imagination to stock levels.*

Investment: *A phrase frequently used by partners in relation to a desired but totally unnecessary domestic object which will yield nothing and* *which will be put in a cupboard, within two days of purchase, before being given to an unpopular relative three years later.*

Mean: *A retort from those whose plans for investment have been rejected.*

Merger: *The name applied to a new alliance of companies, after a takeover, where both companies wish to disguise the fact that a takeover has occurred.*

Moving average: *An emotional reaction to news that your salary is below the national average.*

Present value: *The sum realised by selling unwanted Christmas presents.*

Random sample: *A sample of people just like you, taken in the office, to save costs.*

Seasonal or statistical adjustment: *A modification to ensure that the figures always fit the prejudice.*

Soft currency: *Laundered money that has not yet fully dried.*

Think outside the box: *Ignoring the impact of television.*

Yield: *What happens to an investment when the owner gives way to a bull or a bear.*

Henry enjoyed studying his fellow passengers. One eccentric had tried to engage his fellow passengers on the subject of porridge consumption. "They tell me that you can eat it during the day now." Henry speculated on the identity of the informers and porridge inspectors, roaming the land, wearing caps indicating that they worked for the Porridge Inspection Group, PIG, looking for illicit consumption of the stuff.

When he could find nothing to interest him, he worked out the percentage of those around him who wore white shirts, black lace shoes or, for example, wore glasses. His mental arithmetic was improving fast.

When away on business, Perkins booked into expensive hotels. One night, staying in Boychester, he switched the television on. A man was chatting to an attractive girl on a park bench. He remarked that she must be very hot as it was such a fine day and she was wearing a heavy sweater and jacket whilst most people, although more modestly attired, still looked warm. Eventually the girl agreed that she was hot and acted on the interviewer's suggestion that she should remove her jacket. To Henry's astonishment, the girl not only took off her jacket but everything else. He peered at the screen and realised that he had inadvertently tuned in to an adult film.

Gradually, he started overcoming the challenges posed by hotels. Why, for example, at breakfast time, is the spoon used to heap fruit and juice on the diner's plate riddled with holes so that no juice can make the required journey? Why is the yoghurt spoon always coated with some sticky substance which ensures that the only way to take possession of the yoghurt is to flick the spoon vigorously with potentially disastrous results?

Henry disliked televisions that came on, unbidden, in the middle of the night, liquid soap so adhesive that copious volumes of water proved inadequate to remove the offensive substance, ludicrously exaggerated room costs on the back of bedroom doors, heating controls that controlled nothing, brown water, alarm calls that came long after he had awoken, which could not be cancelled and came at a crucial stage in ablutions, badly-worded notices on how he could help the environment by using towels more than once, extortionate phone charges, light switches for the room that were some distance from the bed, lights that could only be activated by inserting a card in a box on the wall, that you could never find if it was dark when you went in to the room for the first time, pre-programmed room card keys that didn't work, curtains that never met in the middle, shaver points that did not work and those garish welcome notices on the television set as soon as entry to the room was eventually secured.

One trip to Woodbull to discuss the region's budget was particularly memorable. Anticipating fog, airline strikes and vehicle breakdowns, he had arrived just after lunch on the day before the meeting. Having completed his work, Henry visited an exhibition of vintage sports cars in the hotel's large ballroom. He had always wanted one when he was young but could not afford it. Now, with the latest rise, he could but no longer lusted after one. For no apparent reason, he suddenly recalled how, when young, he rescued a wasp from drowning and it promptly stung him. He was soon ogling some very truly beautiful models and admiring their curvaceous lines and seductive sparkle under the lights. One, stroking an elderly Jaguar, said "Isn't this beautiful?" Another girl, in a white trouser suit addressed him. "Hello Perky, how are you? What are you doing here? Long time, no see. Do you remember me?"

Surprised but recovering swiftly, he didn't but was reluctant to sound churlish, especially after such a friendly greeting. He smiled and the gorgeous girl, sensing his dilemma, revealed that she used to work in Broadoak transportation department but had decided to move into "publicity". Henry assumed from her posture that today, at least, that involved being draped over an old car. Her name, the girl, that is, not the car, was Dana Littlebottom and that name was familiar to Perkins. She had changed significantly since he had last seen her, some two years ago, when she was about 18 but still justified her surname.

"What are you doing here?"

"I've been promoted so I'm in town for a meeting tomorrow." Like nearly everyone in Broadoak Oil, Dana had always felt sorry for Perkins, who was widely seen as a decent human being who deserved more from life. On hearing his good news, she instinctively hugged him and kissed him affectionately on the side of his face, unaware of the presence of a cameraman from the local paper.

Henry recovered from this unexpected and pleasant experience and engaged in idle chat. Dana had done some modelling work and had participated in two television commercials for a floor polish and a sun cream. Henry said weakly that he hoped that they had not been confused, as covering yourself with furniture polish was not a good idea. Dana laughed generously. Perhaps Henry had seen the commercials? No, he had not, but maturing by the minute, he assured his attractive friend that, if he had, he would have remembered. This week, she had been hired to adorn two elderly MG cars, which was appropriate as her boy friend had an old MG so she knew something about them.

Henry thought that he should invite her out to dinner although he was not quite sure why. His conscience interrupted. Yes, he did know why. Of course, it would be fun, but totally innocent fun. After all, she had already mentioned that she had a boy friend and he would tell Mrs Perkins when he called her at about 6.30. They arranged to meet at 7.30 pm.

A few hours later, Henry felt guilty and nervous. It was absurd, of course but many years had passed since he had been alone with a single attractive female. Jill didn't remember Dana and Henry, perhaps, had not done his former colleague justice when asked for a description.

When Dana approached, he and every other full-blooded male in the lounge, looked up, aroused by the click of high heel on marble floor and the most seductive of perfumes. She was of medium height, with a figure that was made for modelling. She had a young and mischievous face, her green eyes twinkled and she greeted Henry with a smile and hug that would have made even the most rabid of MG owners forget their cars. Her long red hair was arranged immaculately and her discreet but effective make-up immediately confirmed to the panting uninitiated that she was definitely a film star.

Henry gulped. She was wearing a short light blue skirt and a silk cream blouse under a white shantung jacket. Henry wallowed in the moment and wondered how he could ever have forgotten a colleague who could look like this. "Would you like to eat here?" he squeaked, "I think that they have quite a good restaurant." "Fine by me".

They repaired to the bar, ordered drinks and booked a table for 8.15. Perkins' confidence was increasing, and he settled down to what he was sure would be a pleasant evening. Dana was intelligent and ambitious and although she was doing well in her new life, she really wanted a job in the United States. Having worked in Broadoak, she thought that her knowledge of oil, "although, of course, not as deep as yours, Perky," might help her to find work representing companies at oil exhibitions. Since Henry's elevation, his mind was working much faster than when such activity was discouraged. Presumably, it was because his brain had been resting for years. "I've got a full listing of all the major exhibitions and shows in the US over the next year, in my brief case, in my room. I'll get it and you can keep it. I don't need it."

Dana, having noted some rugby types leeringly lasciviously at her, said that if Henry didn't mind, she would like to accompany him to his room. She felt a little nervous about being left by herself in the lounge, surrounded "by all these overgrown schoolboys overpowered by their adolescent testosterone". It seemed a reasonable enough request to the innocent Henry although their joint departure towards the lifts was clearly misunderstood by the schoolboys. A mechanical voice announced that the lift had reached the second floor and Henry waved an arm indicating that their destination had been reached. The bars which constituted the gates, black and elderly, moved together to allow Henry and friend to leave the creaking lift and walk to his bedroom.

Henry knew that, even in good quality hotels, any attempt to regulate room temperatures often induced precisely the opposite of what was required. Consequently, when he had gone down to the exhibition, little thinking that he would later be having company, he had not touched what was optimistically described as the "temperature control unit".

Opening the bedroom door, Henry had to acknowledge that his room was as hot as an oven. Dana suggested that it might help to open the window. Normally, Henry would have readily concurred but these were not normal circumstances. He had tried earlier and had retired, defeated by decades of accumulated paint on the elderly frame but it would seem unmanly to admit that he was not strong enough. So, whilst Dana was avidly reading the fascinating notice on the back of the door, which offered instructions on what to do if fire broke out, Henry stood on a chair, close to the window sill, prised open the lock on the window, and jumped to the floor, whilst still grasping the reluctant frame. He was successful. The sudden gush of fresh air prompted Dana to spin round. "That's much better", she said, unaware of how the window had been opened and how Henry's imaginative effort had resulted in a strained shoulder. Being British and with a lady, he admitted nothing and hid his pain which eased within a few minutes.

He gave the list to a grateful Dana, who had removed her jacket because of the heat. That was when she noticed that some MG grease had marked the left sleeve. Henry, the new man of action, knew what to do and immediately summoned a representative from the in-house laundry. A few minutes later, a formidable woman of advanced years, whose youth might well have been spent playing rugby, arrived and announced herself as "the laundry". She sneered at her interpretation of Henry's morals, took the jacket and mumbled "I'll do the best I can but I can give no promises. I'll be back in 10 minutes." She left, treating

Henry to another disapproving look of unmitigated contempt for an offence that had not even been enacted in his mind.

Having surrendered the jacket, Henry and Dana were obliged to wait in his room for its return. She accepted a gin and tonic from his mini bar and he sipped an orange juice. He might be maturing fast but some things would take a little longer. Conversation flowed. She was lively and wanted to know what had happened to some of her old friends.

Henry wanted to cough so, being a gentleman, turned towards the open window. It seemed to be becoming foggy and he could not even see the cars just two floors below. He turned to resume the conversation but was rudely interrupted by a clanging of bells that could have aroused a somnolent world to a Martian invasion. Henry ignored the noise but Dana was concerned.

"Isn't that a fire alarm?" The experienced Henry confirmed that it could well be. An alternative conclusion would have been difficult and Dana, collecting her vanity case, was already preparing to retreat. Henry sought to assure her. "I stay in hotels quite a lot now and almost all of the alarms are false alarms." Precisely on cue, the noise ceased, he smiled and Dana looked impressed. The conversation continued although Dana had some doubts on the wisdom of remaining in the room. She said that it was becoming foggy outside, as if it were to be distinguished from the internal kind of fog, which was very unusual for the time of year. In fact, it was also becoming foggy in the room and there did seem to be a vague smell of smoke.

Suddenly, the clanging commenced afresh and the door was flung open by the former rugby player. Throwing the jacket to Dana, she barked out aggressively, as if chiding the members of the scrum, "sorry, can't help and can't stop. Can't you hear that firebell? I've got to get everybody off this floor. Get out now". The last word was conveyed with an insistence that brooked no delay.

Henry picked up his brief case, took his friend's vanity case and together they left his room, minding Dana's injunction, read from the notice on the back of the door, that "in the event of fire, guests are required to use the stairs". They moved briskly to the main staircase. As most of the guests were British, there was an orderly queue. It stretched all the way to the second floor landing but it was moving steadily and without fuss. Henry and Dana took their places.

The queue moved down the spiral stairs slowly, and, although formal introductions had not been made, such was the potential gravity of the situation that complete strangers addressed each other. A pensive Henry suddenly became aware that the girl on the stair below the one that he and his friend were occupying was addressing him. Looking at Dana's vanity case, which he was still clutching, and staring at Dana, she asked Henry "caught you in the middle of it, did it"? Her male companion, who looked like a well-groomed vole, but not many people would have realised this as the vole, frankly, is not particularly well-known, creased his face in what was presumably supposed to be a smile.

Henry had never been particularly mature on such matters and it genuinely took him a few seconds to work out what was meant. He was guided to a conclusion by Dana who now added a most seductive chuckle to her impressive armoury which transformed men into lusty teenagers.

"No, it was nothing like that, at all. As it happens we are old colleagues." The female, not as shapely as Dana but no slouch in the looks department, as Henry had heard one of his young colleagues say recently about Jane Lewis, was eyeing Mr Perkins quite closely.

Somehow, and she couldn't work out why she thought this, he looked so naïve and helpless. It might be fun to see how embarrassed she could make him. Ignoring the silent Dana, she told Henry that she was her male companion's mistress. Perkins knew not what to say so said nothing. Moving down another stair, the female confided that she was bored by her boy friend who was soon to be ditched. The male smiled wanly and Perkins felt sorry for him. Julie, for she had now identified herself, had moved closer to Perkins, as if to emphasise her comment that she would be leaving her boy friend soon. Perhaps it was to be sooner than he realised.

"What do you do?" "I work for an oil company." Dana, making a telling contribution to the conversation, sought to give the modest Perkins his due. "He's a very senior executive but he's too modest to tell you that." Julie's eyes sparkled.

During this bizarre exchange, the queue had reached the ground floor. It appeared that all was well. The manager was speaking. "Ladies and gentlemen, we're very sorry that you have been inconvenienced and thank you for your patience. Fortunately, the fire's now out but as it occurred in the kitchen I'm afraid that means that we can't open the restaurant tonight. I do apologise for that and for the trouble that you've experienced."

Dana was some feet away, trying to listen to the manager over the general hubbub of chatter. Perkins, trying to think where they could dine, had completely forgotten Julie. Suddenly, a warm small hand was tucked in his and a room number was whispered in his ear. He turned, to see a smiling and enticing face. Just at that moment, the cameraman from the local paper took a pic of the happy guests who had just heard that the fire was out.

The following day, after a very successful meeting, the regional Broadoak manager passed him a copy of the local paper. Smirking broadly and inexplicably tapping the side of his nose, he suggested that Henry might like to look at the photographs on pages three and five, devoted to the exhibition and the hotel fire. A blushing Henry assured his colleagues that the pictures definitely gave the wrong impression. The more he protested, the more his colleagues praised his modesty. The reputation of Henry Perkins, general manager, was growing.

Chapter 10

One Friday evening, Jill and spouse, slumped on their elderly three-piece suite, were chatting. Henry was happy in his new job but Jill remained worried about his lack of training and experience. Apparently, his promotion, in part, was based on his honesty but she knew that practicality and pragmatism intrude in the business world. Henry's self-confidence had advanced, stimulating his wry sense of humour. She sensed that this, too, could create problems. Telling the truth and having a sense of humour were not ideal characteristics for success in business.

A few days ago, whilst dining locally, Henry had told the waiter that the Pana Cotta and raspberries, as listed in the menu, justified the use of the plural by the narrowest possible margin. Then when the bill came, after noting that the minimalist nature of the portions were not reflected in the charge, he had caustically expressed relief that prices had not been increased during the long wait for the meal.

Jill still worried about her own job security but hadn't discussed it with Henry in any detail. Because of his promotion, her worries about money were receding. Over the years, she had invested wisely and if Henry had joined the ranks of industry's unwanted, having carelessly reached his mid fifties, the results of her prudence could have sustained them whilst they re-organised their lives. Conscientious and hardworking, Jill had held a senior position for some years and this was why she underplayed her work. Despite the usual irritations, office life had been agreeable until a new director had implemented changes in response to the deteriorating performance by Jill's division, industrial conferences. More cuts were in prospect and some staff had already left. Would she have to join them? Previously, she had reported to her friend and general manager, Elizabeth Budd but she had moved into publishing and had been replaced by Denis Wiltshire. His reputation had been established when wielding the corporate axe in the company's newsletter division.

"You know Henry, Wiltshire is abhorrent. He's so cocky and so stupid that he doesn't even realise that he knows nothing about conferences. He never asks us for our opinions and he's so patronising. He always calls me 'darling' or 'love' and refers to us as 'his women'. He thinks that he's God's gift. He oozes around the office, occasionally patting us on the head or putting a supposedly avuncular arm around our shoulders. And another thing, he wears white socks with his black shoes."

Henry reeled. "My god. That's really serious. Was he a car salesman in a previous life?" Then he added, conspicuously belatedly, "has he tried anything on with you?"

"So far, no, but I'm sure that it's only a matter of time. It's no wonder that he hasn't a wife. Before long, there's going to be real trouble."

"If he's molesting you in the office, you should report it."

"If we do complain about Wiltshire, he could cause trouble for us. We've decided to do nothing yet but we'll take action if it becomes any worse. The swine takes our best ideas and then presents them to the board as if they're his. I know that because one of the directors' secretaries, who's a friend of mine, told me that the board was very pleased with one of his ideas which was really mine. He must have overheard me talking to the girls about it."

"Have you told anyone that it was your idea?"

"No, I may want to set a trap for Dirty Denis so I decided not to".

Henry tried to be positive. "Perhaps he's just nervous and he realises that you all know more about conferences than he does and maybe he's just trying to be friendly?" Jill did not think so.

Jill had not told Henry that some redundancies had already occurred and more were probable. She and her colleagues knew that Denis was remarkably influential and, whatever the injustice, anyone who crossed him could be ousted. Jill had no desire to leave. She enjoyed the work, the company of her colleagues and friends, some modest travel and, if she forgave herself for the cliché, the opportunity to meet people.

It was Saturday and Henry was accompanying Jill to the local supermarket, mainly to stock up for Lynda and Wendy, who were coming to lunch on the following day. Regrettably, the entire population seemed seized with the same idea, to go shopping, that is, not to be with Jill. Henry was unhappy and moaned about how he hated shopping.

"How often do you go shopping? The last time you were surprised to find that the store had converted to self-service and that happened in the eighties. It's amazing that you understand decimal currency. I hope you don't think that I really enjoy shopping?"

"A recent survey suggested that four out of five women enjoyed shopping." Jill observed that she was the fifth. Henry resumed his grumbling by noting that the car park could only accommodate one car. Jill looked blankly at him and, against her better judgement, asked him what he meant. "On that sign, the apostrophe's before the s of customers, not after, implying that only one customer can park."

"If you're like this in the office, you must be driving poor Rose mad."

"There's a space. Quick, the old boy in the Metro isn't looking and he's decided that it's his space. Shall I go and stand in it?"

"Just calm down, Henry. It's perfectly all right, I'll…"

Henry lowered his window to shout at Metro man as he narrowly avoided the front wing of Jill's car and swung triumphantly into the space. "Silly hatted old fool". Henry believed that all drivers who wore hats in their cars were dangerous.

"You might be old one day. Anyway, there's plenty of space at the far end."

"What kind of trolley do you want? Large or medium with wheels, or a basket?"

"Don't be silly dear, you know that a basket won't be big enough. As I have such a jolly little helper and I'm stocking up, we'd better have a big trolley." Perkins tried to persuade one of the larger trolleys to detach itself from about 25 of its relatives but his initial efforts proved inadequate. Told to "come along", he pointed out that the trolley was proving unco-operative. Rousing himself to yet greater efforts, Henry shook the line backwards and forwards causing his chosen trolley to part from its relatives which moved, still linked, at an increasing pace, down the gentle slope towards the car park, chased by a panting Henry. A supermarket employee halted the runaway trolleys, thus avoiding a confrontation with incoming cars, and wryly observed that "most customers seem happy with just one trolley"!

Henry thanked him and joined Jill who was now peering expertly at identical cabbages, seeking out the best. Gradually, the trolley was filled but Henry could not persuade it to move as he dictated. "I push it in the direction I want and these absurd wheels move in any way that they want. Who's in charge?" "The trolley, dear. It's a well-known fact."

"Sorry madam", he intoned, forcing a smile as his trolley collided with one propelled effortlessly in the correct direction by an elderly woman. "That's all right." Elsie Watson, a friend of Jill, smiled at Henry. Having nothing to say, Henry smiled again, thus reinforcing the view that he was a little simple. "Henry, you remember Elsie, don't you? " Henry was grateful for Jill's prompt and smiled for a third time. "You'll have to forgive Henry. He's suffering from shock. He doesn't come shopping very often and isn't enjoying the experience, are you dear? Anyway, how are you?"

"Better now, thanks, after the op. It really was grim and for a day or two, they wondered if I'd pull through." Henry nearly asked if she had. "Still, I've got to take it gently so I mustn't overdo things." Mr Perkins sensed that he ought to say something. "So it's no more cricket?"

"Pardon. I always have difficulty hearing what people are saying in this noisy place."

Jill rescued the situation. "Henry said that's the ticket. Anyway, we mustn't keep you. I'm glad you're on the mend."

Within the next few minutes, Jill met other elderly acquaintances, many of whom had had recent operations. Henry thought that, between them, they had lost enough body parts to make a new human being, but wisely said nothing.

Mrs Perkins was in hot pursuit of a bargain. "Buy three jars of coffee and get one free". Henry was then asked which of two bottles of orange juice represented the better value, given the different prices and volumes, but pretended not to hear. His wife greeted another friend a few yards away, leaving Henry by himself. An elderly lady, whom he recognised as Elsie was walking towards Henry. Anxious not to appear rude, he smiled and said "hello again" to a complete stranger.

The problem was that many people dressed alike. Elderly bulk was contained in trainer-type clothes, often of a hideous hue, implying that after shopping, the inmates would be representing the UK at an international athletics meeting. Most were probably bald but he couldn't be sure because they were wearing the compulsory baseball caps. The other group that Henry had identified, on these, admittedly rare, shopping marathons, were those normal people of his own age who were more sensibly attired in Marks and Spencers casual trousers or skirts, shirts or blouses, sweaters and anoraks. They would never wear a uniform. Henry was normal but, of course, he would always defend the rights of the middle-aged and elderly to look ridiculous.

"Look at these prices. They're supposed to be competitive here. Someone must have altered all the prices without management knowing." Mrs Perkins ignored him. Henry's shopping excursions were so infrequent that he had no idea of prices and always boringly made a remark about someone changing all the prices.

Jill skipped up and down the aisles, returning merely to dump more goods into the trolley and to order Henry to remain where he was. Wherever he stood, he was always in the way. On her return, he asked whether mandarins had plum jobs and why it was raspberries that were blown, instead of, for example, strawberries. She responded that the answer was a lemon. His suggestion that it might have been easier to put what they didn't want into the trolley and they would buy what remained on the shelves failed to provoke an answer.

It was time to pay. They chose what seemed to be the shortest queue whose shoppers had the fewest purchases but the leading customer was challenging the price of a small lettuce. The spotty-faced and seemingly illiterate child, the type on whom the supermarkets depend on a Saturday, clearly bereft of ideas, thumped an innocent bell repeatedly, presumably to alert an adult member of staff that there was a bit of a problem on the lettuce front. None came so the Perkins moved to an adjacent queue. He felt that it was legitimate to claim an advance position in this line but was immediately dissuaded by Jill and hostile glares from the elderly trendies.

As the Perkins moved to the rear of their new queue, the lettuce problem was resolved. The customer, tired by the tedious tintinnabulation, said that his time was more valuable to him than a lettuce. He also suggested that the so-called managers of this supermarket, and here his emphasis on the "super" bordered on the sarcastic, were so incompetent that they might have difficulty giving away ice creams in a heatwave. Stirred by his own rhetoric, he then lobbed the unpriced lettuce accurately towards the vegetable area. An elderly man saw the lettuce fall neatly in the correct section and looked up, as if expecting more. "Did you see that?" he asked his female companion, encased in a very large bright yellow tracksuit that probably doubled up as a marquee. She hadn't and on hearing what had happened said that if that's the way they filled their shelves, she would only be buying tinned stuff there in future.

The Perkins reached the head of the queue. As Jill assiduously unloaded the contents of the trolley on to the conveyor belt, leading to another spotty teenager at the till, Henry sidled up to Jill. "I think that you should keep a very close eye on what is rung up. This girl doesn't seem to know what day it is." She overheard and the parts of her face that were not already red assumed the colour of a traffic light at stop. Slowly, the items started running down the slope and Henry, having had some considerable difficulty in persuading any polythene bags to open, put the meat into one already housing a bottle of bleach.

Jill, looking three ways simultaneously, patiently removed the meat, explaining why and continued to put different items into different bags. Henry had some difficulty in undoing the tops of the next three bags which he claimed had been welded together. The remaining purchases started building up. "You're useless. Here, give me them." He handed the three unco-operative bags to Jill who then rubbed them in her hand and immediately they succumbed to the female touch and parted at the top. Henry meekly filled them up, trying hard not to comment on the bill of over £130.

Saturday dinner was over, the dish washer had been activated, the house shone in the golden sunlight of early evening and Jill was doing some cooking for the morrow. Henry offered to help but as there was nothing he could do, he ambled around the garden, taking pleasure in the colour, perfume, texture and proliferation of the flowers. He had cut the lawn on Thursday evening and the whole garden looked a picture. The so-called "copse", a triangular section at one right angle corner of the garden, opposite the pond, looked particularly splendid. The idea had been to plant trees on all sides of the triangle to create some privacy. He had chosen some slow-growing Goldcrest conifers and in the front garden, to minimise the impact of the wind, Henry had planted some Leylandi, which usually grew so quickly that they were perceived as a threat to society. The slow-growing trees had outpaced their allegedly faster growing relatives by about three feet in just three years. This really irked Perkins because, when he was buying the trees, an old lady, noting his barrow loaded with the offensive Leylandi, tutted noisily, observing that they were the most unsociable of trees and that he should know better.

A hot Henry inspected the repaired greenhouse, re-built from his salary increase, and retreated to the conservatory. He sipped an orange juice, turned on the radio and coincidentally tuned in to the weather forecast. It was to be cold and wet on the Sunday and the recommendations on suitable clothing prompted Henry to mumble his customary rant.

"Did you say something, Henry?" He moved towards the internal door of the conservatory and shouted so that his wife could hear. "Not really, I was just moaning about these so-called weather forecasts."

Sunday, of course, was dry, bright and hot. The sky was as blue as a Tory poster and even the birds couldn't be bothered to fly around looking for food. Presumably, they were all busy covering themselves in sun cream. Jill was addressing her day-dreaming next of kin. "As the weather's so good, shall we sit outside, just retreating for lunch?" Unfortunately, she had listened to an early forecast and had planned a roast, rather than a salad, which now would have been more appropriate.

"What time are Lynda and Wendy coming?" "I told them about mid-day."

Lynda, one of Jill's best friends, was short, vivacious, very trim, which reflected regular visits to the local health club, and blonde, which reflected regular visits to the hairdressers. Her husband had been killed in a fire many years ago and Lynda had worked since then in a local hotel. Henry knew little about Wendy, her daughter, not having met her for some years as she was either away at school or with friends whenever they met. However, when she was younger, he had indulged her, almost like the daughter that he never had. Over the years, he had spent a small fortune on presents for her birthdays and Christmas. She remembered this and always had a soft spot for her favourite "uncle".

"What's Wendy up to now? I don't want to put my foot in it." "Well, in that case, you must be careful. Lynda told me that she's ruled out going on for a degree, although she did well enough in her exams to walk into most universities. She really doesn't know what she wants, although acquiring lots of money is one of her immediate requirements."

"How old is she now?"

"Let's see. She must be about 20, I suppose. She still lives at home and is working at a local office but hates it. She really doesn't have any idea of what to do. Occasionally, she talks about going abroad but, as Lynda says, that doesn't necessarily solve anything. She still seems to be in a rebellious period and I suppose that's natural as she was normal when everybody else rebels." Henry said that, so far, he had never rebelled. Jill stayed silent. "Lynda doesn't want her to go abroad, but if that is what Wendy decides, that is what Wendy will do. Apparently, once she's made up her mind, there's not much that will change it."

At precisely noon, the doorbell at Chez Perkins heralded the arrival of Lynda and Wendy. Jill welcomed her friends and kissed each on the cheek. Henry was never sure about the correct protocol. Over the years, he had realised that the older and, frankly, the plainer the woman, the more they seemed to want more than a formal peck on the cheek or the aimed kiss that narrowly missed all contact. Equally, the younger females in his life, and they could be counted on one finger, namely Alison, a contact in another company, seemed to think that unless an intended peck on the cheek missed by at least 305 millimetres, he was bent on lust. It really was difficult for a chap from Henry's generation.

He need not have worried about how to greet Lynda. She put her arms around him and, to his visible embarrassment, muttered "how great to see you again, Perky". He had forgotten that she had always called him this and she kissed him gently but so innocently on the lips.

126

The embrace over, Henry turned to welcome Wendy. Despite the hot weather, she was encased in battle dress and was wearing formidable and military-looking black boots. Henry's first instinct was to wonder which international conflict was about to be blessed with her presence. His second was to fear for their carpets. Thank heavens it was a dry day. Wendy was also wearing a black beret. She thrust out a hand in greeting. Clearly, there was to be no kissing here. At least, Henry knew what was expected of him and shook the proffered mitt. "Hello, uncle Henry. How are you? I haven't seen you for years."

She removed her beret, shaking loose her long blonde mane and suddenly looked very attractive. Even her baggy uniform could not entirely conceal what Henry imagined was a very shapely figure. She reminded him of Goldie Hawn, for whom he had lusted some decades ago. Why did she hide everything in that uniform? Uncle Henry was convinced that there was a girl inside that outfit and he thought to himself what fun it would be to help her escape. Ashamed and genuinely astonished that such thoughts could even enter his head, he immediately banished them and tuned in to the conversation after providing the obligatory drinks.

Jill and Lynda were talking about holidays. "I presume you'll be going back to Westhaven later in the summer?" "We thought that we'd be more adventurous this year so we'll go abroad in the winter." Wendy wondered if that meant that meant that the Perkins would go mountain climbing in Nepal, or white-water rafting in Africa. Lynda told Wendy not to be so silly. Henry, meanwhile, had lapsed into silence wondering what white water shafting was.

Lynda apologised for not saying anything earlier about Henry's promotion. "I think that congratulations are in order. We were both delighted, weren't we dear", she said looking at Wendy who smiled approvingly. Then, to Henry's great surprise, Lynda leaned over, took his hand and kissed him on the cheek. He was rarely kissed by anyone, except occasionally by Jill on special days, and, innocent and mild as it was, it made him feel just a little bit younger.

"Yes, someone left suddenly and, to my surprise, I was offered his job."

Did Henry do much travelling in his new job?

"I've discovered that business travel is not very exciting. You see an airport or station, a hotel and restaurant, if you're lucky, and even then, you're talking shop, so it's more business chat and you can't appreciate your surroundings. There's also so much more to worry about. But I'm hoping to go to Houston in Texas before the summer is out. It's supposed to be an exciting city and it's where all the major oil companies are based, so it's a very wealthy city and they really like Brits, apparently. I think…"

Jill interrupted. "I don't know how he manages by himself. Only yesterday, we were trying to find a parking place at the supermarket and he started fretting as if we were on the verge of World War Three. When one poor old man took the place that Henry thought was ours, he even shouted at him."

Lynda resumed. "I know that you collect funny stories. You must have heard some on your travels." Jill groaned. "For god's sake don't encourage him. It's getting worse and if he doesn't ease up on these stories I might have to sue for divorce. Would you like to look round the garden, Wendy?" Undecided whether to upset Jill or Henry, Wendy decided to support her own sex. Unfazed by the loss of two thirds of his audience, Henry continued.

"The most intriguing comment I've heard on trains recently was one chap saying 'it reduces the chance of being arrested', but I couldn't hear what they were talking about. Then there was the chap on the train who told a complete stranger that it was most humid for the time of year. His fellow passenger, clearly reluctant to become involved in a conversation, merely nodded. Bore number one then suggested that it was similar to the humidity experienced in Singapore. The second man, who obviously had never visited Singapore, said that it resembled Cairo's. They continued like this for several miles, each trying to show that they were men of the world. "

Lynda smiled politely and, suggesting that it would be a shame not to see the garden, which was looking particularly attractive, offered her arm and they marched into the afternoon sunshine like an old married couple.

A few minutes later, Lynda and Jill were chatting and as Wendy seemed left out, Henry began a conversation with her. "It must be difficult, nowadays, trying to find a career?" "With respect, uncle, what I don't want is an office job." Henry understood and said that the most important jobs have all been eliminated. Seeing Wendy's pulchritudinous face pucker with puzzlement, he explained that he meant car park attendants, tea ladies, lift attendants, photo-copy operators and those who supervised the signing-in procedure in each office to allow latecomers to be suitably reprimanded.

"You had tea ladies?" "Yes, they propelled their trolleys, bearing massive urns and looking rather like World War One tanks, down the corridors over quaintly-smelling lino-covered floors. Apart from appropriately named rock cakes, they dispensed tea and coffee, virtually indistinguishable, except by the timing of their deliveries, and widely believed to have been pumped direct from the nearest oil refinery." Wendy smiled and said that, surely, he was too young to remember such things. Henry, momentarily flummoxed, having noticed her deep blue eyes, muttered something about being so old that he could remember when people answered phones. The young blonde, imitating at least part of her mother's earlier reaction, stretched across and squeezed his hand repeating that he was too young to have been in an office in those days.

The rest of the day passed pleasantly. When their visitors were leaving, Henry embraced Lynda, in accordance with earlier precedent and being a consistent chap, stretched out his hand to Wendy. She took it, drew him towards her and kissed him firmly on the cheek. Henry suddenly noticed how hot it had become during the day.

On the following evening, Jill said that Lynda had phoned to thank them for such a pleasant lunch and that Wendy had decided to go to America soon, hopefully to work there for a year or two. Henry, as usual, pre-occupied with thinking about his own job, half heard what his wife had said.

Chapter 11

Jill was happier. Henry was coping well, the conference on which she was working was attracting more interest than anticipated and, remarkably, Denis was becoming a very understanding and agreeable colleague. Rumours of further redundancies had faded and the summer was sunny and hot. It was time something went wrong.

Despite the heat, Jill, intrinsically attractive, favoured a long navy blue skirt and nondescript blouse. Her shoes were flat and ugly but comfortable. She seldom wore much make-up and Henry often thought that his wife resembled the before part of an advertisement in which the model was later transformed. Years ago, he had protested occasionally that Jill did not make the best of herself. Her standard retort was that she didn't dress for him: being herself was more important. Not, even for a few minutes, had she dressed or behaved for Henry, even in the early days. He didn't want her to look seductive nor to be uncomfortable but after her blunt rejection that there could be an occasional compromise, he had given up. His youth had conditioned him to be acquiescent and his inexperience with females, reinforced by regular and comprehensive failure in his so-called formative years, meant that he lacked the confidence to take the initiative. All emotion, long since repressed, had not been channelled elsewhere.

The peace created by not confronting such a serious issue was costly. In Henry's world, taxes, the pain of sustained sexual frustration and death were inevitable. He knew that his life was unbalanced and he still yearned for the intimacy, fulfilment and excitement, an alien emotion for him, that a more physical relationship would bring. Now, as the days accelerated, he knew that it was too late. He would never know the stimulation of a complete and normal relationship that millions assumed automatically.

The marriage had become more like a brother and sister relationship. Each of them had considered talking about it but nothing had happened. The lack of communication had converted the union into a near platonic relationship, which, backed by sustained inertia, had taken root so it seemed that each accepted the relationship. This suited Jill. She assumed that her husband, although obviously fond of her, was not, and never had been, passionate. Surely, no man would tolerate the lack of a real physical relationship unless it suited him? Henry assumed that his wife had never been particularly interested in the physical side of things so rationalised his failure to act as a kindness to his wife. Her failure to discuss it or take the initiative confirmed his view.

Denis, Jill's new boss, was in his early forties and had gained more experience of women in a month, in his early twenties, than Henry had obtained in a lifetime. Denis had earlier intended to put this experience to advantage in the office but had started so badly that the plan was abandoned. Now he wanted to know Jill much better and he had revised his approach. Even the white socks had been discarded.

"Good morning Jill, you're looking particularly attractive this morning", he oozed. Denis had sensed that Jill's marriage might not be entirely satisfactory and he knew just the man to improve things. She was potentially very attractive and winning her would take time but failure for him was as common as success for Henry. It was time for the first overture. "Would you like to have a drink this evening"? Jill and the other three girls in her office had anticipated this. Acting on a well-rehearsed cue, they all said thank you, they would. Denis, too experienced to explain that he just meant Jill, smiled weakly and said that he'd see them at 5.30 in the Cardigan and Pipe.

Later that week, Denis took Jill to lunch ostensibly because they were both very busy and had to discuss work before Denis went abroad for a few days. She felt guilty for previously disliking Denis. He had behaved impeccably at the collective drink and the solo lunch. He had not made any advances and his conversation could have been taped and replayed in front of anyone without causing even the most sensitive of eyebrows to twitch. She was beginning to like him. He had a dry sense of humour, was unfailingly courteous and always looked well-groomed.

Henry, working long hours, was to visit the US shortly so Jill almost welcomed Denis's innocent attention. He was the perfect gentleman: Henry had long since abandoned the customs that single men bestow on their intended partners, until they are under contract, such as opening doors and buying flowers. Scarcely realising it herself, Jill began to dress less conservatively, which made her appear younger, prompting the usually unobservant Henry to note "you look very fine these days". He could not bring himself to say "attractive". Nothing had happened between Jill and Denis and she would have been outraged at any suggestion that she could have contemplated a physical relationship. She told herself that she was only having the occasional drink or meal with a colleague and they spent most of the time talking about work.

Her phone rang. It was Denis. Could she please spare him a few moments in his office? This was odd because he usually visited her so, curious to see what he wanted, she left immediately. He was sitting at his impressive desk and waved a hand in the direction of a leather chair. Having poured her a coffee and established that Jill was well, Denis told her that the company was doing better than expected but there could be problems later in the year if the market declined, as he anticipated. Denis then passed her a leaflet advertising a weekend event, on how to organise a successful conference, to be held at Newton Tickerton in the country. Jill thought that this was one way of ensuring that a conference was successful and wished that she had thought of it herself.

"I know that weekends are precious, but I wondered whether you could possibly come with me? It could be very valuable and, at least, we'd have a few decent meals. Would you like to think about it and have a word with Henry, to see what he thinks?" "When is it?" "The last weekend in July." Jill thought quickly, checked her diary and confirmed that, as Henry would be in the States then, "that would be fine and thanks for asking me".

Henry was confronted by a mountain of work. He seemed to be the most important person in the company, judging by the pile of papers staring at him. Rose had thoughtfully imported a second in-box and, with irreproachable logic and mathematical accuracy, had labelled it 2. That kind of initiative, which BF would have claimed a success for empowerment, made Broadoak what it was. Unless Henry reduced the piles, there would soon be a happy event as number 3 arrived. Previously, most of his mail had been outdated magazines and circulars announcing the retirement of colleagues whom he had never met, re-organisations of sections that had been created only weeks before and exhortations to reduce costs. Now virtually everything was genuine work and, so far, he had nobody to whom much work could be delegated. His initial view, that he would be involved in most of those really difficult tasks that others shunned, was right.

Henry had been summoned by HB. Instead of walking conventionally, he was letting his feet slide through the thick carpet in the few feet of corridor that separated his new home from the chief executive's. He was fascinated by the wake left by each shoe as it cruised through the rich brown pile. A young secretary, watching his antics, smiled. Henry grinned. HB asked Henry about his latest trip, ignored his reply as senior people always do, and invited Perkins to call him Hubert. This big step confirmed to the still-bewildered Henry that he was now in the cabinet.

"Now that you've survived for a few weeks, I thought that I ought to tell you in a little more detail why I wanted you in the job, and of course, I want to hear from you on how it's all going. Frankly, Henry, I need to be in several places at once, doing about three difficult things simultaneously and competently. I can't do that any more, not at my age." Henry nodded, unaware that his gesture could indicate that he agreed that HB was becoming old. He also wondered at what age the ability to do three difficult things simultaneously and competently vanished and why HB, who spent so much time in the pub, thought that he was overworked.

"I understand."

Hubert continued. "What I really needed was someone that I could trust without having to spend ages explaining what's required. Frankly, we haven't attracted top quality younger staff for some time, and we've got a reputation for being the company for which most graduates would least like to work. I still think that they're biased by the hostile coverage of the chemicals spill, the cancellation of the pensioners' party just after we announced record profits and BF's plan to charge staff for the use of coat hangers, but that's all history. Our recruitment policy must change but it'll take time and meanwhile I need to make sure that our problems are considered by someone who I can totally trust."

Henry noted the incorrect use of the word "who" and the split infinitive but remained silent.

"I want a trouble shooter with safe hands. That's you and that's one reason why I want you to take on the responsibility of speaking to the press. I don't want some jumped-up expensive little twit from an agency speaking on our behalf any more. It makes sense to do it in-house and, of course, you're responsible for all external relations."

Henry, who had already assumed that this was part of his responsibilities, was worried to hear his fears confirmed. "That's a big responsibility, HB, er Hubert, but I'll do my best, but please remember that I haven't had this job for long and it will take time to learn and I know absolutely nothing about the media and how they work." It was time to indicate his commitment, and straining hard to think of what BF would have said, he asserted that "this represents a window of opportunity for the company and for me, that I will not allow to slam shut, at least until the bottom lines have been achieved and a cap has been put on any unfortunate publicity resulting from the winds of change". He also averred that the upside potential was significant and, for good measure, added that there was also potential for a win-win situation.

HB's purple pallor paled. He stared at Perkins and then smiled. "I know you're joking and it was a fine example of pure BF but please, never talk like that again. It makes me feel ill. Henry, I understand your reservations but your long experience has exposed you to many aspects of our operations. I also know that you're completely honest and that you learn quickly and know how to improvise. Anyway, you read newspapers and watch television, don't you, so you know what's what and how they work."

Henry, feeling that he should not challenge the assertion that he knew what was what, stayed silent.

At this point, Hubert's secretary, Benita Harris, entered to provide more coffee and biscuits. She was about 30, auburn-haired, brown-eyed and slender. However, nature, having decided that it might have been too generous in the looks department, had endowed her with what could only be described as a very generous hooter. Benita understood Hubert and his ways so well that it had been rumoured that she was planning to write a satirical novel about business. Executive cups replenished, Benita withdrew and, with his back to the door, and thus unaware that her retreat had not been completed, Hubert said "damn fine secretary, Benita. Lucky to have had her". Unaware that he had ever had her, she smiled and shut the door.

"By the way, Henry, talking about the media, I want you to look into our emergency planning. Some managers have been pressing for the development of an emergency plan but little's been done. Our non-execs, whose every decision I respect", and here HB allowed himself a minor smirk, "felt that a major accident was extremely unlikely as we've never had one and they also believed that training against a practical plan could cost money in preparing for something that would probably never happen. Some bright spark also said that no two accidents are the same, so it's best to make it up as you go along. As you know, to keep costs down, all that we could do was to hire a consultant for two days. He was over-weight, a former army man, who knew damn all about business. He was the sort of chap whose troops would only follow him through a sense of curiosity. Sort of fellow who would have been out of his depth in a bowl of porridge. Wore a blazer, smoked a pipe and went around the 8th floor, twanging his stolen military braces. Need I say more?"

Henry shook his head and grinned.

"All he did was to copy a fat and mainly irrelevant manual, doubtless compiled for other clients, change the company name and a few minor details, put Broadoak logos on the cover and send us a big invoice. Shifty fellow, never liked him."

"What happened to the report? I never saw it."

"I asked Fricker to distribute copies but I learned only last week that he graded them so highly confidential that nobody outside this floor saw it. Apparently all the other copies, securely bound up in box containers, were used to keep doors open in hot weather. Worst of all, there was no follow-up, training or exercises. I want you to take this on board urgently, read the report, here's my copy. Let me know as soon as poss how you're getting on. You've got a training budget. Ask Benita what it is, I forget."

Later that day, on his homeward journey, Henry read a letter in his management magazine which frightened him. It was a letter from one consultant to another, written after an emergency exercise.

We shouldn't reproach ourselves for the mass defection of participants during the early morning coffee break. After all, we had only given two presentations and the delegates had not undertaken any role-playing. Frankly, if our lectures had been less interesting, I think that the scale of the revolt could have been greater.

We must also remember that the course started promptly at 7.30 am., at the request of the managing director, who maintained that accidents usually happen at this time. I don't think that the delegates accepted his logic although it was good of him to come in to welcome everyone to the course when he arrived at 10.30.

It was certainly regrettable that we lost nearly an hour, during the breakout, whilst the managers rounded up their colleagues from local cafés, but we must compliment them for their professionalism when looking for the missing delegates. It is an eloquent comment on their understanding of the local geography that we lost only four participants. I agree with you, however, that whilst four doesn't sound too many, having to re-organise the remaining four fifths of the attendees did create problems.

I hope that the girl who had hysterics is now better: it certainly was harrowing seeing her in that state but I really don't think that you should blame yourself. She could equally well have gone berserk in one of my lectures and nobody believed the bizarre allegations that she made against you. Obviously, she totally misunderstood what you had said. Frankly, she should never have been on the course and I think that we can congratulate ourselves for having exposed her temperament in private. Imagine if that had happened in a real crisis!

Happily, the defection and the consequent delay did not have too great an impact on the programme after the MD decided, at 5.30, just before he went home, that the course should continue after dinner. I think that the antagonism that we noted was directed against him, not us.

I also think that the MD was wrong in barging in during the morning, to claim, wrongly of course, that there was a real emergency offshore and that the participants should remain in their places in case they were required. Frankly, it wasn't funny to see ashen faces and I think that was why two more participants left. It was, as you said at the time, with such a telling phrase, unlucky that we were then down to 13 delegates.

Our problems were compounded by the fact that lunch was so poor that another four delegates sought tucker elsewhere. Although, I'm still not sure why they failed to return, like you, I heard the rumours.

I felt sorry for the telephone responders, being cooped up in a small room for the exercise, and it's not surprising that five of them disappeared before the end of the day. Those who remained tried hard but the fact that they all sat with their backs to the information boards, was, I think, the main reason that they were unable to provide any new facts during the entire exercise.

I had sensed a degree of anarchy as soon as we arrived and nobody, apart from the MD, seemed to have any effective authority. You noted that the Public Relations manager was away. According to one of his colleagues, he always takes a holiday at this time of year, unless an exercise is held in a different month, in which case he alters the date of his vacation. He argues that he could be away when a real crisis occurred and it is important for his colleagues to have experience of coping without him.

I think that we were right in telling the company that the scenario on which they insisted was unrealistic. Frankly, the world's media will not be interested if one man breaks his arm offshore when taking evasive action to avoid an allegedly bad-tempered seagull. It's true that the MD, who insisted on doing an interview in front of the camera did quite well but the company deluded itself in thinking that Newsnight would cover such a story, even on the slackest of news days. Furthermore, speculating that the seagull was to blame for what happened effectively pre-empted the results of an official enquiry, which could have had legal and insurance-related implications.

I must also challenge his attempt to inveigle the interviewer with his comment that "you and I, Jeremy, know that these kinds of accidents occur in our gardens and that there is little that we can do to prevent them". I would also take issue with the MD for giving such gruesome details of how the seagull met its end. He really ought to have had more concern for its next of kin.

The press releases were well written but showed a bias against seagulls which could have caused problems. During the exercise, I particularly enjoyed the comment that the next press release would contain nothing new and that "the original junk will be repeated".

If you'll forgive the pun, I thought that they were all at sea when you asked questions on the type of seagull that was involved. It was just their luck that they came up against an expert ornithologist. Nevertheless, they should have accepted that The Seagull Scene, arguably the leading journal of its kind, would be interested in the story and I think they also showed too cavalier an attitude towards the pressure group, ASS, the Association of Seagull Societies. A large oil company should remember that many an ASS member buys petrol.

The house magazine article, in which the company says that it coped very well with the crisis exercise, does contain a good photograph of the surviving participants and all four told me that they thoroughly enjoyed the course.

Missing our plane was unfortunate and the only hotel with available accommodation would not have been my choice under any circumstances. I hope that the medicine has restored you to full health.

Henry would start planning on how to cope with a crisis during the next three weeks.

Some two weeks later, the new general manager leaned back in his leather-smelling plastic-covered executive chair, put his hands behind his head, placed his well-shod feet on the desk and looked around his new office. There had not been time to accumulate any meaningless management trophies and the bookcase was still empty but the thick carpet and new furniture confirmed that they were in the office of someone important. The walls were covered by totally incomprehensible paintings, inherited temporarily from Fricker. Henry intended to order some works by Thomas Kinkade, some of whose work he had seen in a local shop. He was reminded of them now as the sun slanted in through the clean windows, gently illuminating the pretentious rubbish currently on display.

The range of digital clocks showed that it was Friday and nearly 12.45 in London. Henry was not interested in the time in Singapore and Washington. He had nothing against the good people of these cities but what mattered to him was London and 12.45. Then the phone would ring, announcing that his company car and chauffeur were ready to spirit him away to an expensive and doubtless lengthy lunch in the city. Henry, learning something about wine and good food, relished the prospect of an enjoyable lunch. Apart from HB, most senior managers were out of the office, on some continental junket, so he could anticipate a quiet, relaxing afternoon and early departure. As it was the end of the week, he would buy some fine wines on his way home. Life was good.

His feet swung off the desk and he grabbed the phone. "Thanks, George, I'm on my way", he said blithely, without really listening. It was not the chauffeur. The voice asked if that was Henry Perkins. The startled general manager, having difficulty in hearing the caller, confirmed his identity and demanded to know who he was talking to.

"Charlie Naughton from Wavepuddle South depot. It's awful, we've got dead and injured and …"

"Hold, on, tell me what's happened?"

"We've had an explosion and there's a bloody great fire that's out of control. The fire crews aren't here yet."

"Has everyone been evacuated?"

" I don't know, its chaos. We need help. I've got to go."

He rang off. What should Henry do? No crisis plans existed. Perkins had just hoped that there would not be a serious accident, especially after Fricker had reduced staff numbers dramatically and some maintenance had been postponed…Henry shouted for Rose to cancel his lunch and then remembered that she was sick. Her replacement was outside on the pavement, ironically, having a smoke. He sent for someone to bring her in. Suddenly, the office of the second most senior employee in the building resembled a London underground station in the rush hour. Both phones jangled discordantly, increasing the sense of drama. Henry, who realised that he must tell HB as soon as possible, picked up one phone.

It was Charlie Naughton again and he wanted Henry to listen carefully.

"It's getting worse: it's Armageddon. I'm ringing from the Paradise Hotel because we've all been evacuated. The depot's ablaze. Seven guys have been killed, six are injured and at least 12 are missing."

"Are the emergency services on site?"

"Yes, thank God. They were delayed by tourists in the lanes around the depot. We couldn't even use our own fire engine. The blasted thing had a puncture."

Henry tried to interrupt but was halted in his tracks.

"Hold on, we've got a new problem. Someone's just said that there's a huge purple cloud and it's drifting towards Snooterton Major. The airport's closed and local television says that some chemicals are in the shipping canal, turning the water yellow. The press are swarming all over the place and one of our junior guys has already told local television that we reduced maintenance and fired so many people he's not surprised that there has been an accident."

Henry interrupted.

"Give me the phone number of the hotel." He took it down and then asked for details of the dead and injured to be faxed to him immediately. "I also want an update every 15 minutes."

"Sorry, no can do. We can't cope with what's happening here. We need help, especially with the reporters, who are interviewing anyone they can find. It's absolute hell."

Mr Perkins said that he would try but even if he could find someone, they would not be at the depot for some hours. Charlie rang off. What Henry did not reveal was that nobody had been nominated and that the company did not even have train or plane timetables available and driving would take some hours.

His office was now full of very agitated colleagues. Most of them wanted answers to questions that they had not anticipated, let alone solved in advance. Questions, questions. The company was being besieged by the outside world. Henry was sinking fast. If only he had more pairs of hands and knew what to do. One colleague, who acted as a part-time PR in-house person, asked what to do about demands for radio and television interviews, which were "streaming in because that idiot at the depot has already said that the accident was our fault, and, if we can give interviews, who will it be?" Henry had no idea. This had not been discussed in advance and he did not know who would be any good in front of a camera or microphone. The semi-PR man also wanted to know who should deal with the flood of telephone calls from the media and what could they say? He should do his best.

Then the temporary personnel manager wanted an up-to-date list of those working at the depot. Henry exploded. "Good god, man, why should I have that?" BF's temporary stand-in also wanted the names of those who had been confirmed as dead, injured and missing. His team of two was being attacked over the phone by anxious friends and relatives. Perkins had no idea of how to help or who should do what but, if he survived this disaster, he must organise the new division as soon as possible, bringing in more people. The investment manager sought Henry's advice on how he could stop the plunge in the group's share price.

Henry's temporary secretary returned and put a large note on his desk. "The local MP, Simon Heartless, wants a prompt update." Henry knew that, even by the standards of the unthinking automata now dominating Parliament, he was a particularly silly little man, whose intelligence would have been challenged if required to supervise at a little-used car park. He wanted to know what the company was doing "to mitigate the impact of this truly horrendous accident" and "why wasn't I informed? I am, after all, your local Member of Parliament". Allegedly, the company had his telephone number. They did not.

Another message floated into view. "The secretary of state for Trade and Industry wants an immediate one page report of what has happened and what you are doing about it, to be sent within the next half hour. I said that you would do that", the temp trilled, thrilled to be involved but not responsible. Perkins groaned.

Around the building, his colleagues were trying to respond to myriad other calls from contacts, other companies, health, safety and environment officials, people from Brussels, financial analysts and companies who were offering their services or equipment which could help mitigate the impact of this disaster.

Downstairs, journalists, unable to glean any information from the company by telephone, were mingling with relatives who lived in the London area and who, like the scribes, unable to find out what was happening, were now surrounding the lone receptionist. She did not even know what had happened…Another new note was placed on Henry's desk. The telephone exchange was jammed so normal business had been halted.

Henry turned on the television to hear the latest news. An elderly lady, standing in front of her old cottage, now distinctive because it lacked a front door and windows, sobbingly told the interviewer that her Jack had been blown up. "Here for breakfast, gone by lunch. He always said that it was a dangerous place to work because nobody cared about safety but there's nothing else round here, since the cement works closed, know what I mean?" Without waiting for confirmation that she had explained herself adequately, she continued.

"He gave that company 15 years of his life and now they've taken the rest. What about me?" She then confided to the nation that this was not the end of her tragedy. "Rufus has also been killed. At the end of the day he was a brilliant friend and I really loved him. He had such a loving personality and I really will miss him, he's my dog you know, and I'll miss my Jack too, of course, but in a different way. I really don't know what I shall do without them. They were my best friends. I'm totally gutted, that's what I am, totally gutted."

Apparently, hundreds of local people had been evacuated to the local village hall where they would have to stay overnight. All those within a 12-mile radius of the site, and whose windows were still in place, should stay indoors, because of the smoke, and boil all water because chemicals leaking from the site had penetrated the watercourse.

Henry turned off the television to take a call on his mobile phone from a non-executive director who demanded an update on what had happened and what Perkins was doing about it. Henry could only report what Charlie Naughton had told him and what he had just seen on television. The board member also wanted to know "why the blazes" and Perkins felt that was an unfortunate phrase, he had not been contacted. Everyone seemed to think that they had a divine right to be fully appraised.

Perkins pondered suicide. What he did not know then was that an active pressure group concerned with industrial safety was already organising a boycott of the company's petrol stations and that the leading trade union had called out its members at the company's other locations in protest against the cuts in the maintenance budget. If he had known this, his decision to remain alive, at least for a little while longer, might have been reversed.

The phone rang again.

"Henry, Hubert. Come in, immediately."

Perkins had known HB for years but had never heard him so agitated and he did not even think what an odd name Henry Hubert would be. Jacketless, he left his office and hastened to see the chief executive, whom he had briefed, briefly, some 10 minutes before. Courtesies were ignored.

"Henry, listen carefully. We've got a major crisis on our hands. Crisis management is in your patch, so find out as much as you can, as soon as you can." The modest Henry had already thought of that but what he heard next filled him with fear.

"We've had a request to go on television for a live interview which will be shown nationally. I want you to do it and do the best that you can. I'll try to cope with all the other problems. We must get our side of the story over as quickly as possible before we're completely crucified. Here are the details. Call them and say that you will come in about 40 minutes. The depot and the local emergency services can deal with the physical and operational aspects of the fire and Don Padson there is a good man and will handle things well. We must look after the wider corporate implications. I'm organising all the managers here to deal with the most serious issues and we've asked all regional offices to send help to the site as soon as possible but they won't be there until early evening."

Henry pleaded that he was new in the job, had not had sufficient time to organise things properly, had never spoken to a journalist and had not been trained.

"Nonsense, Henry. Any fool can cope with some ill-informed inexperienced jumped-up interviewer. Most journalists are unreliable idiots who only know about pop music, the royal family and football. You'll have no trouble. Above all, make sure that you have the latest information and for god's sake, say sorry and, above all, be honest. Do what you can and ask Benita, on your way out, to tell all managers to report to my office for a crisis meeting immediately. We've got to work out how to cope."

Apparently, Henry had no choice. He was to appear on television. Hubert waved a hand indicating that the chat was over. "Good luck and keep me posted."

When young, Perkins had equated appearing on television with playing cricket for England. This latter ambition had only been abandoned when, in his mid twenties, he realised that failing to score a half century for his village team, for over 10 years, was the kind of consistency that England did not want.

As he padded out through the secretary's office, Benita smiled sympathetically and asked if HB had told him that Hugh 'Fergie' Norton-Williams, an external public relations "crisis expert" had been summoned and was in Henry's office. The company had paid him a retainer for many years but he had been totally inactive apart from submitting substantial invoices. Having been briefed by HB, he was now supposed to spend a few minutes advising Henry on how to cope with the interview.

Henry took an immediate dislike to Norton-Williams. He seldom made instant and unfavourable judgements but this was one occasion when he must make an exception. The PR man, in his mid twenties, looked about 15. That was not good: what could he possibly know? He reminded Henry of an estate agent with whom he had crossed swords and that, too, was not good. Norton-Williams was wearing a vivid yellow and red spotted bow tie which looked as if some egg and tomato had failed to complete the journey to the owner's mouth. The thick blue vertical stripes of his shirt shouted at his yellow, green and brown three-piece tweed suit, the sort that people wear when they are just about to shoot something and then proclaim the death of an innocent animal as a "damn good show".

Norton-Williams began slowly, showing no sense of urgency, and condescendingly, with an affected aristocratic drawl so pronounced that it endangered understanding said "we in public relations, or as we now prefer to call it, stakeholder and community relations, SACPR for short, feel that the most important thing in a crisis is to pay tribute…" Henry interrupted but resisted the thought that sacking PR was a good idea.

The repetition of the word relations reminded him that he had not told Jill that he was to be on television later that afternoon. She had just heard, on the radio, about the fire and she wished him luck and warned him to be careful. Henry assumed that his wife was concerned lest he fell over some of the cables that litter studio floors. She need not worry. He would be careful. He was too overwhelmed by adrenalin to pay much attention to the odious little bow-tie. Nevertheless, Henry thought that he understood the essentials and his confidence was reinforced because he knew about the depot and its procedures and this would give him a big advantage over the interviewer.

An excited Perkins remembered reading somewhere that the secret of a good interview was to ignore the audience and to pretend that the only person watching was one's partner. That was not good advice: Mrs Perkins had already said that she would tape the interview as she was too nervous to watch it live.

Henry dismissed the PR child and sought a final briefing from his colleagues at the Paradise Hotel. They gave him the latest news, confirmed that the plant had been evacuated and summarised the nature of local media coverage. The explosion and fire had occurred at what, just hours ago, was a very attractive location, just outside a picturesque village famed for its high proportion of elderly citizens and even more elderly cottages. Apparently, the cottages now looked distinctly less picturesque. Nine depot workers had been killed, nine were injured, some badly, and at least four were missing. About 30 local people had been evacuated to a hall in the neighbouring village. The fire was still raging but the emergency services were on site in some numbers. Because of the delay caused by local traffic, the fire had taken hold. The local radio station, somehow, had picked up a plaintive cry from the depot to the emergency services. "For god's sake, come immediately, we can't cope. Unless we cool some of the storage tanks, the whole lot's going to go up. We've got about 40 minutes, that's all." Fortunately, the tanks were cooled and a worse disaster had been averted but the situation remained critical.

According to the local radio, although his colleagues could not confirm this, some chemicals had escaped over the dry fields into the river. The agricultural community was already talking of massive compensation because their livelihoods were in jeopardy. The radio report also said that environmentalists intended mounting a blockade against Broadoak filling stations.

Perkins reminded himself that his chief executive had said that the journalists were unreliable and immediately felt better. Surely, it was exaggeration to say that a purple cloud was spiralling up from the depot and was being blown towards Snooterton Major, a town of some 100,000, dominated by retired military men, about five miles away.

The car to take him to the studio had arrived. Henry rushed out of the building. He was worried about what was happening but, curiously, did not feel nervous. He had temporarily forgotten that millions of people would be watching. It was as if he was being swept along by events and had relinquished control. That said, Hubert was right. Yes, he did know about the company and he certainly knew more than any interviewer.

Chapter 12

Henry used the few minutes in the car, en route to the studio, to think what he would say during the interview. If he did well, just possibly, this could be the beginning of a new life. As the adrenaline started to flow, he forgot the little that he had been told by the bow tie. He had distrusted the pseudo-youth: he did not need prompting on what to say and had never liked wearers of bow ties.

Henry accepted a generous sherry whilst the famous interviewer, Robin Knight, assured him that, although he had never appeared on television before, he would be fine. Henry was inclined to agree. After all, his only task was to answer questions and he had seen countless politicians being interviewed. The sherry, undiluted by lunch, introduced itself to the adrenaline. Guided by the studio manager, Henry walked carefully to his seat. It was hot in the studio and Perkins permitted himself a quick look round before settling down for the moment, when, recently rejected by his company but now in a senior position, he would address the nation.

The studio manager asked for silence, a red light came on the nearest camera and the famous face started reading the introduction from the auto cue.

"A few hours ago, a serious accident occurred at the Broadoak Oil depot at Wavepuddle South. With me in the studio is Henry Perkins, staff supervisor at the company.

"Mr Perkins…"

Henry, proud of his new status, immediately interrupted. "Let me correct you there. Actually, I am general manager, CRAP"

"I beg your pardon?"

"General manager, corporate reputation, assets and planning."
The interviewer, taken aback, persevered.

"Early reports say that nine people have been killed in the fire and explosion. Just how many have lost their lives and have been injured in the accident?"

Henry knew precisely what to say. He had to start on a positive note. He must praise someone.

"Before I deal with your question, which I welcome and I should like to thank you for inviting me on to your programme, I would like to pay tribute to the emergency services and the work that they have done in this disaster, in very difficult circumstances", he intoned, with the pomp and pomposity of a phoney premier.

Turning away from the interviewer, and addressing the audience directly by staring inanely down the camera lens, he confided to the nation that "we in this country are fortunate in having such a fine body of men", and then, thinking of Mrs. Perkins, belatedly added "and women".

He sighed, sank back too far in the chair and tried to turn again to face the interviewer. He was confident that the worst was now over but forgot that the question remained unanswered. Suddenly, he heard the interviewer pressing the point on the number of casualties *"in this disaster, as you have just described it yourself"*.

Perkins knew the answer. He had expected this question and was fully informed. However, in his enthusiasm to tell the nation the news, he forgot to say how sorry the company was. He was inexplicably paralysed with the thought of how dreadful it must be to be injured in an accident and then wake up, in hospital, aching in parts that you didn't know you had, to be confronted by some obnoxious politician, blinded by lights and television cameras as the little pipsqueak created a photo-opportunity.

Instead of answering the question on the casualties, and doubtless pre-occupied with the dreadful picture conjured up by his imagination, he aped a politician.

"My company, Broadoak Oil, which has a safety record", he thought that there was something wrong there but continued, "and which has contributed significantly to the country's export trade over many years, has to confirm that five of its employees have been killed and that at least nine have been injured".

Somehow, as he listened to himself, it seemed that something was missing, but nobody would have noticed and Henry, curiously beginning to enjoy the experience, was not really aware of what had gone wrong. He was feeling increasingly confident. This was easy.

The famous face, listening intently, said that all the reports that he had seen said that nine men had lost their lives and that nine were injured. Henry, flummoxed temporarily and showing a little irritation, contended that he had just said that. Henry also volunteered the thought that "we all trust that the other four men who are missing will soon be found, but, being realistic, there's little hope. I fear that they are probably dead."

"Can you tell us who lost their lives?"

"I'm sorry, but the next of kin have not yet been told, so it would be wrong to reveal this, I mean them, on radio, I mean television." Then, trying to be helpful, he said "all the men who have, so sadly, lost their lives in the explosion and fire worked near the seat of the explosion and fire".

Where was that? That was easy. Henry had asked his colleagues the same question. "It all started where gasoline, that's petrol, you know, is loaded on to the tankers."

"How many people worked there?"

"Just the nine who have been killed and those injured and the missing, I mean unaccounted for."

He didn't realise the significance of this admission for the families and friends of those involved who were watching. When responding to the next question, he heard himself ill-advisedly trying to put this into perspective. "That may sound as if today's disaster is really serious, and, of course it is, and we all in Broadoak regret it but I should like to put it into perspective."

The famous face remained passive. Experience had taught him when to speak and when to remain silent. This was a time to be silent. Henry dutifully filled the pregnant pause.

"Of course, all of us in Broadoak regret the deaths and injuries that happened today but, I can tell you that it's only a very small percentage of those who work there at the depot and in the office there, for Broadoak Oil over the course of an average year. Let's put it into perspective. Even if they had all been killed, and everybody in the company is glad that they haven't, it would still be less than the numbers who die on our roads in, say, two weeks, but I don't see many people on television discussing that. Let's remind ourselves that the vast majority of those on the site at the time of the disaster are safe and well."

Sensing that somehow, he had lost the advantage and he was saying things that he would not have otherwise contemplated in a thousand years, and deciding that honesty was the best policy, he volunteered that "the fire at Broadoak's depot, which is more serious than you may realise", would "probably be out within three days as there'd be nothing left then to burn."

Looking for something positive to say, he claimed that "the prospect of major pollution is already receding as the fire is burning everything in its path."

"What about the reports that a purple cloud, containing poisonous gas, is heading towards the nearest town, causing the police to warn the local people to remain indoors and to keep doors and windows shut? There are also reports that the water in the local canal has turned yellow."

"You surprise me there. I thought that the cloud, if it exists, was yellow and that the water had turned purple but we in Broadoak cannot comment on the colours. I'm inclined to doubt the report of pollution in the canal because it probably came from inexperienced local journalists, but if you want any information on that, you'd better ask the police.

"I must say, Robin, that it's a pity that the media concentrates so much on bad news. Hardly surprising everyone's so depressed. Let's remind ourselves that the majority of those who used to work in the depot and live in the nearby village are safe and well and that it won't take too many weeks to restore the homes that have been damaged. I'm confident that they'll be back before the winter sets in."

Henry was becoming less confident that he was saying the right things.

HB had retreated from the onslaught briefly to watch the live interview from the relative calm of the Thirsty Fox. His face, already maroon, went a deeper shade of purple. A fellow-drinker said that, for one of his age, to jump so high, from a stationary position, was, and the comment loses something in the translation, not least in the omission of the adjectival alliteration, a fantastic feat. "For God's sake, why does he keep mentioning our name? Is he trying to emphasise that

150

it's us who've had the accident?" Why on earth had he ever promoted Henry? If he continued in this way, the company would soon be out of business. BF would have been better. At least nobody would have understood a word the damn fool uttered.

"Have all the villagers been accounted for and are they safe?"

"Broadoak is very sorry that some pensioners have been taken to hospital, suffering from toxic poisoning from the smoke and we all, of course, hope that they will survive this terrible ordeal, although we have to be realistic. Many of them are not as young as they used to be, but that applies to us all, doesn't it?"

Grudgingly, under further questioning, he conceded that their condition, like that of their homes, was not good. "It will take a few weeks to patch up, I mean repair their homes but that's not as bad as it sounds because I expect that they'll be in hospital for the bulk of that time."

The FF wanted to know if the local inhabitants and those who were injured were critical, especially those who had breathed in what Perkins himself said was toxic smoke.

"I haven't spoken to them myself, but I imagine that they're not very happy. Some are probably very cross."

"What I meant was are they in a critical state as far as their injuries are concerned?"

"I'm sorry, but I haven't had time to find out."

"Why did this happen and is Broadoak Oil prepared to accept responsibility for the accident?"

Henry was beginning to think that the interview might not have gone precisely as he had wanted, and, although he could not pinpoint it, he sensed that he might have said a few things that, perhaps, might have been better unsaid. The problem was that Henry had no idea of what he had said and he had little concept of the duration, thus far, of the interview. He felt mildly intoxicated but imagined that the end was in sight. The phrase bothered him. If his performance had been as dire as he was beginning to think, it could well be the end in more senses than one. He must finish on a more contrite but open note and, for no apparent reason, he suddenly felt better. After all, Hubert, and how strange it was after all these years, to call him Hubert, had stressed that he must be honest.

His brief reverie over, he prepared to deal with the question of why the accident happened. Meanwhile, HB stared at the screen praying that Perkins was not about to inflict more damage on his company.

Henry collected himself together to rescue the situation. "I feel very emotional about what has happened at the Broadoak depot and that may have influenced some of my comments. I am not really myself at the moment. Please forgive me but I knew some of the people involved and even worked with them and I know their wives and friends. I feel as if members of my own family have been killed. I'm in a state of deep shock and I really wonder why I'm here now. I should be with my friends, trying to comfort them and then working hard to ensure that, as far as possible, this sort of accident can never happen again. Please forgive me for anything that I have said which may cause offence. I truly feel awful about what's happened and it is very difficult to concentrate at the moment. Anyone who has recently been bereaved will know how I feel now.

"This is an appalling time for everyone involved and I want to say how sorry I and my colleagues are that this has happened and that we all are thinking about those who have lost their loved ones. We deeply regret the deaths and injuries and that elderly people have had to be evacuated from their homes. We're also sorry about the pollution and we'll do all we can to ensure that normality is restored as soon as possible. We intend to learn from this tragedy and shall try to ensure that it never happens again. I also thank the emergency services, who, as usual, have done a marvellous job."

The famous face, sensing that the interview was about to become more conventional as Perkins was now more composed, asked the question again.

"Yes, we can understand that, Mr Perkins, but my question was why did the accident happen and do you accept responsibility for the accident?"

As he repeated the question, the producer spoke directly into his earpiece. "I think that this interview could develop. He's very emotional, follow up on the cause and responsibility angles and go softly with him to encourage him to be candid. I'm going to gamble.

Give him an extra three minutes and we'll drop the piece about the man who bit his dog."

On reflection, this seemed an easy question and Henry wondered why he had not previously replied direct. He had no doubts on how to answer.

"What are the facts? The accident occurred in our depot, during working hours and we have no reason to believe that there was sabotage. The carnage, pollution and evacuations would not have occurred unless something went wrong at our site, so it must have been our fault. We are a responsible company and so we take full"... Henry paused, seeking an alternative word to responsibility, but failed. He never knew whether it was a fleeting moment of prudence, or a concern at using similar words twice within a sentence. Whatever the reason, at that moment, the financial future for Broadoak, like HB's blood pressure, took a distinct turn for the worse. Within seconds, the increasingly generous Perkins had promised handsome compensation for everyone involved, because, as he readily repeated, "it was an explosion in Broadoak's depot, during working hours, so of course, it was ultimately our fault. If we did not have a plant there, it would not have happened".

Henry was sure of this because, quite simply, he could not think of anyone else to blame, besides, Hubert had told him to be honest. Later, he did wonder whether, before the cause of the accident had been determined, it had been wise to have promised adequate compensation, to pay all extra expenses of those forced to stay, as he readily admitted, in a village hall where only "only public-school boys would feel comfortable" and to provide all drinking water, free of charge, until the public supply was re-connected.

"What caused the accident? I know that it's very early in the evolution of this disaster but you must have an idea?"

Henry did not know, but a general manager could not be seen to be ignorant by millions of viewers. Obviously, the interviewer was trying to help.

"Was it human error or equipment failure?"

The general manager paused. "As you say, it's too soon to know for sure and I don't want pre-empt the results of the enquiry, but, if you're pushing me to speculate, I'd say it was probably a combination of both."

The interviewer, manifestly a very pleasant man, who had hardly started to persuade Perkins to speculate, again tried to help.

"Why do you say that, Mr Perkins?"

This was the moment of truth and for some honest speaking as HB had recommended. ""It's a complex issue but let me try to summarise the position that we and our competitors are in. Petrol margins are very low because of intense competition and demand has fallen because the greedy government keeps on increasing prices at the pump and we only have a few pence per litre to find the crude oil, often in very inaccessible areas, bring it to shore, refine it and market it.

"That's bad enough, but this truly dreadful and ignorant government, supported by its sycophantic toadies", a phrase that he had heard HB use, so it couldn't get him into trouble, "has little idea of how industry is run and with the help of those daft un-elected Brussels bureaucrats", (another HB phase), "who are equally ignorant, they continue to impose ever more stringent and costly environmental requirements on us, irrespective of how effective they are. In many instances, we in the industry, and we all want a better and more healthy environment, have offered alternative, less expensive but equally effective schemes but they are automatically rejected, often even before these people, with no knowledge of industry, or anything else as far as I can determine, have had time to consider them objectively."

FF, scarcely able to believe his experienced ears, let Perkins continue.

"Society demands that we sustain high levels of employment and produce more environmentally-acceptable products cheaply whilst maintaining the highest possible level of safety. We want that too."

HB, hearing some of his phrases on national television, prayed that Perkins would not mention him. So far so good but...

Henry had almost forgotten where he was but HB, helped back into his seat from which he had fallen after the latest Perkins comments, was all too aware and was wondering where he himself would be able to find work at the age of 63. His shares in Broadoak would soon be valueless. He pictured Henry selling tickets for deck chairs at Westhaven and felt a little better.

"The problem is that society is not prepared to pay a reasonable price for our products to achieve all these objectives but, let's be quite blunt here, the main culprit is the government which takes more than four fifths of the pump price of petrol. If they're so keen on safety, they should be less greedy and let us keep more so we can introduce new, safer equipment and pay for more training for our people. We need to maintain our equipment to the highest possible standards and this is becoming increasingly difficult for all of us.

"Pressure groups, if they really wanted to alleviate the situation, should spend more time listening and learning and then helping us to formulate answers. The difficulty is that they have enormous power but prefer to be part of the problem, rather than part of the solution. That's how they recruit more members. "

The interviewer, stunned by Henry's candour and sensing a scoop, pressed the point in the hope of provoking Perkins to resume his tirade, *"from what you say, the government is largely responsible for this accident and Broadoak Oil is unhappy with this state of affairs?"*

At that moment, a glamorous film star, soaked in the most enticing of perfumes, and wearing the briefest of skirts, wafted in to the studio. It was unfortunate that Henry, being asked this leading question, but seduced by the scent, looked away from the interviewer, thus creating the impression for the viewers that he was reluctant to continue with this theme. His gaping jaw and rolling eyes reduced his shrivelled credibility.

Henry resumed and tried to look less spellbound and more serious.

"It is a dreadful, regrettable, unacceptable, intolerable, appalling, unpalatable state of affairs", he intoned. Then, becoming almost regal, he added "it's been an annus horribilis for the company because, like other groups, we've had a few accidents around the country and we feel very bad about that. However, accidents will happen, especially in this potentially dangerous sector and society must decide that if it wants improved safety, higher environmental standards and the maintenance of jobs it has to pay more for the products or the government must lower its tax take. Quite simply, we want to provide jobs, look after safety and the environment and to supply reliable, low-cost products but we can't do everything at today's prices, after the government has taken so much."

The famous face attempted a summary of the story thus far.

"You are saying that your company accepts full responsibility for this disaster and will meet all the bills and pay compensation because the accident at your depot was probably the consequence of poor maintenance and inadequate staff training. You are saying that this is because prices are low and that the government takes too much in tax so, in a way, this accident is their fault. In this difficult situation, you are trying very hard to stay in business, and to maintain levels of employment and make more environmentally-acceptable products."

Henry, impressed that his interviewer had grasped the key points so satisfactorily, nodded vigorously and smiled broadly, to be friendly. HB was right: he could cope with an interview without any difficulty. Honesty had been the best policy.

"Thank you Mr. Perkins of Broadoak Oil."

HB had returned to his office and the chaos. He was sitting at his desk, with his hands around his head, as if he were protecting it from the corporate axe which, wielded by the board, would surely descend soon. He had appointed Henry.

The crisis on the ground was being overcome, thanks largely to the emergency services and the dedicated staff and their colleagues from a rival company. HB was trying to assess the damage done by Perkins. That could well prove more expensive than the destruction of part of the depot and the consequential costs. He failed: it was too awful to contemplate. How else, in so short a time, could anyone have alienated so many groups? Perkins had attacked the government, when the company was seeking new offshore exploration licenses, Brussels for being incompetent, society for expecting too much for too little and pressure groups for failing to co-operate. Various comments during the interview would doubtless eliminate any possibility of recovering some of the expenses from the insurance groups and there was much else that would exercise the lawyers.

HB pondered moving abroad. He would not see Henry until he had determined what to say before dismissing him. In his present mood, he would probably have hit him and the doctors said that any physical activity would be bad for him, and given the intensity of his wrath, it would not have been too good for Perkins either. Hubert began to rehearse the arguments that could be used publicly for Henry's sudden departure. After apologising for what had been said, the company would have to distance itself from his comments. Broadoak enjoyed a very close relationship with Brussels, the UK government, pressure groups and, of course, society, based on mutual respect and understanding and the company hoped that these constructive links would continue. Naturally, the oil industry, like all industries, did face some problems but all parties were working hard to overcome them and the company was grateful to all those external groups that were co-operating in the interests of the people.

The company had not realised that Henry had known so many of the casualties and their families and had therefore not appreciated the emotional stress that he was suffering. That had prompted the unfair criticisms which, under normal circumstances, would never have been made. Indeed, Henry had played a leading role in recent months in advancing the relationships with the groups he mentioned in his interview. Meanwhile, he had accepted two months' leave to recover from what had been for him a very harrowing time and to allow him to spend some time with his friends at the depot. One of his tasks, which he himself had suggested, was to set up a charitable trust to look after all children who had lost a parent following an industrial accident. Broadoak would be actively supporting the fund.

Perhaps something on those lines would suffice?

Tired by the unaccustomed use of his grey cells, Hubert replaced his head in his hands and summoned Benita to whom he dictated a draft press release which he would submit to the bow tie for his comments as soon as possible on the morrow. He did not realise that he had to issue the statement now to ensure coverage in the following day's editions.

Perkins returned to the office and was worried about the absence of comments on his interview but it was late so most of his colleagues had gone home. He tried to see Hubert but apparently the chief executive was unavailable. After doing what he could to ensure that the emergency was under control, including contacting the depot manager, Henry headed for his train.

The drama, especially the television interview, had left him feeling totally drained. Instead of buying the evening paper, as was his wont, he opted to dip into a very undemanding novel. If he had bought the newspaper, he would have been interested in page two. If he had not been so tired, he would have noticed that many fellow passengers seemed to be staring at him.

Mrs Perkins, who had been too nervous to see the interview, live or recorded, said that they could see it together after dinner. "How did it go?"

"I think that, on balance, it was OK. I know I made one big mistake and a few others but I don't think anyone noticed. I just followed Hubert's advice to be honest."

Jill shuddered.

The only telephone call was from Lynda. She congratulated Henry on his performance. "You were very good, especially at the end. I do wish you well." Henry suppressed a groan as he really wanted to forget the whole afternoon but rallied to thank her. "Yes, I'm afraid that I was very emotional and I made a monstrous mess of the first half of the interview and in the second half, the adrenalin took over and I said a few things that I probably should not have said and that's that. I really was most embarrassed and my comments were totally out of character but you can't put the genie back into the bottle. I expect that I'll be fired now. I don't know what on earth I can do. I'll never get another job." Lynda disagreed and then said that Wendy wanted a word.

"Uncle Henry, I thought you were just brilliant. You said a lot of things that needed to be said. Big business and the government are colluding to deceive the public and the ordinary people should speak up. You did just that. You spoke for millions of us and I'm very proud of you and I'm going to tell all my friends that you're my uncle." Henry thanked her and rang off.

Although tempted to watch the interview after dinner, as Jill had taped it at work, the Perkins, both fatigued by the day's events, opted instead for an early night. Henry now realised that the interview had been an unmitigated disaster from which he would never recover professionally. The longer he could delay watching his visual obituary the better.

The following day, Perkins deliberately caught a very early train as he thought that Hubert would want to discuss matters with him and he wanted to take the initiative in relation to the media. Yesterday, he now realised, he had probably given the worst television interview in the entire history of the medium and the clip would be used time and time again on training courses. He would be permanently notorious. Although Henry did not know it at that stage, the depot manager and his team had done a very good local press conference and follow-up interviews.

It was too early for the papers and Henry did not see any of his usual travelling companions so he tried to work out his most likely future. Was fate now about to take revenge and snatch back what he had wanted for years but had enjoyed only for weeks? Although having sterling virtues in such matters as stroking passing dogs, giving to door-to-door charity collections and being polite to double-glazing salesmen, perhaps he was not meant to be a general manager?

He puffed up the static escalator at the station, strolled to the office, mechanically mumbled a greeting to an unrecognised security official at the reception desk, waved his pass in the girl's face and went to his office. A few minutes later, the papers were dropped on his desk by Taffy. "I really enjoyed your interview. You really told them. Mrs Taffy and I saw it on the late evening news." Perkins thought that enjoyed was an odd verb but smiled appreciatively and wondered, once again, what he had said. He was still too frightened to watch the video and he remained convinced that his dismissal was imminent.

It wasn't fair. Pitched unexpectedly into his current position, he had warned Hubert about his inexperience but he had been honest, as HB had wished. He also resolved to tell HB, he could no longer think of him as Hubert, that doing an interview was very difficult. Absently mindedly, Henry started looking at the papers. He began by looking at the tabloids. April had returned to page three although she was now called June and was wearing a very tight and inadequate top which allowed the caption "June's busting out all over". Her career ambitions had changed: now, she wanted to be an astronaut. He turned the page and stared at the heading which greeted him.

Oil blaze boss slams 'ignorant' government

Who was this brave eccentric? It was he! What followed, astonishingly, was apparently a summary of his interview. The article acknowledged that Henry, "clearly emotional because of the tragedy, slammed the government's stance on taxes, safety and the environment and won praise from fed-up consumers". Henry could hardly believe what he was reading. Had he attacked the government? He did recall saying something towards the end of the interview. He made a note to ask Rose to obtain a transcript as soon she came in. He really should have watched the video which he had left at home.

He opened one of the broadsheets. It contained a straightforward report on the accident and conveyed the gist of Henry's remarks which were in line with the comments summarised in the tabloid. There was also a note at the bottom of the piece which referred the reader to the editorial on page six. Henry, hot and cold simultaneously, tremblingly turned to the first leader.

Truth at last

It is a sad reflection of both society and industry that only long after a major accident, if ever, are candid, sensible and relevant words uttered and action taken that might prevent the recurrence of such a disaster. It is even worse when, as in most instances, those words are spoken only in the knowledge that few members of the general public will hear them, despite the media's vigilance. Cynics will argue that this is too often the intention. We are in many ways a cosy, secretive society, afraid of genuinely open comment because it will either offend an influential group or invite an expensive legal reaction.

Yesterday was different. Henry Perkins of Broadoak Oil, whilst speaking in a television interview, visibly distressed and understandably emotional that some of his friends and colleagues had died in a fire at the company's depot, nevertheless courageously overcame his grief to offer a balanced, sobering and honest picture of the pressures on an industry that is widely expected to be all things to all people.

The government looks to oil to collect huge taxes on its behalf, gratis, whilst imposing ever greater financial burdens for all those who have no alternative but to run cars because there is no adequate public transport. Similarly, it threatens the long lead-time industry with so-called windfall profits taxes if its rate of return briefly goes into double figures. We cannot recall similar disgust when such a rate is achieved by a supermarket whose activities, as far as we know, are not as risky as exploring and producing oil and gas from the North Sea.

Society is angry when the companies 'have to let go' thousands of workers because their jobs no longer exist. Environmentalists and international bodies demand the most stringent regulations governing the manufacture and marketing of oil products. It is fashionable to maintain that the oil companies have sufficient cash to sustain jobs as well as providing the safest possible environment for the workers and the community in which these operations are carried out. Yet the return on capital of these so-called giants until recently has often been so derisory that if applied to a building society, there would be no savers and thus no mortgages. The big companies may make impressive-sounding profits but the per unit margin is slender.

Henry Perkins, whilst admitting that his company must accept ultimate responsibility for the accident, nevertheless drew overdue attention to the hypocrisy that permeates society and government.

The problem is, as the brave Perkins noted, that society wants too much for too little. It is encouraged in this by a government composed of individuals very few of whom have ever worked in industry. This is apparent by their incessant and unnecessary demands on the oil industry, in particular, wrongly perceived as the golden goose with a permanent and unceasing ability to lay golden eggs.

The causes of yesterday's accident will be determined by the official enquiry but we must hope that those charged with this responsibility will think hard about the various demands put on the industry. We have no right to expect companies to be able to produce economic miracles. Society, backed by a properly informed government, must make choices. It cannot continue to have everything and Broadoak Oil has performed a valuable service by pointing this out.

We must also hope that the conservative management of a company seldom identified with major initiatives, in an industry not known for open comment, will not tell Perkins that they have to let him go. Instead, they should realise *that they have one of the most honest industrialists we have encountered for years.*

Henry was stunned as surely as if someone had hit him on the head with an oil drum. Nervously, he opened other papers. Although the language differed, and some were markedly less fulsome, most praised Perkins.

Henry's phone jangled all the morning. Opposition politicians, oil industry lobbying groups, senior executives from other companies, including chairmen, all called to congratulate him. The general theme was that Henry had said something that should have been said out loud many times in the past. Invitations to lunches flooded in and HB, initially determined to fire Perkins, ended up by congratulating him, saying how pleased he was at the interview and the outcome, even if the words could have been chosen more carefully. Indeed, the chief executive received many calls from his colleagues in other companies and Hubert soon told them that he himself was delighted because he had always encouraged free thinking and speech in his company and had personally selected Perkins for the role.

Broadoak Oil had not received such publicity since a recent local hospital rag week when some nurses posed, fully naked, in front of the company logo before being arrested.

Jill was delighted for her husband, but, over the next few weeks, saw much less of him because he was always addressing industry groups and conferences. Perkins himself remained surprised at the fuss. All that he had said had been said before, in the company corridors and at meetings with other companies. It was true, of course, so why not say so? His mother, as well as Hubert, had always encouraged him to tell the truth. What a pity she was not around to see and hear the consequences of her early teaching.

Chapter 13

Henry was anxious to tell Jill his news. "I'm going to an important conference in New York for a couple of days."

"You're not speaking are you?"

"Yes, it is I, your husband, who is currently addressing you." "Don't be silly. I meant are you speaking at the conference?"

"No, I'm just going to listen. I'm going with Nigel Read, head of investor relations, because I've ultimate responsibility for IR."

"Judging by the time that you spend working, you seem to be responsible for everything. Does this mean that your later trip to Houston is cancelled?"

Henry said that it didn't and Jill reminded him that she was going to the conference that weekend, with Denis. She was pleased that Henry would not be speaking. His last presentation, fortunately given at a badly-attended conference, was not successful. At HB's behest, he had avoided controversy and had spoken about the industry in the seventies. One trade journal described his presentation "a depressingly outdated speech from an old-fashioned company". The critic argued that oil companies must look to the future and acknowledge that people now demanded more from oil groups than "just providing the market with refined products at a reasonable price". The power of the international groups had to be deployed to the benefit of the people in the developing countries more effectively. It was "an act of huge self-delusion" for the companies to pretend that this was not their concern. Increasingly, they must use their influence to improve the lot of mankind, particularly where human rights were brutally suppressed by arms bought by governments from their oil revenue. Henry read the article three times and was impressed by the thoughts that mirrored his own.

On Monday, an excited Henry was sitting in his office with Nigel, awaiting a car provided by the airline to take them to Heathwick. Nigel, for whom travelling was routine, was already fretting about the likely workload on his return. "You know, travelling on work, even to the States, is over-rated. I don't want to spoil it for you Henry, but it's not fun. You see airports, hotels, offices and restaurants but that's all and even then you're talking shop for most of the time, so you can't really even enjoy a good meal." That sounded plausible to Henry but he was still excited.

The flight was due to take off at 18.00 and the limousine called at Broadoak House at 15.15. As the car purred to the airport, Henry savoured the journey to the full. He had never expected to travel in a big black limo, or, indeed one of any colour, let alone fly to the US on business. At the airport, matters began to deteriorate. A member of the airline, taking their luggage to check-in, apologised "again" for the expected delay of three hours in their flight. Nigel asked "what do you mean, apologise again? Nobody has told us anything."

The embarrassed girl apologised for the lack of an earlier apology and said that efforts had been made to advise them but they could not make contact, prompting Nigel to explain "we are a large company which uses a modern telephone system, the success and efficiency of which may be judged by the fact that we receive many hundreds of calls daily. Indeed, such is our grasp of modern technology that we can even make calls out. Our people, all of whom know how phones work, can and do pass on messages and some of us even have mobile phones with fully-charged batteries". Here he brandished his, as if suggesting that this be entered as exhibit A. "Furthermore, I know that our limousine driver had a phone because he used it repeatedly during the journey and his addiction to the instrument occasionally threatened our safety. I've piles of important work that I could have done in the office, but instead of that, because of your company's incompetence, I've got to sit here waiting for the flight, without even knowing when the plane will take off. Anyway, what's the reason for the delay?"

"I can only apologise again for what's happened. I'm sorry but I don't know the reason. Please complete the check-in and then ask my colleagues in the executive departure lounge for more details. I'm sure they'll be able to help you."

Comfortable-looking brown leather furniture was scattered around the large executive lounge. Paintings of aircraft, that had managed to take off, although how late was not revealed, adorned the dark brown wood-panelled walls and a discreet bar was hidden at the back of the room behind some expensive palm trees in expensive containers. Glass-topped tables covered by up-market business magazines and airline publications were placed close to the main chairs. The large room was like an old London club. Was talking allowed?

As the evening unfolded, the problems increased. Frequent exhortations to take full advantage of the free nuts and drinks were interspersed with further pessimistic warnings about when the plane might take to the skies. Henry and Nigel agreed that re-booking with an alternative airline was one possibility but this could be a gamble as the next relevant flight was scheduled to leave at about the same time as their delayed flight. It was decided to do nothing, at least for the time being.

Henry idly picked up a newspaper and glanced at some silly season stories. The BBC had appointed an atheist to head religious affairs and the authorities were debating plans to make pedestrians on Oxford Street walk in lanes. A minimum of three miles per hour would be enforced for the fast lane. Picking up one of the magazines, Henry glanced at a business quiz.

Compare and contrast NVQ, IT, ISO, CPD, BSI and BSE. Illustrate your answer with examples from Prussia in the period 1401-1413.

Is it now square to be involved in quality circles and should they be ring-fenced?

Discretely envisage the kind of house that has Chinese walls, a glass ceiling, windows of opportunity and, outside, critical paths.

Write sentences to show that you understand the differences between EMU, ERM, EPU and EFTPOS.

Explain FIFO, ESOP and EFTA, as if to a child.

Offer as many euphemisms as you can, in just 30 seconds, for losing your job, being fired or dismissed, made redundant, let go, displaced, outplaced, downsized, given a P45, re-organised out of a job, being surplus to requirements, prematurely retired, given the push, allowed to seek out and pursue other interests, pensioned off, given the boot, asked to clear your desk, shown the door, allowed to spend more time with your family, de-hired etc. etc.

Suggest cures for fiscal drag.

Newly-arriving passengers were now complaining to the increasingly flustered receptionist who summoned reinforcements. A fat balding man, about 45, shuffled in. His ill-fitting jacket perched precariously on his shoulders and his face resembled corrugated cardboard that had been left out in the rain. He did not inspire confidence as he eased himself behind the desk.

Henry phoned Jill who expressed surprise at the clarity of the line from the plane but warned him about the costs. Gradually, the announcements became more optimistic and confirmed the duo's decision not to seek real food for fear of missing the flight but then the euphoria was punctured by confirmation that the flight would take off at 22.00.

An angry Henry asked for some proper food to be brought in. "We're effectively prisoners here, discouraged from seeking a seat on another airline and denied real food. This is totally unacceptable and I shall be complaining to the head of the airline at the appalling way that this incident has been handled." Mr Perkins was beginning to enjoy being more assertive but learned that more food could not be provided because the catering staff had gone home.

Nigel's reaction was drowned by yet another announcement. Silence descended.

"Our engineering staff have completed their work on the plane but the pilot has refused to fly it across the Atlantic. Consequently, this flight is cancelled and is re-scheduled for 15.30 hours tomorrow. We deeply regret this. We are making arrangements for an overnight stay in local hotels and are organising limousine transport for you. It will be necessary for you to collect your luggage but meanwhile please stay in this lounge so that we can give you more information. We apologise most sincerely for any inconvenience that this may have caused you."

Nigel's face assumed the same hue as HB's. It was not clear which of so many major mistakes had riled him the most but he spluttered several times, "any inconvenience, any? Do they think that I can sit for hours, without food except that favoured by monkeys, being denied accurate information, being effectively prevented from re-booking, with a real airline, being punished by their sustained incompetence and that despite all that, I may, 'may', mark you, have been inconvenienced? Bloody hell". It was the first time that he had sworn since Norman Lamont was chancellor.

He stormed up to the desk and after some strong words with the presiding official, persuaded him to book the Broadoak pair on Concorde with the tickets paid for by the airline. That success was to be followed by further setbacks. The only available accommodation was at Gatrow airport, some 30 miles away, the promised limousines were not available so the journey had to be made in conventional London taxi cabs and the hotel could not supply them with any food until the morning. Any hopes that Henry had for some rest, before their car took them back to Heathwick, were undermined when a note was pushed under his door telling him that his "breakfast" was outside. It consisted of "plastic" food in a plastic box, similar to that provided by severely financially-pressed airlines. The meal was free but coffee, not included, could be bought at the breakfast area on the ground floor. Unfortunately, the beverage would only be available some two hours after Henry and Nigel had left for the return ride to Heathwick.

The car arrived on time and the two executives were eventually whisked to New York, although Henry fell asleep on the plane, thus missing the trip of a lifetime. Within what seemed like minutes, he was back in the UK, having seen a US airport, hotel, office and conference centre. It was even difficult to make out buildings on the way to and from the airport because of heavy rain. The conference and the meeting with his colleagues were boring. Just briefly, a weary Henry thought that his old job was not so bad after all. He had not enjoyed his first trip to the New World.

Chapter 14

Henry's local newspaper relied on stories about puma-like animals stalking the countryside, oddly never photographed, the dangers posed by youths riding cycles on the few pavements in the village and, of course, the problems of inter-planetary travel. One article told of a local company which claimed that two thirds of dog owners took their animals to work to reduce stress. Henry wondered about those employees who disliked dogs. After his television interview, the paper had included a profile of Henry in the first of a new series on local celebrities. However, the village lacked well-known inhabitants so the series began and ended with Henry.

Mr Perkins, as the only celebrity, was asked to open the annual fete and there was a hint that the famous oil executive would be invited to say a few words at the opening of the local art exhibition. However, Colonel Fotheringham Smith-Jones, (retd.), the embodiment of the establishment figure, was unsure if the renegade businessman could be trusted to open his month without inserting his foot in it. As he told the organising committee, "the man's a loose cannon..." He was interrupted at this stage by the snoozing vicar whose reverie had been interrupted by an allegation that someone in the church, apparently a cannon, had been behaving in an immoral way. The misunderstanding resolved, the colonel resumed. "The blighter attacked our party and I for one, think that his onslaught was unforgivable. In my day, these things were resolved quietly and privately, not in front of the television cameras."

Despite the colonel (retd.), Henry did open the art exhibition and, under Jill's steadfast gaze, managed to avoid criticism of the rubbish on display, saying, truthfully, that he would long recall the standard of the works that he had seen. He also offered the thought that the village might one day produce a Thomas Kinkade. The locals, who had never heard of the American artist, were appropriately impressed.

The Perkins were visiting neighbours Ian and Shirley one mid-week evening, for "a drink and nibbles". "Now, you will behave, won't you, because I think that, one day, your odd sense of humour will get you into trouble." Jill secured Henry's assurance as she pushed open her neighbours' gate. The house was much older than Chez-Perkins. It had started life in the twenties as a small home with a very large garden but had become a very large house with a small garden.

"Hello, dear, how good to see you." Shirley, just 70 but still spry physically and mentally, leaned forward, kissed the air, muttered mmm, wafted a knarled hand in the direction of the lounge and invited Jill to sit. "And it's very good to see you, too, Henry, we're looking forward to hearing about your new life now you're so famous."

Ian said "don't worry, old man, we won't talk shop all the evening, will we"? He had been a bank manager but promotion had come late in his career. Ian was a contented man and probably would not have minded if he had finished almost where he started provided that the adjective "senior" had prefaced the title "clerk". Henry identified with Ian in that he could understand how the vast bureaucracies that propped up banks and big business could become the most dispiriting of organisations for any employee with the merest hint of enterprise. So often, the spirit of "get up and go" was only satisfied by doing just that. Promotion was restricted to those of a certain age, who, irrespective of merit, were favoured by those in power who unerringly chose vacuous people, like themselves, to run the business.

Shirley, like her husband, had worn well. Her neat, dyed hair was brown but she had almost retained her figure. Before bringing up a family, she had been on the stage and had appeared in several popular post-war American musicals in the West End of London. Photographs of her with well-known stars of the period adorned the study but were modestly excluded from the lounge, where guests were entertained.

Drinks and some snacks appeared. "Please help yourselves."

Ian opened the conversation. "Well, Henry, I know that you won't want to talk about work on a pleasant evening, but how are things after that interview?"

"Really, Ian, as you say, Henry shouldn't have to talk about work now, especially as Jill tells me that he doesn't have much time off." Shirley felt that she had said the right thing but she was as keen as Ian to hear more. Instead, she turned to Jill. "We never hear much about your work. How are you getting on, dear?" Jill smiled and repeated the comments she had made recently to Henry.

"The conference business isn't so good. You know, I really think that the days when you could persuade hundreds of people to pay good money to sit in near darkness, all day, with boring colleagues, to listen to mediocre speakers, telling them what they already know, may be over. People can't spare the time to be out of the office."

"I hope that your job's secure, dear?"

"As far as I can tell and I certainly get on well with those running the group, if that counts for anything. I've been in my present job for some years now and I would like promotion, but, knowing my luck, the company will probably fold immediately if I'm given a leg up. Anyway, I'm booked in for a week-end conference in the country soon."

"Will Henry be going with you?"

"No, since his elevation, he's always told me that it's difficult to combine business with pleasure, and he hasn't let me go anywhere with him so I shan't be asking him! Anyway, he'll be in Houston for a conference."

Ian smiled. "So you'll be paying a lot of money to sit in the dark all day, with hundreds of boring people to listen to mediocre speakers, telling you things that you already knew or will you be one of the speakers that hundreds of people will pay good money to listen to? That was about it, wasn't it?"

"That's about it." "Anyway, how are you both?"

Ian admitted to having occasional back problems which severely restricted him. "It's odd. If you tell people, for example, that you've a bad leg, they'll ask lots of questions and hope that you're better soon. It's different for backs. There's no sympathy and all you get is a deep wistful sigh and a long monologue on how they, too, have had back troubles. They always end with the comment that backs are funny things." Shirley said that she had nothing to grumble about although looking after the house was becoming something of a chore and "even doing the garden tires us now, doesn't it dear? But that reminds me why we were particularly anxious to see you.

"Ian wants to tell you about the visit from a local builder who may want to develop this area." The Perkins had a long garden and a part of that and, say, half their neighbour's, would have made a decent building plot. There was already adequate access to a lane at the end of Ian's garden and it would have been easy to widen it to accommodate a new house. "I don't suppose anything will come of it, but they wanted to know if we might be willing to sell."

"How much of the garden did they want?"

"It wasn't just the garden that they were interested in. It was the house. They would knock it down, add our garden and, ideally, some land from our neighbours on the other side for three new so-called executive houses. I don't think that they wanted any of your garden."

"Good grief." Henry didn't want any more houses in the area, especially next to their own peaceful garden. He and Jill liked things as they were.

"What did you say?"

"Being a banker, I told them that unless I had an idea of how much they would offer and the terms of any deal, there was nothing I could say. But then they said that they would pay a premium of 60 per cent on the average valuation offered by three independent estate agents and that they would meet all our expenses involved in moving, contingent on their deciding to proceed."

"How long ago was all this?"

"Only a few days ago." Jill and Henry asked the obvious question. "How do you feel about it now?"

"Frankly, at our age, we'd have to consider it but we're inclined to say no. We both enjoy living here and I don't suppose that we'll hear any more about it but, having said that, the money would allow us to buy a small modern bungalow with a sensible garden and have some money left over to enjoy. We'll keep you posted."

The Perkins, concerned at what they had heard but realising that there was nothing more to say on the subject, then asked about their neighbour's adult children.

Eventually, Ian could desist from asking Henry about his job no longer. Perkins obliged with a quick overall summary, illustrated by acidic and mordant comments on the quality of management in some companies and punctuated by sporadic efforts to avoid having his apparently desirable ankle being chewed by his neighbour's small and aggressive dog of unknown manufacture. The dog's attentions reminded him of a recent radio telephone phone-in that he had done for a London station and he summarised what he described as an odd experience. "The programme started in time-honoured tradition. The first caller said that he was Clarence of Kingbury Eastgate. He said 'good evening' to the presenter and me and we duly returned the courtesy. "Yes Clarence, what is your question for Mr Perkins?"

"To my astonishment, Clarence told the world, or at least those people listening to this programme, which may not be quite the same, that, before posing a question, he wanted to tell the listeners that his neighbour had a dog with three legs. Perhaps anticipating an incisive challenge from the presenter, but guessing wrongly on the nature of the interruption, he assured listeners that his neighbour had authorised him to reveal the dog's loss of a quarter of its legs. The presenter tried to hasten his question but, clearly, additional details of the hapless canine quadruped had to be revealed. Having only 75 percent of your leg allocation was bad enough but having this man for a neighbour was downright cruel. Having a dog's life took on a new meaning. Suddenly realising that he was to be cut off if he didn't pose a question, he asked me to summarise my views on the changing relationship between the US and Saudi Arabia. I'm sure that Clarence was a malevolent friend, but I still don't know who he was."

After some more agreeable but inconsequential chat, Jill said that they really ought to be going. "Thank you for a really enjoyable evening." Back in their own home, the Perkins speculated on what it might be like if the house next door was pulled down and became a building site. They were not in favour.

Chapter 15

"You remember that you're going to tell everyone about the new organisation today?" "Yes, thanks, Rose."

Henry and Hubert had spent many hours on this project which HB said was central to the company's future. This worried Perkins. Wally Dickenson, an outsider with considerable experience of human resources, would lead the new Personnel and Training (PAT), division. His arrival meant that Henry, freed from direct responsibility for staff matters, could spend more time worrying about his other responsibilities.

Henry's old division, MAD, was eliminated and absorbed into a new Planning and Economics (PE) division, which would be headed by the reliable Stan Gray. John Scanlon remained as did Mike Horton, the creep. Henry had warned him about being sycophantic. "I don't want yes men. Is that clear?" Mike, confused, said "yes, or should I say no?" Eventually, they would be joined by new young graduates. Jim Holmes had retired and Simon Plummer and Frank Williams would be leaving soon. When the company could afford a replacement, Jane Lewis was to be promoted and would assist Rose.

The third division would be External Relations, (ER). Nigel Read would remain as head of Investor Relations, (IR), within ER but a new PR person, like new PAT and PE people, could not yet be recruited because of budget restraints. Broadoak would be losing three people so, like all big company re-organisations, fewer people had have to do more work. All that had happened was that some existing members of staff had been grouped together under a new name and given more work.

A hectic Henry had to prepare for the annual general meeting. He was also concerned with revamping the company magazine, organising an employee opinion survey, over-seeing the initial introduction of internal electronic communication and ensuring that employees could not look at pornographic material on the internet and considering whether to institute a dress-down day, which some seemed to have embraced already. Meanwhile, "the dinner" loomed ominously. Henry was to speak at the annual dinner of a leading trade association.

Jill reminded him, almost daily, that he must be much more restrained than he was on television. "You were lucky then. You spoke the truth as you saw it, in a very difficult situation and many people respected you for that. Others tolerated what you said just because you were very emotional, as they would have been if they had lost friends and then had to discuss it on the box. But, and please listen to me, Henry, there will be many industry people only too pleased to see you make one attack too many. Looking at it from our own selfish point of view, my job isn't all that secure and it's really important that you keep yours. Please promise me, you will be discreet, won't you?"

Her husband nodded. He didn't want to lose his job and he knew he couldn't afford to make a mistake. He would be on his best behaviour and would use the very anodyne speech that he had written and which HB and Jill had approved. Her final words to him, as he left for the event and as she prepared to visit some friends were, "remember, stick to what we've agreed, whatever happens. Promise!"

General manager Henry Perkins was standing in the foyer of one of London's biggest hotels, like a self-conscious penguin, in hired plumage, destined to address the allegedly good and the great of the industry at the year's premier function. Broadoak held a cocktail party before the dinner began, but HB said that Perkins should visit some of the other parties, as that would be good PR. Henry sallied forth obediently. Jill had instructed Henry not to drink alcohol, so, as he went from party to party, he only consumed orange juice, although at his final port of call, he had been persuaded to have a very small sherry, or was it three?

His senior industry colleagues, lacking the wise advice of Perkins J, were very merry indeed, even although margins had fallen by two cents a barrel in the last week, thus forcing them to decide how many thousands of staff had to face redundancy. Indeed, one jolly executive, whilst simultaneously plying friend and foe alike with expensive champagne, confided in Henry. "Old chap, don't tell anyone that I told you, but we're going to let about half of our Head Office staff go." Henry replied that was "tragic because your chairman said recently that people were your biggest asset. Things must be serious for you to get rid of so many assets".

Everyone was so light-hearted that Henry was concerned. The organisation's president had asked him to make a serious speech and, in the interests of self-preservation, he had prepared one, on the current state of the industry, that was undeniably soporific. Jill had agreed that it was boring but that was precisely what was necessary. Henry knew that he had to be bland but he did want to indicate that some of the thoughts that he had expressed on television were worth pursuing and were not the product of emotion. He genuinely felt that the industry should be more open and honest with society. This would be an excellent event at which to advance those views. Indeed, he might never have such an opportunity again. It was tempting, but no, he must obey Jill. Too much was at stake. He would be boring but perhaps…?

It was curious how his acquiescence had become ambition. After years of silent toil, characterised by his knowing, to a day, how long he had to wait before drawing a full company pension, he wanted to influence people. It was as if all the frustrated ambitions, hopes, desires and much else had been corked up in a secure bottle for years. The full extent of his frustration had not yet escaped but the cork was under increased pressure.

Judging by the comments and handshakes, even before he had surrendered his coat to the obsequious flunkey, it seemed that everyone knew him. As one of the guest speakers, he was on, or, more accurately, at the top table at the industry's annual dinner. The personnel nominated for this honour had congregated in the "blue" room, for a final drink and Henry, listening to the conversations, thought that the room's name reflected not the colour of the décor but the nature of the jokes.

Whilst he sipped a final orange juice and convinced himself that he was sober, the diners were making their way into the main ballroom which held 1,500 people. Tonight it would be full and more people were located further away, on balconies, which were served by an army of non-English speaking waiters and close-circuit television. Finally, some 25 minutes after dinner had been announced, the top table contingent emerged, to be led into the crowded main ballroom. As Henry and the entourage swept down the grand stairs and as rhythmic and embarrassing clapping accompanied their progress, he suddenly felt sick with fear. Nothing had prepared him for this. Then, as quickly as it had come, the worry vanished, banished by a sudden rush of adrenalin, excitement and some sherries. Henry knew that he was on the brink of a key moment in his career.

He was the penultimate of four speakers so he had partaken, modestly, of course, of some wine to accompany the kind of tucker that was not served nightly, or even monthly, at Perkins Palace. This was the first time Henry had attended such a glittering event, and, as he remarked later to Jill, he was one of the few people whom he didn't recognise.

Henry had accepted the invitation to speak without any of the heart-searching that characterises the reaction of the experienced. He saw it as belated confirmation, that, towards the end of a very ordinary career, his virtues had been recognised. However, sitting next to a famous executive, Henry realised afresh that he had nothing in common with these people and his confidence again drained away as swiftly as the alcohol at the tables in front of him. Desperately trying to sustain the conversation, the FE had tried a number of topics, all of which failed to ignite any prolonged conversation. Consequently, the meal was punctuated by long monologues from the famous executive after which he devoured his lukewarm food. During these quiet periods, Henry had turned to the very attractive red-headed lady on his right, who was nearly wearing a shimmering black dress and who was the guest of a managing director, sitting on her right. Georgina soon told Henry that she had seen him on television and, in her (penetrating and green) eyes, he was famous. She proved quite capable of sustaining a monologue. Henry was happy to bask in her blandishments but she, too, had to eat and to talk to her friend occasionally so Henry was forced to look to the FE again.

Patently out of his depth, Henry justly feared the worst, when the executive asked "ever seen a camel race?" Without waiting for a reply, he claimed that it was a most exhilarating experience. In short, it came fully recommended by the FE. As conversational gambits go, this one

176

went, speedily, probably as quickly as an enthusiastic camel. Perkins dolefully conceded the truth and, keeping a very straight face and tone, said that until recently he had not been abroad on business so the only time that he had been able to go abroad had been on holiday abroad. He sensed that this sentence might have been less than perfectly constructed which boded ill for his speech. He and his lady wife usually spent their holidays at Westhaven, and, notwithstanding its numerous attractions, which Henry enumerated slowly and with some animation, to create the illusion that he was fully engaged in a conversation, "there is a very noticeable absence of camels. Indeed, in my 15 annual visits there, I've not seen a single one, or indeed a married one, so racing was not a realistic possibility." The humourless FE peered at Perkins as if he were a grub that had just emerged from the executive grub and turned elsewhere.

The speeches were about to begin. Henry checked his notes and was satisfied that he had prepared precisely the presentation that he had been asked to deliver. He had included just a few jokes, sanctioned by Jill, but the balance was overwhelmingly serious. Secretly, Henry fancied his ability to deliver a few, carefully crafted lines. At last, he had a large audience. He would not let them down. The redhead, trying to give him confidence, gave him a long, lingering articulate look which comprehensively undermined him. She implied that he was the only man worth bothering with in the entire world and possibly beyond. Even Jill, pre-nuptials, had never looked like that. Simultaneously, she leaned across and, staring into the Perkins eyes, stretched out an immaculate hand which squeezed one of his which was conveniently but accidentally placed for such a gesture. Coincidentally, this was just the moment that some trade magazine photographers chose to capture the scene.

"Good luck" she intoned seductively, "I'm with you all the way." The modest Henry had no idea what, if anything, she meant so contrived to look both bemused and grateful. If the Perkins vocabulary had included the word "gobsmacked", he would have agreed that neatly summarised his reaction. His experience, or rather the lack of it, apart from that rather unfortunate event in a garden shed when he was 12 and the more recent incident during the Glasgow hotel fire, had not prepared him for any such behaviour. Struggling to regain his composure, and having just finished the main course, he settled back to listen to the toastmaster introduce the first speaker. The professionally sanctimonious red-coated toad told the audience that the president of the industry association was so well known that no introduction was necessary. He then proceeded to spend some time introducing him.

As toad had predicted, the first speaker was, indeed, the president who, just by standing up, excited the audience. He was a very popular man who was to political correctness what dry weather was to umbrella manufacturers. This was to be his last public performance, as the toad had indicated when inviting the audience to show their appreciation of his services, and expectations were high. Indeed, the approbation, signalled by fists banging on tables, caused gravy on an uncollected plate to bounce neatly on to Perkins' shirt, creating a very obvious brown stripe. Henry attacked it with water, a napkin and vigour whilst the president began reminiscing.

"Do you remember, how, in 1969, no, hold on, it was 1959, memory plays tricks when you reach my age, we hired a boat when we had our jamboree in the south of France and Puffingham-Buller, or was it poor old Porky Smythe, acquired that crate of sherry which was washed overboard and when that girl lost...".

The stories drifted on, becoming increasingly blue. Perkins felt even more of a trespasser. He didn't belong to this world and he was becoming worried about his serious speech. He neither could nor wished to match this style of humour. If this was adult humour, his was puerile and he was proud of it. Suddenly, the president resumed his seat to enormous applause and the up-market redcoat was introducing the next speaker. Surely, the energy minister would raise the tone?

Henry, alternately rubbing his shirt, which was now predominantly brown, the gravy having been distributed over a wider area, and listening to the president's speech, which was predominantly blue, had been re-writing his notes, to include more jokes. He surmised that the politician's speech would be both lengthy and clean. It was neither. The serious part called for greater co-operation between industry and government and exhorted companies to seek work in parts of the world which, as far as Perkins knew, were areas where UK foreign policy meant that the prospect of securing export orders was virtually nil.

Within minutes, after hearing more blue and very well-received jokes, it was Henry's turn. He glanced at his now confused notes and jokes, which, unlike his shirt, were clean.

Henry's confidence was further undermined by the introduction. Toady, having told the gathering that the next speaker, almost overnight, had become a household name, then forgot it. A hurt and annoyed Henry rose reluctantly to his feet. His morale had been further dented by what he thought was an unfortunate link of the word "more", with "interesting" when the president interrupted to say that Perkins would be followed by one more-interesting speaker.

Henry started in traditional fashion. "My lords, ".. Here he paused, looking around to see if he were justified in using the plural for the female of the species, for he certainly knew that one was there. Yes, there was another so he swiftly added "ladies" before finally adding, after a similar pause for the sake of consistency, "and gentlemen". The predominantly male audience, from an industry which endorsed the principle of equal opportunities but did little about it, deduced erroneously that Perkins was implying that they were not gentlemen. His completion of the phrase induced massive laughter and sustained applause from the well-oiled audience. Henry beamed, as much with surprise as with gratification. He was still smarting from the introduction and having been so misled by the president when discussing the type of speech that he was supposed to deliver.

Intoxicated with the unexpectedly favourable reaction from merely saying what everybody says, he then thanked Mr "whoever you are" for the introduction. This induced much table thumping and the new general manager, reacting to the heady combination of sherry, wine and applause, noted that the president had a joke for every occasion and "we enjoyed hearing it again tonight". The applause was deafening and the redhead looked at him adoringly.

Henry, by now really high on adrenalin, even offered a joke that he was unaware that he knew. The president was a man of rare gifts. "I know that I've never received one." He continued in the same vein. "He is usually well received but the last time that he appeared, he told me afterwards that the previous speaker was so unpopular that they were still booing him when he, our president, was on his feet. He's a good friend, but, fortunately, not one of mine". After a few seconds, necessary to allow the thrust of this sally to reach home, the laughter and table banging resumed.

Then, becoming serious, he said slowly. "You know, I'm very fortunate these days. I'm invited to many dinners and I can reasonably and totally truthfully say that tonight" and here he paused for a few seconds, "is by far... the most recent." This, too, was well received. Henry was enjoying this. He then observed that he was very grateful for such a short introduction because he recalled the famous statesman who, having to wait for the completion of a particularly long introduction was finally asked to give his address. He replied that it was "care of the Carlton Club, and that's where I'm going now". This, too, went down well. This could be easy, even if he had no dirty jokes. Then he recalled his first day at work. "I arrived at the office at 10.00, to be met by a stern departmental manager, who told me that I should have been there at 9.00. Why, I replied, what happened?"

Scarcely pausing for the laughter from the merry audience to subside, he immediately launched into one of his favourite questions. "How is a supermarket trolley different from a non-executive oil company director?" "The trolley has a mind of its own but the non exec. holds more food and drink." This went down rather less well, especially on the top table, prompting Henry to wonder why some people did not understand such a simple joke.

Perkins recalled that one of the secrets of a successful after-dinner speech was to make a self-deprecating joke. Pointing to his shirt, he said that what had happened to him tonight had demonstrated that, having sampled both, he preferred the gravy train to the gravy boat. The representatives of the European Union showed how humourless they were by not even smiling but the majority of the audience roared appreciatively.

Henry sensed that this speech would be rather different to the one that he had rehearsed. The well-lubricated audience seemed to be prepared to laugh at anything. Then, thinking about top executives, immediately recalled the unlamented BF. What would he have said at this point, as it was now, clearly, time to be serious? Perkins knew. "I am glad to interface with you, not just on a networking basis, but on a level playing field, before further downsizing means that our core message and mission will have to be unbundled to release a synergy which can only work if we analyse the feedback from our stakeholders."

The audience, understandably failing to comprehend a single word, received this nonsense as a brilliant parody. They actually cheered and Henry, pleased at the reception, nevertheless did not understand why they were laughing when he was being serious. He moved to safer ground, daringly using up his remaining jokes.

"An explorer, unusually for a major oil company man, went to Heaven, but, on being accepted there, complained of over-crowding. The authorities said that they could do nothing to alleviate the problem, so, to create more space, he circulated a rumour that oil had been found in hell, prompting many colleagues to leave the check the story. Our friend left too, and, on being asked why he was joining the exodus, said that the rumour might just be true."

That went down well but Henry wondered why some people, sitting at tables reserved by the larger companies, did not understand such a simple joke.

He then reminded the audience about the management consultant, who had died in his thirties. Complaining about his premature death, he was told that the authorities, on checking his invoice file, thought that he was in his eighties. The laughter was prolonged, although some people did not understand such a simple joke.

A man wanted a new, good quality brain, weighing four pounds. If they came from oilmen, the price would be £500 but scientists' brains cost £200. Was this because the oilmen had superior brains? No, more oilmen are needed to make up the weight."

Intoxicated by the applause, Perkins moved on. Now it was the turn of the public relations people, whom Perkins, frankly, loathed, little realising that he was, effectively, in charge of Broadoak PR. He asked why public relations people, instead of rats, were being used for live medical experiments. There were three reasons. "There are more PR people than rats. There are some things that rats won't do and finally, you don't become emotionally involved with PR people." This, too, was well received, although Perkins did notice that some rather severe looking people around the room were not laughing. Why was not such a simple joke understood?

Then, having wracked his brains for some other jokes, he recalled one that he had heard in the office. "Do you realise that half the population has sex twice a week, so they're having a better time than you?" Then he wondered why there was only one monopolies and mergers commission and why kamikaze pilots wore protective helmets and how you could see an invisible repair to a jacket. Then he suggested that people played golf only because they could wear clothes that otherwise they would not have been seen dead in. This last jibe did not receive the warm response that Henry had anticipated.

The audience was eagerly awaiting some more-adult humour. Henry had none and knew that the best had gone and that he now had to concentrate on the serious part of his presentation.

"I must now be serious and say a few words about the changing structure of our industry." The audience switched off instantly. They were not interested in such a topic now. Henry knew this and struggled to make himself heard over the increasing hubub which toad could not quell.

At least one colleague, at the Broadoak table, was listening: as Henry glanced in his direction, he was greeted with a cheerful smile and a thumbs up sign which Henry took as encouragement. What he did not know was that his young friend was still in the running to claim the sweepstake on how long his leader would speak. Perkins continued without really knowing what to say next. So he muttered "before I end" and his young colleague suddenly looked downcast.

Looking around the room, Perkins was angered by the fact that the minister was dormant. Earlier, Henry had heard him say, "oh god, it's that ignorant twerp, Perkins. Damned silly so and so. Out of his class and depth. Should have stayed at home". Whether he had dropped off because of the amount of alcohol that he had consumed or whether it was because of his unremitting toil on behalf of the people, Henry neither knew nor cared. It was rude and his mother, apart from drumming into the little Henry the importance of telling the truth, had taught him to condemn rudeness.

The audience was ignoring the very subject on which he had been asked to speak. However, he remembered Jill's words as he wondered what to say. He would never know what the decision would have been because, as the programme had been running late, the cabaret, consisting of some particularly odious morris dancers pranced prissily into the ballroom. The last speech was cancelled. Perkins gazed at the dancers, tore up his notes, scattering them over the top table, collected his coat and left, just in time to miss his last train home. Later, he told Jill that all had gone well in the first part of his presentation, despite having to improvise, but lack of time had effectively precluded the chance of speaking about more serious matters. He did not mention the comment from the politician but he would not forget it.

Chapter 16

Henry Perkins' taxi was stuttering expensively towards the Barbican, in the City of London, for his company's annual general meeting. He felt uncomfortable. This was not because he was to sit on the stage, or, to be more accurate, on a chair on the stage nor was it a reflection on the vehicle. It was a reflection on Perkins himself and it resembled the lack of confidence he experienced when visiting the bank, even although, thanks to ingrained prudence, or meanness, as Jill maintained, he owed the bank nothing. Oddly, Henry was always embarrassed when withdrawing money from the bank. He almost expected the clerks to condemn him for taking away cash that could be better utilised on, for example, alleviating the suffering of starving suburban bank employees or helping to keep the company yacht afloat. He would not have been surprised if the clerk said "going to spend some of our money, are we?" Perkins never used the hole in the wall as he feared that his card would be eaten and he didn't like holes.

He tried to relax as the cab threaded its way slowly through the busy traffic. The company, of course, would be paying what seemed a big price for a small journey and sitting at the traffic lights, in a queue of paralysed vehicles, had already cost £3. Henry should have accompanied his colleagues, who had crowded into several large company cars, but, delayed by a phone call, he had to use a taxi. Henry often felt uncomfortable with taxi drivers and tended to remain silent, which was construed as arrogant, or talked too much, inviting the charge of being patronising.

Usually, as soon as Henry was comfortably positioned, the driver would initiate a conversation. It was odd that they all spoke quietly or just when a large truck was wheezing past. This meant that Henry had to lean forward to participate in the chat and this, in turn, usually prompted the driver to advise him to sit back on the seat because "there're a lot of loonies around, mate".

Early in his new life, Henry had realised that it was prudent to respond positively to drivers' opinions. Silence or disagreement could prompt the driver to select a short cut, which "should save time, gov", although he and Perkins knew that this was precisely the opposite of the alleged intention. Consequently, a life-long liberal, he had vigorously endorsed dramatic plans to eject all those whose grandparents had not been born in this country and he supported automatic jail sentences for theft of goods worth more than £50. He was deeply committed to the restoration of both corporal and capital punishment, preferably imposed simultaneously. He also favoured severe reductions in government-provided assistance, especially for "those who've come to the UK just to scrounge off the welfare state" and readily accepted that most, if not all, of Britain's political and economic ills were caused by the totally uncontrolled influx of millions of foreigners.

Henry felt guilty in espousing this nonsense, but talking of spouses, he had learned that, in matters domestic, it was wise to agree with everything that was said at Perkins Villas and then to do nothing. It seemed logical to apply this to the outside world and taxis resembled home in that he lacked influence.

Why were so many London taxi drivers so right-wing? He'd discussed this with some of his colleagues, who, for many years, had spent the company's money travelling slowly around London. They were astonished at Henry's analysis and said that they'd never detected any such bias. Indeed, most thought that taxi drivers were versatile conversationalists with a sound view of life and politics.

Many drivers stressed that they had not always been drivers and that soon they would be gracing a new profession. Apparently, few of them had ever intended to drive a London taxi. They were surprised to learn that, after chugging around the capital for many months in all weathers on a moped, to learn the geography, they became taxi drivers! Such intensive preparation, surely, had implied that they could reasonably expect to become accountants or zookeepers? It just shows that none of us knows what lies round the corner, even if you have spent many hours sitting astride a two-stroke engine, trying to find out precisely what does lie around the corner. Most drivers were either resting from a more demanding occupation, such as nuclear physics or selling newspapers or were merely awaiting the call to greatness in a new and much-respected profession, such as televised weather forecasting. They were well qualified to undertake this for, as one confided, "we see it all, mate".

The taxi swerved violently. The driver, pre-occupied with his speech on the "the new diseases brought in by foreigners", nearly struck a motorcycle messenger. By now, H. Perkins knew what to say. His "damned lout" came out almost before the driver offered his own view of the innocent motorcyclist's behaviour. Henry did not know what epithet was employed because the comment coincided with the offended messenger kicking the taxi noisily.

Just as Henry had agreed that all MPs were corrupt and ought to do a proper job, so that they knew what real life was like, the taxi arrived at the Barbican Centre. The company annual general meeting would be starting soon and the sports jackets and twin sets and pearls were already queuing to enter the main auditorium. The next challenge was to find his way around a building that was obviously designed as a test for applicants wanting to join MENSA. It was for Henry "un moment historique", as Ted Heath, the former prime minister, not the band leader, once tried to say, although it's possible that the latter also made such a comment. It was just that it was never publicised. That's the price you pay for being a bandleader.

Henry had only been to the Barbican once. He had become lost and took 15 minutes to return from the gents to the floor where he had left Jill and some friends. Tactlessly, Mrs Perkins had demanded to know whether he was all right, although her enquiry was not so delicately worded. "The black banana that I ate yesterday, I can assure you, has not caused any ill-effects, despite your dire forecast. Quite simply, I got lost." "Yes dear", Jill said, disbelievingly. It always puzzled Henry that bananas, although bought fresh, were usually only eaten just before their fascist hue recommended imminent disposal. He blamed his being lost on the original architect and those who organised the signs but spoiled a reasonable case by hinting that there could be some people still trying to leave the building after lengthy involuntary incarceration. This fanciful imagination could doubtless be traced to Henry's youthful dedication to the splendid "Just William" books.

Perkins was a little nervous at the prospect of being on such a large stage but it was most unlikely that he would have to speak. His more senior colleagues would do all the talking. His main task was to stay awake and applaud at the right time. Above all, he must not yawn. He had dismissed the PR bow tie and the temporary external consultant had sought to anticipate shareholders' questions and to organise draft answers. They had spent no time with Henry, saying that the chief executive would field any questions relating to his responsibilities.

Trying hard not to be nervous, Henry moved briskly through the foyer, past the desk prominently labelled "Press". It was surrounded by journalists, keen to secure copies of the main presentation. Predictably, the desk was unmanned and there were no copies of any speeches, which had annoyed them. Why couldn't the scribes just listen and then write up the presentations? His musings on the laziness of the fourth estate were abruptly halted when he realised that he was ultimately responsible for his company's links with the media. Some of the waiting scribes recognised him and questioned him on the company's safety policy. They also wanted copies of the presentations and the chance to speak to some of Perkins's senior colleagues. He assured them that HB and others would be available for informal conversations after the meeting and that he would chase up his colleagues immediately for copies of the main speeches.

One journalist asked Perkins a more difficult question about the company. The inexperienced Henry foolishly joked, "don't ask me: I only work here". Sometimes, but not now, the media is condemned for misquoting.

Perkins joined the first queue leading to the main auditorium, but soon realised that he had joined the slowest-moving line, as he always did when there was a choice. Worried about being late on the stage, he tried to walk past the shareholders. This was unwise. Hearing the startled upper-class growls of "here, I say", from the sports jackets, a security guard, whose arms had been folded, in the tradition that dates back, well, for several years, sprung into action. Without apparent pain, he effortlessly disentangled his arms, grabbed Perkins, abused him verbally, saying that his father fought in the war "to stop people like you" and tried to march him to the back of the line, to the unambiguous approbation of the shareholders who accepted that one reason for the outbreak of global war had been to ensure that queue jumping was banned.

Then the security guard noticed Perkins' badge. His demeanour and facial colour changed immediately. Grovelling apologies and speeches of regret tumbled out. "This way, sir", he oozed unctuously, guiding Perkins past the startled shareholders, now perceived as the opposition by the security man, who commanded his erstwhile allies to stand back. Henry was propelled gently in the direction of the Green Room. Then, as if re-assuring a recalcitrant child, the security guard told the general manager that he would find his friends in there. As Perkins headed in the right direction, he noted that a company video was playing to the faithful in the main auditorium, but, because of a mistake in the overall programme, the band was still playing. Unfortunately, the musicians, charged to play something cheerful, were rendering "food, glorious food", from the musical "Oliver", just as the video was showing the impact of famine on rural communities in the developing world.

Henry's colleagues were re-rehearsing possible questions and answers. Alex Gardner, a professor of economics, appointed as a non-executive director to add gravitas to the board, was incapable of taking life seriously for more than a few minutes. As Perkins entered he was suggesting an "obvious" question that could arise. He was surprised that the PR people had not thought of it. "Could the chairman explain why the real dividend, in relation to cash flow, liquidity ratios and capitalised value, has fallen, especially as most sales are of Giffen goods? Is it not time that the company adopted a strategy of Ramsey pricing, which would enhance the input-output matrix whilst satisfying influential analysts who favour the Heckscher-Ohlin principle?"

HB appreciated neither the question nor the humour. The eccentric offered the correct response. "You should say I'll pass that one to my financial expert, but before I do, let me thank you for your very interesting question. I know that these are topics that have exercised my colleagues for some time."

Henry listened intently to the last-minute preparations. Earlier, Jill had tried to comfort Henry by pointing out that he was more knowledgeable than the audience, otherwise they would be on the platform and he would be in the audience. She had advanced the same line before Henry made his television appearance. This was not the best of omens. Henry took another sip of coffee but, seconds later, the backstage master of ceremonies announced that it was time to move to the platform, gentlemen, and, noting a single skirted person, a kilted Scot, erroneously added "lady". He did not notice Shirley Church, the company secretary, who was wearing a trouser suit.

As the contingent walked on to the stage, the band retreated and some sycophants applauded. Henry was positioned two rows behind the chief executive and the main board members. Behind them, in dark suits almost to a man, except the Scot, were other managers and some specialists, mainly hidden from view for the majority of the audience. The auditorium was full and the average age was probably well into the sixties. Even if all the males lived in the same small area, a barber with a monopoly would not have prospered.

The shareholders had been buried deep in the annual report, even although it had been sent out months ago. Henry, closely involved in its production, had insisted on reducing the number of photographs of the board and HB, respectively, to just two and one. Too many pics of HB would imply that it was a one-man company and, as the chief executive observed, "we don't want them to rumble us on that". Henry had also insisted that they all wore jackets and the clinching argument was that appearing shirt-sleeved made them look like security guards, or, worse still, the prime minister.

One problem was that most companies used the same jargon. Last year, so many spoke of twin-forked approaches that the cutlery business must have been most enthusiastic. Henry had also persuaded HB to drop the all-purpose tosh that had characterised the previous report. Last year, an annual report for the industry might have read as follows:

Most companies are taking steps, often one at a time, while passing milestones, although some directors are stepping down. Programmes are being refocused and the emphasis is increasingly on commitment and teamwork. Margins remain restrained and profitability has been hurt as the new era approaches but winning results are being achieved. Portfolio management is being intensified and some projects qualify for special stewardship. Goals will become more challenging and the future, which lies ahead, can be rewarding and exciting but much remains to be done. We can be confident as culture and values are adjusted to the new environment. Our roles as corporate citizens are being re-assessed in the appropriate time frame and many groups, with their steady vision, are acutely aware of the main drivers of change which will permit the enhancement of asset values. Above all, the future will be based on firm foundations and the commitment to sustainable growth will be similarly soundly based.

HB had agreed that it was unnecessary to review all the economic and political news, country by country, over the last year. Some companies believe that the annual report should resemble an encyclopaedia whilst others, including Perkins, responsible for Broadoak's report, regard it as a necessary evil that should be as slim as the law allows.

The buzz of conversation faded as HB stood up, cleared his throat, reshuffled his notes and prepared to address the strings of pearls and the sports jackets. Hubert looked particularly imposing today in a new and expensive double-breasted dark suit. Apart from his trademark knitted tie of a rather violent shade, he doubtless conformed to most people's views on how a senior executive should look. His piercingly blue eyes, surely close enough together to have alarmed Mrs Fricker's mother, shone out from under bushy eyebrows that had ignored the passing years and remained jet black. HB had used haircream regularly for decades. Consequently, his silver hair, like HB himself on most afternoons, was well plastered. His white shirt could have been used in an advertisement for a washing powder but his executive face was almost purple, which reflected not his tight collar but his efforts to ensure the survival of the local pub.

"First of all, I must pass on to you our chairman's apologies. He can't be with us today because he's unwell. I'm sure that we all wish him a speedy recovery and return to his rightful place at the head of this great company." The pearls and jackets murmured their agreement.

"I'm delighted to see so many of you here today, especially given today's weather. In particular, I should like to welcome so many of our old friends that I can see in the audience."

Henry, told that HB always began like this, wondered if he would remember to adjust his speech if the weather was acceptable or if the meeting was badly attended. Furthermore, because of the subdued lighting, HB could hardly see anyone in the audience, let alone specific friends. The audience, hearing the chief executive's appreciation of their efforts, murmured afresh with reciprocal appreciation. HB smiled and then introduced the other members of the board before continuing.

"This has not been an easy year for us, or indeed any of our competitors in this great and essential industry. We have all suffered. Yet I am pleased to say that we have emerged in rather better shape than most of our competitors." He waited for the inevitable applause which was not long delayed. Apart from eating free company sandwiches for lunch, the sports jackets and pearls had come to hear good news.

"It has been a painful period for all of us and I want to pay tribute, immediately, to my friends on the board. They have worked long and hard, on your behalf, to ensure that we have taken full advantage of all opportunities of increasing share value." Henry thought that it sounded as if they received no pay and were banned from owning shares themselves.

"In particular, I want to thank Peter Nascott, the former MP, who, as you know, has decided to leave us, after just two years as a non-executive director, to spend more time with his families, I mean family." This slip was only detected by the lazy media. "I also want to thank all my other colleagues who have worked so tirelessly to ensure that we have achieved excellent results in difficult circumstances. I must emphasise that our biggest asset is people and we are fortunate in having some of the most dedicated and knowledgeable people in the industry. I pay tribute to them and consider myself fortunate to be part of a team, their team."

Henry winced.

Once the applause had faded, and without a trace of irony, bearing in mind what was to come shortly, HB continued. He was pleased to welcome some new non-executive directors who had joined the board since the last AGM, to bring it up to its usual numerical strength.

"We have been reluctantly obliged to let some of our colleagues go. This has been necessary to allow our company to become more cost-effective and efficient. Like so many companies in so many sectors, regrettably, we've had to reduce overall staff numbers significantly in the last two years, to safeguard the future for the remainder of the employees. I should like to thank all those who are affected for their services over the years as they have built the company into what it is today.

Henry nearly smiled.

"As you know, I cannot say any more now, because of the legal cases pending against us, alleging unfair dismissals, except to say that we believe that we have behaved honourably, fairly and legally and will respond vigorously to the charges made against us. I would like to take this opportunity to appeal to those employees, now working to rule at our refinery and main terminals, to resume normal work, so that meaningful negotiations can begin. We have embarked on a series of major improvements since the depot fire and when repairs have been completed in the next few weeks, it will be one of the safest in the world." Restrained but positive grunts stumbled around the hall.

"We are pleased with our performance but we have a long way to go. We are not complacent: we are not at the end of our journey, nor are we at the end of the beginning or the beginning of the end. We are only at the beginning of the beginning."

Was Hubert stuck?

"We have many miles ahead of us. Some will be very difficult but we are comforted, as we prepare for that journey, by knowing that you are with us and that together, we shall strive purposefully to the light that we can now see at the end of the long tunnel."

Henry knew that this pseudo-Churchillian management-babble would bring applause and the Barbican was soon ringing with the approbation of those who felt that their savings were in good hands. Pearls nudged sportsjackets and sports jackets nudged pearls to confirm that HB was a good man. The good man resumed. "Real prices have done us no favours in the last few years. Indeed, they have fallen by more than 15 per cent." One member of the audience, who had fallen asleep, awoke suddenly, thought that he had heard HB say that costs had fallen by more than 15 per cent, and applauded lustily before stopping abruptly as his neighbours shushed him into silence.

HB continued. "We have to depend on our own efforts: we cannot look to prices to assist us, at least in the short term, but I'm confident that the measures that your board has instigated will deliver the desired results, providing that we do not waiver in our resolve. We shall continue to strive to add value through the undoubted skills of our dedicated and loyal staff. We no longer see big as automatically beautiful but we shall keep our corporate eyes peeled for sensible acquisitions. We are concerned with adding value, and not being all things to all people. We shall return to our core business, concentrating on our core specialities and areas, out-sourcing whenever we feel that this is in the group's overall interests."

"We believe in the need to communicate our mission statement clearly, unambiguously, purposefully, meaningfully, objectively and, above all, succinctly." He paused whilst the audience, who had no idea of what he was talking about, but felt that it sounded impressive, put their hands together, clearly, unambiguously, purposefully, meaningfully, objectively and succinctly.

"We shall continue to invest in those geographic and functional areas where we can maximise shareholder return. I know that we have been criticised by some so-called experts in the media for investing heavily in some allegedly autocratic states, where, I'm proud to say, we were often the only western company. We invested because we believed in their potential but, as you know, we had to withdraw, hopefully temporarily, from some countries after major and totally unexpected civil uprisings. I'm confident that our policy will be vindicated and our media critics, some of whom would not recognise a barrel of oil if they fell over it, will be shown to be as seriously ill-informed."

The attack on the media, inevitably, went down well and HB was unable to resume for some moments until the laughter and applause subsided. The scribes duly wrote down the comments and resolved to follow the company's activities very carefully in the following year.

"I'm going to leave the presentation of the financial results to my friend and colleague, Alan Stewart, our treasurer, but before I ask him to address you, I have a few more comments that I would like to make.

"In the exploration and production sector, your company is making strenuous efforts to reduce costs by forming strategic alliances with other large groups. This also enables us to take advantage of complementary skills. We share expertise and experience and that is very relevant in these difficult times of lower prices and margins and high initial costs of implementing new technology. So far, we have lowered expenses by more than 30 per cent in the last four years. I believe that such alliances are the way forward and that we must continue to reduce costs. We have no alternative, if we want to deliver results to you, our owners."

HB, his first task done, and Alan Stewart having been introduced, sat down to a rapturous reception. Usually, most people, seeing the treasurer for the first time, assumed that he was in charge of the few remaining messengers employed by the company. Today, however, Stewart, just turned 55, had forsaken his usually scruffy look and was wearing a new blue suit, with a white shirt and striped blue tie. Like HB, he looked the part. Broadoak was fortunate to have his services. He was at the top of the list of most major headhunters who could not understand why he remained with such a lacklustre company. He had acquired a reputation for some very astute moves in raising investment and now his usually casual appearance was part of the act and a challenge to the establishment. He commenced his address with some routine comments on the group's performance in the last financial year. His presentation was enhanced by the sensible use of coloured charts, projected on to a very large screen. He then emphasised some key features, using an electronic pointer. Initially, seeking to line the pointer with the screen, he directed the resulting large red dot on to HB's forehead, making him look like a wealthy Indian.

"We shall need to invest heavily in new technology, if we are to remain competitive. Raising the large sums involved will be more difficult and more costly, unless we make sure that our own house is in order." The audience nodded wisely.

"Our costs must be reduced further, until we're acknowledged as the most efficient company in the sector. We must divest all non-core assets in the near future and leave areas where we cannot produce a critical mass."

He rumbled on, touching on many of the responsibilities of his senior colleagues who seemed indifferent to his trespassing meanderings. Then he talked about growth, investment, dividends and a range of financial targets. "Our gearing, frankly, is unacceptable and I suspect that many in this audience realise this and, possibly, have been anxiously awaiting action. I can promise that we shall taking action before the year is out."

Was this good news? The audience really did not know, but, somehow, it seemed that the announcement called for applause so they did. Lower gearing, clearly, or was it higher gearing, was a good thing and they wanted more, or should it be less, of it.

Stewart was concerned about a number of other issues, and the audience encouraged him to believe, that they, too, shared his worries. Apparently prices had more upside potential than downside and profits on a replacement cost basis should continue to improve. The company was making prudent and successful use of the futures market for currency trading.

Throughout this long and often incomprehensibly turgid presentation, the audience took their cue by looking not just at Stewart, but also at HB. Whenever he looked pleased, which was often, because his script had the favourable comments marked in green, they applauded. Henry and his colleagues, at the back of the stage, and in relative isolation, also had marked scripts so they too, knew when to nod appreciatively like well-trained puppies. Thus was the company united within itself.

One or two other executives then pontificated briefly, before HB announced that he would now take questions. He explained the procedures and pointed out the location of the microphones. He then invited the first question, which he would take from the blonde lady at microphone number three on the upper level of the auditorium. That was not the happiest start.

The intending questioner approached the microphone but it soon became apparent to all, except HB, that the "lady" was a well-built young man. HB, ill-advisedly having dispensed with his glasses and perceiving that the blonde was now in place, asked madam to put her question. Before a word was uttered, those in the immediate vicinity of the mike began to giggle and some of HB's colleagues swiftly pointed out his error before the question was posed. HB immediately apologised but, embarrassingly, implied that he was not entirely responsible for the mistake, as he had not expected male shareholders to have such long hair.

The question was potentially devastating and it was one that, oddly, the PR people had overlooked. "Given that the company has made hundreds of people redundant and that there are several legal cases outstanding alleging unfair dismissal, why was the board's compensation increased by 25 per cent last year?"

HB swallowed hard. His brain ceased functioning before he heard himself mumble that the company had to pay competitive salaries, wages and fees, on an international scale, otherwise it wouldn't attract the skills and experience necessary to ensure that it prospered and, "indeed survived in these difficult times". Henry wondered how many of his senior colleagues would be of any value to a competitor.

Gaining in confidence, HB then earnestly explained that the company's approach to executive remuneration was in line with the recommendations of the Waring-Plummer committee. Nobody thought to ask about this committee which was just as well, as HB had just invented it. The chief executive also explained that if non-returnable and liquid share option pension fund allowance rights, on a pre-tax basis, and allowing for superannuation contextual payments, were taken into account, the directors had actually experienced a decline in real remuneration. The rise of "just a quarter" was supposed to compensate for all this.

"Furthermore" said HB, "on a per capita basis, and adjusting for inflation, directors' fees have gone up over the last five years by less than the average for senior admirals of the fleet and experienced surgeons". Nobody understood the relevance of this point but none was prepared to challenge HB when he looked so authoritative. HB then added that what really mattered, and doubtless this was what the questioner really was getting at, was profitability. "On this basis, your company has consistently been in the top quartet for some years." HB had intended to say "quartile" but somehow it didn't seem to matter: perhaps he was concerned with blowing his own trumpet.

The questioner, who knew precisely what he wanted to ask, was about to put an obvious supplementary but was deterred by the general mumble of approval from some nearby sports jackets. The next questioner indeed, was a sports jacket. "Your lordship", he grovelled, "first of all can I congratulate you and your colleagues for another splendid set of results in a very difficult year? We're all grateful to you. It's good to know that the company is in such competent hands."

Henry stifled the results of a chemical reaction in his stomach, which owed nothing to black bananas and much to the fawning shareholder. HB, recalling the man's name, for he made the same comments each year, irrespective of the results, thanked him but said gently, that he was not a lord unless, "Mr. Cedric Arbuthnott-Harrington Smythe", who had now vanished from behind the microphone, "you know something that I don't, but thank you for your observation. Now, please could I have another question?"

Arbuthnott-Harrington Smythe, whose voice was so weak it hardly seemed adequate for a Smythe, let alone an Arbuthbott-Harrington Smythe, was a very small man for such a big name. Indeed, his voice and size justified his confession that he was a small shareholder. He vanished from sight, to re-tie his shoelace but returned to say that he had a question.

"Many of us have known better days, so we want to know whether you are going to be able to maintain the dividend on which we rely so heavily."

HB swiftly passed the question on to Alan Stewart who said that he was pleased that the dividend had advanced faster than inflation over the last five years, not least because, "like you, I am a shareholder. It would be wrong of me to make specific forecasts, but I am confident that you won't be disappointed with your overall financial return. We must also take into account the share price which, as I'm sure you know, has risen by nine per cent in recent weeks." The questioner seemed satisfied but Henry knew that this rise was largely because of press rumours of a series of possible take-overs within the sector although nobody had mentioned Broadoak.

The questions flowed for several minutes without taxing even HB. One shareholder wanted to know why the company did not sell petrol in the UK, as he was sure that it must be a large and lucrative market. Even HB blinked in quiet incredulity whilst deciding how to respond. Without a trace of anger or superiority, he said that he agreed with at least part of the shareholder's observation and that was why the company had been marketing in the UK for 30 years and now had a share of about five per cent, achieved through sales via some 400 outlets. "Profitability, I must confess, is not very good but we are doing all that we can to improve margins."

The next sports jacket, having blown lustily into the mike, to ensure that it was still working effectively, wanted to know why, in the photograph of the board in the annual report, only HB was sitting down. "If it's because you need more chairs, I would like to be considered as a supplier and I could offer you a very reasonable rate." There was always one comedian at an annual general meeting.

The next question came from a string of pearls which dangled just below a grey and elderly face. Her name, like that of many in the audience, was double-barrelled. Lady Hastings-Eastbourne told HB and his colleagues that this was the first time that she had attended an annual general meeting and it had all been very interesting from the moment she entered the Barbican to when HB and his colleagues, all of whom were more handsome than in the pictures in the annual report, explained, as she put it, "what they had been up to in the past year". She was very pleased to be present and to meet so many interesting people, some of whom actually lived near her in Trampshire.

Then, apologising for her doubtless very simple and facile question, she said that according to the annual report, the volatility of crude oil prices had cost the company dearly. "Why doesn't the company hedge on the IPE, especially as we have already heard that we use the futures markets for hedging against currency rate swings? Equally, given the volatility of both crude and refined product prices, and the high cost of storage, which is, in effect, a gamble on future prices, why doesn't the company reduce stock levels, as many other groups in the industry have done, at a time of backwardation in prices?"

HB, who had never understood the concept of futures, swiftly passed on the question to Stewart who gave an answer that seemed to satisfy most of the audience, none of whom knew what the questioner was talking about but seemed to be pleased by the answer. HB then assured the lady, to her apparent satisfaction, that inventory levels were under review. That was his normal tactic at annual general meetings. If any suggestion seemed sensible, and the company had not even thought of the idea, he always thanked the investor and assured him or her that the matter was, indeed, already under review. Sometimes he would accompany this with a happy grimace and a few words to the effect that he was delighted that the owners and the management were thinking alike.

Henry was bewildered, not knowing whether to be dumbfounded by the daft nature of most of the questions or astounded at the occasional complexity of some challenges. Suddenly, as if waking from a dream, he heard his name being uttered by HB.

A questioner was asking about the group's environmental record at some location that Henry assumed to be overseas, on the basis that he had never met anybody from that region. A polo-necked sweater wanted to know what the company said to the people of Lesser Snipica who claimed that normal environmental standards had been abandoned, to their detriment, in Broadoak's quest for profits. Henry tried to rise and failed. He quickly recovered and thought faster than ever before in his life. He was handicapped by his ignorance. He didn't know where Lesser Snipica was, and if under pressure, he would have had to admit that he was unaware even of the precise location of Greater Snipica or, for that matter, any other Snipicas. Furthermore, he did not know what the company was doing there, if it was there at all or what the allegations were. However, he was learning fast and realised that ignorance cannot be an obstacle to management on these or other occasions, as HB and others had shown over the years. He began.

"I know that you are concerned about the environment. So are we all on this stage. I know that I am. I'm not ashamed of it and neither should you be. We are all environmentalists now. It doesn't matter where our operations are based, near or far, in Europe or further afield, in exploration and production or in refining or marketing, in the desert or offshore, in city centres or in the jungle."

Henry thought that that dealt adequately with the location and nature of the company's activities.

"It is the same, indivisible environment. Nature doesn't acknowledge national boundaries and neither do we in our quest to do the best that we can to ensure that we pass on land, and, indeed, water and air, in the best possible state for future generations, who are the future for all of us. I make no apology for my interest in preserving the environment and, as I said a few moments ago, neither should you. We are in an extractive industry but that does not give us the right to ride roughshod over any group's interests and that's an important point."

The audience, not understanding this meaningless prattle, did recognise that this was an important point, for Henry had given them an important clue by pausing and telling them just that. They applauded.

"We are aware that we are but temporary guardians of something that is of fundamental importance. We have a responsibility and we have a duty. We shall neglect neither and I give you my word that...". At this point an embarrassed Henry suddenly heard himself and had no idea of what he was saying and how to finish the sentence. Indeed, just briefly, he was not entirely sure of his whereabouts. Lamely, he added "I shall keep my word, as that is the kind of person that I am and that is the kind of company for which I have the pleasure, no, the honour, to represent. I know that some people think that we should do more to look after the environment. I know, too, that we can never do enough. I think all this too but we must also take into account the need to ensure that we don't lose your financial confidence. We are not alone in facing this dilemma: other companies have the same problem but, in providing per cent of our income directly to environmental remediation, I think that we can say, without any false modesty, that your company is an industry leader."

Henry had deliberately coughed just before inserting a figure before uttering the magical words per cent. He knew that nobody would ask him for the statistic. HB looked pleased and expected Henry to sit down.

He didn't.

"I should be delighted if you would see me after this meeting and could give me your thoughts on what is happening and what ought to be done, I promise that I shall consider, most seriously, all that you say." With that, Henry sat down, determined to find out what, if anything that the company was doing wrong and to rectify it. The applause was prolonged and Henry mused that some aspects of senior management were easy.

Chapter 17

A few days later, Hubert asked Henry to attend a big oil conference in Houston at which some sessions would be on crisis management. "I know it's short notice but it could be useful. We must improve our reaction to emergencies after what happened at the depot. Absorb as much as you can, but Henry, and I mean this, under no circumstances, must you discuss any aspects of the fire, whatever the pressure from the local media or anyone else. I don't even want you to see our own people. I'll tell them you're coming, out of courtesy, but that you won't have time to see them. The insurance people have calmed down and they may now be prepared to talk about money. We cannot jeopardise that."

Henry nodded and vowed silence. Jill had already imposed similar standing orders on him. Frankly, this suited Perkins. After the television interview and the after-dinner fiasco, he wanted a low profile.

He was already becoming disenchanted with travelling, as he explained to Jane. "I used to envy businessmen who stayed in expensive hotels, in erotic, sorry, exotic locations, dining well, seeing new cities and spending the company's money on luxury living, with a little work inserted to justify the trip. Now, I think more about reporting to airports at inconvenient times for a plane that, with luck, may leave three hours late, adjusting to going to bed at odd times according to the body clock after a cold shower because there's no hot water. Then, just as you're almost asleep, having overcome the temperature control system in the room, which either boils you or freezes you, revellers stage a party immediately outside your door or political dissidents will thoughtlessly mount the country's first-ever coup."

Jane looked quizzical at this last comment. Henry admitted that this had happened to a friend, not to him.

"Then you have to cope with the difficulties of eating food for which the refined British stomach is ill-accustomed, working almost 24 hours a day, seeing nothing of the country except offices and hotel rooms and then, returning, laden with expensive junk for family and colleagues, and faced with a mountain of work to be done and having to listen to inane remarks that it must be wonderful to see the world at the company's expense. Even in this country, at hotels near railway stations, you'll be disturbed by rehearsals for the annual nocturnal wagon-shunting competition, and, of course, it's inevitable that just when it's least convenient to leave your room, the fire alarm will sound.

"Some hotels want to know your occupation. I'm tempted to say brain surgeon, although knowing my luck, this will provoke the reaction that 'mine's been hurting lately, can you do anything for me? The answer is that there's been a lot of it around at this time of the year and you shouldn't worry.

"The more luggage you take, the greater the delay in the arrival of the final case off the carousel, after the others spilled off in the first few minutes. However much luggage you take, it will be the newest and most expensive case that is severely scratched."

Jane said that she really ought to be back at work "but it was interesting to hear about your experiences, Perky, I mean Mr. Perkins". Henry smiled and corrected her. "Perky's just fine."

Henry's first American trip, to New York with Nigel Read, had been particularly taxing but his complaint to the airline's chief executive had yielded two free return tickets to the US as compensation. Hubert had generously said that as it was "Perkins the honest" who had been inconvenienced, he should have the tickets. Henry and Jill, who had denounced his letter as a waste of time, would visit the US next year. Despite all this, he was eagerly anticipating his first visit to Houston.

Life had taught Henry how to suppress frustration and that, if things could go wrong, they would and this made him nervous. He could find ambiguity in the simplest instruction. For example, confronted by a warning that the "front three coaches of this train will be detached at Tickerton Magna junction", he had to ask whether that meant the first three in the direction of travel or the first three to enter the station from which the train left, because it reversed on departure. An official with 25 years' experience admitted that he had never been asked that question. Henry seldom read instructions so doors that should be pushed were pulled and doors that anticipated being pulled were always pushed.

Even before the Houston flight was called, many intending passengers had formed queues in the departure lounge, apparently fearing that the plane would leave without them but with their luggage. When the first formal invitation "to come forward", in the best traditions of American television evangelists, was extended to handicapped people and those with young children, there was such a surge that Henry thought that he must be the only mercifully fully-fit passenger without offspring.

He lowered himself into the executive seat alongside the window. As usual, judging by the size of the seat belt, it seemed that the last occupant had been a child with the girth of a toy waste-paper bin. A much-travelled colleague, the appropriately named Ian Michael Anthony Pratt, had given him some advice. "I always prefer an inside seat because sitting alongside the window should mean that you won't be disturbed by a fellow passenger wanting to pass you. When I occupy an aisle seat, I've worked out that my neighbours want to get past every 1,000 miles, except during the night, when the rate falls to every 1,200 but that doesn't matter because they're the only people in the entire plane who keep their reading lights on, so I can't sleep anyway."

Henry was sipping an orange juice, having been offered nuts for munching, headphones for listening, newspapers for reading and a menu for pondering. His neighbour was staring at what looked like a small but apparently blank television screen which seemed to be a part of his seat. Fearing an embarrassing failure, Mr Perkins decided to postpone efforts to release his. When the time came, he would ask for a Bucks Fizz, having enjoyed his first ever at a recent reception after a conference on cost-cutting. A crackling loudspeaker system derailed his thoughts. Oddly, announcements in foreign languages always took at least four minutes whilst the alleged translation in English took but seconds.

"Good morning, ladies and gentlemen, this is Captain Jack Grace. I would like to welcome you all on board and to introduce my colleagues, Len Larwood, my co-pilot, and second officer Don Border. The cabin crew, headed by Patsy Hobbs, are here to help you and if there is any way in which they can make your journey more comfortable or more enjoyable, please just ask."

Henry's neighbour, eyeing a shapely brunette member of the cabin crew hovering near him, indicated that he had already thought of something. Henry forced an understanding grin and looked away. The pilot had not finished. "I'm afraid that I have some bad news. For technical reasons, we'll be taking off a little late today. My latest information is that we shall have to sit here for at least 30 minutes. Now, please just relax and I'll pass on any more news as soon as I have it. Sorry for the delay."

The neighbour, about 35 years old, dressed in a crumpled tracksuit and exuding confidence, spoke. "Can I introduce myself?" Without waiting for approval, he said that he was Cyril Hutton. Henry had no reason to doubt that that he was telling the truth. "I just knew that there was going to be a delay. Funny, isn't it," he said, without waiting for an answer, which would have been difficult as it was not clear what he thought was funny, "no plane ever takes off on time, unless you arrive late at the airport".

Henry agreed that it was odd. Hutton continued. "I was waiting for a plane the other day, to go to Paris, or was it Rome, no, wait a moment, it was to Los Angeles, yes that's it, LA, and they told us that we were boarding late because there had been a problem in cleaning the incoming aircraft. Had the cleaners vanished? Had the vacuum cleaner broken down or had somebody lost a duster? What do you think about that?"

"I'd rather not think about that at all."

Henry's gaze drifted as he watched a battle developing between the overhead luggage locker and a determined but late-arriving passenger with what looked like a small piano. A diminutive member of the cabin crew was content to watch. Soon the luggage locker was tacitly declared the winner and the piano was towed down the aisle by the stewardess who stressed to the distressed owner that he must remind her "when we reach Houston that we have your instrument in one of the holds".

Perkins had some sympathy with a fellow traveller who had been wrestling to recover his jacket from the overhead locker. Denied sufficient space in "his" locker, because of the presence of what appeared to be a small rowing boat, Henry had tactfully placed his brief case on the floor near his feet. This provoked Patsy Hobbs, she whose desire to assist passengers had been so recently publicised, to adopt a stance that combined the worst characteristics of lance corporals and car park attendants. "You can't leave that there" she boomed in a voice that suggested that it could exceed the decibel levels produced by the noisiest of aircraft engines. "That's not allowed and anyway, that's an escape route, as you should know if you'd read the instructions as we told you."

Apparently, in the event of an evacuation, the fate of hundreds of passengers, including the rowing boat owner, was in the hands of Messrs Perkins and Hutton. The old Henry would have accepted such abuse. Not now. Withdrawing a pen and small notebook from his jacket, happily not consigned to the overhead bin, he asked for her name. She confirmed that she had not married since the pilot had introduced her a few minutes ago and that, astonishingly, no moniker changes had been effected by deed poll. Henry made a detailed note and subsequently found a space overhead for his briefcase.

After 28 minutes, the pilot's voice crackled into life and confirmed that take-off was imminent. The journey was mainly uneventful and mercifully Henry's neighbour was asleep for virtually all the flight. Perkins worked out how to release the television monitor but encountered problems with his table, which, not being precisely horizontal, created a challenge for the dishes. His intended liquid consumption frequently coincided with some unexpected turbulence.

Henry belatedly recalled I.M.A. Pratt's advice. "Always concentrate when preparing to eat airline food. Many talkative adults release the mayonnaise and pour it over their salads. That's a sensible use for mayonnaise which is a product with very limited applications if not dedicated to enlivening a salad. Unfortunately, many passengers don't notice that the chicken-tasting salad, and incidentally everything on a plane tastes of chicken, is still covered with a transparent wrapping. The mayonnaise then trickles over everything on the tray."

Henry had some difficulty in filling in the visa form and the customs declaration. Smugly, he had noticed that many passengers had to recover passports from the overhead lockers. His was in his shirt pocket and he started to complete the form carefully but stumbled when he came to country of residence. The explanatory video had obligingly offered UK as an example. "But", as he explained to a puzzled member of the cabin staff, "the UK is not a country, it is a political entity just". He was advised to indicate that he came from the UK.

Whether he was carrying snails, dead or alive, was one of the easier questions but he smiled at the question on moral turpitude and wondered whether recent American presidents would be re-admitted to the country if this question were considered seriously. He rather fancied the idea of a little moral turpitude. Perhaps, one day?

The plane landed with scarcely a jolt, precisely where the authorities and the pilot had intended. Perkins was in Houston. He joined the long line to enter the country and then recovered his luggage which embarrassingly aroused the curiosity of a small but fallible drug-detecting corporate dog. He booked a seat on a van, apparently the American for minibus, direct to his hotel. Tired after the long flight and aware that although it was 5.00 in the afternoon, his body felt that it was 11.00 in the evening, Henry took in the sights greedily and, above all, marvelled at the sunshine and the space. The airport seemed to be as big as Oakshire.

After about 50 minutes, the minibus stopped at a dusty building site which closer examination revealed to be an elderly hotel undergoing demolition or renovation. If it was the latter, Henry immediately pitied those booked in there. Then he noticed the name. It was his hotel, his home for the next three nights. His eyes flashed a disapproving message to his stomach, which registered horror whilst his feet assumed the characteristics of boiling water. Quiet, dignified British panic. He left the minibus, carrying a briefcase under his arm and humping a heavy case, which, judging by its efforts to remain in the vehicle, shared his apprehension, and strolled hesitatingly into unaccustomed heat and humidity. Henry's fellow passengers, having maintained monastic silence thus far, came close to voicing sympathy. Skilfully carrying his luggage over the impedimenta of construction, and pausing to read the signs indicating that the temporary reception area was on the far side of the building site, Henry tried to convince himself that this could not be as bad as it seemed. After a modest walk during which he only hit his leg twice against unseen obstacles, he hobbled towards what was now called reception.

The area was covered by a generous layer of elderly brick dust and the walls were hidden by large wooden boards festooned with notices revealing that they concealed construction sites to which access was strictly prevented. Apart from the brave receptionist, Perkins seemed to be the only person who was not wearing a hardhat. Once upon a time, just possibly, at about the time of the Civil War, the hotel might have been great but what would the bedroom be like now? Perhaps renovation had commenced there? Henry was clinging on to all kinds of vague hopes but he knew instinctively that this was the beginning of a disaster.

"Good afternoon sir. I'm Frazer Nash. Can I check you in?" The receptionist handed Perkins various forms to "fill out" which he filled in. One was a declaration that if he did not complete his agreed sentence in the hotel and escaped early, he would pay a penalty. This seemed odd before he had even seen his room, but the fatigued and yet increasingly assertive Henry was sufficiently confident of his ability to challenge this if the rest of the hotel was anything like what he had seen thus far. The temptation was to move elsewhere immediately but he was too tired. If his first impressions were confirmed, he would leave in the morning.

Henry's hopes that his room would be acceptable were soon dashed. It was very dark and the furniture, whilst doubtless appealing to an antiques specialist, was as uncomfortable and unwelcoming to the tired traveller as a closed bar in the desert. The bed was hard and the bathroom was medieval. He turned on the light, because, although the sun was still shining, the cell remained dark, partly because the single window was coated in dust and cement which had missed its target. He read a notice which informed the hapless inmate that the room had some "special amenities". Allegedly, there was a coffee maker, with coffee. What astute planning! So many hotels provide only tea or orange juice with coffee makers. There were 100-watt light bulbs, not just by the bed but also on the desk. What generosity! Could there be more? Yes. There were wooden hangers and every phone had a long cord. Many hotels might have long phone cords on perhaps one instrument, but on every phone! How truly wonderful it would be to hang his clothes on genuine wooden hangers! After slogging for decades, Perkins really felt that he had arrived. The trouble was that he wished he hadn't.

Some planning was required if he was to satisfy his appetite, so Henry, picking his route carefully between the bricks, planks and discarded pipes, navigated his way to the dining room. It was located so far from the main area that the walk was clearly designed to stimulate appetites. Henry's first impression was that the restaurant was closed because it was so dark. Presumably, all the 100 watt bulbs were in the bedrooms. Henry just wanted a light snack. Some soup perhaps? No, there was none. Just an ice cream? No, supplies had been exhausted. Some diners earlier in the day, so impressed with the quality of the stuff, had scoffed the hotel's entire stock. A few minutes later, a dissident employee confided that the real reason for the lack of ice cream was that the freezer had failed. A cappuccino, perhaps? No, that machine had broken as well but the waiter expressed the hope that Perkins would have "a truly wonderful evening".

Later, at about 4.00 am UK time, Henry successfully booked accommodation for the rest of his stay at another hotel. That done, Perkins went to bed, basking but briefly in the warm glow of the 100 watt bulbs whilst marvelling at the long phone cords and admiring his clothes, resting contentedly on wooden hangers.

On the morrow, the world was transformed. He left a message on the Perkins Mansion voice mail and another in the London and Houston offices to tell them that he was changing hotels. Henry then received an apology after his uncompromising refusal to pay the cancellation penalty. Another guest, inspired by Henry's stand, was demanding a discount.

After checking in at the new hotel, the bellhop, whose huge Texan-style silver name badge claimed that its wearer was called Copper, seized Henry by the hand and clasped it to his vast stomach, saying that he just wanted to touch base.

Henry arrived at the conference for the afternoon session. The event was well attended and the four presentations on crisis management fully justified Henry's attendance. He enjoyed a comfortable night at his new hotel and as the following day was hot, Henry was pleased to be able to sit in the cool, listening to more helpful presentations, before taking a strolling around the associated exhibition.

At lunchtime, Henry followed the crowd out of the main conference building into the adjacent hotel for lunch. He was briefly exposed to a temperature that was in the nineties, in old-fashioned Fahrenheit, and a humidity that augured well for local dry cleaners' commercial prospects. Conference lunches can be valuable for the chance to hear a leading industry executive. Today was not such an occasion. The speaker was dwarfed, in more ways than one, by a fellow diner. The large and well-painted lady, swathed in a brown polka dot dress and decorated by several tonnes of jewellery, bore down on Henry as he pondered which space to occupy at a table near the speaker. Introducing herself, she gave Perkins a card which failed to indicate the nature of her company's business but which showed the company's address in English and Russian. Her job title, Global President, might have impressed the gullible.

Staring at Henry's lightweight dark suit, she told him and his fellow intending diners, that he must be important. They were understandably indifferent. Receiving but a polite smile from Perkins, she turned to another hovering diner and informed the less-than-impressed individual that he was so handsome "why, he just ought to be in the movies. Don't yawl agree?" The remark was received in silence. It seemed that he preferred commerce and did not want publicity. Indeed, he looked so abashed, he might have been British. Doubtless an honest man, he would have been the first to admit that he did not share the lady's opinion. The polka dot then busied herself in collecting business cards from the other surprised diners, thoughtfully ensuring that each person had a card from everyone else around the table. She then astutely assessed the likely supply and demand for butter and informed the gathering, which, curiously, evinced no gratitude, that each person had their own supply but, if necessary, some sharing could be arranged. Henry sighed with relief. A butter shortage was one of those things that could completely undermine the enjoyment of a business trip.

She manoeuvred her way towards the handsome man who wasn't and the intending diners felt for their new colleague but not sufficiently strongly to assist. However, a tall, fair-haired young male then strolled to the table and innocently appeared to be about to sit next to the man whom Hollywood missed. The polka dot saw this and soon re-organised the table again to ensure that she had the prime and apparently coveted position. She addressed the newcomer. "You must be Dutch." Clearly a gentleman, he apologised for the apparent carelessness of his parents on the matter of nationality, and, coming clean immediately, confirmed that he was, well, American.

Henry watched all this from the far side of the table which remained largely unoccupied. The PD, clearly a sympathetic character, noted that he lacked companions. This mattered little to Henry but it did to the lady. She announced that it seemed as if he was to be alone. There was no rush to join him. Henry Perkins, general manager and patriotic, good-naturedly assured her that Britain was accustomed to standing alone, especially in 1940, although the full force of his remark was lost because he was then sitting. However, he assured her that his position was essentially temporary and that he was hovering until she had finally landed. The word "hovering", was seized upon and Henry was praised accordingly. "Don't yawl just love how he talks?" His fellow delegates remained indifferent.

The kindly lady offered to sit next to Perkins later in the meal, "if you're still alone". He thanked her but insisted there was no need. Apparently relieved, she landed between her new friends and told them about her son in such detail that the Dutchman who wasn't, understandably confused that one person might be involved in so much, asked how many sons she had. The answer was one. He, the son, was very successful, handsome, unmarried but, and she stressed this, very fond of girls, and six foot four.

"How tall are you?" He conceded that he was only six foot.

"Never mind. I'm deeply honoured to be sitting alongside a young new graduate, you're a graduate aren't you?" He confessed that he was and Henry, the non-graduate, sitting some way from the PD, hid behind the jug of cold tea.

Henry had enjoyed his lunch and was padding around the associated exhibition. A slim, brown-haired girl glided sensuously towards him and smiled. The modest Perkins turned around to see the undoubtedly handsome and giant brute who had inspired such a friendly gesture. There was nobody there.

As Henry wondered why he had been favoured, and before he could work out what was what and why, very important in such circumstances, the girl was hissing seductively in his left ear. "Wouldn't you just covet this beautiful electronic organiser?" She spent some seconds mouthing the word "beautiful" stretching out the adjective for so long that she might just as well have said "pulchritudinous", but Henry did not want to quibble. He was amazed that anyone could apparently lust after a non-human organiser. Henry had never coveted an electronic organiser but liked them sufficiently to own three, half the total used in Broadoak, but he could not really go beyond liking them. Being British, he had always held passion in check. Having feelings about an electronic organiser, frankly, sat awkwardly with his upbringing. Suddenly, the mood changed. Forsaking the seductive whisper, the girl bawled out "it's showtime in just a minute, folks, and then you can win one of these great electronic organisers!"

On the last full day of his trip, Henry attended the presentations, had lunch and then packed. The lunch was the main event because it was when the industry presented itself with awards. The occasion reeked of show business. Ordinary mortals, such as Henry, temporarily important, had to walk to their tables through serried lines of respectful waiters and waitresses marshalled as if greeting a visiting head of state. Only with difficulty did he resist the temptation to inspect them, pointing out the odd gravy spot on their uniforms and lump of cheese tucked behind the ear.

The large room was plunged into darkness, spotlights played on the leading figures at the top table, two large screens showed videos, accompanied by strident music, of the award winners at work. This was followed by shiveringly embarrassing laudatory remarks from colleagues. The dignitaries about to be honoured were asked to sit down so they could stand up when presented by the chairman. He then requested that the audience held its applause until everyone had been introduced. Understandably, some individuals collapsed under the strain and clapped loudly and unashamedly until silenced by colleagues. Yes, Houston was an interesting place.

Chapter 18

It was early Saturday morning in late August and Henry was ensconced in a deep brown leather armchair in the lounge of an expensive olde-world country hotel near Kingly Trustworthy. The only sound came from the few animals which had astutely avoided the nation-wide cull of almost anything that moved during the recent foot and mouth epidemic. The empty fields and hills meandered peacefully into the future, illuminated by a fitful sun, unsure whether it was a weekday or a weekend and thus whether to shine or hide.

Henry was flicking through the newspaper delivered to his room. Apparently a multinational group, trying to meet new European Commission safety regulations, had spent millions on producing leaflets in five languages, explaining to its London-based employees how to gain access to their office building safely via revolving doors that had functioned without incident for many years. A chief executive who, had taken his company to the verge of bankruptcy, was claiming £15 million compensation after being dismissed for incompetence and three young adults were suing their former school for inadequate teaching which, allegedly, had resulted in their having only mediocre jobs.

Mr Perkins, sipping his coffee, was thinking about the day ahead. He was wearing a suit, as was recommended not by the hotel but by Broadoak Oil and this, doubtless, had also confused the sun.

Hubert Bennett had convened an urgent meeting of key staff. Henry, whose first such meeting this would be, knew that they met about three times a year, over a weekend, to discuss matters that HB deemed sufficiently important to take his colleagues away from the excitement of shopping, housework, gardening and family visits and to impose on them some golf, swimming, good food and drink and a little work. Henry was curious on the reason for this meeting but, as HB enjoyed these sessions, there was not necessarily cause for concern. What was mildly annoying was that he would be in Houston the following weekend and Jill would also be away on business. Some weeks ago, HB had told Henry that one of the advantages of these weekend jaunts was that confidential matters could be discussed "without the staff knowing that we've met". HB did not realise that when accounts department paid the bills, there was usually a sweepstake on the size of the wine bill.

Gradually, Henry's colleagues, most of whom had breakfasted in their rooms, mainly because it was more expensive, filtered into the hotel lounge. The males were conspicuously suited and a large notice in the reception area said, "Welcome to the executive management of Broadoak Oil". So much for corporate secrecy. Indeed, some guests were already speculating on what was happening and one resident, waiting for his coffee, was scribbling in a notebook.

The suits gathered in the Winston Churchill Suite adjacent to the more basic Attlee Meeting Room. The tables were covered by green baize cloths and each place was allocated a glass, a bottle of sparkling water and enough boiled sweets to satisfy the greediest of consumers. Also present were a thin pad, bearing the name of the hotel in large black type, to the detriment of any notes that might be written, and a pencil which also bore the name of the hotel. The wallpaper, which looked sufficiently expensive and tasteless to have been chosen by a leading left wing politician for his office, lacked a logo but was loud enough to deter slumber.

HB opened the proceedings. "Gentlemen, first of all", he interrupted himself as Benita Harris sustained a sudden secretarial splutter and glanced meaningfully at Shirley Church, "and ladies". He started again. "Ladies and gentlemen, first of all, thank you for coming and I'm sorry to drag you out on a weekend. I hope that you all slept well after our little dinner last night."

Henry smiled the smile of the sycophant. The dinner had been the best he had ever had and, even although he usually drank very little, he had fallen victim to the atmosphere and had consumed about six months' rations in one night. Fortunately, he felt quite normal and his fellow managers seemed well. Perkins looked around at his colleagues.

The ambitious Lance Boyle, the marketing director and nominally the managing director, was chewing the logo of the hotel pencil. His verbosity in the office had prompted his erstwhile secretary to devise a trophy which was awarded each month to whoever had been lectured for the longest. The average for the last year was more than one hour. Uncharacteristically, Boyle seldom said much at these meetings, but exuded a sense of superiority which HB, who distrusted him, interpreted as opposition. When asked for his opinion, he usually intoned that the topic was more difficult than seemed initially and that it should be considered in detail, from all perspectives, and there were many, before any definitive decision.

Alan Stewart, company treasurer, could not attend and he was represented by his deputy, Pat Head, whose monosyllabic approach and unchanging expression made other accountants seem exciting.

Dick Wood, head of operations, looked expectantly at HB awaiting the reason for this conference. Henry respected Dick whose wooden and clipped style, developed from his military days, invited and received ridicule from junior staff. Dick knew what he was talking about which distinguished him from many of his peers. Predictably, he was wearing a white shirt, regimental tie and his usual suit.

Monty Llewellyn-Tripster, who had replaced Peter Nascott as a non-executive director, sat next to Dick. Tripster was another former MP and his appointment to the board reflected the fact that he and HB had attended the same minor public school. Subsequently Hubert had, entirely coincidentally of course, added to his own list of non-executive directorships.

Nigel Read, head of investor relations, who had accompanied Henry to the US, sat opposite Perkins. In the City's eyes, he was a safe and competent pair of hands. Broadoak was lucky to have Stewart and Read.

Shirley Church, the company secretary, was aged about 45 and did not slavishly try to look like her male colleagues. Instead of a suit, she was wearing a smart navy blue dress and a white jacket. Her long auburn hair, which many would have cut short in an effort to look masculine, roamed freely.

Stan Gray, responsible for planning and much more under the new organisation, but still lacking support, seemed over-awed by the occasion, but Henry, also making his debut, told him that "anyone who's been around as long as us can keep up with this lot". Sitting next to him was Professor Alex Gardner, a non-executive director who was clearly under-awed judging by his casual demeanour. He was already leaning back in his chair and Henry wondered when gravity would overtake the well-known and acerbic university economist. Alex, who had written a series of well-received studies on business, had accepted a position on the board to help him understand how a medium-sized company operated. His initial plan to write a detailed analysis of organisation and decision-making had been ditched in favour of a satirical sitcom for television.

Sir Willerby Wistleton-Nugget, another non-executive director, was a former junior minister in a long-forgotten government. After losing office, he had run a bank and then a publishing group, conspicuously badly but with very considerable compensation. When asked his qualifications for running a bank, he replied "I've used a bank all me adult life". Unfortunately, when joining the Broadoak board, asked by a journalist why he was joining an oil company, he replied "I've used petrol all me adult life".

The other attendee was Wally Jones who had represented the staff at these meetings for many years. He was indubitably one of the group's most astute members. His appointment, hailed as a victory for common sense by the trade union, was how HB had resolved a labour dispute at the refinery some years ago. Wally's contribution extended far beyond conveying employees' views: he sensed how companies operated and how they would react to particular circumstances. He had read business publications avidly and had done particularly well on the stock exchange. Like Fricker, he favoured the simultaneous use of braces and belts and it was widely surmised that this caution resulted from an unfortunate trouser-related mishap at a psychologically crucial stage in his earlier life. His lack of confidence, reflected in the trouser tale, extended to pens. He always carried a range of not less than six, all of which were neatly clipped into his breast pocket.

HB resumed.

"I needn't tell you that the sudden slump in crude oil prices, which could last for some time, has caused some major problems. Every company has had to economise and to challenge every item of expenditure." Henry, looking out at the acres of garden around the hotel, nearly giggled.

"We have had to let some of our colleagues go. Over the last few months, our return on capital would not appeal to a greengrocer. Worse still, our share price, like those of our competitors, is falling. Apparently, the financial sector cannot understand us and, even if this is because of the ignorance of the callow red-braced jacketless brigade of so-called analysts, we all suffer the consequences of their ignorance and inexperience. We all feel the pain from this."

Heads, including that of Pat Head, nodded vigorously and a few "hear hears" were muttered. This was because the remuneration committee, consisting of some board members and a few outside consultants on very gratifying retainers, had decided to give shares and options to some senior staff only a few months ago. This had caused a short-lived debate in some newspapers but HB had brushed it aside, arguing, once again, that there was no such thing as bad publicity. "I believe that we've done all that we can to reduce costs and that there's only limited scope for further divestments."

"You mean sell something?" enquired Willerby.

HB nodded.

"We've cut back investment but the scope is limited because, as you know, over the years, we've always distributed a high proportion of our earnings to those who created them." Grateful nods indicated support for such a policy. Broadoak had not done particularly well lately, even during the periods of high prices, mainly because of under-investment. "That said, and bearing in mind that we are not alone in our struggle to stay profitable, I've been thinking hard about how we can reduce our expenses. Frankly, apart from some modest divestments, I can think of nothing. I should like to hear your views later this morning. However, I've some much more important news. Personally, I believe that crude oil prices are cyclical so it's important that, unlike the rest of the industry, we don't panic. We're surrounded by takeovers and mergers and I wondered if we could reduce our costs by seeking a partner in an agreed merger. I was inclined to reject this but before I could even discuss it with you, I had a call from Chuck Charles, who as you know, heads Muswell Petroleum of Houston."

Nobody had ever heard of Charles but most nodded sagely.

"I think he wants to merge with us."

HB paused. A young waitress, busily pouring out more coffee for his colleagues, had not quite finished. It would have been rude to continue whilst his audience's attention was diverted. She completed her task at 10.45 precisely, left some sandwiches, for a mid-morning snack, which bore the legend, in bold red letters, "to be eaten by 10.35 am today" and legged it. Henry, aware that any "merger", a euphemism for takeover, would almost certainly mean the end of his career, felt the blood draining from his face and put his head in his hands, partly to return some colour to his face and partly to ensure that his head did not fall off.

HB continued. "He was not specific but it was clear that he was sounding us out for a friendly merger." He paused for a sip of coffee. Alex said that he assumed that the call came late in the afternoon. HB nodded, unaware that the point behind Alex's suggestion was that HB might conceivably have been just marginally below his best at that time of day.

"Yes, but, to my surprise, he also sent a very short and personal note. I've go it here." HB waved it above his head like Chamberlain after the Munich talks with Hitler. Would it be peace in our time? "I'll read it to you.

"Dear Horace",

Lance interrupted. "Horace?"

"We must remember that he's American and anyone with such an odd moniker as Charles Charles might reasonably be excused for getting others' names wrong."

Lance persisted. "If he can't get your name right, is he the kind of man we want to talk to?"

"May I continue?"

"It was good talking to you again. It's a long time since we met and we should try to organise a lunch the next time that I'm in London which should be real soon."

Henry frowned involuntarily at the absence of the correct adverb.

"I'll get my girl to ring your girl to fix something up. Meanwhile, as our industry's going to face continuing financial difficulties, we agreed we should consider linking up. I think that we could create some pretty good synergy. We're sure as hell keen on this and I'm mighty glad you seemed keen too. Why don't you and your guys kick this around and then we can meet to discuss details? In the meantime, I'll keep this idea confidential and I know that you will too. It would be fun working with you, all the best, Chuck."

Dick was the first to speak after a long pause.

"HB, I think that we must all have the same question. He says that you, I think the word was 'agreed', that we should consider linking up. Did you and were you aware that 'linking up' is a euphemism for a full-blooded takeover because they're so much bigger than us?" Alex nodded his support. Nobody noted that Dick had asked not one question but two. It was to be that kind of meeting.

Unfortunately, the call had virtually coincided with HB's return from the pub and he was feeling rather fragile. He had a vague recollection of Chuck saying something about unions and alliances but sadly, try as hard as he could, he recalled little of what had been said. How could he admit this?

"Frankly, I think that Chuck is exaggerating and that all that we agreed was that the industry faced a difficult future. I did agree to meet him in London, the next time he comes, because he's a leading member of our industry and it would be interesting to hear his views on what might happen over the next few years."

Sir Willerby Wistleton-Nugget, who had recently been given some massive share options, felt the need to speak. It mattered little that what he had to say was obvious: it was unreasonable to expect too much from such a rich buffoon. "I think", he said, which, in itself, was of interest, "that we have to decide what we want for the company, what is best for the company, I don't just mean, us, around this table, I mean the company, not us, and then decide how we do it". Flushed with the effort of such cerebral activity, he sat back.

Nigel Read offered an opinion. "HB, I think that what was said or not said is almost irrelevant." Hubert sighed with relief. He had always liked Nigel.

"What we know is that Charles has a large cash mountain, after absorbing, no, let's call a spade a spade, buying smaller companies and then stripping out unwanted assets and getting rid of hundreds of staff. We must assume that, whatever was or was not said on the phone, he intends to buy us if the price is right. Let's not deceive ourselves. This would not be a merger of equals. We're not equal and any alliance would inevitably be one-sided. We have several choices. We can surrender, fight or find a white knight."

Sir Willerby, most of whose friends were white knights, looked puzzled as Nigel continued.

"We must not assume that he'll just go away. We must also ensure that, whatever happens, our shareholders benefit to the maximum. "

The shareholders present agreed.

Sir Willerby still did not see how he or any of his friends could help but remained silent.

HB, in an unnecessary summary said "we're all totally opposed to succumbing to any early blandishments?" Heads were nodded in assent.

Shirley Church then joined the debate and her colleagues turned to listen intently to her because she was widely respected and had considerable clout with influential outsiders. "Mr chairman. At this stage, we have no confirmation of whether Muswell Petroleum are interested in us or not. We must assume, as Nigel says, that they are. We should also try to work out why they might want to buy us, as there's no overwhelmingly obvious reason, apart from the opportunity to make significant but one-off reductions in costs. I should be interested to hear my colleagues' views on this. Clearly, we must prepare for the worst, a hostile bid and all that that implies. However, we must not lose sight of our main objective." Here she paused to pour some hotel water into the hotel glass before resuming.

"Our main objective, as in our day-to-day work, as we have already agreed, is to do the utmost for our shareholders. If, one day, and I certainly hope that it does not happen, the best that we can offer is to sell to MP, that's what we must do. But we really must work out our overall strategy. What are our weaknesses, what are our strengths? If it comes to a fight, how do we conduct our campaign? What are the relative strengths and weaknesses of our opponents? What is it that we have that they want, beyond, as I just said, the opportunity of cutting costs to impress the easily-impressed financial institutions, albeit briefly?"

Her colleagues, who were mostly big shareholders, agreed but what should come uppermost in their minds, jobs or shares? Henry's main worry was his job, but what about Lance Boyle and even HB who was close to retirement and who might welcome a large golden handshake and a rise in the value of his shares?

In the main lounge, the man with the notebook, a handsome young fellow with one of those faces that seem destined to be famous one day, engaged the pretty young waitress in conversation. "I feel sorry for those guys in there, don't you, cooped up in their suits discussing some boring piece of work. She smiled. "I'm not sure about that, it seemed to me that they were discussing either a takeover or having a bid from an American company."

"Well, well. Are you sure?"

"Yes, I'm just finishing my business degree course and I'm working here at weekends to give me some more cash. As it happens my tutor is an old oil man, so I've become interested in the industry and I recall the name, Muswell Petroleum, because I used to live in Muswell Hill, in North London." Realising that she had said too much, she immediately offered him another coffee. He made no further reference to what she had said and merely remarked that it was now possible to see the distant hills more clearly so perhaps the afternoon could be fine after all. Relieved, she agreed. No damage had been done by her indiscretion.

"Well, what do we want to do and how do we do it?" Hubert Bennett wanted something more specific.

Henry felt that he ought to speak. "Is there anything more that you can tell us HB, er, Horace, er Hubert, that would help?"

What HB had forgotten was that Chuck had said "as we all know, companies must continue to cut costs and that many of us, like you and me, Horace, have done all we can internally, so now we, that's you and me, have to think about mergers, alliances and other ways to reduce costs." A fuzzy HB recalled little of what had been said, let alone agreed. What he did realise was that a sale of Broadoak could make him rich. Only last evening, Mrs HB had said that they could not afford to buy a pub for his retirement and, as she memorably concluded, "that's that". Clearly, none of this could be revealed and he must appear to oppose the takeover with all his might.

"I wish I could help but I've told you all that I can."

Henry recommended that the group should follow up Shirley's suggestion and then conjured up a few ideas as he rambled on. "I think that we should work out how we can make our company more appealing to the City. I don't want to trespass here, Pat and Shirley, but I suspect that we're perceived as a rather old-fashioned company, whilst MP is seen as progressive."

Shirley and Pat both nodded.

"We've always relied on organic growth and, now that's dried up, maybe it's time to consider a few carefully-chosen acquisitions ourselves, to strengthen our position in those parts of the business where we've already got an advantage? Perhaps we should sell some parts of the group that are under-performing but which could be of more value to other companies?"

Henry, aware that he was coming close to discussing others' areas of responsibilities continued. His new job and way of life were under threat. He could not go down without a fight. "Maybe they want us because we've built up a useful position in the UK and European gasoline market. That's petrol", he added for the benefit of Sir Willerby, "whereas they've been involved mainly in exploration and production and, of course, most of their oil comes from the Middle East, Russia and Venezuela, all potentially volatile. Unlike us, they're not involved in the North Sea.

"Perhaps we should consider buying an industrial fuels marketing company here in the UK, so we can optimise our depots. We've got to secure more economies of scale but we don't want to attract other potential predators. Maybe they want us for our upstream activities, especially in the North Sea and Ireland, and, incidentally, I see that some trade journals are already speculating that we might be sitting on a major oil find there, and our enhanced recovery technical knowledge." Here he broke off to explain to Sir Willerby, who had been on the board for only five years, that upstream meant exploration and production and that downstream meant refining and marketing.

"Could we form a few cost-saving alliances in the North Sea, not fully-blown mergers, that would allow us and the other party, to save on costs? Both companies could operate more efficiently. Above all we need to make MP either pay a very significant sum for us or we must remain independent."

Wally endorsed what had been said and emphasised that they must not be fooled by any soft approach. "Whatever their rhetoric, they will probably want to buy us out and we know their policy of stripping the companies bare and chucking people on to the scrap heap."

HB wanted to resume so he did.

"MP have always boasted that they recognise the reality of the respective values of the companies. Their style is to propose a cash payment and an exchange of shares which usually incorporates a premium of about 10 per cent on the share values of the victim company just before the offer was made. I don't think that such a premium would be acceptable to us."

Alex chimed in. "Perhaps I could just remind you all that detailed and objective academic analysis of all kinds of mergers, in different industries, shows that more than half fail."

Hubert looked at his watch. He knew that curried turkey, a favourite of his, was on the lunch menu and he fully understood Nigel's reason for leaving his last employer who had carelessly removed curry from the staff restaurant's menu. HB wondered whether the list of desserts today included his much-favoured rum and raisin ice cream. He must remind Mrs Bennett to buy some on her next outing to the supermarket. "Outing". That was an odd word. Why was it used to describe somebody admitting to being homosexual, as well as a visit to the shops?

Perhaps he ought to say something: nobody was talking and everybody was looking at him. It was time to lead. Putting his hands together, so that they formed a triangle, he placed the apex of the triangle under his nose, breathed heavily, partly because he had inadvertently blocked his nasal passages, and tried to imply that he was concentrating. He stared at an innocent spot on the wall opposite him and delivered himself of a comment that distinguishes such executives from ordinary people.

"What do we all think about what we've heard so far?"

All agreed with everything.

HB resumed. "Frankly, it might be in our own selfish and personal interests to be the victims of a generous takeover as most of us have very acceptable golden parachutes, and let's be candid, are substantial shareholders." Judging by the happy smiles around the table, many had apparently forgotten their compensation clauses if the company were taken over. Henry was neither a shareholder nor a parachute owner.

"We must forget that. Our only objective must be to secure the best for our shareholders. If their best interests are served by the sale of the company, because that's what it would be, then we must work towards that end by ensuring that our company, their company, I mean the company, attracts the highest possible price. Alternatively, if we genuinely believe that we can achieve more by remaining independent, we must work to that end by increasing our value.

"I suggest that, taking up your valuable suggestions, that, for the remainder of this weekend and we're not leaving until after an early lunch tomorrow, we form into two sub-committees. One should candidly consider our strengths and weaknesses and make recommendations on any disposals or acquisitions that we could make in the short term. The other should come up with a list of cost-cutting measures that we should be considering, irrespective of any formal bid that may or may not come, and our strategy if one develops, which must also take into account the weaknesses of the opposition. As you know, ladies and gentlemen, we have on retainer some very expensive, I mean experienced, corporate experts and, in anticipation of your agreement, which I trust I have", murmurs implied assent, "I asked them to meet us for lunch and then I'll brief them immediately after that before joining us in these committees. Naturally, I wanted to have this confidential meeting before we divided into groups and met our friends. In the last few minutes Lance has been working out who should be in which team. Have you finished?" Lance nodded.

"Now for lunch, which I gather is being served next door in the Attlee Meeting room. We'll convene again as a formal group next Friday but we can meet earlier than that if necessary and in any case, we'll have an informal session over dinner tonight. This work must be given top priority. Finally, and I know that I don't have to say this, what we're discussing must remain absolutely secret. I don't want to read about this in the papers. Tell nobody. Much depends on our ability to keep this highly confidential. Now let's eat."

HB shuffled a few papers together, stood up, stretched and wondered how he could ensure that a generous takeover bid was received so that he could buy that pub. As Henry moved to the door, HB beckoned to him. "I've been thinking Henry. We need someone in the US, to see if our colonial cousins can help to get the best possible offer for the company, I mean to see how they could help to defend our group. Why don't you go over there for a few days, see what they think, feel the temperature of the water, so to speak and see how MP is perceived there?"

A surprised Henry, flattered that he should be entrusted with such an important task, immediately agreed but reminded his chief executive that he had already been booked to attend another major international conference in Houston. Indeed, he was due to fly out the following Friday for a few days, so he would miss the next formal meeting of the group.

HB, who really had dreamt this up all by himself, said that was fine but there was one condition. Perkins had heard it before. "Henry, you must not, under any circumstances, make any speeches and whatever happens, don't talk to the media." HB could not afford to have Henry, a loose cannon, in the UK at such a crucial time and, providing he behaved himself in the US, HB felt safe.

Chapter 19

The following Friday saw much activity at Perkins Place. Henry's executive car had taken him to the airport en route for Houston and Denis Wiltshire had arrived about an hour later to pick up Jill, an unfortunate phrase perhaps, to take her to the weekend conference. The born-again neighbours' curtains had twitched when Henry left in a limousine and they twitched afresh when Denis arrived in his bright red BMW convertible. Jill stared at the car, sparkling in the unpredicted sunshine, and wondered why she and Henry had so little to show for years of work. They never had expensive holidays and their house had been bought with the assistance of a relative's endowment. She decided that they should save less in future, provided, of course, Henry kept his job. There had to be a change: life was passing them by.

Denis pretended to heave her weekend case into the boot, observing that it was so heavy that Henry must be in it. After about an hour, they drew up at an old worlde pub at Willow Ferrers, in the heart of the country, some 70 miles from their destination of Milton Snodgrass. Jill chose a table in a small alcove created by two rich blue hydrangeas whilst Denis ordered coffee. The sun was illuminating the nearby hills and the fields in the foreground were deep green, as if freshly painted. Cars in the distance, chugging up narrow and dusty lanes, twinkled as they reflected the sun's rays. Houses, perched on severe gradients and seemingly successfully challenging gravity, oozed serenity. Apart from the occasional twittering of an apparently contented bird and the gurgling stream flowing past the pub, this was serenity. Jill felt mildly guilty that Henry was not there to share it with her but he would soon be relaxing besides a pool at a luxurious hotel.

She and Denis chatted amiably about nothing and everything, except work, and discovered that they had much in common. For example, both enjoyed films but Jill said that most of her information now came from newspaper reviews. She was seldom "allowed", as she put it, to visit the cinema, as Henry was not interested. Immediately, she regretted saying this. It was wrong to even imply any criticism of Henry. Denis noted the remark but said nothing. He was treating

Jill with more courtesy than she had experienced since before her marriage. He was handsome, she had to admit, and the cockiness that had antagonised her and her colleagues had gone. By her standards, even his clothes were more sensible. Today, for example, he was wearing clean brown shoes, light brown trousers and a pale cream shirt. His hair was no longer plastered down in a way that had justified his nickname of Slimy Denis. His conversation contained no puerile and sexist quips. In short, he seemed the perfect (and single) gentleman. Nevertheless, she must not let her guard down.

Had she misjudged him or was he a reformed character? It didn't really matter.

For the first time for decades, she was going away for a weekend with a single man. Even thinking this aroused her yet she felt guilty although it was, and would remain, totally innocent. "Why don't we take the country route to Milton Snodgrass? It's such a fine day and we've plenty of time. We don't have to be there before 4.00 so we might as well enjoy it." Denis agreed and although Jill thought that she had chosen the country route, it seemed that Denis had planned it in advance. He suggested that they had lunch at a fine rural pub at Hayes Snogwart.

The gardens around the old thatched building were spectacular and a rockery and waterfall could have won a prize at the Chelsea Flower Show. The two chose a table which Denis guarded whilst Jill "freshened up". He now knew that she was a deeper person than she seemed in the office. He was definitely attracted to her, not just physically, as he realised some months ago, but mentally. They laughed at the same jokes and had some common interests. He was not really sure but he sensed that she and Henry, whom he had met only once, were not entirely at one. It seemed odd.

Jill, engaged in the euphemistic rite of freshening up, was thinking about her permanent partner. Although she would never, never, admit it, Henry did not excite her and had not for many years. He was solid and seldom wasted money but even his ability to make reasonable jokes occasionally was being slowly submerged by his job which was turning him into a tired workaholic. Henry treated her more like a sister and, as she made herself look more attractive, merely by renewing her lipstick, she reflected that their physical relationship was virtually non-existent. That was bad enough, but she had no idea of why it had apparently ended so many years ago, and, sadly, it was never discussed. Now sustained abstinence somehow made it seem rude to even raise the subject. She knew that this was absurd and that her life was incomplete but she seemed unable to make the first move.

Denis watched Jill as she returned. She was wearing a cream-coloured silk blouse and beige trousers which flattered her figure, so often disguised by her choice of office clothes. A white cardigan was hanging limply around her shoulders. Henry was a lucky man even if he didn't know it.

They ordered lunch and talked about this and that but definitely not the other. Denis declined wine as he was driving but insisted that Jill imbibed. The food was good and well presented without being excessive.

"Thanks for that, Denis, it was just right. I really enjoyed it." "Good. It was an enjoyable meal and I hope you don't mind if I say that I enjoyed the company, too." Jill smiled, acknowledging the gentle compliment. No, she didn't mind. It didn't happen very often because Henry took her for granted.

Denis had recalled some distant conversation in the office about music and, remarkably, had some of Jill's favourites on CDs. Even with the competitive sounds of the open lane and, later, the open road, the effects of the wine, the sun, still beating down, and the music elevated Jill to levels of innocent but rarely-experienced pleasure.

The conference was being held in an old but well-modernised country house. Denis held the car door open for Jill and carried her case and brief case to the reception area before returning for his. Jill, accustomed to looking after herself, unthinkingly opened negotiations with the elderly male receptionist. "I'm sorry, but I have no record of either of you and there is certainly no reservation for you." Denis returned at the crucial moment and produced a fax from his trouser pocket. The old man stared at it, as if seeking some hidden message and, after detailed scrutiny, announced "that doesn't help. It's from you to the conference organisers and what I need is something from them to me booking a room for you." Denis and Jill both noticed that it had been assumed that irrespective of the names on the fax, they would be sharing a room.

Over the next few minutes, a determined but diplomatic Denis discovered that the confusion had been created by an incompetent temp working for the conference organisers but all was eventually resolved satisfactorily. Jill was most impressed with how Denis had handled an annoying situation. She had also noted that he had insisted on separate rooms. Although reluctant to admit it, Mrs Perkins was gradually feeling drawn to him but she was married and was therefore disqualified from having such emotions.

The Friday night dinner was most enjoyable. The food and wine were excellent, Jill had met some friends whom she hadn't seen for years and Denis was the ideal companion. After dinner, he suggested a nightcap on the moonlit patio and she readily acquiesced. Although articulate, Jill could not explain adequately how she felt in under several thousand words. She was sober but had consumed sufficient alcohol to loosen inhibitions just a little. For her, even a little was so unusual it was intoxicating. The real world had been expelled and she was in a novel region that was exciting but safe. She knew that nothing serious was going to happen, was it, how could it, and this gave her the confidence to enjoy herself. Feelings buried decades ago, seemingly permanently, had re-surfaced. She had forgotten that exquisite sense of youthful desire, pleasure and pain, aroused by maturing sexuality. Now, as nothing significant could happen, there could be only pleasure. Diminished by an early marriage and later crushed by apparent indifference, the sensation of sexually-based pleasure now, so many years on, was very powerful. She was so grateful to Denis, still behaving irritatingly impeccably, for reminding her of emotions long gone. It was worth the sense of immediate frustration to recall those feelings that belonged to a time when the world was almost innocent and males competed for her attention.

At 1.00 in the morning Denis said that he ought to go to bed. Jill, busily chatting to an old friend, didn't hear this and only realised his intentions when he took her hand and said "thank you for a very enjoyable day, Jill. I hope you have a good night. I'll see you at breakfast at about 8.00 o'clock?" Jill nodded. Denis leaned forward, still holding her hand gently and kissed her, equally softly, on the cheek. With that he was gone and Jill felt strangely annoyed. He hadn't even tried to make a pass yet she knew that he was attracted to her and there was a part of her that wanted some physical attention.

In Houston, on the Friday evening, local time, Henry realised that he had mislaid the telephone number of Jill's hotel. At about 10.00 pm, local time, about 04.00 am on Saturday, UK time, he left a message on the voice mail at home, hoping that she would check for any messages. Perhaps Jill might ring him sometime on Saturday.

Henry had told his main contact, Daniel Druff, that he would be in town on the Saturday. However, this was inconvenient for the Texan who apologised that he could not show Henry the sights as he was already booked to watch his son play baseball and then he had to go to the airport to pick up his parents, whom he had not seen for six months. Henry, who quite enjoyed his own company, was not displeased. He had a guidebook, a wallet full of dollars and time.

Mid morning on Saturday, he took a cab from his hotel on the Katy Freeway and headed for the Galleria area, home to the best departmental stores and many smaller but interesting shops in the huge and cool indoor complex. He was fascinated by the range of shops, the architecture, especially the curved glass roof, and carpeted wide corridors between the shops and the cleanliness of the huge complex. Knowing his ability to become lost in his own back garden, he used the ice skating rink as his benchmark.

His watch and stomach suggested that it was time to eat so he sat down at a bar by the rink and ordered a large Coca-Cola. This arrived almost immediately in a bucket carried by a diminutive waitress who was blonde, shapely and wearing blue denim shorts and a white top. Presumably, Coke was so popular that it was then poured from the bucket into individual containers. Henry was wrong. Joy, for that was how she had introduced herself, showed surprising dexterity for one so small but certainly well formed. She hoisted the bucket on to the table, apparently effortlessly, and gave him a pipeline cunningly designed to resemble a straw. She then confirmed that she was ready to help him in any way she could, including returning "presently" to record his food order. He requested a beef sandwich. "It'll be "along real soon, jest as soon as we can get it to you."

It had a nerve to call itself a sandwich. The description was as misleading as calling a double-decker bus a scooter. An adult cow had been compressed between two floors of bread. It was surrounded by a tropical forest and Joy wanted to know what he would like to pour on the forest which she described as a salad. Henry was in Texas. Some 15 minutes later, Henry was convinced that, as he unfolded successive layers of meat, more remained on his plate than Joy had delivered. Following some serious eating, having devoured the bulk of the cow and the coke, apart from half a tonne of ice at the bottom of the bucket, Henry ambled around the shops.

He wanted something for Jill and kept an eye open for anything that he fancied. Henry smiled to himself as a blonde he certainly fancied oozed past. The place was full of them. Henry thought of himself as totally married, whatever the physical state of his union, and thus officially banned from even noticing other females. Still, this was America and there was no harm in just glancing. He spun round as another evocative perfume glided past. This was going to be an innocent but enjoyable week. He was surprising himself and had forgotten that he could soon be unemployed.

Jill liked brooches and pendants so the intrepid Brit entered the first jewellers that he saw. The middle-aged female assistant said "hi there, can I help yawl?"

"Well, that's very decent of you", he intoned but the rest of the sentence was lost in a flurry of excitement.

"Wah, jest listen to that accent, ain't it jest great? I jest luvv your accent. Hold on there, I want ma daughter to hear you. Jew mind?"

A bemused Henry shook his head. A fat teenage girl, dark, plain and sullen, thus disproving Henry's new theory that all young female Texans were blonde, beautiful and happy, entered the shop from the rear.

"Talk some more, ok?" Henry wanted to oblige but couldn't think of anything profound so merely just said that this was his second visit to Texas but the first time that he had been able to visit the shops for something for his wife.

232

"There, ain't that just too suede for wards?", asked the mother who then addressed her daughter triumphantly, as if she had just advanced her offspring's education by several years. "I thawed you'd want to hear this. Where do you think this gennleman comes from?"

It was clear that the daughter was as indifferent as she was ignorant. "Australia", she answered aggressively. Henry was not sure if he should participate in this game, but as the only really accurate accent he could manage, this seemed a good opportunity to impress. "No", he whined in passable Aussie, "they speak more like this".

The mother saw renewed educational opportunities for her daughter if this quaint Englishman would offer a few more unusual accents. She invited her daughter to have another attempt.

"Italy?" she offered. Henry obliged afresh.

The next choice, suggested with declining conviction, was "Patagonia, I mean Germany?" Henry knew nothing about Patagonia so was pleased to hear the European alternative. He attempted a very English version of a Teuton before indicating that she was now on the right continent but should move north. In the next few minutes, Henry tried out his Irish, Scottish and Welsh accents although the last owed more to Bombay than Cardiff, before England was correctly identified. The mother, clearly, enjoyed the show and thanked Henry and, as he left, having forgotten why he went in, said "now yawl have a good time, jew hear?"

The adjoining emporium was an up-market shoe shop. A purple-haired woman and a person of the same gender, but whose hair was dark mauve, were staring at some shoes in the window. Purple spoke to mauve. "Don't you jest luvv those shoes? I've never seen them in person before but I've just got to have them." Henry, never formally acquainted with his shoes, belatedly muttered an introduction to them and apologised for not having spoken before.

The next shop sold model cars, trucks, trains and planes. Henry, steadily buying back his youth, had a collection of some 400 vehicles, entered. "How are yawl today?" Henry assured the man behind the counter that he was very well, thank you, although he was forced to admit, that having flown the Atlantic yesterday, his body was not too sure what time it was and he intended to have an early night. Henry belatedly realised that this was not quite the answer that was expected, smiled and showed considerable interest in a petrol tanker of the thirties.

Henry then paused at a shop which sold adult gadgets with which he was unfamiliar. He had never experienced a desire to own a musical toothbrush or even one that doubled as a penknife. The predominant device in the window, extensively publicised, apparently removed unwanted hair from nostrils. This seemed a popular product and Henry wondered if there was some strange virus that promoted excessive growth of nasal hair in the US. If it spread, could it snuff out democracy?

Mr Perkins found a bracelet for Jill and then drifted into a computer shop. Children, scarcely able to reach the keyboards, were apparently landing jumbo jets safely. Henry's first effort resulted in very realistic emergency service sounds being blasted around the shop, causing knowing adults to smile and children to sneer. His second attempt, probably misguided in the circumstances, resulted in the screen becoming blank. When a message flashed up, indicating that he had "performed an illegal operation" he left the shop as fast as he could without drawing attention to his retreat. Too many Americans were lawyers.

He took a cab back to the hotel, showered, changed into some lighter clothes and sat by the pool. Two families were splashing around and the children were screaming, as children usually do when confronted by water in bulk. What would it have been like to have had children? Even now, the pain was considerable and when a small boy offered him one of his biscuits, Henry, with no other emotional outlets, felt the tears welling up. Why couldn't he have had children? What had he done that the gods had decreed that he was to be denied what he had wanted most from life? If he still felt like this, what about Jill? He rationalised this, as usual, by thinking of some of the young horrors they knew but this was not an honest answer.

After, a modest meal, he had another shower and went to bed early, hoping to be entertained by the large television set parked in a corner of his room. A news bulletin was "coming right up".

According to the anchorman, Hank Hanks, an earthquake in the Far East had killed several thousand people, an important political leader in the Middle East had been assassinated and there was more evidence of global warming as two islands had vanished in the Pacific. "We'll have more details of those stories later but first here's Chuck Chuckson with something of interest for cat lovers." What followed was an extended piece about a local kitten that, thinking it was a monkey, had climbed up a tree, necessitating rescue by the brave boys of the local fire service. Henry sat spellbound, awaiting the real news. Now it was his turn.

"As we reported earlier, there has been a very severe earthquake in the Far East. Now over to Frank Franks who is in the devastated area now and speaks to us live. Frank, where precisely are you now? We understand that this has been a very severe earthquake?"

"Yes Hank, I'm in the earthquake area now and it has caused much devastation."

"Frank. What can you tell us about the people involved?"

"The reports so far say that thousands may have lost their lives and, clearly, there are many more who are injured."

Astonishingly, that was the end of the piece, because Hank was thanking Frank for his contribution, and lest the message had been too complex to absorb, the former repeated that there had been an earthquake in the Far East and early reports suggested that thousands had been killed. Henry, still ignorant on where the tragedy had occurred and subjected to a straight repeat of the headlines relating to the other more important stories, groaned and tuned in to another station. Some enormous people were being cheered by a moronic audience for having lost so much weight. He turned the set off, extinguished the light and sought sleep even although it was still only 8.00 o'clock on Saturday evening. His body clock was demanding the chance to offset delayed jet lag.

Earlier that Saturday, in the UK, Jill went down to breakfast. Denis, already in the dining room, immediately offered to bring her a coffee from the buffet whilst she decided what to order from the menu or helped herself from the laden tables.

One meal later, Denis remarked that he thought that the morning's presentations had been very constructive. Jill agreed and admitted that she was really enjoying everything about the whole weekend. Denis noticed her slight emphasis on the word "everything". He was feeling ashamed. His original intention had been to seduce Mrs Perkins but, the more time that they spent together, the more reluctant he became to undermine what, hopefully, could become a real and lasting friendship, with a crude physical approach that would be rebuffed anyway and which could cause all kinds of problems.

Jill felt guilty. She had never contemplated being seduced: indeed, she never felt that she was sufficiently sensuous to stimulate such a possibility. Even her husband made no physical overtures. She would have tried to prevent a seduction but now, for the first time in her married life, she could not have guaranteed that she would have resisted Denis. Part of her wanted to hear him say the crucial words: part of her was glad that he had not, but there was still another evening to negotiate. Why had this massive change occurred? She couldn't blame the wine, not now. Nor could she blame the romantic day that she had enjoyed yesterday. It was lunchtime on a Saturday, effectively a working day.

The afternoon session was of a high standard and a formal conference dinner was scheduled for the evening. Denis had reminded her to "bring a posh frock". Jill seldom attended such functions and felt that buying a new dress was an unjustified luxury. Instead, she chose a knee length, four year-old-black dress with a belt that emphasised her figure and added some jewellery. Apart from doing her hair slightly differently, she spent more time than usual making up. The result was stunning: Henry would have had some difficulty in recognising his own wife.

Denis, looking immaculate in a dinner jacket, was overwhelmed but vowed that, despite increasing temptation, fuelled by an absurd idea that she was trying to impress him, he would not succumb. It was difficult. They were sitting opposite each other at the dinner and although both felt obliged to speak to colleagues, somehow each sensed that they really wished they were alone. The wine flowed, inducing a sense of well-being and it gave Jill more confidence. She was no longer Mrs Perkins. Just briefly, she was someone else, perhaps herself when young, who was only vaguely familiar. She leaned across the table to make some comments to Denis in a most alluring way and, taking courage in both feet, made sure that occasionally she caressed his trouser legs with the toe of her high-heeled sandals. Initially, Denis, already captivated by her perfume, could not believe it and assumed that someone had accidentally brushed his leg under the table. When one such move coincided with a radiant smile from Jill, he began to wonder what should be done. About three quarters of him knew but the remaining quarter counselled caution.

The course was to end after lunch on the Sunday and Denis, who lived about 15 miles away from Perkins Villa, had gratefully accepted Jill's invitation to dinner before he went home. That was tomorrow but, dinner and drinks over, Saturday had not yet slipped into history.

Jill and Denis and six other delegates, who either knew each other before the conference, or who had made spectacular progress the previous evening, gathered for drinks on the terrace, which overlooked the hotel's richly-striped lawns and colourful flower beds now illuminated romantically by spotlights. The night was warm, the air was still and apart from the laughter and talk, the only sound was the just audible background music which was playing in the hotel conservatory and on the boat moored at the bottom of the garden. The darkness shut out the real world which, for the second successive night, was exiled for a few hours. One couple went off to dance in the ballroom, adjacent to the conservatory. Jill, who rarely had fun, took Denis's hand and announced "we're going to dance". Denis, keen yet reluctant, allowed himself to be wafted away. Her hand tightened around his, as if she was determined not to lose him.

Later, Denis checked the time. It was about 2.45 on Sunday morning. They had been dancing, talking and drinking, albeit modestly, for some hours. "I expect that you're tired", he suggested and put his left arm around her shoulders in a gesture that was only partly fraternal. Jill nodded and placed her arm around his waist. She felt in some strange way as if she had been reprieved. Condemned to eternal boredom with the same honourable but physically dull man, she had been allowed just the slightest glimpse of another life that she thought had gone for ever. She felt no guilt now and told herself that everyone should be allowed one or two indiscretions every 20 years. It was time for her first.

Freed of her conscience and Henry for the first time for decades, Jill invited Denis into her room for a final drink. It was not really an invitation. She took him by the hand and pulled him in. He could no longer tolerate the pressure and he spun her round with his free arm and hugged her. Even then, he almost believed that he was intending nothing else, although few would have believed him. Jill took the initiative. She kissed him passionately and drew him ever closer. Both were aroused as Jill pulled him on to the bed.

In Houston, a weary, jet-lagged Henry had woken up again after his very early effort to sleep. The defects of the air conditioning system meant that he could choose either noise and a comfortable temperature or silence and heat. A change of tactics in the night would wake him up. Having opted to turn the air conditioning off, Henry dozed but briefly before waking again to find that the inside of his throat had been sand-papered. The room temperature would have permitted an egg to fry on the window sill. Although lacking eggs with which to test this theory, Henry was fairly confident of his prediction. Having turned the air conditioning on, he lay on the bed, drinking a Coca Cola, wondered what Jill was doing and hoped that she was having a good time. He checked the time. It wasn't even 9.00. He picked up the phone and left another message on their home voice mail, saying that apart from being boiled, he was fine and he hoped that she had enjoyed the conference and that Denis had behaved himself. "And if he didn't, I'm sure you knew what to do."

Henry would be a tourist again on the Sunday. Monday would be spent at the major conference and the rest of the week would be passed in the Houston office and around the city, seeing other executives and analysts whom HB had carefully selected. Henry intended to use the time between meetings to think out how he might save his own job and those of so many friends. He didn't know what he could do but he certainly was going to try. He would fly home on the Friday.

The more he thought about the possible takeover, the more angry he became. It was so unfair. He had waited all his life to reach a reasonably senior management position and now, after just a few weeks, it would be snatched from him and, worse still, he would be confronted by unemployment. Life was really cruel. He must think of something to defeat Muswell Petroleum but he knew very little about corporate finance, or, indeed, anything that could derail their bid. It seemed hopeless.

Having made himself totally miserable, and thinking that he might never see Houston again, he decided that on Sunday he would have a huge American breakfast, hire a cab and take in as many sights as he could. He wanted to see Clear Lake, NASA, downtown and the old houses in Sam Houston Park, the George Brown Convention Center and much more. Henry knew that all this would exhaust him but he would have many photographs to show Jill. Jill! Suddenly, he remembered where he had put her telephone number. Pleased by his discovery, he dialled immediately, without thinking about the time difference.

A sleepy Jill answered the phone, pushing a still fully-clothed Denis out of the way.

"It's me, Henry. How are you, has the conference gone well? How has Denis the menace behaved?"

"Hello, Henry, don't you know what time it is here?"

Genuinely surprised that it was so late in the UK, he apologised but he never knew what the real time was.

The spell was broken. Jill, her short-lived dream over, had been catapulted back into the real world. Denis, close to exploding with frustration, sighed, shrugged, sighed again, grimaced, mouthed that he understood, kissed her again, this time more like a Henry, and said goodnight.

Later that day, he took Jill home and she repeated her invitation to stay for dinner. He thanked her but said that he really ought to be getting back. Subsequently, whenever they met in the office, their relationship was correct and friendly. Denis and Jill, having tasted a magical freedom for a few hours, had been returned to what passed as normal. Jill could only guess what might have happened if Henry had not rung but she sensed that Denis had not accepted final defeat. Perhaps..? Anyway, like a true Perkins, she contented herself with the rationalisation that at least she had been given some unexpected excitement for which she would always be grateful.

Chapter 20

Tim Robertson was an ambitious young journalist on a local newspaper in Coryville in Blackshire in what used to be the industrial north before manufacturing yielded to do-it-yourself stores and supermarkets. He had enjoyed his weekend, a week ago, at the Kingly Trustworthy hotel managed by his brother, Tony, and patronised by Broadoak Oil.

The last few days had been hectic, testing his patience but not his intellectual ability. He had covered a meeting of the local Conservatives, allocating generous space to the thoughts of the three members who had attended, the annual general meeting of the bowls club and a village flower show, enlivened by a fracas between the runner up in the main category and a judge. Tim had also written about three road accidents and two thefts from the local church. He had also edited the letters page where the contributions covered the desirability of re-introducing dog licenses to the need to de-criminalise all drugs, thus reducing crime and allowing the police to catch burglars and louts "who terrorise our old folk". Finally, he had reviewed a book written by a local resident, *Pavements in rural communities* and had checked an "advertorial" for local estate agents, in which glib and favourable editorial was accompanied by several advertisements.

About three years ago, Tim had decided to gain experience in the provinces but nothing had happened locally, yet, to justify sending a story to the major broadsheet newspaper for which he was a stringer. How much more of this boring local work should he do, could he tolerate, before moving on? Now he had some spare time and he pondered what he called the Broadoak mystery. Nothing had appeared in the papers so possibly there was nothing to say but he had to find out.

He knew that Broadoak was a regular client but why was the company at the hotel that weekend? Judging by the cars in the car park, these Broadoak people were very senior. Intriguingly, he had also seen some other suited individuals checking in late on Saturday morning before joining the executives for lunch. For no particular reason, he had checked the register and noted the names and addresses of the newcomers. They all worked for companies with long names, some of which Tim recognised as firms of corporate accountants and lawyers. Nobody had provided a home address. Then there was the brief conversation that he had had with Louise, the waitress, and her claim that they were discussing a takeover and she had mentioned Muswell Petroleum. It was time to make some discreet calls.

On her return to the office on the Monday, after the weekend away, Jill's colleagues had besieged her with questions. "Did Denis behave himself?"

"Depends what you mean by behave" Jill countered, immediately regretting that she had strayed from her carefully crafted script, devised on the journey to work. They persisted but Jill returned to her planned comments. "Denis was a good companion and we both enjoyed the conference, which was really interesting. Let me tell you about one interesting comment we heard..." Henry had phoned and all was going well. Apparently, the weather was very hot and humid and he was having difficulty sleeping and working out UK time, because he had phoned her at about 3.30 in the morning.

"Were you awake then?" asked one percipient colleague.

Jill ignored this and said that Henry had wanted to hear about the conference. She parried more questions, feeling increasingly miserable, as what had, or had not, happened was not a subject for discussion in the office. "Denis behaved just as I would have wished." Nobody asked what Jill had wished. The rest of her week proved uneventful.

One week on from the weekend sojourn in the country, Hubert Bennett was so worried that he had abandoned his usual lunch routine, opting instead for sandwiches and, astonishingly, orange juice. The expensive consultants had not been in contact, nothing more had come from Chuck and informal office meetings, to discuss strategy and tactics, had revealed little new thinking. Surely, Chuck had been serious? Broadoak had not taken advantage of the delay. Still, there had been no press comment on the possible merger. The company must seek the best future for its shareholders but what was best and how could it be secured? Should it fight on, as a small independent company, surrounded by giants enjoying economies of scale or should

Broadoak, after securing a high price, sink gracefully into the arms of the American predator?

In the afternoon session at the hotel, Hubert had sensed that the consultants were more concerned with increasing their time spent, and thus their bills, than formulating a solid response to any bid. They also talked in jargon such as the Pacman defence which HB had believed was how to silence the presenter of the *Newsnight* television programme. It seemed that the main creative thinking to fight the bid, or, as he liked to think, increase share prices, would have to come from within the company. Feeling depressed, he added a little something to his afternoon tea.

Clearly, the first bid must be rejected because it was the first bid. Having some shares himself, he knew how shareholders would react to an initial offer. The prime objective had to be seen as trying to save the company but the real objective had to be to increase the Broadoak share price so that Hubert could buy his pub. If Muswell did bid sensibly, HB was confident that his board would not be able to justify Broadoak's continued independence unless the offshore Ireland well yielded oil or gas. Fortunately, drilling would not be concluded in the near future.

What really mattered now was the view of the inexperienced financial analysts who were interested only in short-term return on capital employed. However, the industry was characterised by high risks and a long lead-time for new capital-intensive projects. So the only way to appease the red-braced and ignorant brigade was to hope that crude oil prices soared whilst companies curbed investment. This increased the rate of return on capital so share prices moved up, thus giving directors bonuses and higher value shares simultaneously. The future would have to look after itself and, of course, by then, the current managers and financial analysts would be long gone.

HB knew that there was little real scope for further cost-cutting or informal alliances without inflicting serious damage on the company. Unfortunately, little of Broadoak's crude oil production was in the prolific and low-cost Middle East: the bulk of its output was scattered around the world although the company had retained some holdings in mature but expensive fields in the UK North Sea.

HB enjoyed being chief executive and the life that went with it so what were the options? If Broadoak challenged the takeover and it proceeded, he would be dismissed immediately. Equally, even if he supported the proposal, as he was now a certain age, there would be no place for him on the new board. He was lucky still to be in employment. The industry had convinced itself that, even in their fifties, most peoples' experience was increasingly irrelevant and that their elderly brains could no longer learn new skills. Then, smiling broadly, he recalled that, last year, he had astutely agreed with his senior colleagues that they should be provided with golden parachutes. Like all leading executives, they also held many shares each and thousands of options. The compensation for loss of a job, after a takeover, and the higher price of the shares, was more appealing than being chief executive of Broadoak for another two years.

It was clear: he would be much better off financially if the company were sold for a good price. The chief executive rolled up his knitted tie, as in the old Laurel and Hardy films, smiled and stroked his modest moustache. He had decided. At some point, he would recommend the sale of the group. He wanted the bid to succeed and would do what he reasonably could to achieve that result. Typically, however, he gave no thought to the hundreds of junior personnel who would receive little compensation and who might never work again.

Hubert, pleased with the results of his deliberations, retired to The Thirsty (F)ox to meet some friends for an early evening drink and to debate important issues such as the need for additional controls on immigration and whether ballroom dancing was about to stage a comeback on television.

Lance Boyle had not slept well since the Kingly Trustworthy meeting. He had to be seen defending his employers and playing a leading role in fending off any bid from Muswell Petroleum but, unlike many of his colleagues, Lance was relatively young and ambitious. Even replacing HB when he retired, which was virtually certain as he was, meaninglessly, called managing director, fell substantially below his objectives. Certainly, he was interested in boosting his savings but he was equally keen to have a big job. He did not want to be unemployed at such a difficult time in the industry.

One of his friends happened to be the managing director of Muswell Petroleum in London. Coincidentally, both lived in the same part of Surrex and had the occasional pie and pint, just to be sociable. Lance checked his diary for the second half of the week and picked up his phone.

Henry, having woken early, felt refreshed as he descended 15 floors to the restaurant. He had not intended to eat much because he still felt full after a solo blow-out the night before but the spectacle of the buffet and of others devouring huge piles of hash browns and assorted eggs proved predictably irresistible. He would stint himself over lunch and work up an appetite for the evening by walking around the exhibition linked to the conference. As he waited in the humid heat for his cab, to take him to the convention centre, he worried about the threatened take-over. How could he help maintain Broadoak's independence and hundreds of jobs, not least his own?

At the George Brown Congress Center Henry paid the driver, asked for a receipt, was given three blank yellow ones, and entered the cold building, wondering where he would find the executives' meeting room, where he was to join his local colleagues. It was still only 8.15 and few of the predicted 10,000 delegates had arrived. Indeed, the Houston police, present in force because the US president was booked to open proceedings, outnumbered the intending participants. Henry always arrived early at all functions and for trains and planes, anticipating problems that others could not even conceive.

The police were glancing at all those who were seeking admission. A large notice indicated that those carrying any "sticks or poles that can be used in a threatening or injurious manner", would be denied access. So far, so good, thought a bemused Perkins, astutely unencumbered by either a stick or pole, as he headed for the ground floor reception area. He had received mailed confirmation of his status as a transatlantic invited senior executive (TISE) and, according to the reception clerk, his badge awaited him in the executives' meeting room on the first floor. Henry, heading off in the correct direction, did notice that other participants were already wearing badges. Feeling almost naked and certainly vulnerable, he put a tentative foot on the escalator. It was as if his foot triggered a reaction from a fully-armed Houston policeman, who sought to arrest his progress.

"Excuse me, sir, where do you think you're going, without a badge? Come down immediately."

Unfortunately, the swiftly-moving escalator had already taken the hapless Perkins up to about a fifth of the distance between the ground and first floors. His comment that his badge was on the first floor failed to reach the official and Henry sensed that a promise to come back, immediately, but on the down escalator, would be unacceptable. It would have delayed his return and, for a few seconds, he would have been increasing the distance between himself and the policeman, which seemed unwise. Henry's instant analysis, as he continued to rise, also had to acknowledge the policeman's emphasis on the word "immediately" thus effectively eliminating the desirability of further ascent before embarking on the down escalator.

Henry would have to walk down the up escalator whilst informing the official that he had been told that his badge would be on the first floor. By talking and walking in the wrong direction, he showed himself to be manifestly superior to the former President Chevrolet, who could not walk, even on flat ground, and chew gum simultaneously. More correctly-badged individuals were now heading for the first floor, so Henry's descent was difficult. One man told his female companion that "you always get one like that, and at his age!"

Back where he started, Henry explained his dilemma afresh. The policeman had been told that, under no circumstances, must he allow anyone without a badge to go to the first floor. It was simple, he explained patiently to an impatient Perkins, "you have no badge, so I cannot let you go up. I was also told that badges must be collected personally, by the person involved, in person, not by any other person, before they step on to the escalator, so that's that, sir."

"My badge is upstairs so on the basis of your logic, I can never go to the first floor, which is rather embarrassing, as I happen to be a TISE."

"I don't care who you are sir, or whatever you call yourself, you're not going up there without a badge."

Perkins suggested that he should be escorted to the executives' room and after a short delay, whilst the police discussed the proposal

246

before nominating who could be entrusted with such an onerous task, a more mature-looking officer arrived. They ascended together and their proximity implied that Perkins had been arrested and was assisting the police with their enquiries. This view was reinforced by the fact that the policeman was now carrying his gun in a manner that implied that he thought that Henry could be about to scarper.

The cop seemed genuinely happy when "I'm Laine, I'm here to help you" announced that Perkins was not "in the computer" in the executives' room. That was true: he was standing by a photocopier, angrily waving various accreditation documents and a copy of the programme in which he was clearly billed as a TISE.

"I can see that name in the programme and I can see your documents but unless I can link the face to the name, and that's why we asked everyone to send a photo so we can feed it into the computer, you're not going nowhere." Henry, assaulted by the policeman's double negative and angry at the organisers, was preparing a short speech when Laine confirmed that he was, indeed, "in the computer" but his pass was on the third floor. The policeman bravely concealed his regret as Henry's authenticity was proved and legged it to prepare for the arrival of his president.

Perkins was then joined by a US television cameraman, looking like a mobile Christmas tree as he was wearing most of the equipment he owned. He, too, was seeking his badge that, allegedly, was on the third floor. The policeman had been replaced by an elderly lady, "I'm Esmeralda, I'm here to help you". She would unite them with their badges. Suddenly, the immediate area smelt of smoke which was being emitted by the cameraman. This seemed an exaggerated response to his frustration but one of his lights had inadvertently been switched on and the "fur" around his boom microphone was on fire. What would have happened if the policeman had been escorting them? Henry had visions of headlines such as "Vet UK oilman 'slain' in US presidential security scare". "Speaking from his lawyer's office in downtown Houston, a shocked but unhurt Perkins said that he had been saved by his wallet, which took the main brunt of the bullet. He intended to sue for several trillion dollars and he was confident of an early settlement. Ally McBeal has been retained."

The panic was over. Henry had received his badge, an apology and tickets for the opening ceremony. An official escorted him to his seat and he belatedly greeted his colleagues from the Houston office. The opening ceremony was about to begin. The massive hall was plunged into darkness and spotlights played on to the flower- bedecked stage.

The ceremony combined the worst of an Olympic games opening ceremony and the Eurovision song contest. The opening comment was delivered with such self-important gravitas that Henry hissed to his neighbour that he was relieved to discover that the speaker was not announcing the outbreak of the Third World War. Then two delegates from each of the participating nations, in turn, were introduced by one of their colleagues. "Welcome from the mumble delegation. My name is mumble mumble and I would like to introduce my two fellow delegates who are... We award nine votes for the United Kingdom entry"... Perkins' imagination was straying. One delegate proudly announced that his country was represented by "our honourable minister". The stress on the word "honourable" implied that he was the only minister who could be so described. Knowing the country, Henry agreed.

Each national delegation, including the chief mumbler, marched behind a young child holding up a banner indicating the identity of the nation. Now yawl know that everything in Texas is big and that includes the children, so it was no surprise that many delegations were hidden by the big banner-bearing bairns. As the giant children and the delegations that they had concealed moved away from the presentation area, Henry noticed that the males in the delegations, and females were conspicuous only by their rarity, were sporting red roses. This gesture recognising Lancashire's feats in English cricket showed how keen the organisers were to please as many delegates as possible.

When all the procession personnel had filed off, the speakers welcomed the large audience to Houston. The repetition became tedious, although real ennui set in as each speaker congratulated everyone else for their part in organising what was indisputably the major oil event in the last year, decade and probably in the history of the industry. Henry mused that if there had been, say, just two more speakers, the event would have been described as the most important in the history of man... The enraptured audience, except for Perkins, struggling to keep awake, was told that the planning of the conference had taken six years. Why, therefore, had Henry encountered such difficulties in finding his badge?

Next was a video of Houston seemingly narrated by one of the UK's television chefs. This concept became infectious. A few minutes later, Perkins was convinced that a Japanese dignitary looked just like an England cricketer and later he was certain that an official at his hotel was formerly secretary general of OPEC. Eventually the ceremony ended and Henry thought that some of the children had grown since its beginning.

Before strolling around part of the accompanying exhibition, Henry listened to some of the early presentations with his US colleagues, and was pleased to hear the occasional familiar word. Apparently, crude oil prices, like the security arch at the entrance to the conference, were being "recalibrated".

Henry was thanked by one company for his visitation. Later, his dictionary confirmed that a visitation was an official inspection by a superior, a calamity regarded as a punishment sent by God or a prolonged visit unpleasant to those being visited. He was impressed by some visitors' dedication to public service. Asked how they were, many told Perkins, proudly, that they were doing good.

Perkins headed for one of the luncheon presentations. He and his American colleagues had decided to go their different ways to "maximise our presence, publicity-wise" as one expressed it so eloquently. After an interesting and very filling lunch, an inflated Henry returned to the main conference hall. Delegates were drifting in to the darkened and cool room. When about 1,000 people were present, the chairman asked the first speaker if he was ready. He then blew on the microphone, waking up some delegates who looked up at the black ceiling and doubtless thought that a storm was imminent. The chairman, a US academic, notorious for what she called her imaginative wit and which others described as rudeness and ignorance, was about to introduce Bruce Grove, from a small UK independent company.

"This morning we had a frankly disappointing paper from Will Barrow, whose latest book was, I believe, misguided and misleading. Our second presentation was from Timothy Pott who re-introduced us to concepts that I must admit, I thought were discredited some 30 years ago. Still, it was a pleasant if idiosyncratic approach and our third speaker, Alexandra Pallas, offered us a paper that can be best described as 'memorable', even if for the wrong reasons."

Bruce knew this woman was tactless, unfair and rude but he had no idea just how acidic her comments could be. His short introduction referred to his "experience which has been gained entirely in a small company and which is thus largely irrelevant as the majors dominate this industry. However, I'm sure we all look forward to his presentation". Grove then thanked the academic for his introduction and said that, having listened to her comments on the earlier speakers, he was reminded of George Bernard Shaw's comment that "he who can does. He who cannot teaches". The audience, consisting entirely of oil industry personnel, roared their approval. Although what Bruce delivered was routine, he won a most appreciative reception.

Henry had arranged to meet two of his American colleagues, Richard Richardson and Skip Skipperson at his hotel at 7.00 for drinks, dinner and discussion. Precisely at the right time, a luxurious car drove up, Henry got in and the car glided away to a leading restaurant. After three rounds of enormous cocktails, which the near-teetotal Henry thought were very weak, they adjourned to dinner and it soon became evident that his friends were more interested in eating, drinking and making merry, rather than discussing the future of the group. However, Henry was here for a few days, so, perhaps, it was not crucial to launch into a major discussion tonight, especially in a public place. No, it would be better to get to know his colleagues and then to have a full discussion.

Having had a big breakfast and some lunch, Henry was not hungry. The waiter announced his presence. "Good evening gentlemen. My name is Darren, but please call me Karl. I shall be looking after you tonight. My first pleasure is to welcome you here to the Superior restaurant and to express the hope of the owner, management and indeed yours truly that you will enjoy your evening here and have a great time with us. Tonight we have some specials and it is my pleasure to list them for you."

Henry could not keep pace with this long list which the dutiful Darren/Karl threw out at a speed much favoured by racing commentators. With some difficulty, he resisted the temptation to say "pardon, Darren, could you please repeat that?" as the recital ended. Fortunately, there was a long wait which allowed Henry to develop a modest English appetite but when his main course arrived, he recoiled. He would do his best to eat it, if only to honour the memory of the beast whose life had been apparently snuffed out just for him, but it would be difficult.

The three talked generally about nothing in particular but, in Frickerese, they were bonding. Eventually the meal was concluded and Henry looked forward to some sleep. Perhaps, no definitely, he had seriously under-estimated the power of US drinks. He was exhausted and wanted to have a good night's sleep before a taxing day in the office. Indeed, apart from seeing some other contacts and perhaps another visit to the conference, that would be the pattern for most of the rest of the week. If he was to survive this schedule and, more importantly, to find a way of thwarting MP, he must have more sleep. Consequently, when Skip, with a mischievous grin that Henry missed, suggested that they should have a nightcap, Perkins tried to indicate as tactfully as he could that he was reluctant to participate. Unfortunately, he was so diplomatic and typically British that his views were deemed to be a vote in favour of the motion.

They drew up outside a large square single storey building, the outlines of which were illuminated by pink lights. A flashing neon sign indicated that it was called Hotspot. All this seemed odd to Perkins who failed to detect any similarities with the Hammer and Toothbrush pub near his home. For example, it was odd to have to pay an entrance fee of $8 each merely to have a drink but a very weary Henry reminded himself that this was America and that they were very different people, indeed, so different that they were foreign. Henry's naiveté was almost visible and, of course, this had been detected by his American friends, pleased to have a night out on the company. They had developed a fondness for the unworldly Brit and they intended to have some fun.

The cool entrance hall was only modestly illuminated but the overall opulence suggested that this was not an economy measure. The carpet was so thick that it made the eighth floor office carpet seem almost threadbare and heavy and seductive throbbing music challenged those ill-advisedly bent on conversation. His nose detected an appealing scent which he imagined was something that they put in the air-conditioning system. The dark wooden panelled walls could have graced one of London's most respectable clubs but what Henry saw, even as his eyes were adjusting to the gloom, would have caused mass apoplexy amongst the members and therefore a big reduction in the length of the waiting list. He could not help noticing that their waitress, "hi, I'm Kelly, how are you guys?" was topless. They said that they were just fine and asked her how she was. "Just perfect." From where Perkins was sitting that seemed a very accurate reply.

Henry tried not to stare and to ensure that his expression implied that this was a routine event in his life. He was naïve but he must conceal that from his colleagues whom he guessed had taken him to this expensive club partly to see his reaction and partly to give him a treat. He would react carefully. Like his friends, he ordered a beer from the brunette whose heels were so high that, although she seemed slight and short, she remained above carpet level. She cruised off in the direction of the bar rather like a shapely periscope on a determined submarine.

"What do you think about this then?" Skipp enquired. "Anything like this back home, Henry?" Perkins had no idea but decided against a straight denial in case his new friends had visited any such places, if they existed, in the UK.

"Let's just say that I haven't spent much of my life drinking in such places." He managed to say this without sounding patronising.

Not looking around and not seeming bewildered was difficult. There were hundreds of attractive girls, not over-dressed and progressively moving towards near nudity, prancing provocatively for males near small and individual tables. As he watched, feeling both guilty and excited, one girl sat on her customer's lap and became distinctly friendly, seeking to multiply the points of contact. Then he saw four huge television screens on the walls, showing basketball and baseball matches. Why on earth would men be interested in watching this if they came to a place like this? He decided not to ask. Emerging from his coma, Henry recalled reading about such places in a quality Sunday newspaper. He was in a lap-dancing club.

As he looked around, looking as if he was not looking around, he saw that there was a main stage and two smaller ones, in the corner of the huge room. On each, attractive, topless girls were gyrating, unencumbered by excessive clothes and patrons were putting dollar notes in what remained of their attire. His new friends told him that the purpose of this was not just to offer a token of appreciation but to ask the girl to come over to the table after her stage appearance to perform a personal dance. The girl would also sit and chat with you, his friends told him. Henry suggested that it would cost an arm and a leg and he unwittingly stressed the word leg as one girl on the stage managed to undertake what Henry would have thought was an impossible manoeuvre. "$20 per dance and that lasts about four minutes."

Mr Perkins suddenly realised that he was significantly less sober than he had expected and his condition could reasonably be described as just this side of emotional. Additionally, he had an urgent need to avail himself of what the Americans call a "comfort break". Threading his way carefully past the thrusting, heaving congregation in this chapel of Eros, he found what he still called the gents, did what he had to do and flung cold water over his face in an effort to stimulate a little life.

Whilst he was away, his friends, sensing that he needed a little encouragement to really enjoy himself, called over a particularly sensuous blonde. Dick took the initiative. "Hi there gorgeous. A friend of ours, who's never been in this club before, and is a bit nervous, will come back from the john real soon. He's wearing a dark suit and will be sitting in that chair next to Skipp there."

Skipp waved, thus confirming the necessary geographical details.

"We'd like to buy him three dances with you. Come back real soon but don't let on that we booked you. Will you do that?"

The girl grinned. "Sure, will, it'll be a pleasure. I'll make sure he has a real good time." Dick handed over $60.

Henry returned. He felt excited but guilty even although all he had done was to look. Merely being present was stimulating and reminded him of The Wasted Years. That was painful but he was here now, for the first and last time in his life so perhaps he should enjoy it. The likely loss of his job was forgotten. Henry spun round, reacting to a new perfume, and accidentally stared straight into a spotlight. Blinking and temporarily blinded, but being an astute chap, he realised that the gorgeous scent was now sitting on his lap. His eyes readjusted to reveal one of the most attractive blondes he'd ever seen.

He stared at her.

She squealed. "Uncle Henry!"

Chapter 21

Tim Robertson felt that he was close to a major story. He was convinced that Broadoak had been discussing a link with Muswell Petroleum. A long chat with an industry analyst, who had been happy to exchange comments on the background in return for Tim's information, had been valuable. Some restive US shareholders of MP were putting pressure on the board. They saw other companies merging and securing big cost reductions but their own company, which had built up a cash mountain, partly by not paying a dividend for some years, had done little recently. Its share price was lagging the sector and opportunities to merge and to lower costs were diminishing. Ironically, some Broadoak shareholders felt the same but their concerns had not yet surfaced and at least their dividends had been satisfactory. MP shareholders worried that their company's oil production came mainly from Kuwait, Iraq and Venezuela. Their investment in Russia was a financial disaster and analysts had criticised the company for not taking a stake in some of the more mature fields in the politically safe North Sea. The bigger companies, dogged by high unit costs, were leaving and other smaller companies had secured bargains.

MP had also gambled by taking a significant position in Aipotu, despite US government pressure to withdraw, and the company was perceived as a leading supporter of the military regime. Their involvement was influencing public opinion and some of MP's gasoline sites in the United States, where they were strong, were feeling the effects of a burgeoning boycott. MP had also defied public opinion by taking acreage in other so-called pariah states but even ignoring politics, many months would pass before new discoveries influenced revenue.

Muswell Petroleum had a share of about 2 per cent of the UK petrol market but was successfully pioneering a new type of filling station that offered many other services. Broadoak had about 5 per cent of the market but its sites were old-fashioned and the analyst said that a combination of the two networks could yield substantial cost savings and the opportunity to exploit economies of scale in a flat market. In the exploration and production function, apart from diversifying supply sources for a new combined group, Broadoak's advanced technology, which enabled it to maximise recovery from old fields, would be most appropriate for MP's onshore US fields.

Apparently, it would not be an "earth-shattering" merger but it would create a more successful group. The biggest advantage, attractive to both companies, would be reduced costs, not least on office buildings. Broadoak owned its London office and MP (UK) operated from a prestige building it owned some 20 miles from the capital. Because a European Commission regional division was moving to central London, at least half the MP building was now vacant. The analyst estimated that a successful merger would result in high job losses, especially in the UK.

Tim checked everything meticulously and phoned his national paper contact who spoke to his colleague on the business desk. Yes, he was interested. A few hours later, Tim emailed the story and subsequently heard what he wanted. "We've checked several details, talked to a few knowledgeable contacts and we're happy. We're running it in the paper tomorrow, Wednesday, under your by-line. Meanwhile, many thanks and keep in touch so I can let you know what's happening and we'll talk later in the week about money, if that's ok with you." It was ok with Tim.

In London, Hugh Mungus, the editor of an influential political and business magazine, was lunching at his club with a life-long friend, Sir Montmorency Carlton-Terrace, who was a senior figure at the Foreign Office. Apparently, the FO knew that some members of the United Nations Security Council were planning another effort to cancel all the sanctions imposed on Iraq. The UK and US, implacably opposed to any concessions, were becoming increasingly isolated and convinced that they would soon have to capitulate, thus giving victory to Saddam Hussein. Once before, in an effort to deter "Iraq's friends" on the Security Council, according to Sir Monty, an elderly report on Iraq's ability to construct weapons of mass destruction had been modestly amended and re-released at a crucial time to help defend the "allied" position. Eventually, however, this had caused a few problems.

"Now", he said with studied casualness, "we have genuine reason to believe that Saddam is about to move his troops to the Kuwait border but I doubt if anyone would believe us until they can see his army poised to attack". Hugh looked dumbfounded. "Are you serious, Monty?"

"Yes. I can't give you the physical evidence but you can take my word for it. Saddam's troops will move towards the border within a few days." Perhaps it was the sherry in the trifle or the presence of the attractive waitress but he forgot to mention that this was only a routine exercise that Saddam had planned some time ago.

Hugh's magazine would reach its readers on the Friday, in time for a leisurely read over the weekend. He would contact as many confidential sources as possible then write a draft. On Thursday, unless there was substantial evidence to the contrary, he would finish a carefully worded piece. Monty had never let him down.

In an office in New York, Hamlyn Pye, a new employee of the Petroleum Industry Statistics Service, (PISS), was preparing the statistics on supply, demand and stocks that the group published weekly. This was not an academic exercise: the volatile oil market was significantly influenced by the data and traders anxiously awaited figures on stocks. The Americans called them inventories which always amused Henry who called them inventions. Oil prices frequently moved in anticipation of the likely direction of the data, but, for example, when stock levels moved in an unexpected direction or more dramatically than the market had predicted, prices changed significantly.

Ham was conscientious but knew nothing of this. He was not a statistician and he neither knew nor cared about the oil industry. He just processed data but this was not an occupation that he intended to follow for long. Meanwhile, he was re-living last weekend, which was the best of his short life. He had been away with Jackie, his new girl friend, and this was the first time that he had ever spent an entire night with a girl. He had never been successful with females who were deterred by his shyness. Continuing failures made him more shy and thus even less attractive. Now, the cycle had ended and life was sweet. In his daydreaming, he did not notice that one leading company's data had some figures transposed nor did he note the warning message flashing on to the computer screen. He merely pushed a key, as he had been instructed…

He passed the printouts of the statistics to Martha Goodbody, a colleague who was good with figures, to write a few words to accompany the release of the stats. She only had the aggregate data and, having done this job for three years, was accustomed to the very wide variations in the weekly statistics. Not only did their own figures bounce up and down each week but they often differed significantly from those prepared by her friends in the American Statistical Service, (ASS), even although the definitions were identical. She often wondered why anyone bothered about the figures but millions of dollars changed hands as traders used them to push the market in whatever way they wanted. One week it would be turn of the bulls and the following week the bears would be in control. If only they all knew how the statistics were compiled!

She smiled to herself. Minutes later, she had finished a draft release which was promptly approved by the press department. Martha glanced at it again and authorised its global distribution for the following day. Apparently, crude oil stocks had plunged seriously, by 10 million barrels, in the previous week and gasoline inventories were at their lowest level since 1979. The lazy Martha had not bothered to find out why there had been such declines: like airlines explaining delays, she attributed the fall to technical factors.

Very early on the Tuesday morning, an exhausted Henry was in difficulties. His breathing was irregular and his brain had ceased functioning. His American colleagues, having temporarily abandoned Texas for cloud nine, were now being pampered by two other stunning girls so had not heard Wendy's squeal. Mr Perkins remained silent. The mechanism for devising thoughts and then uttering them, hitherto in good working order, had failed. Wendy, similarly astonished, reacted first.

"We must pretend you're just a customer, otherwise I'll be fired. We can chat with the guys but we're encouraged to sit very close to you otherwise they think that we're not really trying to part you from your dollars, so, if you don't mind, I'll stay on your lap."

Henry tried to speak but nothing happened so his young friend assumed she had his formal approval to remain where she had landed. Actually, management only put pressure on the girls to dance on the stage and to encourage customers to buy expensive drinks but now was not the time for such details. Whether clients bought dances was of no concern to the management but she thought that saying that might help Henry to revive and, besides, she had always liked her "uncle". After what seemed an eternity, Henry croakingly asked what Wendy was doing there, although the answer was fairly obvious. She allowed for his obvious state of shock.

"We can talk later and I'll tell you about my new career. Do you like my outfit?"

The little that she was wearing hardly justified the word "outfit" but it was skilfully distributed to maximise interest. Henry tried to speak but composing a full sentence was still too demanding a task so only laudatory grunts emerged. She was wearing a pleated red mini skirt, split to waist level on each side, a white shirt, open almost all the way, and white thigh-length boots. He gulped, nodded and, making a supreme effort, squeaked approval.

"It's rather hot in here."

On the verge of self-combustion, Henry nodded vigorously.

"I think I'll take something off."

The choice was distinctly limited. "What do you think?"

Henry, totally flummoxed, abstained. It seemed that his vote was not essential.

She wriggled out of her skirt and then the discarded shirt was wrapped around his neck as she squirmed, seductively, affectionately, topless and only wearing a G-string, on his lap. "Anyway" she said, "your friends have already paid me to give you three dances, so you might as well have them otherwise they'll wonder about you."

His vocal chords returned to duty.

"They're American colleagues but I've only known them a short time", he said defensively, as if anxious to pass his guilt to others. Beginning to adjust to his unique situation he attempted what, by recent standards, was a speech of Castro-like length. "I suppose it would look odd if I turned you down." Then, gaining in confidence, he said pompously, "I've always believed that blood runs through my veins and I have every reason to think that I'm a normal, full-blooded male, so, pray proceed".

Wendy smiled as her "uncle" remained covered by her shirt and confusion.

"When my colleagues aren't looking, give me your telephone number as I'd like to take you to dinner tomorrow night, if you're free, and then you can tell me all about your new life."

"I'd certainly like to have dinner with you but I can't as I'll be here again tomorrow night. A girl has to earn something to keep her body and soul together." Henry winced at the mention of the word "body", not least as it was now being slowly wrapped around him like a beautifully scented erotic scarf. The dance had begun. Nobody, as far as he could recall, and he suspected that he would have remembered, had ever knelt on him before and then pushed him back close to the horizontal before stretching out on top of him. Being British, his immediate reaction was concern for his suit. This was not the way that it was usually pressed. He also worried lest he sustained an injury that might be difficult to explain as the sultry Wendy started slithering seductively down his prostrate body. Having commenced with her head some feet above his, her journey of discovery had now taken the blonde bonce close to his. She whispered seductively in his ear "could you possibly make it for lunch?" Henry had forgotten his name, where he was and, above all, why he was having this wonderfully realistic dream, whilst still wearing his suit and, apparently, without having gone to bed. This was more fun than he had ever had, with or without clothes.

He rallied. Aware that he ought to be seen playing this odd game, and because of the loud music, he was forced to go even closer to Wendy's ear to convey his hotel name and telephone number. Wendy hissed in Henry's auricular appendage that she would pick him up at 13.00. During this brief exchange Henry was overcome with guilt. A giggling Wendy had none.

Raising her voice so that the US oilmen could hear, and adopting an amazingly realistic Texan accent, she asked Henry if he came from Australia. The absurdity suddenly appealed to Henry's sense of humour and he asked her a few routine questions as he continued to revive. It was difficult to hear because the music was so loud and Wendy tilted her golden head close to Henry's mouth so that she could hear. Mr Perkins, surprisingly, resisted the temptation to kiss her on her cheek. Such discipline could not be guaranteed on any subsequent occasions.

As the music softened just briefly, Dick chuckled and said, "it looks as if we've done Henry a good turn". The UK executive, suddenly recalling that Wendy was only sitting on him because of their generosity, shouted out his thanks and smiled so broadly that a medical man might have wondered how close he was to splitting his face.

"That first dance didn't count. You'll have to have a proper dance now, you know."

"Proper? What do I do?"

"Just sit there, do nothing and don't touch me, officially, but it's just possible that I might touch you."

Henry, now resembling a blushing and suit-creased statue, had absolutely no intention of touching her, lest he gave offence or committed one. It was too late to ask what "proper" and "officially" meant because Wendy, who had put her skirt on again, had gyrated into action after saying, "of course you must come back again, later today. We're open until two in the morning but try to come early and then we can find somewhere more secluded so we can… ". Her voice faded as she gave up trying to complete with the music. Perhaps it was because the noise became intoxicatingly louder or perhaps it was the mischievous look that Wendy directed at a rejuvenated Henry but he knew that tomorrow evening, or, as he suddenly realised, later today, could be unique. At that moment, even thinking became impossible. The music was affecting Wendy. Now minimally clad again, she had pushed Henry's chair back against an obliging wall, so that he could not stray, and was beginning to move sensuously, swaying seductively and slowly from side to side some three feet from him before gradually moving ever closer until their two bodies were virtually entwined. Henry worried that he might have a heart attack. Her dancing was somewhat removed from the ballroom concept that had blighted his early adult life. Being required to do nothing, he sat back and tried, unsuccessfully, to avoid the impression that he was having the happiest few minutes of his life.

One problem was where to look. Every inch of her brown body merited the closest attention. Perhaps, he thought, as Wendy continued to stimulate him in parts that he did not realise were his, he was going mad. Henry was convinced that everyone was staring at him but the truth was that other males were similarly occupied.

The music faded and Wendy put on her skirt again. The music, sounding the same to Henry, revved up afresh. Presumably, a new dance was about to begin. Perkins, general manager, had rather more on his mind than whether the disc jockey had placed a different record on the turntable. Wendy was becoming yet more physical. She turned her back on him, asked him to unzip her skirt, which he did falteringly. Seemingly defying gravity, it fell only tantalisingly slowly to the floor, before once again revealing the red G-string. Next, she bent double in front of him and then reversed to lie on him as he sat slumped but supported by his friendly wall. Slowly, and almost reluctantly, she slipped sexily to the floor, thoughtfully checking on whether Henry was enjoying himself. He was.

Then the exercise was repeated except that this time Wendy started by facing the hugely embarrassed Henry, caught in a foreign land without his passport. During her descent, she fixed a penetrating and apparently meaningful stare at her "uncle". Henry assumed that this was just part of the act and that all customers were so treated. Wrong. The next artistic movement brought Wendy into a kneeling position, balanced carefully on Henry's knees. She then leaned forward, facing him and allowing her blonde hair to caress his executive face, before taking his hands and holding them to her breasts as she retreated gracefully. Once on the ground, she turned round, with her back to him and bent over, retaining this position for several moments. A few gyrations later, Henry, who had forgotten his own name, returned to this world. Life would never be the same but he was so exhausted that he was feeling ill. He told Wendy that he really had to go.

"I still owe you one more dance. You can have that later today, so you must come back. You will, won't you?"

The new Henry was dumbfounded to hear himself say that he doubted if the Chinese army, suitably trained and equipped with the latest American technology, would be able to keep him away. The pungency of the remark was submerged in its pomposity, but the astute Wendy detected a certain alacrity on the part of uncle Henry. She kissed him gently on the cheek, like an affectionate niece, and whispered that she would see him later that day for lunch. Then, in a louder voice, and waving her shirt as if it were a trophy, said "thanks you guys, see you again I hope".

Henry watched her sway commercially towards a new victim and wondered where his brain had gone. Despite having removed his jacket and tie between dances, he was hot, bothered, dishevelled, excited, ashamed, proud, exhilarated and hugely guilty. He had never experienced so many intensive emotions simultaneously and he feared that he might implode. He had suppressed emotions since his youth but this was different. How could he suppress what he felt now? He had never been so aroused. It was truly sad that he was experiencing such intense feelings for the first time well into his sixth decade. He did not know how to cope and what was astonishing was that some males probably experienced this excitement not once in a lifetime but once a week. What remained of his brain was in conflict with his body. He felt everything: there were too many conflicting emotions to determine the identity of the winner but guilt was probably marginally ahead of excitement.

His inexperience must be kept from his colleagues and it was time to thank them but he had to wait. They were intermingled with a redhead and a brunette, respectively nearly dressed as a cheerleader and chorus girl and, although Henry sensed that it was bad manners to watch, he could not help noticing that his colleagues were taking a manual initiative. Admittedly, they lacked a supporting wall but their hands seemed occupied in rather more than preventing their female chums from falling out of the chairs, the designer of which was to be congratulated for creating such a robust item of furniture. Testing the chairs to withstand these pressures must have been very exciting. Henry heard the redhead instruct Skip to fondle her breasts. He obeyed.

Perkins turned away swiftly, wondering what might happen later that day if he returned. Should he come? It was a stupid question. He knew that he would be back. His colleagues disentangled themselves from the girls as the music ended and the DJ invited the audience to put their hands together to thank "these gorgeous gals here at the Hotspot".

Henry told his new friends that he had really enjoyed himself and he wanted them to know how grateful he was, not just for the dances but for bringing him to this place. He had intended to say what he thought about "this place" but could find no appropriate words so merely puffed his cheeks out before allowing his mouth to hang open. He looked quite ridiculous, of course, but his friends appreciated his silent eloquence. Most visiting Brits, obviously all sex-starved, had the same reaction. Henry thanked his friends again, for a most unusual and entertaining evening, and said that he would see them in the office some time in the morning to discuss the possible takeover. He was lunching with a friend but would continue the brainstorming session in the afternoon.

They all headed for the exit and, having established that a cab was readily available for Henry, his benefactors walked to their cars. Henry fell into his cab enthusiastically. It was now 1.35 am and he had never been so happy with the causes of his fatigue. After a quick shower, he fell on his bed, still reeling from an experience that might well have been commonplace for many males but which had been unique for poor Henry. It was not just the sheer erotic if ephemeral pleasure: it would be the treasured memory that he could take with him into old age, if he survived another evening in the club. The dances were being replayed in his head and he doubted if he would ever be able to concentrate on anything else ever again. Although his mind was whirring round, like a toy windmill propelled by an energetic child, sleep gradually claimed the born-again adolescent.

When he woke, at 7.30 am, it was difficult to recall during the first few nanoseconds of consciousness whether he was emerging from a dream or whether he had actually been to the club. He had always liked Wendy but never, ever, could he have contemplated meeting her in such circumstances. She had been very tactful and had judged the dances accurately. Anything more erotic or physical, and Henry had seen some other girls behaving more physically, could have been embarrassing, especially in front of his colleagues.

Naturally, Henry and Wendy had agreed that news of their meeting must never leak out. Although it had been innocent, well, fairly innocent, the implications could easily have been exaggerated and misunderstood. Some people could twist anything.

He spent the bulk of the morning with his colleagues and became increasingly disappointed at their lack of ideas on how to defeat any bid from Muswell Petroleum. They said that the group's statements should be positive, highlighting the advantages of staying independent and that information from MP should be examined closely and then strongly condemned. All this was obvious. Perhaps more positively, Broadoak should sell any peripheral businesses, or non-core activities, as they put it, and reinvest in projects where they had a comparative advantage. Henry remained acutely worried. Unless something big happened soon, his career would be over, just as the frustration of years in a boring job was being eradicated.

At 12.15, after two disappointing hours, he left the air-conditioned office and emerged into a typically humid Houston. His cab arrived promptly and Henry had a quick wash in his hotel and drifted down to the reception area to await Wendy's arrival. He did not have long to wait. Wendy saw Henry in the reception area, bounded up to him, embraced him warmly and greeted him in her Texas accent. "What's up Perky?" Henry, pleased and embarrassed to be so greeted in public, muttered, sincerely, how good it was to see her again.

She was wearing a yellow top that promised much, but revealed little, and jeans. "I thought that we might go to the other side of town. There's a small restaurant and a few shops that you might want to look in if you're going to get something for auntie Jill. Hearing his wife's name returned Henry swiftly and brutally to the real world. Wendy walked up to a blue open-top Mazda. "This belongs to my flat mate, Laura, although she's not, if you know what I mean." Henry did not, for at least some seconds.

Wendy drove confidently and swiftly, taking full advantage of any openings in the steady stream of traffic but the noise of the road precluded any real conversation. After about 10 minutes, she turned right and pulled into what looked like a service road and leapt out with admirable agility.

Henry, whose brain was still functioning below normal, stumbled as he got out of the very low car. Wendy extended a protective arm and in one move, arrested his progress and steadied him by holding his hand. A photographer caught the occasion. He was covering the story of a nearby gasoline station that, as a protest against a new and cruelly punitive government duty of two cents per gallon, which surely infringed the constitution, was selling gasoline at just 40 cents a gallon. The queue extended for some miles down the main road but a startled and guilty-looking Henry and a beautiful blonde made a better pic. What Henry didn't know was that the local television station had filmed the line from the air and had also recorded Henry's near fall. He did not see the local news so missed the usual cliché-riddled voiceover saying that motorists were really falling for the cheap gasoline.

Henry, unable to concentrate, saw little of interest in the local shops. When he was not fantasising about Wendy and his return to the club, he was worrying about the possible takeover and the absence of ideas on how to counter it. Perkins opened the conversation over lunch. "I really thought I was too old to be surprised, but, when I saw you, I thought I must have been dreaming. What prompted you to come to Houston and work in a club?"

She looked at him as if he were the only male in the world. Clearly, she was very good at her new profession. Henry, who, only a few hours ago, would not have even noticed the intense expression, was now only mildly disconcerted but he was astounded by her reply. "Actually, it was you, uncle." Henry hastily suggested that she drop the title.

"Actually, it was you, Henry."

"What? Me? We've never discussed the subject and if we had, I wouldn't have been any help, because I didn't know such places existed here until my colleagues took me to your club last night."

"Earlier this year, when we came to lunch, you told mummy and me that one day you hoped to visit Houston. You said it was the capital of the oil world. So, when I was thinking about where to live for a few years, I thought that Houston sounded like a good place to start. I've always thought that I could easily get to like rich people."

"Your trouble is that you've been watching too much television. The industry has had its share of hard times but, anyway, that doesn't explain about the club and your…" and here Henry stumbled over the word, which somehow did not adequately express her contribution to the happiness of men, "dancing".

She smiled.

"You may remember, I was trained as a dancer and when I came to Houston, just a few weeks ago, after a boring spell in some grotty coffee bar, my friend Laura, I've known her for some years, well, she lives here, suggested that I should try to get a job in a club. I'd never been in one but I'd seen a programme about one on television. Laura, who used to work in one in Dallas, took me to the Hotspot and I was invited to do an audition. She had told me what to do and how to look and I was given a job immediately. To start with I was terrified but I soon realised that the girls are in total control and we choose what we do, and who we do it for."

Henry, fascinated, didn't even notice that Wendy had ended a sentence with a preposition.

"After all, it's quite dark and most of the men have had a drink, which eases the tension. The loud music and the lights also make it seem as if we are in a different world. When I danced on the stage for the first time, I didn't even look at the audience. I must confess that I did have a drink before my first evening and I did tell my first customer that this was my debut. He was most understanding."

Henry averred that he did not doubt that but "why the Hotspot?"

Wendy smiled.

"That's easy, I was told that's where the oilmen hang out and they like spending on the girls. Even in difficult times, these guys seem to have plenty of money and I presume that they're fiddling their expenses. I don't think that what they pay us comes from their own pockets. I wonder how they list our charges on their expense sheets? I s'pose that's why you went there because you're a rich oil company executive who just wants a good time? "

"Me, with plenty of money? Ha ha. Don't forget that I'm British. The only reason that I found myself in the Hotspot was that I suspect my new American colleagues wanted to have a laugh at their expense, if you'll pardon the phrase."

They both smiled.

"Anyway, I'm earning a lot of money now and I owe all this to you and I want you to know how grateful I am, but please, please, don't breathe a word of this to Auntie Jill or mummy." Henry, aware that such a revelation could just conceivably cause him a problem, vowed eternal silence.

"You know I won't but what does mummy, Lynda, know?"

"I've told her that I'm staying with Laura in her apartment. She met her once in the UK, so that cheered her up."

"Yes, but what about the job?"

Wendy frowned.

"Yes, that's been a bit more difficult, especially as mummy used to ring me at tea time in the UK, which is breakfast time here, when I was usually asleep. Now, I've trained her to call just at sensible time during the weekends, when I have the time off, completely."

"What have you told her about your job?"

"Well, I've got a work permit and I decided that I had to adjust the truth a little, so that she doesn't worry. I'll tell her the whole truth when I go home, well, possibly. For the moment, she thinks that I help to look after executives in a bar."

Henry suggested that was quite accurate.

The odd couple enjoyed a memorable meal. Henry was intrigued about how the club operated.

"We get irritated when we're called strippers. We're not, we're dancers or entertainers. What attracts us is that we can earn big money by charging men who want to look at beautiful girls in a safe, secure and friendly place, without their being hassled, well, not much. They may want a lot more, but they know, and we know, that's not possible. We try to make it seem like a party, which is why you'll hear whoops and whistles, as if everyone is enjoying themselves. One advantage of these big clubs is that any male can find the kind of girl who appeals to him. We've blondes, as I think you noticed, redheads, brunettes, bimbos, intellectual types, every kind and we dress differently, to turn on different kinds of guys. It's not men exploiting the girls. If anything, it's the other way round. It's easy to find their particular weakness and then exploit it. We make them feel good and forget their day-to-day troubles."

Henry nodded understandingly, having been reminded that he had forgotten the takeover.

"Some girls can earn up to about $1,200 in a night and their secret is to be what the men want them to be. We treat all the guys equally and pamper them, single, ugly, married or handsome. Some girls start work at about 5.00 pm or even earlier and only stop when the club closes at 2.00 in the morning. The most successful girls are always looking around, whether on the stage or doing a dance, seeing who's interested so that they don't waste time strolling round, looking for the next guy. We must never look bored. We all have some regulars and get to know them well."

Apparently, most clubs charged the girls $30 per session for permission to do lap dances. They had to perform on both stages around the club but, if they declined, a financial penalty was imposed. Texan law required dancers to be no closer than three feet from their customer. If the girls were seen to transgress by plain clothes police, harshly forced to visit the clubs as part of their job, they were fined not less than $500 and might even spend a few days in jail. The man and the club went unpunished.

A recent high-profile case, mounted by a self-styled guardian of the public morals, Marie Blancmaison, had resulted in the girls having to retreat to three feet from the customer. However, this had such a devastating impact on the revenues of the clubs and the girls alike that the rule was now totally ignored. Most good clubs, like the Hotspot, attracted about 2,000 customers most evenings. They drank expensive but harmless concoctions whilst watching or dancing with up to 200 girls. More recently, the club had introduced a restaurant and that was doing well partly because customers could come earlier and stay longer.

The biggest spenders came from the Middle East. "About two weeks ago, a group of five arrived, to celebrate a birthday and they got through $5,000 in just one hour. We like them and there's usually some competition when we see them coming in", she added unnecessarily.

Some girls were on drugs, some were hookers. Seeing Henry's innocent look, she said, "I mean prostitutes, not rugby players", and some were lesbians. "But you know Perky, the majority are ordinary decent girls who are bringing up children by themselves, saving to go to university or who want to make as much money from their looks whilst they can. Not many can go on after they're 35. I've heard that there can be friction between girls in the smaller clubs but here we all get on well. Many girls are very bright and a darn site brighter than the guys. For example, Anna, a good friend of mine, who you must meet, is a trained secretary and now she's studying law. Incidentally, that's her real name. We all use made-up names, for security. Her work name is Martina and mine's August.

"A few girls are grade one gullible bimbos who can be seduced by the English accent. One believed that the man she was talking to was a friend of Prince Charles just because that's what he'd told her. He also claimed to be stinking rich and to have a castle in the north of Scotland. Last Christmas, he had cut down 3,000 fir trees and they had hardly noticed the impact on his forest. It was some time before she realised that he hadn't been telling the truth."

The girls tended to hunt in packs or pairs, especially if they had targeted two men. Few guys went to the club by themselves. Waitresses tended to follow the girls, aware that one of the first questions posed to the target males would be "why don't we have a drink"?

"Waitressing is hard. I tried it for a few days and managed to earn $500 in tips during an eight-hour shift. That's about half what I would have got from dancing. My feet ached and my brain didn't have the rest that I'd expected, compared to dancing. When you're dancing, your brain is always active and you run the range of emotions every few minutes. You go from innocent curiosity, what does this man do for a living, to fear, is this guy a vice cop or is he dangerous, to self-doubt. Am I becoming too fat, too old? How long can I remain fit and able to compete with the teenage girls? The girls always sit down with a potential client, put an arm around him and then introduce themselves, giving their work name and asking for his name. They even shake hands, as if formalising a new relationship, which is what they hope will happen. Then, after a few minutes flattering chat, when a new record is put on by the DJ, the usual line is 'this sounds like a good record for me to dance to for you'. It's a brave man who says no. Then the next move is to turn your back on the customer and ask him to undo your bra."

An emboldened Henry asked whether the dancers were ever turned on when they were performing for an attractive male.

"Sure, it's happened to me a few times. I say 'I'll be right back and I go to the dressing room and, well, you can guess." Henry could not but looked understanding.

Any girls who went out with a customer or gave phone numbers were fired as the authorities might think that the club was employing hookers. Managers wandered around the clubs to ensure that all was well and Wendy had never heard of any real trouble. Henry attributed that to the weakness of the beer but said nothing.

"Security is important for the girls, of course, and also for the men. If they feel threatened, they won't come. There's very little crime. Outsiders may think that the whole concept is disgusting and that it's a cover for paid sex. They're wrong. It's just a friendly relaxing place where the girls and the men can feel comfortable and safe and enjoy a few fantasies, free of worries and commitments. We've many regulars whom we know by name and we often go to the quiet room with them, so we can be more friendly. Of course, many guys try to impress us with stories about their wealth but the vast majority are pleasant and polite and I don't see what's wrong with having such a place.

"As I said earlier, my friend Anna will be working in the club tonight. She's very attractive and she particularly likes Brits. You will come, won't you? Would you like to meet her?"

Mr Perkins grinned, distorted his face to suggest that he was thinking hard and then said after the briefest of pauses, "very well, then, but I'll be by myself tonight". It would have been unwise to invite his colleagues. This was his chance, probably the last ever, for some unique excitement. He would enjoy himself and would not allow his conscience to spoil his fun.

Wendy returned him to the office and he thanked her profusely for having lunch with him. He would see her again that evening and Henry was told where to sit so that Wendy could find him. Apparently, it was a darker area than the one where history had been made earlier in the day. He was enjoying the conspiracy and was beginning to silence his sense of guilt. However, the afternoon session in the office on the takeover yielded little, plunging Henry into yet-deeper pessimism.

Later, the unmathematically-minded Perkins, having wrongly calculated that the time difference between Houston and the UK meant that it was early evening at home, phoned his next-of-kin who was listening to the midnight news as she prepared for bed. "Yes, all's fine. I'm seeing a good bit of Houston." He omitted to give details of the bit that he had seen but did say that it was more attractive than he had anticipated.

Jill was well and expected to be transferred to a different job at work but she assured Henry that this could be a good move. After some inconsequential chat, she reminded her husband to reconfirm his flight for the Friday. He thanked her. He had forgotten.

Earlier, Henry had phoned Broadoak House. There had been no material developments, despite some meetings with senior managers, and Hubert was concerned that the consultants, whom he had chased himself, still had apparently done nothing. A major meeting was planned for tomorrow, Wednesday.

Perkins reported that they had had some gruelling sessions locally but the only real idea that had emerged was whether some Broadoak assets, in different countries, could be exchanged for some held by other companies so that both groups could develop critical mass? HB said that it was a reasonable idea that had already been debated in London. Hubert confessed that he was concerned and urged Henry to do everything possible to conjure up something that could save the company. The new general manager felt ashamed for not having had a single new and sensible idea. He seemed to be permanently cloaked in guilt for one reason or another and it was not comfortable. The outlook was grim and the dire prospect that he might soon be unemployed had not stimulated his imagination.

Henry had generously insisted that his colleagues should spend the evening with their families as they were to have a formal business dinner on the Thursday, his last evening. Wednesday evening was to be taken up with another brainstorming session, fuelled by sandwiches. They acquiesced so Henry was spared having to invent some story to cover his visit to the club that night.

He dined early, although he was not hungry, and prepared for the meeting with Wendy and her friend Anna. A cab drew up outside the hotel, to deposit some new visitors and, having checked that it was free, Henry climbed in and only confirmed his intended destination when the door was firmly shut. Allegedly, the driver had never heard of the Hotspot so Henry was obliged not only to read out the address, but to say what kind of club it was. He was not sure whether the driver was deliberately embarrassing him but he knew that Houston drivers' command of local geography was not perfect. Eventually confident that the driver knew where he was going and trying to look confident himself, Mr Perkins slumped into the warm embrace of the seat and speculated on what he was about to do.

The cab turned right out of his hotel, on to the Katy Freeway, before moving right again, to join the 610 West Loop. It passed the Galleria shopping centre and the Post Oak area and Westheimer Road before moving east on to the South Loop, past the famous Astrodome, to join the Gulf Freeway, Interstate 45, which led to Galveston on the coast. Henry wondered whether this was the most direct route but, although the traffic was dense, as it was 24 hours a day, it usually moved well, at least until there was an accident. Then the congestion, caused mainly by myriad emergency vehicles, slowed traffic to a temporary crawl. Tonight the traffic moved uninterrupted and Henry looked at the passengers in passing cars, wondering where they were going, why and who their occupants would see at their destinations. Their journeys were doubtless routine and presumably most of them led normal, well-balanced, uncomplicated lives.

How different his position was. He was soon to be out of work, having tasted management and its fringe benefits for just a few months after years of frustration and, talking of years of frustration, he had been allowed to glimpse what a more normal sex life might have offered. He had an urge to scream out against the injustices of life. This absurd world, pre-occupied with youth, would soon cast him aside, abused but not used, because his turn had come and gone. Why had he not made more of his life? What was his future? Wallowing in uncertainty, pessimism and, yes, some guilt and self-pity, he hardly noticed that the cab, after about 45 minutes of hard driving, had slowed and left on exit 19 for Dickinson.

Becoming increasingly nervous and confused as the destination neared, the callow Henry wondered what to say to Wendy. Of course, a man of the world would have questioned the need to say anything but however hard he tried to ignore it, that wretched tidal wave of suffocating guilt threatened to overwhelm him. It was not just guilt that he was on his way to the club but guilt that he, a general manager, had been able to contribute precisely nothing to save his company and his job. Should he return immediately to the hotel? No, he would make this his wake.

One internal voice reminded him that he enjoyed Wendy's company and the experience of physical contact with a young and beautiful girl. A second voice suggested that they had little in common so why was he returning to see her this evening? What a daft question! It was because he was a normal male, and that such opportunities to look at, talk to and touch beautiful girls had never occurred before. At last, he was having some of the fun that he had missed when young males are supposed to have such experiences. The gods were giving him an unexpected opportunity to build up some memories, relatively late in life, probably just weeks before the end of his professional life. Above all, surely, it was innocent and he derived some confidence from the absolute certainty that nothing much could or would happen. Despite this good talking to that he gave himself in the cab, he was still less than convinced when he handed over a $10 note to the club receptionist, who, even at 9.25 in the evening, expressed the hope that he would have a wonderful day.

A tall girl, wearing a conventional steel-blue knee-length dress, who reminded him of Jane Fonda, asked him where he would like to sit. Wendy had told him that he should sit behind the smaller stage on the right hand side of the club. This was conveyed to Jane and he followed in her wake, convinced that everyone in the club had seen and recognised him. Total disgrace was surely imminent. Henry wanted to order a beer but, confronted with a list of brands foreign to him, he said to the waitress, as she bent low over him, so that she could fulfil his desires, at least in the matter of providing beer, "any kind you like, surprise me". This ordeal over, he sat back in the comfortable but highly manoeuvrable chair to await developments. He did not have long to wait.

Wendy, having just performed for two clients, had noticed Henry as he came in. "Hello, uncle" she whispered seductively and naughtily into his ear.

"Please do drop the uncle bit. It makes me feel both guilty and old and I don't like that at all."

"I'll call you Perky, because that was what you were last night." He graciously said that was only because she made him feel young.

"I really enjoyed dancing for you last night and I still owe you one. I hope that I didn't put you off from having a repeat performance tonight."

The usually articulate Perky snorted.

Part of Henry wanted to be in his bedroom, alone, reading newspapers or watching television. Another part was encouraging him to enjoy what might happen. He reminded himself yet again that Wendy was totally reliable and would not breathe a word of this to her mother or Jill. Silence could be assured, thought Henry as a bright light flickered briefly behind them. He told Wendy that "we Brits must stick together". As Wendy was now sitting on his lap, and as she was nearly wearing a black micro-size PVC dress with a very low neckline, the phrase was particularly appropriate.

"Anna's very keen to meet you. As I said at lunch, she particularly likes Brits. She says that they always treat her as a person, not just as some sexual object." Seemingly on cue, a gorgeous girl, probably in her mid twenties, approached them. Her long blonde hair was curly and her blue eyes seemed to sparkle in the near darkness. Her figure was perfect and she had developed a walk that matched her sexy appearance. Henry, not for the first time that day, was stunned, intoxicated by the sight and perfume of what seemed to be female perfection. The girl was nearly dressed as a cowboy. She wore a short-sleeved check shirt, open to the waist and trousers which, at the front, were conventional except for two large holes in mid thigh but she was exposed to any drafts from the rear. She looked remarkably like Wendy who now addressed her friend who was swaying gently but provocatively from side to side.

"Hi Anna. I'd like to introduce a good friend of mine from the UK who's over here on business. He likes blondes. His name is Henry but he answers to the nickname of Perky. Perky, this is Anna." Anna smiled and the man who had gained a national reputation by speaking fearlessly about business, now mute, just stared.

"Say hello, Perky" cajoled Wendy. Still dazed, he looked straight at the girl and did precisely as he was bid. Both girls laughed.

"Perky, what's up?"

"Hello. I'm sorry. It's just that all this is so astonishing and bewildering I'm really delighted to meet you."

They shook hands.

"Can I sit down?" "Of course. Please do. Can I get you a drink?" He knew that she could have asked for champagne at $100 a bottle and hoped that her taste would be more modest. "Orange juice, with plenty of ice, please."

"What about you, Wendy, I mean August?"

She declined with thanks and, having overseen the initial overtures between her two friends, left them and moved towards a small but lonely group of young men. Before she went, she promised Henry that she would be back as she still owed him a dance or two. A dark-haired waitress, dressed in what looked like a French maid's abbreviated uniform, who had followed Anna to the table, took the order and headed for the bar.

"I'm really glad to meet you, Perky. Wendy told me how you were so honest on television. I respect people like that. We don't speak out on things as often as we should. I think that what you did was very brave."

Perkins nearly blushed but managed to concentrate on Anna's next question. She wanted to know if Perky had ever been to Houston before.

"Yes, once before but this is my second visit to the club. The first was just a few hours ago."

"Do you like what you have seen?"

Henry, prompted by a mischievous grin, realised that this question was intentionally ambiguous so he deliberately commented on some of the tourist sights that he had seen so far and made generous reference to the old buildings in Sam Houston Park. Then, gaining in confidence and feeling that he might as well enjoy himself, observed that what he had already seen so far that evening was undoubtedly the high spot of the trip so far. His reward was immediate. Anna clambered on to his lap and put an arm around his shoulder and gave him a friendly peck just below his left ear.

"So what brings you to Houston, Perky?"

"Well, I work in the oil industry and I wanted to go to the big conference that's on this week."

"Are you a speaker?"

Perkins smiled and said "not this time, Texans wouldn't want to hear me".

His modesty immediately appealed to Anna. She was so tired of brash, noisy egotistical Texans. Henry, unknowingly, immediately capitalised on his standing. "Tell me about yourself. How long have you worked here?"

"I started here only a few months ago but it's ok. The money's good and I meet some interesting people. But really, I'm saving up hard so I can continue to study and then buy my own house. I know that I shan't always have this earning capacity, so I'm trying to enjoy it whilst I can."

"What are you studying?" "Well, I'm a fully-qualified secretary and I spent a year studying journalism but I'm now half way through a law course."

Henry mentioned that he used to work in an economics division in an oil company in London. Anna, who had completely captivated the Brit, looked at him carefully. He was polite, asked her questions about herself and seemed as innocent as anyone she had met. "Ever been in one of these places before, Perky?"

"No, not until last night. I came with some local colleagues and was astonished to meet Wendy. I've known her for many years. I was very pleased to see her. I had no idea she worked in a place like this."

"Do you disapprove of 'places like this'?" This was the second time that Henry had used this phrase. It must be banned from his vocabulary.

"No, I don't. If I did, I would be back now in my room doing something really edifying like watching commercials on television, rather than wasting my time with one of the most attractive girls I've ever seen." His confidence was growing alarmingly. "No, it seems innocent enough to me and if nobody's hurt, why not?" He was not sure what he meant by this last remark but it really didn't matter because another record had finished and the DJ was exhorting "you guys out there, please put your hands together for June who's just finished dancing on the main stage, and ask these beautiful Hotspot girls for a table dance." June had just performed on the stage, Wendy was called August and where, he wondered, was the tabloid girl, April?

"Well, what about it Perky?" Henry knew that he could not refuse as he had happily engaged her in conversation for about five minutes when she could easily have been earning money by dancing for someone else. Besides, he wanted to have a dance. He had decided that tonight would be a night to remember.

He grinned. "Do I really have a choice?"

"No, not really. Sit back and just.."

Her words trailed off into infinity as Henry did as he was bid. He was the first to admit his tragic inexperience with the opposite sex but what happened next, would surely have aroused the most seasoned of libido-worshipping men. Anna called herself an exotic dancer and was professional in that she offered value for money but she reserved a little more for people that she genuinely liked. Henry was in that category. She shed her trousers, shook her golden hair over him and began stroking some areas that oilmen would probably regard as core. Her hands never stopped moving over the prostrate Perkins and he was very, very aroused. She was slim but well-proportioned and there was scarcely a square inch of her brown body that was not thrust against Henry. She slipped down him, like Wendy earlier, and then she sat on him and bounced up and down, whilst simultaneously moving gently backwards and forwards.

Henry did not know whether he was coming or going and the dance, if that is what it could be called, seemed to go on for so long that the sensually battered Perkins thought that he might have to ask for a bucket of ice. A lifetime's experience later, the general manager emerged after a very physical session in which he had been invited, no, ordered, to use his hands to advantage. She had given him the most exciting, arousing few minutes of his life. A gasping Perky was unsure whether his heart would stand another dance.

So, nobly, he told Anna that he knew that she had to earn money and that as a humble Brit, he could not possibly compete with "all these rich Texans so I do understand if you want to go now but please come back when I've recovered and I would like another dance later". She was impressed that anyone should be so understanding.

"That's ok but I'm very happy here with you. I think you're real cute."

Henry had never been so described and he only just managed to suppress a cheer. He ordered more drinks and Anna perched on his lap and put her arm around his shoulders. He asked if she ever became tired. "Tarred, why, no, not me when there are guys around like you. What's it like, being an important oilman?"

"I'm not important at all, just lucky. I happened to be, as they say, the right man in the right place at the right time. I can't claim any credit for that. Anyway, what are you going to do when you finish your law course?"

"Well, I thought that I might dance for another year or so and then look for a job in an oil company but the way that they're getting rid of people, I changed my mind. I wondered if I should put my year studying journalism to good use so I could then write about law and current affairs."

Henry injected what was intended as a joke. "I could tell you a few things about oilmen and their affairs but that's not quite what you had in mind. Anyway, good luck. How long have you been in Houston?"

"Just two years now. I used to live in New York but I prefer the people here." Henry agreed but did not reveal the length of his stay in the Big Apple.

"They're so much more friendly and I've got a good condominium just around the corner. I can even walk to work." Henry recalled from his abortive days of studying that a condominium was the common rule of a territory by two or more nations. Talented as she undoubtedly was, surely, she was not ruling a part of Texas?

After about another 10 minutes of idle chat, Anna asked "fancy another dance?" Henry was besotted by this intelligent and attractive girl. They both knew the answer. "Yes please but do be gentle with me. I nearly caught fire last time."

Perkins was astonished to hear himself speaking in this way but he no longer cared. He was a different person and he was enjoying himself in an unimaginable way. Four minutes later, having touched a few more distant stars, a rather ragged-looking Henry was slowly returning to earth. Anna, obviously, was not anxious to seek other clients but Henry had made the offer and she was an intelligent girl so he was not bothered. However, she sensed his apparent discomfort.

"I know that you feel guilty that you can't pay me to stay with you for the whole evening but I'm happy. It makes a very pleasant change to be with someone like you. Let's just have some fun. It's good to talk with you. Some oil guys come in here and just boast about how rich they are. One guy, for example, wanted me to go back to his ranch, some three hours outside Houston, just to be real friendly, as he put it, and promised me $2,000. I didn't go. In here, you know that, if some guys get too physical, the management can kick them out. I would have been a real ass if I had gone, alone, with him so I told him that I had college early the following morning and couldn't. Anyhow, he still comes here and I dance for him. Look, he's over there now."

Henry followed her gaze. She pointed to a prematurely bald man who, even at this range, in the near dark, looked wealthy. "That big guy with the moustache, wearing a white shirt and a redhead?"

"Yup."

"Do you know him?"

"I don't know him personally, but I do recognise him. He's Chuck Charles, boss of Muswell Petroleum, who're threatening to take over my own company." As soon as the words were out of his mouth, he regretted them and, more importantly, his lack of judgement. He had just told a complete stranger, an exotic dancer in a club, something that should have remained a secret, even although he had not given any details. Hastily and rather clumsily, he added belatedly, "between you and me, please Anna, I mean Martina". That was the first time that he had used her real name and somehow it seemed appropriate but he asked for approval.

"Anna's jest fine. What will happen if he does take yawl over?"

Having started, Henry could see no way out of answering this question, so confessed. "Hundreds of us, especially people of my age, will be thrown out and we'll probably never work again as jobs for people like us, like me, are very difficult to find. We're all very worried indeed. Please, 'though, do forgive me for blurting out something that I should have kept quiet. You won't say anything to anyone, will you?"

She shook her head and for no apparent reason, suddenly stood up, kissed Perkins fully on the mouth and said "gottago, see you tomorrow, handsome, I'll tell Wendy that I've abandoned you. Bye Perky". So saying, she vanished, leaving a very confused general manager with yet something else to worry about. Could he trust Anna?

Henry had been sitting alone for some time. His solitary state was not the dancers' fault. Some amazingly attractive girls had asked if he wanted company. Most of them playfully put an affectionate arm around his shoulders or sat down very close, on the adjacent chair, and asked him his name and where he came from. All seemed bewitched by his English accent but he declined offers of their company, saying "possibly later thanks", or "I'm just waiting for a friend".

As Wendy had told him, the girls often hunted in pairs and seemed instinctively to know who had money to spend. He also worked out the signs that had to be conveyed if you wanted girls to approach you. You had to be accessible. It was negative to have chairs arranged around you so that they had to be moved to allow a girl to approach. Equally, it seemed important to make eye contact with the girls as they passed, if you wanted them to talk to you. During the chair test, Wendy returned. She had suddenly felt guilty, there was a lot of it about, when she noticed that Henry was alone. She had been "otherwise engaged". Apparently Anna had suddenly remembered something and she was sorry to have left so abruptly but she'd see him late tomorrow and, cryptically, she had asked Wendy to tell Henry not to worry.

"What did you think of Anna?"

"She really was most intelligent and we had a very interesting conversation."

"Anything else?"

Henry smiled and thought that it was time to pay Wendy a compliment. After all, without her, his evenings would have been much duller and he would have lacked some outstanding memories to take into his old age. "Like you, she's an absolute cracker." It was difficult to tell who was the more surprised at this: Henry for saying it or Wendy for having heard her "uncle" use such language.

"Meanwhile, what about that dance I promised you?"

Henry was once again transported to an alien but most agreeable world. When Henry returned to his home planet, Wendy looked at him penetratingly. "It's really good to see you, Henry. We're always going to keep this a secret and that's really exciting. I know that I shouldn't say this but I've fancied you for the last two years."

Perkins reeled. Nobody, not even his wife, had ever said that to him and to hear it, for the first time, in his fifties, was astonishing. It was even more surprising because it came from someone young enough to be his daughter. No, he eliminated that thought immediately. He did not want that kind of stuff in his head. His startled reaction sounded extremely pompous because that is just what it was. "That's most kind of you, Wendy and I must say that I am not wholly unmoved by you, as, being the perceptive girl that you are, you may well have noticed. Indeed, I suppose that, to be honest, I must admit that I have had something of a crush on you for the last two years. No, sorry, that's misleading. What can I say?"

Wendy was in no mood to assist and Henry the pompous continued to flounder.

"What I mean is, no that's wrong too, I am and always have been very fond of you. I must admit that the more of you I see, and I have seen more than I ever anticipated, the more impressed I am. You do look rather different from the time you came with your mother to lunch and were wearing battle dress."

"Yes, I remember. I had intended to wear a short white summer skirt but mother said that it was too daring for the tennis court, let alone for visiting uncle Henry and auntie Jill, so I decided to go to the other extreme. Anyway, which outfit do you like best?" Henry was too married to fall for this trick. "Apart from the battle dress, all of them."

"Would you like me to dance again for you?"

"I thought that you'd never ask."

Was it Henry's imagination or was Wendy determined to perform more lustily than Anna? After he emerged for air, neither knowing nor caring whether his three free dances had been completed, he offered her dollars but Wendy declined them, saying that it was wrong to accept money from a friend, especially as she had really enjoyed the dance. It was time to go but Henry had to tell a visibly disappointed Wendy that he could not come the following evening as he had to work until late and he must have some sleep. That said, he intended to be at the club again "late ish" on Thursday, his last night in town, and he would look forward to seeing her and Anna then. Please would Wendy tell Anna many thanks and he'd see her on Thursday night, not Wednesday, as he thought that he had told her.

Chapter 22

HB's idea of dividing his colleagues into working groups had seemed a good idea at the weekend gathering of senior management but that session and other meetings had achieved very little. An angry chief executive had told colleagues and advisers that much more was expected of them and that they would convene again this Wednesday. It was now more urgent because Chuck Charles had phoned yesterday to say that he would soon be finalising his approach "and I'm telling you this Horace, I mean Hubert, because it's a real friendly offer of a merger of equals and I know you're in favour and this will help you to get your guys on board". Before HB could respond coherently, and it was late afternoon, Chuck had vanished. Reflecting the gravity of the situation, HB had scheduled the meeting for 1.30. Each group, as constituted at the weekend meeting, would make a presentation before a more general discussion. Participants, anxious to see how HB behaved after lunch when denied his usual fare, and keen to secure sufficient sandwiches to last through the afternoon, assembled early in the boardroom. HB, who had decided that the only liquid to be served would be coffee, opened the meeting briskly.

"As you know, the *Daily Shout* has confirmed that Muswell Petroleum plan to merge with us. I don't know how they got the story but I assume that it didn't come from any of you and I also assume that you haven't spoken to anyone else about this. So far, the story hasn't stirred up much interest and I don't think that we'll have to take on any other predators." Hubert the shareholder then thought it appropriate to add "but, of course, it's early days and we should not expect much until after MP make their initial bid".

Lance Boyle, fearing that his facial pallor might have implied his guilt, hid behind a document, placed just under his nose, and tried to look loyal.

"All this must, I repeat, must, be handled very sensitively. Jobs and income are at stake here and we have a duty to ensure the best possible outcome for our shareholders. Chuck Charles phoned me last night to say, and I quote, said that 'a real friendly offer of a merger of equals' was imminent." His recollection of Chuck's remarks stopped here. "I don't intend to say much now because I don't want to influence your thinking or your reports. It's important that we have a frank discussion."

Boyle smiled inwardly: that was typical of the wimp HB. To avoid seeming incompetent, he wrapped himself in management democracy.

"There are just two other things that I want to say. "I think that any talk of a merger of equals is an insult to our intelligence."

Sir Willerby Wistleton-Nugget, probably the biggest name in the UK oil industry, hear heared vigorously, under the mistaken impression that Broadoak was much bigger than MP. "Damn fool, that Chuck man and damn silly name. Needs to learn that a tiny company like his can't mess around with someone of our size." HB continued.

"I make no apology for repeating that we must remain mindful of winning the best deal for our shareholders, whatever the impact may be on our jobs." So saying, one of the largest individual shareholders sat down. Restrained assent around the table resulted in several pieces of sandwich being involuntarily ejected. Boyle, in particular, was having difficulties with a maliciously uncooperative piece of ham.

HB resumed unexpectedly.

"I should have added that as you know, Henry Perkins is in the States at the moment and I've spoken to him, several times, on the phone, person to person…" Evidently, HB had nothing to say and had even forgotten how to convey it. "And, frankly, I don't have any encouraging news. It seems that our friends agree that we should reject the first bid but ideas on what weapons we can use, well, have not been forthcoming as yet although Henry told me that he is intending to have another meeting today, US time, and he hopes that something might emerge. Perhaps we can start by asking the committee, charged with outlining our weaknesses, to open the proceedings. I'm sure that this won't take long!"

Morton Hampstead, an independent expert in corporate acquisitions in the oil sector, rose. "Chairman, I think that we owe you the truth, however unpalatable. I regret to say that our brain-storming session at the weekend induced a level of pessimism that was not dispelled even by the occasional sip of wine from the one bottle that was delivered to our room. Last week, we became even more depressed. It'll take a miracle to avoid a takeover because MP has both the cash and the desire to spend it. If they are to avoid a shareholder revolt, and they haven't been paid a dividend for some years, they must make another acquisition, mainly to reduce their costs and we think that something is us, if I may be considered a part of you. So a discussion of strengths and weaknesses is less relevant than in the majority of instances. I should also say, chairman, that we decided that, to avoid repetition, one person should make the initial presentations so that we can spend more time on the general discussion. I am he.

"We believe that our only real hope, and it's a slender one, is to concentrate on those points that the City and others may perceive as major weaknesses in MP and, somehow, to convey to MP shareholders that they would not gain from a merger. We must also take immediate measures that make us more desirable but, of course, more costly to acquire. My colleagues will be working hard for the rest of the week, looking at all the financial implications and calculating rates of return etc. All this is important, but, unless MP shareholders think they're paying a ridiculously high price, we believe they'll buy us. Ironically, if we can push up the price, by emphasising our merits, we may well still go under, possibly to another group, but, at least, we shall have done the best we can for our shareholders. Of course, one very important factor is the very low rate of interest in the States which makes almost any reasonable investment a good long-term buy. In fact, at the moment, the real rate of interest is negative. Borrowing to buy, especially in a long-lead time industry, dealing with something so fundamentally important as energy, makes sense."

Willerby, the former banker, didn't understand this but nodded when he saw HB's head move up and down.

"Frankly, even if we adopt all the usual tactics and conventional strategies, to counter a bid, my colleagues and I think that we shall lose. My US friends say that MP's management is coming under increasing pressure, as I said earlier, and it will be very difficult for us to resist a bid unless it is derisory and I don't suppose it will be. That said, let's compare the two companies and see whether this analysis yields any inspired suggestions."

Morton Hampstead, who had already transformed the atmosphere with his introductory comments, looked at his notes and resumed.

"Frankly, and forgive me for being so blunt, it says something for the strength of oil demand that we're still in business. We have about five per cent of the UK petrol market but we've spent almost nothing on the sites which now require substantial investment, being tarted up and given more cost-saving technology. We're in the wrong areas and we must move more into those regions where demand is concentrated. The policy of having many sites in the Lake District, for example, because of the potential of tourism, just did not work and we have too much capital tied up in sites where demand is, at best, only moderate for a few months a year.

"We have too many small depots for our overall sales so our unit costs are too high and our efforts in the industrial and commercial markets have, how can I say this, not been spectacularly successful. Again, inadequate investment has been a cause. We also concentrated for far too long on the diminishing heavy fuel oil market, seemingly ignoring the increased penetration of a substitute fuel, natural gas."

HB, whose policy this had been, winced.

"But the good news is that within about a year, we shall have the most modern and sophisticated depot in Western Europe." Nobody was tactless enough to point out that this was because the old one had burned down. "Incidentally, MP's old UK refinery is currently being upgraded but the work will not be finished for at least another 18 months. Finally, the flat market prevents us from securing the economies of scale that most of our competitors enjoy. It's easy to understand why the financial sector sees us as old-fashioned.

"Let's now turn to our exploration and production policy. A few years ago, the areas in which we were interested had to be no more than five hours' flying time away." Some of the other outsiders sniggered but Morton said it was true. "I don't think that it would be right for me to comment on such a policy. Admittedly, it was abandoned some time ago, but then we paid too much for mediocre acreage and failed to attract good quality staff. Because we don't pay very much, we still have difficulties in retaining good people, but that's not an issue for today.

"Then the company moved to the other end of the spectrum. Some years ago, apparently, determined to demonstrate boldness, it acquired acreage in, for example, a number of countries shunned by the big companies, mainly for political reasons. That meant of course, that, even if we found oil or gas, we couldn't farm out a share of the license in return for the necessary investment because the big boys wouldn't come. But, in a sense, that was academic as we never found anything in these politically undesirable countries although our efforts were widely condemned not just by pressure groups but also by many other companies in the industry."

HB, whose policy this had been, winced.

Morton was nearly finished. "Our next moves were into the more established areas. We became involved in unconventional oil in Canada, just before oil prices slumped, making heavy oil totally uneconomic until some new technology arrives and our efforts in Venezuela, for example, were widely and, I think, correctly, regarded by commentators as a serious misuse of our funds. What we paid was probably at least 10 per cent over the odds and the impact on the group was even worse as oil prices plunged soon thereafter, forcing us to sell some proven assets in safe areas. Finally, I must mention our propensity for securing acreage in apparently safe countries, just before revolutions topple the governments with which we are closely linked, so we lose popularity and acreage. In future, we must pay more attention to detailed risk analysis.

"That said, we have successful in the North Sea for many years so still have some supplies coming from a politically secure source. Additionally, the board should be congratulated for its continued involvement offshore Ireland, where, I think, an important well is being drilled as we speak. Also I should mention our production from politically secure countries such as Australia and the excellent exchanges the company arranged to provide supplies for our markets in Western Europe. Before I finish, I must also mention our new enhanced oil recovery technology that allows us to extract more, economically, from elderly oil fields. That should help us over the next few years in the North Sea and possibly elsewhere."

HB, whose policy this had been, purred.

"Thank you Morton, for a blunt assessment of where we are now and how we got there. Perhaps it's not as bad as we thought but we must bear in mind your initial comment that MP's shareholders are desperate for an acquisition. This may be one of those occasions where, whatever the target company does to defend itself, there is no solution through, let's put it this way, money."

"I fear you may be right, chairman."

HB, aware that what he had heard boded well for a prosperous retirement based on inflated share values and his golden parachute, concealed his excitement and, forgetting that Hampstead had said that there would only be one spokesman, asked the person who was to present an analysis of MP to begin.

Morton sat down and stood up again, to indicate "it is I, again, chairman".

"As you know, they have some elderly oil and gas acreage onshore US and I suspect that they see our enhanced oil recovery techniques as particularly relevant. By becoming involved in the North Sea, especially using our new technology, they would gain access to a ready supply of quality crude oil for their gasoline or petrol outlets and our more modern refinery, of course, is an added attraction, at least for the present. By combining their two per cent of the UK petrol market with our stake, the new group could realise substantial cost savings which could be ploughed into the redevelopment of a combined network. We must also remember that their distribution and marketing technology, especially at the point of sale, is light years ahead of us.

"Another important factor is that we own our big building, here in central London. MP has a UK head office in the country, near where you live, I believe, Lance, and I gather that they've plenty of space available. Selling our building and moving to the country would yield a one-off savings of many millions and, of course, they would also have two of everything so many staff would be made redundant."

HB, feeling increasingly optimistic, tried to look pessimistic.

"What should we be doing immediately?"

HB, listening to the ideas, predictable and unspectacular, was torn between making the company apparently more secure and not undermining MP's determination to buy Broadoak. He was encouraged by the widely-held view that money was not really a factor. Psychology seemed likely to determine whether his company survived and if MP shareholder pressure were as strong as his colleagues believed, there would only be one outcome.

It was agreed that Broadoak would:

Try to sell some small affiliated non-core companies, especially one that made wheelbarrows and another that sold tents via mail order. (These companies had been acquired in the days when oil companies did not know what to do with their massive profits and believed that they could run any organisation successfully. One large company had considered buying a circus but was deterred by its employees who maintained that the group already employed too many clowns.)

Attempt to form more links with other North Sea companies to save costs.

Investigate the possibility of moving Head Office to the country.

Sell poor-performance filling stations and invest more in the better outlets.

Close some smaller depots

Announce a modest share-buy back scheme.

Seek to sell marginal assets that might be worth more to another company

Withdraw from the very small but costly onshore UK exploration acreage.

Stop some management perks such as providing ice cream with a sweet at lunchtime. Henceforth, managers could choose one or the other, not both.

Cancel pensioners' annual summer trip down the Thames.

The delegates endorsed these proposals enthusiastically and individuals were charged with ensuring that the plans were followed up. Lance spoke. "I've listened to all this with more than a little interest. At last, it seems that we're going to do a few things that I have advocated for years. However desirable they may be, and they are, does anyone here think that they'll make any difference to the outcome of this bid? Anyone with half a brain can see that these ideas are panic moves by a worried, old-fashioned and incompetent company."

HB interrupted him with a serious gaze.

"All right, I withdraw that last sentence but what I'm trying to say is that the impact of any of these measures is going to take some time and will have no immediate relevance to the outcome of the bid. Furthermore, with one or two exceptions, we've pursued a policy of only promoting people when they reach the magic age of 40 plus. This means, with all respect to my colleagues, that we are not so forward-thinking as our competitors. The world is changing, ever faster, and, instead of planning change, we always react to it, too late."

HB had heard enough.

"OK, Lance, what do you recommend that is feasible and effective in the short term?"

"What we must do, despite the low priority accorded it by Morton, who seems to have surrendered before we start, is to prepare a really strong financial defence, concentrating on our performance and MP's major weaknesses, especially their failure to pay a dividend. Given their track record, we can show their limited potential for growth. All this may not be successful in repelling a bid but if we don't do that and do it soon, we shall vanish. Frankly, given the long association between Broadoak and Morton's company, I'm surprised and disgusted that this has not already been prepared in draft. I must ask, therefore, whether Morton and his expensive friends have their hearts in this? If they haven't, we must go elsewhere and quickly."

Boyle realised that what he was proposing could, if was successful, effectively undermine his own ambitions to have a senior job in the merged company but as he would soon be meeting the MD of MP, he had to demonstrate loyalty to his employers. Anyway, he was convinced that a bid would succeed.

HB had not expected such aggressive remarks and waved a restraining hand to Morton indicating that he should not respond.

"I don't think that's fair to our respected consultants, Lance, and I want it known that I fully support them in what they're doing, and, indeed, what they are not doing. Unless anyone else wishes to make a contribution, I think that we should end this meeting now and agree to meet again next Tuesday afternoon, unless there are any other developments in the meanwhile that justify our getting together before then. Many thanks, ladies and gentlemen and let's hope that we all get what we want."

HB was reasonably satisfied. He still was not really sure why MP wanted Broadoak, notwithstanding what he had heard, but he was convinced that a takeover would yield major cost savings for both companies, and in the current climate, that was what really mattered. The chief executive reminded himself that this crucial industry, which had to plan and invest on a long-term basis, was being led by an ignorant financial sector that could only think short term and by pressure groups whose ignorance was only matched by their odd belief that pursuit of their own twisted objectives justified the means. Yes, HB felt, he would be better out of all this.

Hugh Mungus was working hard to finish the draft of his story about Iraq's possible threat to Kuwait. A few insider contacts believed that Saddam was probably about to play a new game but nobody really knew what it would be. Hugh's piece had to be written very carefully so that whatever happened he would not look foolish. This was a story that nobody could confirm or deny in advance. He had received strong encouragement from some contacts in the UK and US delegations at the UN but, predictably, his French sources had ridiculed the piece. He would finish the story tomorrow and run it in Friday's edition.

Lance Boyle, eventually freed from the Broadoak meeting, hurried off to meet his near-neighbour, Jim Karner, the MD of MP UK. He didn't know what he was going to say, despite having spent hours pondering his approach. Only that morning, he had decided to approach TEPID (Top Executive Placement-Industrial Division) to see if they could find a position for him but he was not hopeful. He had to bet on MP. The two men met socially occasionally and saw each other at various industry functions. Jim, in his mid forties, always seemed easy-going, uncomplicated and ambitious and had already reached the top rank. His next move would be to the States to a very senior position. This would leave an important vacancy in a larger UK company if the takeover succeeded. Lance had decided what he wanted and he reasoned it was worth taking a small risk.

They met at about 7.30 in the garden of their local, The Fiddler and the Trader. It was too early for most of the regular customers and the only noise came from two pugilistic pugs fighting fiercely in an adjacent field.

"Good to see you again Lance. Here's to the future." Both men raised their glasses and took a deep draught of the local beer. A nervous Lance, remembering HB's injunction that his colleagues must not discuss the takeover with anyone, let alone meet MP people, was reluctant to begin the conversation. Jim came to his rescue. "I see the *Daily Shout* carried a story this morning that we are to get together."

"I really didn't know that our having a drink was of national importance."

Jim smiled. "You've seen the story, of course? It's by someone called Tim Robertson and he's claiming that our two companies are involved in merger talks. Do you know him?"

Lance shook his head, slowly. That, at least, gave him a few seconds to ponder his next move. Again, Jim helped. "Apparently, we're going to take you over, preferably in a friendly and agreed bid that we might make in the next 10 days or, if you don't agree, we'll make it a hostile bid. Do you know anything about it?"

Mr Boyle parried. "I was going to ask you the same question. Do you?"

"Can I speak frankly and totally confidentially to you?" The senior Brit did not wait for an answer but assumed it to be positive.

"When you rang, I was just about to call you."

Lance looked intrigued. Jim continued.

"We've known each other for some time, so I hope you'll forgive me for saying this, Lance, especially if I'm wrong, but I've sensed that you don't see your long–term future with Broadoak. In fact, I remember that you came close to criticising your board before an industry committee meeting last year. Again, tell me if I'm wrong, but I don't think that you've been promoted for several years have you?"

Lance again shook his head and smiled wistfully. "Not really. For the last six months, I've been called managing director as well as being in charge of marketing but it means absolutely nothing as anyone in the company would tell you. I didn't even receive a pay increase."

Jim noted that his friend had still not answered his question of whether he knew about the likely bid. His silence was eloquent.

"Well, whether you know about the possible takeover or not, I'll tell you that the newspaper story was correct. Furthermore, we know that HB convened a senior management meeting in the country to discuss the bid if and when it will come. I imagine you were there but I don't want to know."

Lance looked at the dogs. The number of participants had doubled but they were not all of the pug persuasion.

"I'll tell you now, it will be coming and we'll be successful."

Lance sighed and looked worried.

"From our perspective, it would be most interesting to know how you guess, and I do mean guess, on how Broadoak will react. After all, if we do buy your company and I'm very confident that we shall, we won't be retaining all the top men but we'll want some of the younger and brighter guys and they'll have great opportunities in a much larger group here and in the US."

Sensing that this could be a definitive moment in his career, Lance opted for a few significant sentences whilst avoiding anything that might come back to undermine his career at Broadoak. He wanted to remain there until a better offer came along. That might be soon but great care was required. He had transgressed HB's specific instruction that managers must not talk to any of their contacts in MP. "Well, where do I start? You certainly were right in saying that, occasionally, like so many people of my age, in so many companies, yours included, I dare say, I've been frustrated by the lack of promotion prospects. That's painful, because I'm sure that I can do more but how can I prove that in my company if they don't let me run the whole show? Yes, I admit to being ambitious and I'm beginning to wonder what I do next if I'm to make progress. I imagine you were involved in the discussions that preceded the informal approach from Chuck to HB."

It was Jim's turn to nod and Lance took a chance.

"Yes, we did have a meeting and I was there although it seemed to me that HB had already made up his mind on what ought to be done." He heard himself and paused. Was this wise? What he wanted to say next must be sensibly and sensitively composed. This was an occasion for coded speech, the interpretation of which could be denied if necessary. He continued more cautiously.

"I think that most outside observers would guess that we would resist any initial offer strenuously, saying that it was totally inadequate. That is precisely what any company in any industry would do in that situation, just as yours would. A board must secure the best possible deal for its shareholders and it must assume that no serious predator makes an initial offer that is also its final offer. So the outside observer would guess that a better bid would follow. You know that Broadoak seldom attracts much attention, and, I suspect that restless shareholders in many companies like ours and probably yours, from what I read, would rather have money, I mean cash, in their pockets today rather than the promise of more some time in the future. I guess that most analysts would be surprised if any white knights rode to our help. An astute analyst would also note that most of the company's senior managers are of a certain age and hold many shares in the company. You can see that in the annual report. It's just younger managers like me who, presumably, will be looking for a job if anyone buys us."

"That's nothing that you need worry about, Lance.

"Now let's talk about this winter's series with the Aussies. Do you think that we stand a chance?" The two men chatted idly for another hour, decided that England would struggle to avoid a series defeat, munched two pork pies and went home.

Within a few minutes of Henry's arrival at the Broadoak office in Houston on the Wednesday, he had a call from Jill. She had seen the *Shout* story and wanted to know if it was true that BO could be taken over. Henry merely muttered that she must not worry. He then apologised but he had to go because the vice-president for external affairs, M. Bargo, wondered if he could spare a minute. Henry, replying in American, said "sure can, Mike, but the meeting about the bid will be starting soon".

"It's ok, this won't take more than a few seconds. We need to talk, now." His tone was polite but urgent and Henry wondered what had happened. They went into the sombre wood-panelled, heavily carpeted conference room, that reminded Henry of somewhere, but he couldn't think where.

"I just wanted to congratulate you on your choice of companion." Perkins paled and his legs turned to hot water. Surely, Mike couldn't know about Wendy? If really necessary, he might have to say that he was taken there by colleagues who had even paid for three dances. No, he could not do that and he was ashamed for even thinking it. Mike then brandished a page from the local paper which contained the photograph of a stumbling Henry being helped out of an open top sports car by a very glamorous blonde. Wisely, he decided to say very little. "Some guys have it and others don't. I just bring out a maternal instinct in females of all ages. Anyway, she's a Brit and friend of the family and has been for years." His British modesty went down well. Other senior members of staff were now drifting in to the conference room.

Mike opened the meeting.

"As yawl know, Muswell Petroleum contacted our head office in London recently to talk about a possible merger. Or, at least that's what they called it. We all know that it would be a takeover. Now, again as obviously you know from Henry here, and welcome to the meeting, senior management in London is opposed to any such deal but they think that MP will go public with a specific bid very soon. Hubert Bennett, the chief executive, whom I guess many of you know, and the other directors are most anxious to devise a strategy to defeat any bid. Frankly, it doesn't look good and I don't have to tell you guys that if a takeover or merger or whatever you like to call it, does come, almost certainly, we're all going to be out on our asses. They're much bigger than us over here and I'm mighty unhappy about all this especially as MP usually pay very little in redundancy.

"Guys, we've been asked by London to do everything we can to assist. I know that some of you have already been talking to Henry about this but I must ask if any ideas have occurred to you. Frankly, I can't think of anything more important to us at the moment. The chips are down and the stakes are high." Henry felt that this sounded like the confession of an incompetent cook.

Silence ensued. The majority of those present had not realised the gravity of the situation and that their jobs were genuinely in danger. No one seemed prepared to speak first so Mike asked Henry for his views. He had little to offer and said so but it had already been established that the Brit was a very modest man so he was pressed to say something. " I really don't have much to add. I know that before I came out here, Hubert and the board were worried enough to bring in a variety of outside consultants…" Mike interrupted him. "I spoke to Hubert at his home last night and he said that he doesn't expect them to come up with anything worthwhile. He said we should have a brainstorming session as soon as possible. Henry, back to you."

Mr Perkins, who had suddenly realised that the conference room looked like the club, removed the blissful smirk that he felt he must be wearing, cleared his throat and said nothing for three seconds before uttering a few worthless words but they were sufficient to stimulate what was to become an interesting debate. The meeting lasted into the evening and through a dinner of sandwiches. No overall grand or even novel idea emerged but there were several thoughts that Henry would pass to HB as soon as he could.

Mike Michaelson, the local energy economist, noting that real interest rates were negative, suggested that the group took out a loan to buy some more assets that would help to develop relatively fast in new and expanding areas. He wondered if this might allow Broadoak to make a reverse bid for MP. Henry noted this. Another suggestion was that the company's enhanced oil recovery system should be made available on the open market, under license, rather than confining its application to old Broadoak fields in the North Sea. All this was fascinating but, as he fell into bed for an early night, Henry knew that something special was needed.

Mr Perkins was not the only absentee from the club that night. Wendy, knowing that her "uncle" would be absent, was having a night off with her boy friend but she had received a call from Anna that afternoon. Wendy listened with increasing incredulity. After thinking hard, she said that providing her friend was careful, it might just work but "for god's sake be very careful and don't take any risks. Nobody would want you to".

Anna arrived at the club at about 9.15, showered, made up and dressed up, or should it be down? Transformed, she emerged into the club through a door at the side of the stage, about one hour later, having changed into a cowgirls' suede top, white leather miniskirt and white knee-high boots. The ensemble was topped off with a jauntily-positioned stetson. Her usual purse, almost the size of a modest wallet, had been replaced by a small handbag. She swayed seductively towards a prematurely balding big man, whose other main distinguishing mark was a big moustache. He was, as usual, wearing a white shirt.

"Hi there, big boy, how yawl tonight? I sure am glad to see you. It's been kinda quiet the last week and I've missed you." Whilst offering this unashamed sales pitch, Anna landed carefully on the executive's lap, ensuring that he could take maximum advantage. She draped an arm around his shoulders and with the remaining hand hid what was still visible of her tiny skirt. This encouraged him to look at her long brown legs as she wriggled on his lap in a bogus attempt to be comfortable. It also reminded the executive of many happy hours spent with her in the club over the last year. She pecked him on the cheek. It was clear that she was not about to give a lecture on the declining role of the vu-foil projector. "Making lots of money, so you can come here and spend it on us poor little girls?" she enquired, like a small child asking a wealthy parent to stump up for an ice cream.

Before he could reply, she put her hand on his head and gently ruffled his remaining hair.

"I've really missed you, sugar. Why don't we go upstairs where there's more space and then we can be real friendly?" Chuck Charles needed no second invitation. Bimbo Anna had not said that it was much quieter. For the next hour or so she needed to have much less noise. Chuck paid another $15 and followed his friend, hand in hand, to another land.

Once they were both settled on a comfortable and commodious leather sofa she resumed the conversation, after placing herself strategically on his copious lap. "The other day, as I was stripping off to go to bed, I was thinking about you." The image roused him. "I was thinking how clever you were and wishing that I was more like you instead of just being a simple girl. What was that really bright idea you thought up to make some more money?"

The oilman, now physically aroused and with his guard well down, looked at the self-confessed bimbo and thought that tonight he might try to take her to a local hotel where he had a room booked for occasional alliances, as he called his one-night stands. She was as dumb as a doorknob but she was really attractive and she seemed to know how to make him really, really excited. His vocabulary, unlike his bank account, was limited. Anna's next judiciously-timed wriggle encouraged him to boast.

"Well, it all happened some years ago. I got the idea from some guys in Britain. I'd just been promoted and I had the power to authorise payment of invoices."

Anna screwed up her enchanting little face and looked puzzled.

"Do you know what I mean by invoices?"

"I think so, no, not really."

"Well, I give you dollars when you dance for me but if we agreed that I paid you once a month, you would have to send me a piece of paper saying how much I owed you and detailing the services rendered. That's called an invoice."

Anna managed to avoid smiling and asked, "what's services rendered?"

"In your case, honey, that's easy. You could put down 'provision of assistance to senior management'. You sure provide some real fine assistance and I want you to know that I'm mighty grateful."

"I remember now. Isn't that what you did? You sent invoices to yourself."

"Sure" said the boss of Muswell Petroleum, surprised and flattered that she had remembered. "I had some headed paper printed with the name of a mythical company".

Anna interrupted. "What's mythical?"

"It means that it doesn't exist."

"and I then sent these invoices on the headed paper to myself at Muswell to approve for payment and then the money goes into the bank account of these non-existent companies and I collect it."

Anna paused and again looked puzzled as she pretended to work out the implications of all this. "And these companies never do any work for you because they don't exist?"

"You've got it gorgeous. These dumb guys in accounts have paid up regularly for years now, without any questions and I guess they never will. They just truss me. There are some advantages, baby, with working with such complete dumbos. They juss pay whatever I send them."

Anna allowed herself to look admiringly enraptured. "Gee, you sure are clever, Chuck. How long have you been doing that?"

"Some years now, I guess. I bought the ranch with it and my collection of vintage cars plus the limo where you and I had some fun last Christmas."

Anna tried not to wince at the recollection but the $500 tip she had been given for some modest physical activity had enabled her to have her old car repaired.

"Anyway, I want a dance. Perform gorgeous."

Anna did as she was bid, having carefully moved her handbag from the table on to the chair next to the one that they had recently shared. This was to be the first of 10 dances for which Anna was paid more than the standard $200 but the final cost to Chuck was higher. It was a good evening.

Chapter 23

In London, Hugh Mungus was busy, finishing his article on the apparent threat to Kuwait. As expected, his contacts had been unable to confirm or deny the story but he knew that his carefully-crafted piece would arouse considerable comment when it was published on the morrow. The oil market was already nervous because the PISS figures suggested that US oil stocks were at a low level.

Within seconds of waking on his last full day in Houston, Henry, once again, was assailed by guilt, worry, joy and, inevitably, fear that he and many colleagues faced unemployment. Furthermore, after this trip, he would never see Anna again and, judging by the way that Wendy was earning money, she was unlikely to return to the UK for some time. Had he done anything that was so immoral or damaging? Why this tireless tedious, demoralising debilitating agonising? Unlike so many men, he had never been unfaithful and what had happened this week was, well, just a brief glimpse of what might have happened in the youth that he never had. That, and the thought that thousands of males enjoyed life every evening, did little to assuage his guilt. Why, just for once, should he be any different? What had happened had happened but the unique memory could not, must not, be undermined by guilt.

He intended to spend most of the day at the office, discussing budgets, sales forecasts and the takeover, if there were anything new to say but, first of all, he wanted to invite the girls to lunch. Fortunately, Wendy was awake and, coincidentally, Anna was lunching with her anyway. Then he phoned HB, who, unusually as it was 3.00 p.m. in the UK, was coherent and told him of the little that had emerged during the long meeting the day before. Hubert seemed oddly sanguine and even happy, despite the real prospect that Broadoak could soon lose its independence.

Sometime today, he really must ring Jill. Whenever he remembered, she was asleep and when he forgot she was awake. Some shopping had to be done later in the afternoon and, on leaving the hotel, Henry had to make a courtesy call on another company in Houston with which Broadoak had a good relationship in the North Sea.

Continuing his review of the day, he decided that, although he was not due to fly out until Friday afternoon, he ought to pack. He knew that taking clothes out of a case, and then neatly folding them again for re-packing, always created a shortage of at least 15 per cent of the original case space. Finally, he had to attend a dinner with his colleagues. After that, as it was his last night in town, probably for ever, he might just patronise The Hotspot.

The normally staid atmosphere at the office had been replaced by some excitement. Apparently, in the last week, US stocks of crude oil and gasoline had fallen dramatically. Crude oil prices had soared by $3 a barrel and seemed destined to rise further, prompted by forecasts of unseasonably cold weather across the US. Oil company share prices were moving up and Broadoak, listed on the New York stock exchange, was rising encouragingly, in contrast to those of MP because Chuck Charles had said only last week that he saw no profit in maintaining high inventories as prices were destined to remain low for some time.

Henry, pleased by the news but seeing no long-term advantage for Broadoak, was looking forward to lunching with his new friends. It would be exciting yet innocent and he was reminded of distant days when a date was in prospect. Then he always failed but now there were no pass or failure levels. Henry would always be grateful to Wendy and Anna for this belated reminder of what it might have been like to be young and successful. The restaurant, recommended by his hotel, was on the outskirts of the downtown area and, judging by the number and quality of cars in the park on three sides of the building, it was expensive and popular. Henry did not care. This was an investment for his old age.

The girls were already at the bar, sipping orange juices. They looked like sisters as each was dressed in short, pink and summery dresses, prompting Perkins to wonder why girls in London apparently thought that wearing faded and dirty jeans and filthy black boots was a legal requirement. When they saw Perkins padding over the ruby red carpet, they slid off their stools elegantly and hugged him. "Hi Perky, what's up?" asked Anna, clearly not expecting an answer.

Henry, to his surprise, was not embarrassed and glowed in the knowledge that several men, about half his age, were looking green. He did not care, even if they thought that he had paid for the treat. If this was what it was like to be a sugar daddy, pass the bowl. A few drinks later, he and the girls moved upstairs to the restaurant which contained more plants than a well-stocked greenhouse. A flunkey, scarcely able to conceal his envy, escorted them to a table in one corner of the garden room. The sun shone through a well-cleaned glass wall and potted palms provided both relief and privacy. If Perkins had had any doubts on what topics might have been ventilated over the lunch, they soon vanished. Being the oldest and the host, Henry thought that he ought to start and, besides, he was anxious to say something. Indeed, that had been the real reason for suggesting this lunch. "Please forgive me for being neurotic about this, but I'm very worried about what I said about the possible takeover. It's true, as I said, that many of us could lose our jobs but if word got out that I had told you, I would be in real trouble. I know that I can trust you to say nothing, can't I?"

Both girls nodded their well-coiffured heads in unison. Henry felt relieved and, possibly quite irrationally, thought that he could trust his life to them. He was becoming silly and recalled that there's no fool like an old fool. For the rest of the lunch, conversation flowed back and forth, on nothing in particular. Both girls were intelligent and more capable than Henry of small, medium and large talk. Towards the end of the meal, they looked knowingly at each other and indicated that their noses were in need of powdering. As they came back, Henry, having paid the bill, heard the end of their conversation. "…I'm really glad that it worked" Wendy said. Anna nodded "yeah, it was easy. I'll pass it on tonight".

Whilst they were powdering proboscises, Wendy had said how sorry she felt for Henry, who seemed such a good guy and how unfair it was that honest, sincere people like him could lose their jobs. He had been really terrific in that television interview, bravely saying things that others funked and he'd treated them as intelligent adults and not just playthings, unlike most guys. For example, he had realised that they had to earn a living and, as he could not afford too many dances, had encouraged them to find other customers. Anna had summed it up. "He's a good guy who deserves a break."

A sorrowful Henry bid the girls goodbye and was particularly unhappy to say farewell to Wendy who could not be at the club that evening. She hugged him and hoped that all would be well. He must visit her again when he was next in town. He knew that he would never return. Embarrassed and emotional, he thanked her for everything. "You'll never know how much I owe you."

The restaurant chosen for dinner that evening was busy and the Broadoak group had to wait before a red-haired vertically-challenged girl, by name Marilyn, apologised and said that they were short-staffed that evening. Henry wanted to say that she was not too tall herself but stayed silent. Meanwhile, the headwaiter spent all his time positioning and re-positioning cutlery on unoccupied tables, ignoring patrons seemingly keen to eat. The dinner was a very staid affair and the gloomy atmosphere reflected the fact that no big idea on how to defeat the takeover had emerged.

Henry spent most of the evening just listening, wondering why his friends delighted in using four words when one would have sufficed so he listened to only a quarter of the conversation. He also tuned in to chats on nearby tables and heard two men discussing colleagues who had been killed at work. Only when they ran out of names when the dessert arrived did they change topics. Most of their comments were preceded by "I want to share this with you". One, clearly almost drunk, confessed that he'd forgotten his friend's name. When told, he nodded approvingly and confirmed "yes, that' right".

Predictably, huge quantities of food vanished as his American colleagues ate whilst still debating how to save Broadoak. Henry tried vainly to keep up.

Eventually, his colleagues drove off into the night, to their loved ones, and, in some cases, their wives and Henry took a cab back to his hotel. There he changed and, inevitably, pondered how the next few hours would unfold. Surely, as this was his third visit to the club in four days, the impact would be much weaker. Diminishing returns, he told himself, recalling his failed economics degree. After changing and showering, he had only arrived at about 11.45 and the suspicious cab driver asked if he really did want to go to the club as it was so late. "You know they shut at two?" "Yes". "You must be a fast worker, man, but if that's what you want, let's go."

Over lunch, when Wendy had told him that she could not go to the club that evening, he was close to deciding not to go himself. Much as he liked Anna, nothing would be gained and it might be better not to subject himself any longer to the bizarre combination of pleasure and pain but something had been said that convinced him that he should go. As the girls left after lunch, Anna had asked Henry to meet her in the club car park at about 2.15 on the Friday morning. Apparently, she had to ask him now because it was confidential and if she asked him in the club, she might be overheard and then she would be fired.

"Will you do that, Perky?"

Perkins was puzzled but Wendy had encouraged him. "I know it sounds odd, Henry, but I promise you, it's all quite safe but it's really important." He had agreed and was told where Anna's black Toyota would be parked. "I'll tell the security guard that you'll be there, he's a friend of mine so there won't be any problems and he won't shoot you".

Despite being riven by curiosity, Henry enjoyed his last evening of fantasy. Intoxicated by perfume, music and mystery, he had been to a place whose existence he did not know even a few days ago. Now the dream was over but, in his mid fifties, he had finally tasted excitement.

Chapter 24

The article by Hugh Mungus on the possible invasion of Kuwait had received substantial coverage in the media and was the lead item on the BBC's main news bulletins. Not only was it an otherwise slack news day but Hugh had distributed a press statement that had attracted interest from journalists who were otherwise wondering what to write.

In the London office of Broadoak Oil, there was little activity. An offer had not yet been received from MP and the chief executive was worried. Nevertheless, the trade journals, which surely knew what was what in these matters, were forecasting that Broadoak would be the next independent to succumb to a large US group. That said, Hubert the shareholder, who had come in early, was impressed with what was happening to the Broadoak share price, propelled by US inventory statistics, the possibility of a new crisis in the Middle East and forecasts of cold weather across the north-east of the United States.

Earlier in Houston, at 2.00 am, Henry, having found Anna's car, wandered around the tree-lined car park. The temperature was in the seventies and the night air was still. The silence was broken by the rhythmic noise of crickets, the distant traffic on the main highway and Henry's thumping heart. Apart from this, the only sound was the occasional clunk of a car door being slammed and then the chesty roar as another expensive vehicle took its female driver into the inner recesses of the night. Some shouted out goodnight to anyone in earshot. Two called out "bye, Perky, come and see us again". Soft grey clouds skidded silently into obscurity, temporarily hiding the stars which invested the scene with their own romantic dimension. Henry recalled waiting for his first girl friend, a redhead, outside school and later, meeting his first real love outside a London departmental store. Why did such apparently irrelevant and elderly images stroll uninvited into his consciousness?

He was waiting under the stars, on a warm Texan night, for probably the most attractive girl he had ever seen and it was at her request. One thing was sure: whatever the temptations or the circumstances, and he was really attracted to Anna, physically and intellectually, heaven help him, he would remain loyal to Jill. He rebuked himself. What arrogance and conceit to think that Anna had asked him to meet her for that reason. "All right, that was absurd, but why did she want me to meet her at such a time and place?"

The reverie ended abruptly as Anna came over. "Hi Perky." The new Henry smiled. It was frightening to realise how much he had changed in a few days and he wondered if Jill would detect any differences. He'd worry about that later. Now was now and the next few hours could be rather interesting, he thought with characteristic British understatement. Henry, demonstrating manners and maturity, held the door of the sport car open for Anna. She lowered herself carefully sideways and then swung round behind the steering wheel. Then, showing minimal grace and even less savoir-faire, Henry fell into his seat. He had miscalculated his descent into the decadence that his parents had always linked with sports cars. Doubtless if they had considered that the ever-young and rather naïve Henry could ever have found himself in the position, they would have also warned him about associating with their drivers, especially at night and if they were Texan, young, very female and blonde. However, their imagination could never have stretched so far and nothing in Henry's past had suggested that he could ever have been in such a situation. Now he was.

He sat for a moment, drinking in what he knew would be unique, however long he lived. He was in a totally different world from which, he, a gawping newcomer, would soon be catapulted into unemployment. He absorbed the atmosphere and circumstances avariciously. He was even able to ignore the pain that reminded him that his youth should have been characterised by numerous memories like this. Instead, there was nothing, absolutely nothing, so he would recall every last detail. Whatever the pangs induced by the realisation of what he had missed, he was once again grateful for the opportunity of adding this memory to his otherwise remorselessly dull collection. He had come alive for just a few hours.

Henry looked at the black shadows of the nearby trees, outlined against the grey skies, the departing cars and their attractive drivers. He looked at the car, too expensive for most men twice Anna's age, and he looked at her. She was wearing jeans, a yellow open-necked shirt and flat shoes for driving. Her perfume was intoxicatingly seductive and, unlike the other girls whom Henry had watched leaving the club, she had not removed all her make-up. Her colleagues had gone to some lengths to disguise their femininity. Most had changed into faded denims and scruffy tee shirts and the bags that they were carrying presumably contained their more alluring wear. Having been spectacularly noticeable earlier, they now sought anonymity.

The piquant impact on Mr Perkins was electrifying, especially as he knew that nothing could happen, could it, and that nothing must happen, must it? The ignition key was turned and the unusual couple headed into the night and the brighter lights of the downtown area.

"Had a good evening, Perky?"

Hearing confirmation that he was part of this new world, thus saving him the task of pinching himself, Henry rallied with some style. "Not particularly, I must admit, it was dominated by shop talk but, as you know, things improved in the second half." She smiled.

"I expect you're wondering why I asked you to meet me here, in the early morning but I didn't think that there would be another opportunity to see you before you went back to the UK. I've something that might help you and I couldn't give it to you at lunch or in the club. I want to take you home, if you don't mind. I want to kidnap you."

A perplexed Perkins certainly did not mind but the "explanation" increased his curiosity. What on earth did she mean? Why had an attractive girl, young enough to be his daughter, no, such thoughts must be banned, invited him to meet her in the small hours of the morning and why he was now hurtling at over 70 miles an hour across Houston towards her home? The comment about helping him was particularly mystifying but he wisely did not pursue this, sensing that all would eventually become clear. It was masochistically pleasant just to speculate. Frankly, he had no idea of what was coming but one thing he did know: no physical activity was on the agenda.

"I thought that we might have a coffee and chat at my place but first I must buy a few biscuits. Is that ok with you?" Henry nodded and looked at his watch. It was 2.50 am and he was just about to go shopping. He recalled oft-repeated words of his grandmother. "What would people think?" He didn't know what he thought, let alone other people. He also remembered her frequent claim that something was not what people wanted. He was beginning to know what he wanted. The physical frustration was building.

He asked Anna if she had had a good night, socially and financially.

"Yeah, I think so. There were some Arabs in tonight and they're always big spenders. I also saw some old friends so I'm sorry that I couldn't spend more time with you. Here, please count it for me." With one hand on the steering wheel as they bumped along, she used the other to extricate a small purse from a big bag. She passed it to Henry, who, tentatively, opened it. He pulled out a wad of dollar bills and began his unique task. She continued to chat, commenting on the behaviour of some young Japanese who had to be rejected from the club for expressing their gratitude towards one of the girls too vigorously.

As he counted and she conversed, the only comment that really registered was how she would miss him at the club. "I know that it's only been a few evenings, but you're so different. You're a blast." Henry assumed that this was good. "You have a sense of humour and you make me laugh. Not many guys do that: they're only interested in one thing, not, of course, that they get it, at least from me."

"I really like you and if the circumstances had been different..." She did not finish her sentence as a bright yellow Mazda sports car screeched past, rather too close for comfort and her speech was interrupted with a verbal torrent which indicated some dissatisfaction with the other driver's behaviour. Showing remarkable reactions, whilst braking swiftly, she stretched out a protective arm to prevent Perkins from moving forward. He was both impressed and touched, in more ways than one. In the sudden but short-lived incident, Anna's financial adviser, still occupied in counting, did not hear how she really liked him and if the circumstances had been different...

A few moments later, Henry was able to announce the results. "As far as I can determine, the total is $950." Anna purred with pleasure. "That's more than I thought. Thanks." She put her purse back in the larger bag and pulled up in a car park outside a brilliantly illuminated hypermarket. Despite the time, several dozen cars were parked there. As they walked around the store, about the size of Oakshire, Mr Perkins, some decades older than his young companion, suddenly felt almost ill with fatigue. Perhaps it was psychological: when the wave of fatigue washed over him, they were walking through the sales area devoted to beds. He made a powerful effort to recover and minutes later, revived in the fresh air as they walked towards her car.

Anna inserted a CD into the car's player and increased the volume so that the whole of Texas could be given this early wake-up call but they were travelling so fast that few would have heard the noise for more than seconds. Roaring down now deserted streets, and occasionally turning abruptly, challenging car, tyres and passenger equilibrium, Anna, clearly an excellent if fast driver, took Perkins towards a crucial chapter in his new life.

They were now in a less developed area and with a final scream from the protesting tyres, the car came to a complete halt on a 40 yard drive alongside a bungalow. "Out you get, we're here." Seeking to help the struggling Perkins, as he sought to leave the very low sports car, she placed a helping hand on an area of his body that even Mrs Perkins had effectively regarded as a "no-go area" for many years and pushed him out. He smiled his gratitude. As he followed his blonde friend into her home, he looked discreetly at his watch. It was 3.30 am and he wondered just how effective he would be the following day. He immediately corrected himself. Today had started and it had commenced in a way that suggested it would be remembered for a long time, whatever happened. Anyway, he had little to do and his flight was not until late afternoon.

They were in the kitchen. "Like a strong coffee, Perky? You look as if you need it."

"Please. I must admit this is rather different from my usual lifestyle and I really feel my age."

"Garbage, you look at least 10 years younger than you are and you mustn't take any notice of me. I'll fade at about lunchtime and go to bed then. That's what my body needs and as it's a good friend to me, I listen to what it tells me."

Henry, whose confused body was transmitting some very mixed and unusual messages, ignored them all but why was he here and what was the big mystery? He accepted his coffee and recently acquired biscuits.

Anna left the kitchen and moved into her bedroom, beckoning him to follow her. "I hope you don't mind coming in here. I'm not trying to seduce you, well not yet", and here she grinned, "but it's the most comfortable room in the house". Henry, his imagination already out of control, demurred. At his friend's invitation, Henry sat on the edge of the bed and Anna began her long-awaited explanation. "Wendy and I were worried that you might lose your job if Muswell Petroleum buys your company and she suddenly realised that we might be able to help. You remember that guy we saw in the club and who worked for them?" Henry nodded. "I don't know if it really can help but I thought that you might like to hear his explanation of how he deceived his company for years and stole so much money from them?"

This was more than Henry could absorb immediately. His jaw dropped, his eyes rolled in astonishment and his head, asked to process this extraordinary piece of information, throbbed with the effort. A few seconds later, having established that he had not fallen asleep and was not in the middle of an odd dream, Henry revived and his imagination started to function.

Anna stretched deep into her cavernous bag and pulled out a small tape recorder.

"You've taped a conversation with him?"

"Yeah."

Henry, stunned, immediately expressed his concern for her safety. "He didn't suspect anything did he? You'll be ok won't you?"

Anna thought that was typical of Henry, that, on the verge of hearing something that could save his company and his future, his first thought was for her safety.

"Absolutely. I made sure that he had a few drinks whilst we were with him, enough to blur his judgement but not enough to cause any problems."

"Are you sure you'll be ok?"

"I'm sure but, anyway, it's time that I changed clubs and I'll probably go to work for a friend who runs one near the international airport. Please don't worry, it's real cute of you to be so concerned, but you mustn't worry. I can promise you that apart from Wendy and now you, nobody knows what happened and I'm sure that you won't use this to blackmail him. You're a clever guy and I know that you'll devise a more subtle plan to take advantage of his confessions."

Henry's mind was in a whirl. "I just can't believe that you've done this for me. I'm very grateful for what you've done and just hope that nothing happens to you." Henry placed his coffee on an adjacent table. Anna sat down close to Henry on the edge of her bed, stretched seductively, grinned and said it was time for action. After only a few seconds, Henry requested a pen and some paper. Anna obliged and started the tape. Mr Perkins started taking notes. Ignoring the verbal by-play, the relevant conversation lasted only a few sentences but Henry, to his astonishment, was already beginning to see how it could be used, without any hint of blackmail and, most importantly of all, without in any way implicating the resourceful Anna.

"Well, what do you think?"

"I don't have the right words to say how I feel. I'm totally overwhelmed. I could not be more grateful. I think that you're a very kind and thoughtful girl. You've tried to help a near total stranger and many hundreds of my colleagues, providing that I use this information sensibly and I'm sure that I can. I'm really moved and very very grateful. I just hope that you'll be ok. I promise you that I'll use this extremely carefully without in any way indicating how I acquired the information. Whatever happens, and it's now up to me, I'm really grateful, more than you can realise. I shall owe you for the rest of my days if this works. Please say thanks to Wendy as well. I've got to leave tomorrow, I mean later today, so I shan't see either of you again, certainly on this trip, although I'll try to return to Houston from time to time, if we survive this takeover bid. But you took a big gamble for me? Why?"

"As I said, I think you're a good guy, Perky, and Wendy told me that she has known you since she was little and you were always kind to her. We both thought that this was an opportunity to help you. That other guy's a crook and I don't like to think that he can chuck people out of employment. He's a louse and ought to be squashed. Anyway, I hope that you save your company. You'll keep in touch, won't you? Here's my address and phone number and I've written my email address on the back. Please let me know how you get on. You promise you'll keep in touch?"

"Of course I shall. It's been tremendously exciting for an old man like me to meet someone like you. You've given me some unexpected and very happy memories to take into old age, apart from probably saving my job. What a week!"

His speech was stopped abruptly. Anna muttered "don't be silly" and dragged him closer, kissing him gently but significantly on the lips before asking him to excuse her for a moment. She returned after a few minutes, accompanied, to Henry's astonishment, by Wendy. Both girls were nearly dressed as cheerleaders.

"Now then, Perky, what about one more dance, for old time's sake?" The two girls draped themselves over the startled oilman and transported him to another world for about 10 minutes. He emerged exhausted, confused, happy and sad as Wendy announced his imminent return to his hotel.

"Mr Perky, come on it's late, even for me, so I'll take you back to your hotel, although I would like to kidnap you for what's left of the night. I really would like to, but I don't think it would be right." He embraced Anna warmly and then Wendy who kissed him more lustily than would have been deemed proper if he had been her real uncle. Just 10 minutes later, Henry, having finally kissed Wendy goodbye in the dutiful manner of a real uncle, once again found a hand propelling him out of the car and back into the real world. "Stay in touch, Perky!"

He waved, forced a final smile and tried to ignore the deep and thudding pain caused by the certainty of deprivation. He had crossed the boundary between collecting a few memories for old age and the frustration of unfulfilled desire. Just when he might have been provided with a solution to his business frustration, he had acquired a deep, deep sense of physical deprivation. He even missed the envious glance of the hotel night staff as he moved reluctantly to the lift that would reunite him with lonely reality.

Chapter 25

Henry left a hot, humid and hectic Houston on the Friday afternoon and reached a chilly Heathwick early on Saturday morning. For once, being exhausted, he slept for most of the journey but was annoyed when, stretching forward to remove his shoes, his head became stuck on a piece of chewing gum lodged on the back of the seat in front of him. This only became apparent when a spider-web like network connected him to the seat.

Some 300 miles later, he had detached himself satisfactorily. Some travellers, dressed for the Texas weather in shorts and T-shirts, were doubtless unpleasantly surprised to discover that temperatures "back home" were not identical to those in the rest of the world. Clearly, that was something that the Administration would have to resolve once the US president had rid the world of all terrorists, crime, ill-health and, hopefully, rainfall during Test matches when England were well-positioned. Presumably, refusing to accept the Kyoto accord was a first and laudable step in this direction.

Jill had met him, Henry, not the US president, at the airport and because he had slept on the plane, the male Perkins spent the rest of the day snoozing, unpacking, accompanying Jill in some modest shopping, walking round the garden, reading the newspapers and doing nothing much before jet lag set in around 8.00 o'clock. Mr and Mrs Perkins had much to discuss but the main conversation was reserved for early evening before Henry flagged.

Television news claimed that Iraq was moving troops to the border with Kuwait and this was linked with the other previously reported factors prompting the economics correspondent to suggest that crude oil prices, and thus petrol prices, were bound to rise soon. One motorist said in an interview that this would not affect her as she always bought £10 worth each time she filled up. All that was the second lead story.

The first concerned the sale of a footballer to a northern club for £95 million. He was "over the moon" and Henry remarked that on a weekly wage of £150,000, he could afford to do that for real. The third story was about a local authority which had cut down all the trees over 1.23077 metres high in a park, lest a falling branch cause injury. There had been no such accidents since the park was opened during Queen Victoria's reign but as the leader of the local council, Anna Logg, apparently a financial adviser, noted, history was no guide to future performance.

A man had taken his wife to court for denying him extra-marital sex. Apparently, he thought that this meant more activity with his next of kin. When the misunderstanding was revealed and the case terminated, he said "basically, at the end of the day, jew know what I mean, I'm coming to terms with it, trust me. It's brilliant, real cool." The US president, still concerned that there were many millions of "my fellow citizens" who had below-average intelligence, was demanding a shake-up of all US statistics after discovering that so many always ended with a series of noughts.

Jill turned the television off before the weather forecast, prompting her husband to warn that "you realise that this means that, unaided, we shall have to decide what kind of clothes to wear tomorrow?" Her predictable husband was back. "I think that we can probably manage without help from that retarded bimbo, Mabel Thorpe, who doesn't even know where Manchester is: when you were away, she relocated it just outside Ipswich."

They discussed the US trip and Henry, who was beginning to feel tired, which prompted him to be extra careful in what he said, conceded that he had seen much more of Houston this time, much more than he expected, and that he really liked what he saw. He must not mention Wendy and Anna and, anyway, nothing had happened, had it?

Jill was more interested in what might happen on the takeover bid and wanted more information than she had gleaned from Henry thus far. "Didn't you get any good ideas on how to defeat Muswell's bid, which, incidentally, that ill-informed twerp on the radio said was imminent?" Henry knew who she meant. He was the man who forecast that a major US trading company was on the point of announcing record profits just before the group went bankrupt.

"Frankly, I'm really worried. The Americans only offered fairly predictable stuff. There's no big idea and that's what bothers me most. Just like the London people, they're very keen to remain independent.

But I really wonder if HB and Lance Boyle, for example, really want to defeat the bid. Perhaps Hubert thinks he'd be better off by retiring and Lance fancies his chances in a merged group. Another thing worries me. The outside consultants have been completely useless. Why? Do they want the merger to go ahead? I don't think that we have a strategy. It's almost as if some managers and even the outside consultants have given up or want us to be taken over. With so many scams these days in so many business sectors, and so many corrupt and incompetent directors, you really wonder, not that I'm saying that this applies to Hubert and Lance. But I haven't given up. I'm working on a new plan."

Jill, really anxious, tried to sound cheerful. "That's my husband. Would it help to talk it through with me? Tell me all". Henry almost recoiled at the thought of telling Jill anything.

"No thanks, not at the moment, if you don't mind, I'm still kicking it around in my head. If I decide to go ahead, could you slot me into your conference on Tuesday and tell the media that it might be worth their while attending?" Jill was unsure but after several minutes' discussion, reluctantly agreed. Henry had to promise that he would do nothing to reduce his employment prospects in the industry. He also had to confirm his participation by lunchtime on Monday, at the latest.

Henry resumed. "Anyway, we still haven't talked in any detail about your weekend away with Denis. I'm afraid I've been pre-occupied with work." He flicked a fly which was showing an unhealthy interest in his gin and tonic and said, "so tell me all". Jill almost recoiled at the thought of telling Henry anything.

"Was it really grim, being with Denis all that time?"

"No, not really". Jill, like Henry earlier, knew that she must choose her words carefully. "As I told you on the phone, he was thoughtful and considerate. Frankly, I was pleasantly surprised. He was a perfect gentleman and didn't do or even attempt anything that he shouldn't have." She smiled inwardly. Only she knew what standards she had imposed and whether he had conformed. "I think that we all misjudged him because he used to wear white socks."

"But I thought that as your friend Janet puts it, he was always "letching about".

"Well, perhaps I don't appeal to him sufficiently, but I can assure you that he didn't overpower me to have his evil way with me." Again, she had to suppress a faint smile. She was enjoying this game and this was her first secret since university. Anyway, nothing had happened, had it? The conference was fine but there's something else that I want to talk to you about. I think that I might have to change jobs."

Henry grimaced. "What? They're going to fire you after so many years just after sending you on that expensive course?"

"That doesn't mean anything. You, above anyone, should know how stupid companies can be. Anyway, I didn't necessarily mean I'm about to be fired. I might be moved to another division. As you know, Denis is a general manager and he told me in the strictest confidence that divisional budgets are being cut and that mine could be next so I should be prepared. Denis thinks that I might be switched to conference promotions. Frankly, that's where I started and I'm not keen on returning. Even 'though I would head the division, because Paddy Field's retiring, I'm not keen because the work is boring and difficult. As I've said many times before, people don't want to sit in a darkened room all day, listening to uninspiring speakers and looking at badly designed, cluttered and out of date visuals, totally invisible at a range of more than a few feet, or I suppose I ought to say metres. More often than not, the machinery used for the visuals fails to work and when slides are projected, the lazy speakers have not checked them, so they are upside down... "

Henry, who had heard this speech many times before and who welcomed the respite, decided against asking if the speakers were upside down.

"And they are in the wrong order. For all this they are asked to stump up several hundred pounds for the privilege. I'm sure that one reason for attending conferences is to be able to boast 'as I said to the minister the other day'. Now senior speakers don't come and there is rather less prestige in crowing 'as I said the other day to Joe Bloggs'. Papers are often boring, bland and unimaginative and usually only cover old ground. I mean, if you had discovered a new kind of mouse trap, would you stand up at a conference and tell your competitors all about it? Broadly, the more senior the speaker, the more likely that they won't turn up. Printed or web versions of the paper are seldom available, so why do these idiots allegedly spend so much time preparing their presentations and then fail to maximise the intended benefits? That's one reason why the press don't come to so many conferences and they haven't the time to cover fourth rate speeches from fourth rate people. Anyhow, journalists can sleep more comfortably in their beds than at conferences.

"Then the staff at the hotels where we mount most of our events, seldom speak English so it's difficult to persuade anyone to provide what you ordered and for which you will be charged a hefty fee. Those who do speak our native tongue, generally, couldn't care less. Conferences are dying, although, of course, the networking benefits remain substantial if you can assemble really good speakers. The trouble is that the audiences are small and often consist of fringe people, who, by definition, are not very well-informed, as otherwise they would not attend in any case."

Henry listened in silence. "I really had no idea..".

He was unable to finish as Jill, having taken a deep breath, was about to continue. "Frankly, Henry, I think that I've had enough of this company and conferences. It may be time to look for something else."

Henry was surprised. Obviously, Jill was serious so he must be tactful but the reality was that his own job could soon vanish if he could not use his new information to full advantage. He hadn't been earning big money for long enough to be financially happy but he must be tactful and he knew only too well the frustration of doing a boring job. "I really had no idea that you felt so strongly about your job or that you were so unhappy, although I know from what you've said recently that everything was not perfect."

"I haven't felt this strongly for very long. I've been thinking about making a change for some time but since I came back from the weekend conference, I've been unsettled, depressed and frustrated." Henry knew precisely what she meant.

"This is bad news, Jill, and I'm really sorry especially as it comes at a potentially very difficult time for us. Forgive me for mentioning the bid again but I think we must assume we'll lose. We haven't moved with the times and HB is out of touch with the modern world. I'm almost certain that I'll lose my job and finding a new one at my age won't be easy. I'm frightened."

Jill swiftly re-assured her husband and unexpectedly held his hand. "I would never leave just like that. I'd stay until we knew more about your future but I think I should look around to see if there's anything else that I can do. I need a change but I certainly won't do anything impulsively, whatever the provocation. Anyway, I'd be due for some money if the company asks for voluntary redundancies. Perhaps one day we could find something that we could do together?"

Henry assumed that this was rhetorical, so said nothing, absent-mindedly sipped the remains of the gin and tonic and spat out a drunken fly.

Chapter 26

Henry spent a quiet Sunday, thinking how he could use his new information to maximum advantage to undermine the MP bid. He was now refining the idea that he had had when in Houston but it had to be thought through carefully. Jill attributed his pensive mood mainly to fatigue and jet lag. Privately, she had given up hope that Broadoak could be saved. This and her own job insecurity depressed her. Some of Jill's fears were confirmed the following day by her friend and managing director, Lisa Carter. "Jill, I'll come straight to the point. As you know, the conference business has not done particularly well lately and our record isn't much better than the competition. We've had to cut budgets by 25 per cent and I've got to reduce the numbers in your division. I certainly don't want to lose you and it's more important than ever that we market our events as effectively as possible. Paddy's retiring at the end of the week, so I'd like you to replace him and head up marketing. I know that's where you started but the jobs' really important. Without effective marketing, the entire UK organisation might sink, so I hope you'll agree to the transfer."

Jill nodded. She and Henry had already agreed that she should stay for as long as possible until Henry's own future was clearer. "I don't suppose that I have much choice?"

"Not really."

Jill left Lisa' office and went immediately to see Paddy.

"I'm sorry Jill". Instinctively, he understood Jill's reluctance to return to her old division, even in a senior role. "The conference world is pretty tough these days and, frankly, I'm not sorry to be getting out. But, if there's anyone that can bring in new audiences, it's you. I really do wish you well and I'm here for a few more days if you need any help after a handover which I thought we might start on Wednesday, if that's ok." Jill nodded. The industry needed more people like him and fewer of the young, absurdly assertive arrogant and ignorant youngsters who address everyone by their first name and maintain that everything is brilliant.

Henry could feel the tension in Broadoak House. According to the financial press, MP was about to confirm that it was in exploratory talks about a link with a UK company. At the mid-Monday-morning management meeting, known as the 4M meeting, which reflected someone's inability to count, HB confirmed that Chuck Charles had phoned him last night, at home. "He apologised for the slight delay in confirming the offer what he called a friendly merger of equals but said that it was imminent. That was the word used last week but he assured me that it would come very soon."

Hubert repeated his concern for the shareholders. "We must not be deceived by the language of these things. If any deal goes ahead, it will not be a merger, it will be a takeover and we, gentlemen, and ladies, almost certainly, will be out of a job. A few minutes ago, one respected financial source suggested on the radio that MP would probably propose an all-share bid, on the basis of the levels at the close of business last Friday. That would be unacceptable because our shares are rising and MP's are falling. If this is the basis of their offer, we should reject it unambiguously. Indeed, I've taken the precaution of drafting a statement in advance. He handed copies around.

"The board of Broadoak Oil confirms that it has received an unsolicited approach from a third party regarding a possible offer for the company. There has been no discussion and the approach has been rejected as it is not deemed to be in the best interests of the shareholders." Henry toyed with saying that it might be wise to consult some of the leading shareholders before drafting the statement but remained silent when he realised that many of them were at the meeting. He was still pre-occupied with what he might do to repel the bid.

Hubert continued.

"When the formal bid comes, many of the our shareholders will expect us to demand that part, probably a large part, of the price should be in cash. After all, some of our shareholders are pensioners and with Christmas coming, a few pounds in their pockets would not go amiss." Responding to an aside from Lance, he said that, whilst it was only September, the Christmas season started earlier each year.

"We all know that oil company share prices are very volatile. Unless the overall industry suddenly wakes up to the dangers of all these insane mergers that are putting cost cuts, short-term profitability and share prices ahead of medium to long-term risk and reward, I don't know what will happen." After a promising start, HB's comment, much longer than his usual utterances and certainly more complex, had petered out as he did not know how to finish the sentence properly and his audience did not understand what he was trying to say.

"And now, gentlemen, tell me your views."

Nigel Read was first. "Like the rest of you, I've been looking at the weekend press. Let me quote the *Sunday Gossip.* *"The management of Broadoak Oil is lacklustre, unimaginative and inadequate but, assuming that this hapless crew is ditched, to be replaced by executives from Muswell Petroleum, it is just possible that a takeover of Broadoak could yield substantial savings and rich pickings for shareholders."*

"This emphasises why we must publicise our views on the relative prospects for each company as soon as the bid is announced. I can't understand why Morton Hampstead and his friends haven't prepared our case in advance. I presume you still haven't received anything yet, HB, and that you'll be chasing them today?" Responding to the two questions, Hubert shook and then nodded his head. Perhaps they were slow to react because of something he had said? HB was upset at the paper's criticism but impressed by the conclusion. Perhaps, after decades at work, no, working, he could now retire, criticised but rich.

Others reported good progress on the plans already agreed. HB did not like what he was hearing. It seemed that his colleagues were now planning action that might just deter MP, if they had sufficient time, but that was unlikely. The last thing that he wanted, at his age, was to preside over major changes that he could not understand and which could ensure the continued independence of the company. He wanted the highest price for the company and the best personal compensation terms.

Henry spoke briefly about his US trip and then HB said that, as nobody else had anything significant to say, he and Henry would now compile a revised statement for the media saying that "very preliminary" talks had occurred. Inwardly, he thought that this would help push up the share price more effectively than the earlier draft statement saying that a bid had been rejected. He decided against revealing what the company was doing to make itself less vulnerable if a full bid were made. His colleagues were then dismissed with another reminder to do their best for the shareholders. The meeting planned for Tuesday was cancelled.

Perkins phoned Jill and asked her to organise a conference slot for him immediately after lunch on the Tuesday. This was convenient, because, as usual, a senior industry figure had just withdrawn. She must not mention Henry or Broadoak but she could reveal that a surprise speaker would be saying something newsworthy. Broadoak must not hear about it. "I do know what I'm doing. This is important for hundreds of people and please do make sure that the press are present."

Very reluctantly, Jill agreed, made the necessary arrangements and phoned some of her media friends. She couldn't imagine that he was suited to the graveyard slot. It needed a charismatic figure, with something to say and with an ability to deliver good jokes with the correct timing. Henry did not rate highly on at least two of these criteria. Still, he had said that his presentation would be newsworthy. Obviously, Broadoak did not know what he was planning but, if he bungled this, both of them could be out of work. How fortunate it was that she had been able to build their savings, secretly, over the years.

She glanced to see who else was speaking. The keynote speaker was the boring energy minister who had been in office for nine months which was a post-war record for any party. His personality, frequently compared unfavourably with that of a lamp-post, and his monotonous tone had often induced sleep in the most severely afflicted insomniacs. The press had received advance information from a government that leaked more effectively than a holed and rusty supertanker. He would be revealing the results of a review of government-industry focus groups which had been studying prospects for the further exploitation of the North Sea. Apparently, he had ruled out a review of review groups by a peer group as being unnecessarily complicated and a waste of taxpayers' money. All of this, of course, he had frequently told an anxious public, had been made "perfectly clear". However, it had been rumoured that a new specialist panel might be set up to ensure that the focus remained on review and peer groups. BF had been involved with some of the early "work". Apart from that, the minister was expected to praise the industry for the contribution it had made to the UK economy and to promise that no unfair taxes would be imposed, although the sharper financial journalists noted that the definition of "unfair" could be a source of contention.

Apart from HP, the UK politician and an unknown OPEC oil minister, it seemed that the usual assortment of boring, fourth rate individuals would be performing. Perhaps it was the news that Iraq was moving troops to the border with Kuwait, the alarmingly low stock figures from the US or the realisation that takeovers in the industry had not finished, but last-minute applications to attend the conference came in at a very pleasing rate. Jill assumed that the attendees expected that some of the speakers might touch on something relevant about the changing structure of the industry, which was the topic of the conference, but she knew only too well, that, however hard organisers try to ensure that speakers deliver relevant papers, there was no guarantee that anyone would conform.

She knew the procedure. "I have been asked by the organisers, and I thank them for the chance to speak to you today, here in... to address the topic of where this industry is going in the next decade. This is a fascinating topic but I believe that it would help if I sketched in some of the key events that have influenced us on our journey to where we are today. Let's start with the crisis of 1973-74." Then, some 35 minutes later, the speaker would suddenly pretend to realise that he had not addressed the topic for which he was hired, so the speech would end, with "I realise that I have not devoted much time to what might happen in the next few years, but, frankly", and here the idiot would smile faintly, as if preparing the frustrated audience for a joke, "forecasting, especially of the future, is very difficult. However, I hope that by sketching in some of the details of recent decades, I have indicated some of the relevant factors, that will, in my view, remain relevant and thus be important determinants, drivers, if you will, of the future structure of the industry in the years to come."

She shivered with embarrassment and hoped that at least her Henry would have something to say that was interesting but not damaging to their careers.

Chapter 27

Oil was still in the news on the Tuesday. Monday had been a slack newsday, apart from the Iraq story. Some business commentators, now convinced that Broadoak would soon be involved with Muswell Petroleum, had noted that the latter remained largely reliant on the Middle East. In contrast, Broadoak still had useful production in the North Sea and it was rumoured that their new well, offshore Ireland, could soon yield oil and good news. Analysts recalled that Chuck had also boasted recently that MP's oil stocks were low. Hubert, who never understood the economics of inventories, had fortuitously decreed that the company should never follow the "daft" policy of "just in time". His thinking had been developed after a bruising encounter with his lady wife over some domestic supplies.

Today's broadsheets had belatedly followed up a small news item from a Sunday paper. An independent human rights group was about to publish a report condemning some oil companies for their involvement in countries that disregarded human rights and actively suppressed their people with arms purchases financed from their oil revenue. One of the companies named in the report, it was claimed, was Muswell Petroleum.

Henry and Jill travelled together by train to London. Jill went direct to the conference where Henry would join her immediately before he was due to speak. He had declined his wife's invitation to lunch, saying that it was best if he arrived as he put it, facetiously, "just in time". Jill, not amused, was tormented by the fear that she would be a party to their collective commercial suicide. The journey was punctuated by Henry's frequent grunts as he tinkered with his notes. Jill did not know what he was going to say. "I'm still not sure myself, it's best that you don't know in advance and then you can't squeal when they torture you. Anyway, I'll want your reaction as a member of the audience."

The keynote speech from the vacuous and patronising minister was precisely as forecast by the media. Indeed, as he rowed through a sea of jargon and clichés, members of the fourth estate gleefully crossed off their predictions of the points that he would make. The end of his speech was greeted enthusiastically. It was unfortunate that the only way that this could be recorded was by applause and the minister smiled, confident that his presentation had been well received. The audience, of course, had clapped in sheer relief because the challenge to stay awake was over. One red-haired and slightly-built bespectacled female journalist applauded with such gusto that it was clear, very clear, that she had won the media's sweepstake on how many of the predicted points, suggested by the press before the presentation, would be made before the minister sat down.

Jill, whilst delighted at the attendance, now in the eighties, nevertheless, realised that, unless someone said something interesting, another 80 people would probably never return to a conference. Could she rely on the OPEC speaker, due next on the platform, or would it have to be Henry? The thought made her pale. Was their world about to collapse? Because an OPEC meeting had just ended, she imagined that the minister would want to discuss it. She was not disappointed. About six foot (1.846 metres) tall and clad in what looked like one of London's most expensive suits, he advanced slowly and majestically to the rostrum. The man had presence.

"I expect you all know that I and my colleagues concluded our meeting in Vienna, to discuss future production and pricing strategy, just a few hours ago." There was an expectant and respectful silence from the audience, although they knew that because the chairman had just told them. "I also expect that you want me to say something about our meeting. There was an early agreement that we should cut crude oil production quotas immediately, for three months, to prop up prices, before reviewing them again and unless there is a marked change in the market, I suspect that the lower levels will be sustained through the winter. I know that some mischievous and totally ignorant journalists like to write that we are always at each other's throats. That is not true nor is it fair to say that we are like a tea bag in that we are only effective when in hot water."

Some in the audience actually laughed at this old and unfunny joke: others, who had not heard the news about the cuts, looked astonished.

The minister continued. "That said, we feel strongly that it's wrong that we have such little support from other crude oil producers and supermajor companies, who are happy to take advantage of the higher oil prices that result from our sacrifices, when we cut output, and then boast about record profits. We rely heavily on oil income and the progress of our peoples, towards the standard of living that you all take for granted, depends on a fair oil price and a just share of the global market. I must warn you that political instability in some of our countries could occur if oil prices remain low. Think about that in the context of security of supply.

"We also deeply resent greedy consumer governments which take more in taxes on products, such as petrol, than we secure for owning and producing the crude oil. We deplore the unfair tax burden being placed on oil because of the campaign against greenhouse gases. We do not understand why, if you feel so strongly about cutting carbon dioxide emissions in the west, you subsidise indigenous coal and tax imported oil. Meanwhile, although oil prices are moving up for what I'll call economic reasons, we shall only be satisfied when they remain at current levels for many months. I expect a lengthy period of sustained low supplies to ensure a price level that is fair for producers and consumers alike."

Jill sat on the edge of her seat. This was, surely, going to be a very important speech. The journalists, aware that something significant had already been said, eagerly anticipated more. The minister looked around at the audience, relishing their sudden interest. After a dramatic pause, he resumed. "Now, I want to talk about something which is of fundamental importance to my people." The interest was almost palpable.

"I refer to the use of firewood."

Some listeners smiled, sensing that this was an example of ministerial humour. It was not. For another 30 minutes, the diminishing audience listened to an amazingly boring dissertation of a subject that was of no interest whatever to them. By lunch, about a third of the original audience had left and the remainder was highly critical of much of what had been heard. Jill felt for Henry. He had a mountain to climb and, almost certainly, he lacked the necessary equipment.

After a brief introduction, Henry, wearing a new dark suit, a white shirt and a Middleshire county cricket club tie, mounted the dais to scattered applause. Few in the audience would have dissented from Jill's view of his unsuitability as the first speaker in the afternoon. Several journalists had stayed but others had already made up their minds and recalled other engagements that demanded their presence. Some were chatting to industry delegates in the foyer but most were busy writing up the OPEC minister's severe warning.

Henry's opening comment seemed to confirm all that his wife, the audience and the remaining scribes had feared. "I have here a speech written for me by some public relations advisers." He did not mention that it was an old presentation that he had just pulled out of a file. He brandished the speech in the air and three journalists buried their heads in their hands, which was unfortunate because they missed Henry's next move. Ensuring that he was in full view of the audience and no longer standing defensively behind the desk on the podium, he tore the speech up and watched the pieces flutter to the floor.

"Let me make it clear, perfectly clear, as ministers tediously say, as if we can't understand basic English, what I've just destroyed was a perfectly acceptable speech. It said the right things, the sorts of things that can easily be forecast and which are often said by my friends in the industry. I imply no criticism of the authors of that presentation. I yield to nobody in my respect for an industry which has played a key role in the development of nations and many millions of people around the world during the last 100 years. It has allowed a life span and a standard of life that would astound our ancestors. I pay tribute to the thousands who have worked hard to achieve that and am pleased to be a part, a very small part, of that group.

"Today, I don't want to recite the massive achievements of the sector which are well known, even if some ill-informed pressure groups deny what they could see if they did but open their eyes. No, today, I want to look at some topics that need to be discussed and are seldom debated in public."

The audience, growing as some delegates returned belatedly from lunch, was silent. An expensive-looking film camera, dormant thus far and perched on a burly man's shoulder, came to life. The red light indicated that Henry's speech was being recorded and this reminded Jill to activate her own audio recorder. The journalists in the foyer returned, summoned by colleagues who sensed that something interesting might happen.

"What I have to say today will doubtless be dismissed by my critics, and I shall have plenty, as eccentric. They may well choose to ignore what I say because of my alleged inexperience. Perhaps I should say that I have worked in the oil industry all my life and I'm now aged 55. Yes, I've become a senior executive only recently but that doesn't mean that I don't understand this industry. Indeed, in some ways, that makes me more qualified than many senior managers who seldom leave their luxurious offices to see how the real world lives."

The atmosphere in the conference hall was electric.

"But, if my remarks are ignored, I believe that the industry in which I have worked all my life and for which I still have the utmost regard, will find itself in even more difficulties than it is today. That may sound boastful, but it's time for some straight talking. We live in an era where transparency is rightly demanded by society. We in the sector cannot, must not, ignore this demand and we must expose what we think is wrong and admit our mistakes. We're not a political party. It's time for honest talking and change and I'd like to make that clear, very clear."

The minister, who had remained to listen to Perkins, was quivering and Jill was shivering. Henry seemed more composed, confident and determined than she had ever seen him, but once on a flight like this, there was no way of predicting his destination. She trembled afresh when she recalled that he had only outline notes and was due to speak for about 35 minutes!

"The main subject of this conference is the future of the oil industry. I want to break with the tradition long since established in the conference world. I intend to speak on the topic that, presumably, induced you all to part with £550. I'm also assuming that you are not here just to avoid going into the office. If that's your real intention, I recommend the local park as some of the autumn flowers there are now at their best. Before I start my detailed presentations, I must emphasise that I cannot comment on the possible takeover of my company. I'm sorry, I should have said merger of equals. If any of you have come just to hear my thoughts on that, you might like to go for a walk in the park, which has now received all the publicity it will get.

"At present, because of the low crude oil price in recent months, although this seems to be changing, thanks to our OPEC friends, who have bravely just cut output, and reports that Iraq might take hostile action against Kuwait, the industry has become infatuated with mergers, alliances, joint ventures and all the other euphemisms that seek to conceal takeovers. If ever in doubt on whether two companies coming together is a takeover or a merger, look at the composition of the new board."

Henry's reference to OPEC's "brave action" was noted by the media. The audience was silent and the only sound was that of journalists turning pages in their notebooks.

"I want to start by talking about mergers in general. Let's begin by noting, as Harvard discovered in a recent study, that more than half of all such 'alliances' fail. In other words, shareholders in both companies, and certainly those in the purchasing group, often end up with shares that are worth less than before the takeover. Cultural difficulties means that historically deadly competitors suddenly must be friends but it's more difficult than that. Different companies have different ways of solving similar problems or coping with political or economic difficulties. Broadly, we use the same technology, but, in some areas, one or another of us has an edge.

"Bringing all this together and pretending, yes pretending, that it is an easy challenge to overcome is to indulge in self-deception on a scale that suggests a need for psychiatric advice. Management is deflected away from unimportant matters such as developing new technology, raising new capital efficiently and negotiating entrance to promising new areas, and towards genuinely important matters such as the design of the new logo and whether the initial letter of the name of the acquired company, once incorporated in the new group, should be in upper or lower case. I need hardly add that the names of the acquired companies are then dropped, usually about one year later.

"Inevitably, despite the dumping of thousands of staff, or should I say human resources, and I'll come to that later, the management structure, initially, is cumbersome, top-heavy and lacking in a common structure, or a basic understanding of culture, policy and experience. It's like expecting an Eskimo, accustomed to living in igloos all his life, to make sensible comments on the design of a tower block." Henry knew the value of colourful expressions and quotes.

"Because the management structure is so big, at least until some of the acquired senior staff can be pensioned off without too much of a fuss or leave because they loathe what they see, the new group is slow and unable to take advantage of the opportunities that it was too inept to accept when much smaller and more flexible. Can anyone tell me why, by merging two sluggish elephants, we should expect to see a gazelle?"

Jill, like the audience, knew that she was listening to a historic presentation. Just a few months ago, Henry was hidden in a dusty office, doing little of importance, whilst his brain and individuality were cruelly suppressed by his unthinking employers. He might be brave but if he carried on as he had started, as he obviously intended, he might soon be jobless.

"Regulatory authorities, understandably, and correctly, in my view, are becoming more suspicious of these huge takeovers. They sense that many of them, probably the majority, are against the public interest. That may often be difficult to prove so, in my view, they should err, increasingly, on the side of severity.

"Low share prices encourage lazy and ineffective companies to buy new oil and gas reserves by acquiring smaller groups. Then the level of drilling fades, with a negative impact on both the numbers of people involved and, of course, global reserves and thus future supplies. Even when two bigger companies merge, using their euphemisms, does anyone really believe that their efforts to find new supplies of oil and gas will be at the same levels as when they were separate? Of course not. Does anyone believe that competition is advanced? Are more jobs created? Of course not.

"This industry justly prides itself on technical innovation but we must remember that many advances come from small companies who have to innovate to survive. They are being bought up or being offered such small margins that many are vanishing. Size is no substitute for innovation. Of course, those individuals who devised and developed

331

that technology are not lost: some of them join the bigger companies but they are no longer the same people. They joined the smaller groups because they were encouraged by the absence of bureaucracy and company politics and because they could see the ultimate impact on their companies of what they were doing. They joined smaller companies because they wanted to work in what for them was a very acceptable environment. If they wanted to work for big groups, they would have applied so to do. Does anyone believe that a tiger retains all his grace and athleticism if he is caged?"

Jill was now shaking and she wanted to cheer Henry, who was obviously making his last-ever speech. She also wanted to shout out 'stop'. The audience was silent.

"Many in this industry have heard senior executives maintain that 'people are our greatest asset'. What insulting rubbish! Why do those who utter such nonsense compound their error by imagining that the people to whom they are speaking are as patently daft as they are themselves? If people are genuinely groups' most important assets, many directors should be fired for disposing of so many assets so often. Clearly, I understand that some people must lose their jobs because of the advance of technology but it's high time that this industry, now over 100 years old, found a better way of securing the right staff numbers and then maintaining that total, subject, of course, to new technology and unpredictable events. What particularly irks me is that staff numbers are augmented excessively when prices are high and then immediately cut as soon as prices slump. Excessive optimism is followed by unjustified pessimism. No wonder this industry has acquired a reputation for hire and fire. No wonder bright young graduates, desperately needed if the sector is to meet the demands imposed upon it in years to come, don't want to go into oil.

"Are we really saying that these companies, the biggest in the world, are forced to cut staff numbers every time that the crude oil price falls by a dollar? Groups know that the level of prices will recover because their own demand forecasts show a steady rise over the years, not least as the developing world develops. If the companies believe their own estimates, why do they remove those people who can assist them to participate in this expansion? Perhaps we should remember that these powerful groups, so many of which are currently badly led, nevertheless, have incomes higher than those of many UN members. One reason for recent high profits, of course, is that by denying the validity of their own demand forecasts, they destroyed much capacity so we shall see relatively high product prices for some time, whatever the price of crude oil.

"I am straying. I shall return to the subject of people later but now I want to turn to environmental matters. Firstly, let me pay tribute to the massive and costly efforts made by the sector to meet increasingly stringent and often irrelevant demands placed upon us by ignorant, unthinking and often unelected politicians."

Jill gulped. Now, having condemned his own industry, he's going to attack Brussels.

"We must fight these bureaucrats who don't realise that many of the measures that they are proposing, allegedly fundamental to health and welfare, could not have been implemented even a few years ago, because the technology supposed to gauge the infractions was not even invented. Now we're allowing ourselves to be manipulated into undertaking some actions that we know are expensive, unjustified and unlikely to achieve their objectives. These bureaucrats even reject the industry's suggestions for cheaper and more effective solutions to what, the officials maintain, are 'problems'. Some energy ministers who are not only ignorant but patently out of their depth should stay at home rather than meddle in matters that they conspicuously fail to understand."

Henry had effectively returned the comments that the minister had made, under his drunken breath, against him when he tried to make the after-dinner speech. Jill winced. What would he do with the rest of his life?

"Unless the industry stands up now, instead of lying down, like a comatose cat, it will deserve everything that's imposed upon it but the trouble is that the customers will have to pay. I genuinely believe that the industry's overall environmental record is excellent and compares favourably with any other in the world. It's certainly much better than our critics would concede. However, our reputation is being undermined by relatively few but unpleasant incidents and the determined efforts of self-appointed, self-important individuals living in academic towers and single-issue pressure groups who have but a tenuous grasp of the issues involved and who sometimes have only a nodding relationship with the truth. To them, ends justify the means, which, no doubt, has comforted the enemies of democracy for years.

"That said, I would like to suggest that companies, when operating abroad, especially in developing areas where governments are so anxious to find oil to lift their people out of poverty do not merely meet the environmental standards of the country in which they are operating. I would like to see them abide by the standards that we set in, for example, Oakshire. That cannot come tomorrow but we should work towards achieving that goal.

"If we are to provide the energy needed by increasing numbers of people in the next decade, we must make sure that governments, pressure groups and of course, our customers, understand our problems and don't erect unnecessary barriers. The price of this is that we communicate more constructively and accept that we are part of society. That is not to advocate that we become mesmerised by communications on each and every issue. Let's ensure that we never become besotted by focus groups, in effect, telling us what to do. Let's remember that management is paid, very well indeed, to manage, and that is what they should do in a democratically controlled context.

"I know that I shall be criticised for what I'm saying today, although I started by paying tribute to the industry for making the lot of mankind less brutish and short. Let my critics remember this. But it's healthy to ponder some issues and to tell everyone that we know that all is not well but that we're learning how to live in the new world and that we shall change. Privately, we know that we must. We cannot automatically assume that we shall always be allowed to do what we want, which is the arrogant assumption of some very large companies.

"I promised a few minutes ago to return to the subject of employment in the industry. Before I do, let me ask a question of those companies operating in countries where human rights are conspicuous only by their repression. You must accept that the government secures revenue from oil production, the development of which you have materially assisted. Don't you realise that this revenue is often used to buy arms with which to suppress the local people? If you do, do you think that your corporate conscience, if you have one, is offset by building a small local school and having discussions with some lowly local official on the need to allow human rights? If you don't, what planet are you living on?

"I want to conclude with some comments on employment, especially in relation to mergers. Nobody in the industry has a divine right to a job. Anyone believing this is out of touch with reality. I may well unemployed myself soon, very soon. Employers do have some responsibility to the community. Before my critics start salivating, let me emphasise, most strongly, that I'm not suggesting, for a moment, that oil companies become an arm of government.

"What I am suggesting is that one of the best contributions to communities is to create and sustain work and jobs. I don't want companies to create bogus jobs but I want my colleagues to have more consideration, during takeovers, for many good and loyal workers, who've been in the sector for years. Bosses can easily say that shareholders' prospects are improved by mergers but that's not always true, as history shows.

"Those leaders can expect substantial compensation for improving profit levels, often achieved by discarding people. Even if they don't reach their targets, our distorted society now pays failures at the top level of business massive compensation following the consequences of their incompetence. Too often, corporate failure prompts personal financial success. In contrast, many of the ordinary workers made redundant, 'because now we have two of everything' to use that insensitive and insulting phrase, know that they'll never work again. The huge redundancies that we have seen are rationalised by the predators as the price for ensuring that they survive. What nonsense! Is anyone really saying that companies with turnovers of many billions of dollars can only survive if they become even bigger?

"The problem is that whilst technology, asset portfolios, cash flow and all the other usual factors are considered, the human aspect is virtually ignored. To make matters worse, some of those taking such decisions behave in what many of us would regard as a totally unacceptable way. Let me tell you one story before I finish. I am not,

I repeat not, suggesting it proves anything nor am I suggesting that what I shall describe is confined to the oil and gas sector. It is not and please note that I am stressing this."

Jill, an ardent agnostic, shut her eyes and prayed. However contentious and serious his remarks, she suspected that Henry knew precisely what he was saying and was gambling on the likely outcome.

"One leading executive in the industry, not in the UK, boasts of how he deceived his group over many years. Apparently, he had some headed paper produced for some fictional companies. Then he sent bogus invoices, on their behalf, to himself. He authorised payment and I hardly need to tell you where the money went and where it continues to go, as far as I'm aware. That man is not fit to determine the future of thousands of jobs but that is precisely what he can now do. Assuming that this story is true, as I firmly believe it to be, and not just the silly and exaggerated boasts of an immature man of overwhelming conceit, he ought to be in jail. What we can also glean from this, and, let me repeat, I believe that his boasts are true, is that either his company is totally incompetent or corrupt or acquiesces in these crimes because it would be embarrassing to admit its incompetence to the outside world. On that basis alone, the company is not fit to make any acquisitions affecting the lives of thousands of other individuals, should it so decide.

"Let me emphasise that I know that all industries have known such characters and that it would be wrong to condemn the entire oil sector on the basis of this story and some of the problems I have discussed here. What I am saying is that we should be more open, more communicative on our faults and embrace change. Above all, we must ensure that people, as employees, members of local communities in which we work and as customers must be treated with greater consideration and respect, not just in empty press releases but in the real world.

"Finally, we must not believe that putting two companies together with massive loss of jobs, will automatically solve problems that could not be solved before when the groups were single. Mergers must take account of people if the industry wants to be understood and respected. We must shun the short-term blandishments so beloved of financial analysts and accountants who can seldom see beyond the end of their red braces. The industry seems to be in thrall to these mental adolescents whose concept of the long term is the bonus that they will receive in three months. Let us think more about people and the impact that ill-advised decisions can have on the thousands who have shown their employers sustained loyalty and hard work, over many years. They deserve better. Thank you for your attention."

Henry sat down. Jill was stunned. After years of sitting through hundreds of conference presentations she had never heard such a speech. The journalists were frantically scribbling down Henry's last comments. Worse still, the audience was silent. It was eerie. It would have been better if they had booed or even walked out. Suddenly, after what seemed minutes but which was but seconds, the spell was broken. A few members of the audience started clapping and to Jill's astonishment, it gave way to cheering. Never before had she seen an audience rise, but everyone was standing, standing for Henry, her husband, who courageously, had just talked himself out of a job because he was so honest. She felt proud. Tears were running down her cheeks. The frustration and irritations that Henry had discussed with her all through the years had come out and they had emerged, not in the privacy of their lounge but in front of an industry audience and the media. Even as Henry stood up, to acknowledge the sustained applause, he wondered what he had really said.

The chairman, a senior executive from a leading overseas company, as shocked as anyone else, thanked Henry for a courageous and stimulating contribution, the like of which he had never heard before in his three decades in the industry. As Henry tried to leave the auditorium, journalists surrounded him, asking questions. Many concentrated on the comment about the executive who had deceived his company but Henry was adamant that he would not say any more on that except that he was certain that the story was true. One perceptive scribe, noting that Henry had just returned from the United States, asked if the man mentioned was American. Perkins merely smiled and said "you may or may not think that: I shall not say".

A few interviews later, Henry rejoined Jill, whose eyes were still damp.

"What's the matter, why've you been crying?"

"I'm afraid that you may have just lost your job but, whatever happens, I'm really proud of you." With that, she put her arm around her husband, just as some of the photographers were pointing their cameras at Henry.

Henry recalled that he had been photographed at the motor show and, more recently, he had been filmed falling out of a car in Houston and being aided by an attractive girl. That had led to some jealous banter from his colleagues. So, this time, he said loudly that this lady was his wife. After all, he thought, most ungramatically, a chap has to be careful on who he is seen with.

Chapter 28

In the cab on the return to the office, an increasingly worried Henry listened to Jill's recording of his speech. He knew that he had been candid but only now did he realise how far he had gone and he was shocked at the number of targets he had identified. What was worse, however, was that he had diluted his key message. Clumsily, he had told the story about Chuck Charles, the real reason for the speech, at the end of his presentation. He should have known better: journalists with early deadlines often did not stay for an entire speech. The most important points should have been addressed early on and he had not been able to provide a copy of his speech because it was mainly spontaneous.

He would be dismissed, Broadoak would be sold and most of his friends and colleagues, whom he had grievously let down, would be made redundant. He was also angry that, after Anna's imaginative and brave action, he had failed to use her recording to advantage. He had let her down too and that really hurt. Chuck would never know about the speech and would continue stealing from the company. If he had been a little more thoughtful, he might just have succeeded in warning MP off.

He felt frustrated, guilty and very worried. He had made a mess of his entire life and ruined his one big opportunity. Even now, in the midst of this new crisis, he realised how much he was missing the girls. The frustration was worse than before he went to Houston. He had done much more than create a few memories: he had slithered over the boundary dividing friendship and physical desire. The huge injection of adrenaline, induced by his speech, was wearing off fast and his swift descent into a deep depression would have aroused the interest of the most seasoned weather forecaster.

Henry was convinced that the effort to save his company would soon explode in his face. For the second time in a few weeks, he faced unemployment because, as he saw it, he had spoken candidly on matters that he thought were wrong. At least, after his emotional television interview, it was accepted that he was grieving for lost friends and colleagues. Now there was no such excuse and he could not reveal his true purpose. He had wanted to secure publicity for the speech, including the comment about the thieving oilman, to warn off Chuck Charles but how could he explain all that to HB and, indeed, anyone else? Too many questions would be asked.

He had said that the industry had done much of which it could be proud and that he would concentrate only on negative aspects but none of that would count. Once again, he had provided ammunition for the industry's numerous critics. The sections in which he praised the industry and its personnel would be ignored and the headlines would concentrate on his trenchantly expressed criticisms. He would be perceived as a traitor and his only achievement had been to unite the industry's critics. Despite knowing that Jill's future was not very secure, he had gambled and lost. Trying to rationalise the situation, all he could tell himself was that MP would have bought Broadoak anyway. At least he had tried.

The taxi jolted to a standstill. Henry, absorbed in his fears for the future, remained seated, unaware that he had reached his destination, if not his destiny. "We're there, mate." Henry, still in a trance, looked at the meter, pulled out some cash and handed it to the driver. "Here, aren't you the guy that made that speech earlier this afternoon? I've just come on duty and I saw you on the news on the box. Good for you. It's about time that someone blew the whistle on these incompetent and dishonest bosses." The taxi driver omitted to mention that he had also seen reports that the UN Security Council might meet in emergency session within the next 72 hours to discuss Saddam Hussein's latest moves.

The driver's comment, intended as a compliment, merely confirmed Henry's worst fears. He really was a traitor and the nation had heard what he said. Now he had to pay more than just the taxi fare. By the time that he reached his office, he had decided against resigning. That would be cowardly but he would stay for as long as possible to allow him to think through his future. He also had a month's holiday entitlement which could be useful for planning. He sat in his office for a few minutes, meditating. For years, he had been obliged to listen to patronising rubbish from incompetent bosses. They were like politicians. They always assumed that they had a monopoly of knowledge and experience. Once he started speaking, the frustrations, simmering from deep within, for many years, had burst into the open. None of this mattered now. He had demonstrated that he was not senior management calibre, that he had no sense of diplomacy or even basic loyalty and was totally unsuited to his post.

Rose was out, visiting the dentist, but Henry's desk was plastered with notes taken by other colleagues and it was impossible to determine in what sequence they should considered. Before he could even embark on the task the phone went again. Could he participate in that evening's edition of *Newsnight*? He promised to ring back within five minutes with a definite response. It might be a good idea to have a word with HB first. He walked down the corridor, smiled weakly at HB's secretary, Benita, and asked if he could see the chief executive.

"Yes, actually, he wants to see you so please just go in but before you do, I must say that I thought that your speech was terrific."

"How do you know what I said?"

"An enterprising PR agency which wants our business sent a transcript round and a recording almost as soon as you finished. I think that they were keen to impress HB with their efficiency. He asked me to play the recording, you know he's not too happy with technical things, so I heard the beginning in his office and then read the transcript before circulating it to the board, as HB had instructed. If you don't mind my saying so, I think you're great." Henry forced a smile, thanked her and asked for a copy of his speech, explaining that he made it up as he went along. He began to feel as if he were watching a film in which the main character ricochets from crisis to crisis, whilst his situation becomes ever more helpless. He had seen many such films and usually felt smug as he anticipated the next serious incident. Unfortunately, he was the central character and this was only the beginning.

"How is HB?"

"Not in the best of moods, I'm afraid. Might be best not to provoke him."

The chief executive, pacing the floor furiously, resembled an extremely angry purple-faced tiger. Earlier, he had been recalled from the pub to meet an unexpected visitor and then Perkins had given an unauthorised speech which gave the company a very high and unwanted profile. Henry had to be dismissed.

Before Perkins had returned, HB had declined to give an interview on a BBC current affairs radio programme, which, on balance, had praised Perkins and thus Broadoak. It was unfortunate that the programme ended with the presenter observing "we asked Mr Perkins' chief executive, Hubert Bennett, for a comment but he declined, alleging that we would only twist everything he said."

Henry, uninvited to take a seat, remained standing in front of his chief executive, much like a child awaiting an angry parent's rebuke. "Look here Perkins, if you want to commit professional suicide, and that's fine by me, in fact, go ahead, as soon as you like, but why attack the industry that's given you your livelihood for decades? Why are you apparently determined to totally undermine all that we've tried to do together, for so many years, in just a few dangerous moments of poisonous talk? What the hell got into you again? Were you drunk?"

Perkins, despite all his frustration and worries, only just suppressed a smile.

It seemed that HB was not entirely delighted with the afternoon's events. This view was confirmed as the managing director's face assumed an even deeper shade of purple which prompted Henry to speculate on the prospects of his leader self-combusting. HB, waving his arms excitedly like a frustrated windmill reacting to an unexpected breeze, continued.

"For God's sake, man, do you have any idea of the damage that you have caused? Don't you realise that our company will now be treated as a pariah? Don't you know that this industry exists on the basis of mutual respect and that co-operation is essential for any group if it wants to survive? The institutions that hold large numbers of our shares know this and they will now, even as we speak, be looking to offload our shares as they know that their value will sink." Henry decided that it was not a good idea to tell HB that the stock exchange had closed some time before and that Broadoak shares had ended slightly up.

"This means that we are an easier takeover target than we were at lunch time and that wretched Chuck Charles will get us for a song and then make most of us redundant and pay us the minimum compensation they can get away with." Henry did not even notice that HB had ended a sentence with a preposition.

Perkins, so keen to save the company, had overlooked the implications of his speech on future co-operation with other groups and the likely impact on share prices. He struggled for breath and gave serious thought to fainting. The only problem would be that HB and not the beautiful Benita would give him the kiss of life. On second thoughts, HB would do nothing and order his secretary to leave him alone. No, he would not faint. Ironically, his speech had been designed to save the company. Not knowing what to say, and unable to identify Chuck as the thief, he said nothing. He was still standing as no invitation to sit had been forthcoming and that suited the hapless Henry. Standing would enable him to summon medical aid more promptly if HB exploded and it also meant that Henry could leave hastily if fighting broke out.

Henry knew what it was like to be an old wall, about to be struck by a huge ball swung by a single-minded crane as the significance of HB's remarks dawned on him. He looked at his feet, expecting to see steam rising as his whole body dissolved in a fit of hot embarrassment. He had probably ensured that his company, after 100 years of glorious independence, well, independence, would be bought by a foreign group for a derisory price. He might even be beaten up by dissident shareholders.

HB had not finished and was revealing an unexpected eloquence.

"I cannot think of anything that could have done us so much damage in so short a time. Even a major environmental accident takes a few days to fully register with the public. What you have done is to ensure that we're on every current affairs programme and news bulletin so everyone knows what you said."

Henry sensed that this was not a good time to ask Hubert about his invitation to appear on *Newsnight* but he had the wit to feign a need to visit the gents from where he told the BBC that he regretted that he could not appear. He returned to HB's room, wondering whether his chief executive had calmed down. He had not. Hubert's mood seemed to have deteriorated. The television set was on and Henry was about to be interviewed. Aware that he had to make his points succinctly, he was leaving out some of the qualifications he had included in his conference presentation.

"What can you say about the possibility of being taken over and can you please clarify your comments about the illegal and immoral behaviour of the non-UK executive that you mentioned in his speech?"

Another question was barked out before he could answer the first one.

"Mr Perkins. You've just returned from the US. Is the dishonest executive you mentioned an American? "

"You would not expect me, now, to say anything about the possibility of my company linking with any other. On the other matter, as I said immediately after my speech, I'm not prepared to comment on the person I mentioned except to say, once again, that I believe that what I said was true."

"Was he in any way connected with the possible takeover of your company?"

"I've said all that I'm prepared to say on that. If the individual in question hears about my speech, he'll know that I mean him but I certainly don't have any wish to undermine a fine industry. All I wanted to do was to point out that a very small minority of the industry's leaders, as in any major sector, is not entirely honest. We mustn't kid ourselves that everyone in senior positions is acting purely on behalf of his fellow workers or even shareholders. Some are behaving in a way that just advances their own interests and those of their friends on company boards. That's all I meant and I think that I'm only saying what everybody knows but seems reluctant to say out loud."

At this point, HB felt uncomfortable.

"You were fiercely critical of your own industry and, by implication, presumably, your own company. Do you expect to have to leave?"

"That is not for me to say. Others must decide but I certainly won't be resigning. I don't think of myself as the guilty man. All I did was to offer a blunt review of some aspects of the industry in which I have worked for decades. I did not say, nor am I saying now, that everyone is corrupt or that all companies are dishonest and untrustworthy. That would be nonsense. There are many thousands of very honourable people working in this industry. They're hard working, very experienced and have together been responsible for advancing the lot of mankind very considerably over the years, as I emphasised in my speech. I feel privileged to have worked with many of them in my own company and in particular I should like to mention my own chief executive, Hubert Bennett, who is a man of massive integrity whom I have respected for years.

"To indulge in a blanket condemnation would be silly. I was only saying that, contrary to the view that many companies try to portray, everything is not perfect and we must pay more attention to communicating what we're doing. In particular, we all must pay more attention to the needs of our staff and not to jettison them purely to meet the short-term needs or whims of the accountants and the finance people in the City, many of whom are know very little about this crucial industry. They are important but the industry should not be ruled exclusively by them. If we continue along these lines, young and talented graduates, that this industry needs, won't want to join us. If making such observations in a balanced, objective way is an offence calling for dismissal, perhaps I'm in the wrong industry anyway."

HB snarled. He knew that Perkins had outsmarted him and what made it worse was that Henry had not done it deliberately. He was far too naïve to manage that. "We'll continue this tomorrow".

Perkins returned to his own office, checked the messages outstanding, now re-arranged by the returned Rose and Jane, whom he had promoted, decided that those that he could deal with could be checked in the morning, ignored all those requests for interviews and went home.

That evening, he and Jill listened to the tape again, very carefully, and agreed that, given the nature of the oil industry and its importance in the world economy, serious repercussions were inevitable. Henry, as he put it, was as tired as a large block of flats, but he could not sleep. What would they do? Buying a bookshop in a small town in the south west seemed to be the best option but more discussion was needed after they had fully assessed their financial position.

Mike and Graham Warren were brothers employed by a leading maintenance company. Both were qualified and very experienced engineers and, over the years, they had worked together on projects around the world in the oil, gas and petrochemicals sectors. Now, as dusk blocked out the shapes of one of the UK's oldest refineries, they were both engaged in one last task for the day. Although they were widely respected for their professional skills and mixed well with their work mates, few of their colleagues really knew much about their background. Both men, in their late thirties, had been able to ensure that they could complete one more job at their current place of work. It was the MP refinery at Tadchester, in the north of England. They had been working there for four months and the security staff at the gates knew them well. As they drove their company truck through the official entrance, the night security man waved cheerfully.

"No rest for the wicked then?"

"Well, someone's got to do it", Graham replied.

He drove up to a parking area near a huge storage tank, holding about five million litres of gasoline and removed some equipment from the back of the truck, aided by his brother. Although the refinery usually operated on a 24-hour basis, there were few personnel around and the immediate area was totally deserted. Despite the MP boast that they cut costs by maintaining low stocks, UK management had gone its own way and, because demand had been unexpectedly weak lately, reflecting another rise in government taxes on petrol, all the tanks in the immediate area were full or nearly full. Other nearby tanks contained kerosene. The brothers took out eight conventional drums off the back of the truck and placed them carefully on the ground. Other equipment was handled even more cautiously and then the operation was repeated outside the temporarily deserted control room.

On the other side of the Atlantic, Chuck Charles shuffled through the thick pile of his rich brown carpet in his sumptuously furnished office, picked up the remote control for his huge 48" television set and pushed the right button to hear the latest business news from CNN. He had missed the headlines so was unaware of what was happening in the wider world but saw the familiar face of the UK correspondent who was just beginning his contribution. Chuck leaned forward. As

MP was close to bidding formally for Broadoak, he must know what was happening in the UK. When the deal was done, he would take Anna to London as his personal assistant for a few weeks.

The UK correspondent was saying something about an oil conference in London. "The oil industry has often been severely criticised by politicians on both sides of the Atlantic and by single issue pressure groups such as Greenpeace. However, this afternoon, speaking at a London conference, Henry Perkins, a general manager of Broadoak Oil, attacked some of the senior individuals in the sector as greedy, incompetent and guilty of putting their own interests above those of their staffs, particularly before major takeovers." Chuck sat on the edge of his chair, staring at the screen. A picture of Henry appeared at the top left-hand corner but Chuck was sure that he never met him in London or anywhere else. He'd never even heard of the guy.

"One of his most serious and specific allegations concerned an executive in the oil industry, outside the UK, who had systematically stolen from his company by setting up dummy companies and then submitting invoices for work that was never done. He then approved the payments and Perkins says that this man is now in a very senior position in his company. The UK executive refused to give any more details but industry analysts are pointing out that Perkins recently visited the US and that the mystery man may therefore be American. Now it's back to you in Atlanta."

Chuck suddenly felt ill. Of course, that miserable limey may not have meant him, but if there was the slightest chance... He dared not contemplate the outcome. All that he had enjoyed through his illegal activities would go. Was the Brit warning him to drop the takeover or was it just a very nasty coincidence? Could he take the risk? Perkins didn't seem very experienced: sensible oil people were not that open in public. Hastily thumbing through a one-year old tome containing biographies of all the senior people in the industry, Chuck could find no reference to Perkins. The worried American decided to go out for a quick early meal, by himself, and think what, if anything, he ought to do. A decision would have to be taken tomorrow, after a good night's sleep had put matters into a clearer perspective. Above all, he must not panic.

The boss of MP turned off the television set so he missed an analyst commenting on the dangers of the low US inventory levels, particularly if the Middle East erupted. He also missed a comment from an OPEC minister that the group's production cuts might be sustained for much longer than anticipated. Already bullish traders, also influenced by forecasts of cold weather, had added $4 a barrel to the price of West Texas Intermediate crude oil and oil shares were reflecting this rally.

At the club, Anna, unaware of the outcome of her enterprise, was parting clients from their money. She had decided on a new look tonight. Some time had been spent curling her hair into a ponytail which she pinned up. Then, when the customer was losing interest, a mass of blonde voluptuous curls would be shaken free to caress the victim's brain, like a warm and friendly puppy. Then, a little sensuous lick of the customer's ear and another $40 would transfer ownership for about eight minutes work.

Mike and Graham were also working hard. Slowly and methodically, as behoved trained engineers, they were setting about the task of blowing up the refinery.

Chapter 29

Henry woke at 6.56 am on Wednesday, precisely 15 minutes later than usual. Just for a glorious nanosecond, his mind was blank: there was no sense of guilt, frustration or even impending unemployment. Jill was still asleep, peaceful and innocent. Then reality struck Henry with the force of a supersonic cricket ball. Still half asleep, he turned on the radio, just in time to hear the headlines.

"Saddam Hussein, the Iraqi president, has been warned by the UN Security Council to withdraw his troops from the border with Kuwait. However, in a speech late last night, the Iraqi leader claimed that the troop movements were part of an exercise that had been planned last year. He said that the UN warning and the US reaction, assuring Kuwait and Saudi Arabia that any military move against either of them would be construed as an attack on the United States, was hostile and totally unjustified. Meanwhile, three American warships have been routed to the Persian Gulf and are expected to arrive shortly. There was also intense diplomatic activity in Whitehall last night and Prime Minister George Minor is expected to offer the US his total and immediate co-operation and backing for any action they might take."

Some moments later, the news item was concluded with a comment on the implications for the oil sector from the business correspondent, John Applecart. "When the markets open later this morning, oil shares are expected to soar. Analysts say that the companies that will benefit most from the crisis will be those with major production away from the volatile Gulf. Apart from the developing crisis in the Middle East, US oil inventories are at their lowest levels for some years just as weather experts are forecasting a period of colder weather.

"It also seems that OPEC will proceed with its plan to cut output for the whole of the winter, to push prices up as some member states desperately need higher revenues. Another factor that will influence the market is the major explosion and fire that occurred late last night at Muswell Petroleum's large refinery at Tadchester in the north of England. It is unlikely that the plant will be at full production for a year. Initial reports say that two contractors were killed. All other personnel are accounted for and are safe and well. Muswell is thought to be planning a bid for Broadoak Oil."

Henry, now fully awake, was trying to absorb all this and to work out the consequences. He grabbed the two daily newspapers that were sitting on the doormat. There was only scant mention of the developing crisis in the Middle East: it had obviously erupted too late for the papers and there was no coverage at all of the refinery fire. He turned to the business pages in his favourite broadsheet. There, staring out at him was a report on his speech and a photograph of him, embracing Jill. Pale and frightened, he flicked through the piece, which seemed to be fairly factual but his eyes were drawn to the last sentence, written in bold. There was an editorial comment on page 12. Trembling, and with a great sense of déjà vu, his face as white as an advertisement for a new and obviously improved soap powder, he sought the page. The comment appeared under the headline:

The acceptable face of capitalism

It is a widespread belief that this country is really run by faceless individuals, taking decisions frequently based more on self-interest than on society's needs. Seldom has any insider confirmed such thinking as eloquently as Henry Perkins, a senior executive with Broadoak Oil. In a carefully balanced presentation he told a London conference yesterday that much was wrong with the international oil industry and that it would be naïve to assume that its leaders always acted according to the book. He cited one alleged conspiracy where an executive, possibly an American, had allegedly deceived his company for some years by submitting bogus invoices to himself, approving them and collecting the money.

Perkins also drew attention to the "hire and fire" policies which dominate the sector, especially after takeovers, and which, in some instances, he claimed, are inspired by the greed of the leaders of the predator companies and not by wider economic considerations for employees or shareholders.

Doubtless, Perkins will be severely censured for providing the industry's numerous critics with so much ammunition, especially as this is his second candid comment in recent weeks. The first occasion was after a fire killed some of his colleagues at a company depot. We believe that, by exposing some of the less desirable practices, he has done the industry a great service and has reminded it of the need to take action before governments intervene, with, assuredly, less success and at higher cost. Whistleblowers are seldom popular and we can only hope that the courageous Henry Perkins is not fired himself. He deserves better even if the industry in which he works does not deserve him.

Henry reeled. He took a cup of coffee to a still drowsy Jill and hissed "look at page 12, dear. I must go, I'll ring you if possible with any news. Have a good day". With that, he was gone before Jill could comment apart from bestowing a traditional and sisterly kiss on his recently shaven cheek.

By the time he had reached the office, some 30 minutes ahead of his usual schedule, Henry was feeling a little more confident and was pleased to learn that HB would only be in the office after lunch. Perhaps, by then, he might have cooled down. Anxious not to inflame the situation any further, Henry declined requests for media interviews. He had bought all the daily papers to see what kind of coverage, if any, he had attracted. Only one other paper, a tabloid, from the same stable as the paper that had praised him, had mentioned the presentation. What they said in an editorial, headed **"SHAME!"** worried him.

We have often slammed the oil industry for its greed at the pump, its disinterest in the environment and for the fat cat salaries it pays. When these giant companies, often richer than the countries they're exploiting, get together, and say that they have to become even bigger if they're to survive, they cruelly fire thousands of innocent and loyal people. In the callous words of one executive, "we don't need two of everything". All this pleases the money men, obsessed with short-term results who don't give a fig about the people involved and the fact that many of them will never work again. All they care about is saving money and lining the pockets of the bosses and shareholders.

WE WERE RIGHT!!. How do we know? Because Henry Perkins, a big boss at Broadoak Oil spilled the beans at a London conference yesterday. He admitted all this and more. Well done Henry! Now perhaps the government will act at last and curb these greedy companies and the fat cats that lead them."

Henry turned on the television set in his office and checked the latest news stories on Ceefax. The refinery fire was mentioned and it was confirmed that two contractors had lost their lives. Suddenly, he realised that, having arrived at the office much earlier than usual, the news programme was still on.

"We are receiving reports that the explosion and fire at the Muswell Petroleum refinery in the north of England might have been deliberately started by two contractors who were brothers. An apparently authentic letter from the two men has been released by the editor of the local newspaper who found it when he opened his office earlier this morning. The men had a mother who was born in Aipotu and lived there all her life. The brothers wrote that she was suffering from cancer and the regime refused their father, who is a UK citizen, an entry permit to take his wife for treatment to the United States. The mother died and the father committed suicide. The note says that the brothers took every precaution to ensure that nobody else would suffer when they caused the explosion which, it now seems, was much bigger than earlier believed. The plant has sustained very severe damage.

"The men said that they approached the management of Muswell Petroleum, which owns the Tadchester refinery and who are the leading foreign operators in Aipotu, for help. They claimed that the company refused to discuss the issue and even returned their letters asking for assistance. The brothers argued that their own deaths counted for nothing whilst so many people were denied basic human rights in Aipotu. They ended by saying that, if what they have done draws attention to the selfish actions of greedy companies which support such despicable regimes, and makes decent people think again, their deaths will have been worthwhile. They ended by saying "all that we would ask of our friends is that they continue the struggle after we have gone".

Henry was so deeply moved that it was some time before he was able to ponder how this and all the other relevant news stories might influence any bid from MP. His morning passed quickly and he received some calls from friends in the industry, offering their "private" congratulations on his speech and expressing the hope that all would be well and to let them know if he needed any help. They, at least, he assumed, had read the full text and this prompted Henry to ensure that a full copy was sent to all staff with a note explaining that this was a direct transcript and it was important that they knew what he had actually said. He emphasised that he had been careful to present a balanced picture and that parts of the media had only selected what they felt was most newsworthy.

Nevertheless, he was still worried about his future and, naturally, that of his company. He went for an early lunch with his old friend and colleague, Stan, who insisted that some good could come out of the speech, but he did not know the source of the story about the US thieving oilman and did not ask. Only Anna, Wendy and Henry knew and that was how it would remain. The next meeting with HB was scheduled for later in the afternoon.

Chuck always arrived at his Houston office by 08.30 but today, concerned at local radio reports that Iraqi aircraft had already bombed Kuwait City, he was in much earlier than usual. He was very worried about the explosion in Tadchester and the bid for Broadoak. Another worry was the possibility, albeit remote, that he might just be the dishonest oilman cited by that guy Perkins. He had convinced himself that although Henry was unintelligent, he should not be under-rated. There were many other executives who were playing the same game as Chuck but could he risk all? At 8.00 he was to address a board meeting and the takeover was at the top of the agenda.

Back in London, HB was attending a meeting of an industry group. Anticipating that the Perkins speech would be discussed, he had decided to distance himself from the hapless Henry. To his astonishment, even before the meeting started, his senior colleagues came over to congratulate him. One said, "I know that the media was bound to misrepresent some of the things that Perkins said but what's important is that the industry has been seen to be aware of the criticisms made by objective external commentators. We needed to admit these things and then we can go on to demonstrate that we're doing something about them. I know for a fact that government was becoming very worried that some of us were seemingly riding roughshod over our critics. What Perkins has done is to show that we are listening, and I think that will deter the government from taking direct action and we all know that such action would have severely damaged us. Frankly, Hubert, I shouldn't be surprised if he was poached for a senior position in some new full-time industry-wide task force."

HB swallowed hard. He had not anticipated this although some doubts had begun in his mind when he read the laudatory editorial that Henry had already seen. All this meant that he would have to be very careful on how he handled the second part of his interview with Perkins. It would be difficult, if not impossible to withdraw some of the comments made yesterday. Perhaps he should start by apologising if he had been a little sharp. Having returned to the office, HB turned on his television set and checked on share and commodity prices.

Most oil company share prices, already encouraged by OPEC's hints, had risen dramatically on the news from the Middle East. Broadoak shares had advanced by a quarter in a few hours. In contrast, the MP share price had fallen, apparently because of the fire at the UK refinery, its low stocks in the US and its dependence on Kuwait for crude supplies. All this meant that it could not profit from the higher prices and would have to buy-in expensive product although the extent of its purchases was uncertain because human rights activists, deeply moved by the brothers' suicides, were organising embargoes at the company's filling stations in the UK and US.

The Broadoak share price had gone up faster than most, as commentators realised that only a small proportion of its oil came from the Middle East. There was also a report from a respected analyst that the well being drilled by the company off the coast of Ireland had found oil in commercial volumes. Some commentators claimed that Henry's speech had reflected well on the company and this could add a few more pence to the Broadoak share price in their fight against the takeover. Another analyst suggested that just as some groups had realised that rather than fighting environmental issues, the most sensible stance was to take commercial advantage of the trend, Broadoak had established a clear lead in its desire to meet public expectations on other important issues. This, she argued, would doubtless be reflected increasingly in their financial results.

HB had not forgotten that he had many thousands of shares and, overnight, he had made a very substantial gain on paper. He decided to wait but he must choose the timing of a sale very carefully: he had to sell at peak prices, before any bubble burst. He must not miss the chance of becoming seriously rich. Apparently, the crude oil price was expected to go higher because the US government had refused to take any emergency supplies from its strategic stockpile, as an emergency had not yet developed. The chief executive pondered all this. He still wanted Broadoak to be sold but, given current share prices, would selling his stake give him a higher return?

The answer was being formulated in Houston even as HB was speculating. Chuck had taken a decision which, in the best tradition of some senior managers, was based largely on his perception of his own circumstances. After some considerable thought, he believed that he was not the thief mentioned by Perkins but it was not worth the risk. The challenge was to imply to Broadoak that the withdrawal of the intended bid was being made in return for their silence. This would not be easy. Another problem was that Chuck had been the most energetic supporter of the intended takeover and his cogent reasoning, backed by his sheer enthusiasm, had persuaded his reluctant colleagues that he was right. Under no circumstances must his fellow board members know the real reason for this volte-face.

Suddenly, it was obvious. Because of the Middle East crisis, low US stocks, OPEC's recent comments, the fire at the UK refinery and the boycotts, apart from the reaction to the Perkins speech, the value of Broadoak had climbed whilst MP's value was tumbling. Now, clearly, was not the time to make a bid. Spare cash would be required to buy costly refined products on the open market.

Chuck began the meeting.

"Gentlemen. I'm real tarred, I guess like you guys, trying to keep up with all that's been happening in the last few hours. Some of you look as watt as a sheet and I sure feel sect to my stomach but ahm glad that yawl on tom today. Yawl know that I was real keen to buy Broadoak and I guess yew agreed. We awl decided that by acquiring this outfit cheaply many of our problems would be solved. It was jes too suede for words. What mattered was price. Now, following hints from those OPEC guys on production levels, and the new crisis in the Gulf, crude oil prices have soared as fast as an escalator on heat. We might lose our Middle East oil and we haven't much elsewhere then we've got the problems caused by the UK fire, especially as we deliberately cut back on our inventories, expecting oil prices to fall further. Now, damn me, we've got a boycott of our gas stations here and in the UK because of our activities in Aipotu. I can barley believe what's happened.

"Yawl recall that Broadoak appealed to us because they had production outside that god-damned Middle East. Now the rest of the market, thanks to that lahr Saddam, one real main man, knows that too. So, at the share price in London a few minutes ago, it would now cost us a hell of a lot more to buy the company. As things are now, I don't think we should go ahead."

His colleagues remained silent.

"There's something else. I thawed that between us, we'd met all the Broadoak guys who counted in that set-up. Most of them seem as lazy as a bump on a log and we decided that they couldn't even mount a piss-up in a bar. As yawl know, their top man is a funny guy who's pissed most afternoons, which is when I give him a bell. I was confident that he would let the company go for a song because he's as thick as a brick. Now it seems that they've got a particularly brave guy called Perkins who gave a very astute speech to a conference in London yesterday which suggested that if we do decide to proceed, we could be facing not that pathetic old relic, Hubert or Horace or whatever his name is but a younger and dynamic guy who seems to have his finger on the public pulse. He talked about redundancies after a takeover and I guess he's got public opinion on his side. If we were discussing this now, for the first time, would anyone recommend we buy this outfit?"

Chapter 30

Hubert Bennett, pensive, pending his next meeting with Henry, wondered whether he had been too aggressive with him. Several City commentators had attributed part of the rise in the price of Broadoak shares to Henry's speech and HB's anger towards Henry had reflected his view that the value of his shares would plummet. The opposite was happening. Over the years, HB had taken advantage of many generous share options which had been readily agreed by the non-executive directors on the remuneration committee. It was, of course, just a coincidence that he had appointed them himself.

When the price of Broadoak shares started climbing, HB had phoned his adviser who suggested that he should wait as he expected the values to rise further, provoked by international events. HB had decided to follow this advice but he had to monitor events, minute by minute, lest he made a catastrophically expensive mistake. After years in the business, HB had sensed that this was, as BF would have said, "a small window of opportunity".

He reviewed the factors that were driving his share prices higher and smiled because he had no influence over any of them. Apart from takeover gossip, there was the Middle East crisis, the developing shortage of both crude and refined products in the US, the refusal of the American government to release oil from the Strategic Petroleum Reserve, OPEC's decision to restrain output, the reaction to Henry's speech, rumours of Broadoak striking oil off Ireland, a long-term weather forecast of colder than usual weather, and, of course, the refinery explosion and its impact on the UK market. HB left his television set on to follow price movements. He knew that this powerful combination of positive factors might never recur and he must take advantage of it. He decided to wait a little longer, providing that prices did not fade.

His thoughts turned again to Perkins. Was Henry more astute that HB had believed or was it a lucky fluke? Whatever it was, it seemed that the new general manager, wittingly or not, had played a part in helping to release HB from the unrelenting drudgery, deceit and dishonesty of the business world. Hubert was staring into space, towards the panelled wall, decorated with numerous photographs in which he happened to feature. One showed him with a former prime minister and in another he was with a young Princess Margaret. It seemed that he had either not met anyone famous for decades or if he had, no photographer had been present. Allowing his gaze to drop, he belatedly saw a note on his desk from Morton Hampstead, the head of the company's defence team, who was now based in Broadoak House. It was terse but said much. "The new circs mean we must reconsider our stance. We're much more valuable now. Pl. can we talk soonest?"

HB remained uncertain about Henry's role in the advance of the share price but had decided that his new potential wealth meant that he could be charitable. There was a knock on his partially open door and being an astute businessman, HB immediately recognised Benita. Simultaneously smiling and pushing the door wider, this multi-skilled young lady advised him that "Mr Perkins is here for his meeting". "Come in my dear fellow" boomed HB and Benita slid gracefully out, having wafted an elegantly ringed hand to confirm the audible approval that Henry had already received, indicating that he could enter the hallowed sanctum.

Perkins was immediately suspicious. Yesterday, HB was angry: now he was friendly. He even asked how Perkins was although he did not wait for an answer. He then thanked Henry for coming. The stark change of mood indicated that he was about to be dismissed. For the second time in a few months, the end was nigh. Clearly, there was no point in being hostile to someone whose career was about to be destroyed. What would be his new life? Already, Henry had received encouraging messages from all the main political parties, each of whom wanted him to assist them. The ruling party was prepared to offer him a senior advisory role, on the newly-formed business, ethics, and society team, already dubbed by the press as "beast". The creation of the new grouping had been announced by the prime minister within hours of Henry's speech, prompting some press comment that the move was "opportunistic" which was grossly unfair according to politicians interviewed on the *Today* programme who sought to make that "clear, very clear". Henry was perceived as "progressive" and "just the kind of man we want".

The opposition had invited him to become one of the leader's main speech writers and adviser on industry because he was progressive whilst being conservative and "just the kind of man we want". He was seen as a natural to be included in the party's inclusive team. The third party was not sure what they wanted from him, but they knew that they needed him, partly because he was "progressively liberal and clearly a democrat" and partly because the other two parties were rumoured to be interested. All this was very flattering but the simple truth was that Henry wanted to stay with Broadoak.

"Sit down, Henry. There's something that I want to say."

Henry shuffled uneasily. He would be very sorry to leave as he was beginning to enjoy his new job despite the problems. Unlike many colleagues, he had not climbed the corporate ladder gradually, acquiring that self-confidence and arrogance that seemingly accompanies every promotion. Instead, he had been catapulted to the senior ranks and felt rather like a mountaineer, experienced on the foothills, suddenly being asked to climb Everest without oxygen before breakfast. However, he was learning and he still thought that he could cope with a really big job. He knew that recent events had changed him fundamentally but he was surprised to realise that he was already wondering what he would say to the media.

"Naturally, you wouldn't expect me to say that I'm pleased to be leaving such a fine company. I've enjoyed working with Broadoak and I have enormous respect for the international oil industry which has done so much good for so long without any real acknowledgement, which, of course, I thought that I had made clear, very clear, in my speech. That said, I must admit that if I had stayed in the company, it could have been embarrassing for them, so I decided that the honourable course was for me to resign. Although I regret nothing and withdraw nothing, I accept that, in a sense, I was the architect of my own departure. That's all that I shall be saying. Thank you."

"I think I owe you an apology."

Henry looked up from addressing an imaginary group of reporters to a real Hubert Bennett.

"Yesterday, I must admit, my back was troubling me. You'll remember that I fell off a ladder some years ago when the damned thing inexplicably just gave way under me. Went to hospital and they told me that I was very lucky to have avoided serious injury but it wasn't all bad. They made me promise that I would never dig the garden again. I agreed."

HB smiled. HP did not.

"Occasionally, I find it difficult to move without some pain. Yesterday was a bad day and I'm sure you realised that something like that made me so rude. I'm sorry." Henry realised no such thing and resented the implied insult to his intelligence. HB's adventures with ladders were of very little interest to him. The phone rang. There was to be a further stay of execution. Henry, as always, trying to do the decent thing, stood up, gestured to himself and then the door, hopefully implying not that he wanted to be on his way out, as would doubtless happen shortly, but questioning whether he should leave the room. HB paused, frowned, nodded and waved his ash-ridden cigar towards Perkins and the door, managing to give Henry's dark suit a rather spotty appearance. Henry tried to brush it off and inevitably only succeeded in converting the spots into lines. At least that made him look more managerial.

Perkins heard HB say "hello Chuck".

This was the man who had threatened the takeover of his company and whose own morals were lower than the deepest well his company had drilled in the autocratic Aipotu. Why was he ringing HB? Was he planning legal action against Henry? Surely, his presentation had offered no clues on the American's identity so there was no possibility of legal action? Even when asked by the media for a clue on Chuck's identity, he had said nothing. Calming down after a few seconds of panic, Henry realised that the obnoxious Chuck would hardly initiate legal action as that would prompt the question of why he had even thought that he was the anonymous cheat. No, it must be about the takeover. Henry waited in Benita's room.

Jill's own life was in a whirl. Her husband had ensured that, even although only a few journalists mentioned the name of the conference organisers, they had secured an enormous amount of publicity. Better still, the trade journalists, whose articles would appear later, in the weeklies and monthlies, were more professional and would mention the organiser's name. Even in these difficult times, attendance at any future oil conferences organised by Jill's group would do better than the opposition. It seemed as if her own business life was destined to prosper even if ironically, the reasons for this would also end her husband's career. Henry had phoned twice already and although she made allowance for his usual pessimism or realism, as he called it, the outlook was poor. Hubert had been very negative yesterday.

HB was listening intently to Chuck Charles. The American began by saying "you know Hugo", which prompted Hubert to deny knowing anyone called Hugo before he realised that Chuck meant him. HB's only contribution to the conversation was the occasional "yes" or "I understand" until he said, "so you'll be putting out a statement in 10 minutes and you'll copy it to me?" HB wanted to finish the call as soon as he could. "Thanks for letting me know and I wish you well, too."

HB immediately phoned his financial adviser and sold every last share he had in Broadoak. After confirmation that the trade had been carried out, at a suitably encouraging price, he rejoiced silently at the prospect of imminent retirement and the purchase of the local pub. Then, realising that some action was required, he shouted out "Benita, come in immediately, please. Call the merger team together immediately and tell them that I want to see them all in my office, come hell or high water, in 15 minutes."

Henry, pleased to be so early for the meeting, sat silently in Benita's room, awaiting a renewed summons that did not come and decided against returning to his own office. HB, trying to suppress his excitement, had forgotten Henry. Perkins knew that he only had to wait for a few minutes but whatever Chuck had said, his own future was much more important to him.

HB sat back in his chair, luxuriating in his new position. Whilst the takeover might have given him a golden handshake, the rise in the share prices was very handsome compensation, and, of course, he had a very good pension. He was so happy that, just briefly, he even pondered ringing Mrs HB to give her the good news. No. He had not phoned her from the office for at least 10 years and she might immediately panic, thinking that something serious had happened. It was best not to frighten her.

Members of the merger team drifted in and by the deadline, only one was missing and he was on a three-day course that, for just £2,500, taught management how to deal with difficult staff. He had not intended to attend this workshop but it was now necessary because he had earlier sent three of his colleagues on a "self-assertiveness in the office" course.

Hubert wasted no time.

"Lady and gentlemen. About 15 minutes ago, I had Chuck Charles on the phone. They've had a board meeting and they agreed unanimously that they would not be pursuing their bid to buy us now or in the future."

HB looked at his watch.

"They will have put out a statement a few minutes ago, so the news is in the public domain and, in case you haven't heard, PISS have corrected their stocks figures for the US, so the oil shortage is not nearly as serious as was thought."

The immediate reaction around the table was one of relief, although Lance Boyle seemed to be having one of his occasional asthmatic attacks. At this point, Benita entered again, seemingly on cue, and gave a note to HB. He read it and light-headily said that he could confirm that it confirmed MP's confirmation that it would not be pursuing its interest in Broadoak. Henry tried to look pleased but it all seemed academic although his speech had been designed to achieve that precise objective. He had, surely, helped to save his colleagues' jobs but he would be dismissed for having spoken out. The ultimate irony was that nobody would ever know what his role had been. That really summed up the story of his life.

HB paused for breath and this gave Alan Stewart the opportunity to ask the obvious question. "Did they say why?"

"Yes, I'm coming to that. As you all know, the oil price shot up in the last few days, partly because of the OPEC decision to curb production and more importantly, because of the Middle East crisis and the supposedly low level of oil inventories. He pointed out that our share price had soared and, although he thought that it was excessive, and that he did not really understand why, he had to deal with realities. Because of the Middle East crisis, they expected oil prices and share values to continue rising and they also had to concentrate on rebuilding the UK refinery and finding alternative suppliers at a difficult time. Then he said something odd and he even spoke more slowly, as if he was keen that I wrote down what he was saying. It almost seemed as if he was reading from a prepared statement. Since then he's faxed it so I can read it to you.

"My board was also influenced by your guy Perkins and his comments on redundancies. It was an impressive speech and it made me think about the ethics of business. I guess I've made mistakes in the past, like everyone, and, although, of course, there are other factors, perhaps I and my colleagues can wipe the slate clean by not pursuing you and the massive redundancies that would result. Please tell Perkins that." Perkins the hero swallowed hard. Lance continued to gasp and Henry's other colleagues congratulated and thanked him.

"Then Chuck told me that we were no longer a sensible acquisition so he was not going ahead with a bid and in today's circumstances, he could not imagine that anyone else would be looking to buy us. I'm sure that we're all very relieved at the news. We shall be discussing this again soon, in more detail, especially why we were so unprepared but now, if you'll excuse me, I have some unfinished business to attend to with my friend Henry."

They all trooped out, leaving Henry and Hubert alone. The former congratulated the latter and said how pleased he was to hear the news. "Now that's out of the way, you and your team can face the future, in the years that lie ahead, in the future, with more confidence." His nerves were beginning to influence his words.

"Thank you. I think that we've been lucky but at least we're safe for the present. What it demonstrates, I think, is that we must be better prepared. The trouble is that we're all so busy that we can't spare the time to think about the medium-term future of the company and, for example, the changing world in which we operate. But you know all about that. OPEC and Saddam Hussein may not help next time. However, I am most anxious to discuss your future."

Henry nodded. He was keen too.

"I think that I explained, and, I hope, apologised, for my strong comments yesterday. I've thought it over and I realise that I reacted much too quickly and I was unfair. I suppose that I've been at the top level of oil industry management so long that I've overlooked some of the basics and my mainly supine colleagues are usually reluctant to point out where we're all going wrong. You did that and I commend you for your courage in speaking out as you did. I must confess that I should have been happier if you'd told me in advance what you were going to say but if you had, we both know that I should have forbidden you to make the speech. There's something that I meant to ask you yesterday but I forgot. When you were in the States did you, by chance, see Chuck?"

"I can promise you, HB, that neither I nor any of our colleagues in Houston had any meetings with him whilst I was there. Indeed, I can say, quite truthfully, that I have never even spoken to the man."

Occasionally, HB could be very perceptive. He noted that Henry had not specifically answered his question but wisely did not press for a response. "I suspect, Henry, and I don't want you to say anything, not a single word, that apart from thanking OPEC and Saddam Hussein, I ought to say thanks to you for the way that things have turned out. Somehow, God knows how, I think that you were more involved than we shall ever know. Say nothing now or in the future. Promise me."

HB smiled and HP nodded.

The chief executive then told Henry that he was to be promoted, to the new post of Director External Affairs, with immediate effect. He would, of course, have a salary rise and seat on the board and would be allowed to recruit up to four new graduates to assist him and he would also be given the funds to bring his overall department up to strength. Hubert extended his hand in a gesture of congratulation and Henry beamed broadly.

Jill's delight at the news was expressed physically and Henry thought that she seemed to be a new person. Curiously, as they lay in bed together that night, she had the same thoughts about her husband. He seemed more mature, physically more imaginative and unusually assertive. She attributed this to his newly found self-confidence. He attributed her more liberal approach to her newly-induced sense of stability. The radio had been left on and the midnight news was beginning. The headlines prompted Henry to sit up.

"After sustained diplomatic pressure and the imminent threat of US and UK military action, Saddam Hussein, the Iraqi president, has withdrawn his forces from the boundary with Kuwait. He maintained that his army was only participating in a training exercise and that, contrary to western press reports, it had never been his intention to attack his neighbour. Saddam claimed that there was absolutely no substance to the reports and the exercise had been planned months before. It was another example of western propaganda designed to influence neutral members of the UN Security Council against Iraq. Governments in the Middle East expressed their relief at the news but the US administration warned that the west must remain vigilant for as long as what it called 'this tyrant' is in office."

Later, having neglected to silence the radio, Henry heard on the business news that the sudden end of the crisis had caused crude oil prices and oil company shares to slump on the Japanese stock exchange and that a big decline was expected when the US and UK markets opened. The fall had also been prompted by reports that OPEC members, taking advantage of the high price that had prevailed after their earlier production cuts, had increased output, despite the accord to cut levels. Crude oil prices could tumble by as much as $5 from their earlier inflated values.

HB, listening to the same bulletin, but fortunately, in another bedroom in a different county, smiled broadly. He fell asleep before the main financial news was broadcast so missed confirmation of the story that the Petroleum Industry Statistical Service had now apologised for issuing incorrect figures on oil stock levels in the US. A "genuinely human error" had led to a substantial under-estimate for both crude oil and refined products. (This was later crudely reported by one UK oil tabloid as "Industry PISSED off".) The last item was from an Irish source that claimed that the Broadoak well was dry and that the rig was to be moved away within a few days.

and then…

Much happened in the next 18 months.

The media, angered by HB's hostile comments at the annual general meeting, were influential in prompting the administration to investigate Hubert's sale of his shares, alleging insider trading. HB, who never thought of himself as an insider, retired as chief executive although he became a non-executive director. Henry was instrumental in securing a very generous financial gesture from the company to acknowledge HB's leadership over many years, culminating in the defeat of the takeover. Nobody within management actually asked what he had done but HB was instrumental in securing a very generous financial gesture from the company to acknowledge the efforts made by Henry and his colleagues for their efforts in defeating MP.

Alan Stewart became the chief executive and Michael Michaelson, the US affiliate's economist, was brought over to the UK to become managing director, to replace Lance Boyle, who left suddenly "to pursue other interests". Broadoak, of course, thanked him for his loyal service. Stewart, Michaelson and Perkins were perceived by the City as the architects of the defeat of MP and the trio was assisted increasingly by the academic economist, Alex Gardner who was now basking in the fame resulting from the television adaptation of his satire on business. The quartet, using their new contacts, and taking advantage of persistently low interest rates and the disarray of Muswell Petroleum, organised the acquisition of the enfeebled American company in a move that was warmly applauded by the financial sector. Henry had not been to Texas since the defeat and then acquisition of MP, but had kept in touch by phone with some of his local friends. Now, with two colleagues, he was visiting the US to organise some of the details relating to the takeover. In particular, the supremely confident Perkins was looking forward to meeting Chuck in his own office, just outside Houston.

The meeting was obviously difficult but Henry, who had done his homework, explained how economies would have to be made and sadly, that meant that there was no place for Chuck. He felt sure that he would understand. The American executive, who had long feared this interview, expected Henry to give some clue that he, Chuck, had been the person mentioned in the speech. He had earlier decided to make a pre-emptive and generous gesture, designed to establish the answer to this vexing question and, simultaneously, to buy Henry's silence. He had even rehearsed his speech.

"You'll know that my contract allows for compensation amounting to two years salary and of course, there are other big benefits that I'm entitled to. I've been lucky in my career and I was genuinely moved by your comments on redundancies. I want to tell you that I don't want any compensation and I'd be grateful if the money could be allocated to others less fortunate than me."

Henry had not anticipated this but reacted very quickly.

"My dear chap, I wouldn't dream of that. You are contractually and morally entitled to compensation and that's that. He then said, with some emphasis, I can think of no reason, absolutely no reason, why I should accept your kind and thoughtful offer, none whatever. Why shouldn't we honour your contract? You will be paid every last cent."

A confused Chuck tried to hide his disappointment at hearing that he would be receiving so much money. Surely, if had been the guy that Henry mentioned in his speech, the Brit would have tried to penalise him through cutting his compensation in return for not revealing his identity? Did this mean that he was not the thief? He was puzzled and angry. Later that day, a distraught Chuck had decided that he was not mentioned in Henry's speech. That meant that he could have proceeded with some modest acquisitions after the Broadoak debacle when the market settled down again. He had banking friends who had already promised him the necessary finance but he had desisted, even when the climate for mergers had improved, fearing that Perkins would reveal his identity. Now he had nothing but his compensation and unemployment. All his worrying had been for nothing and it had cost him more than he dared calculate.

A truly jubilant Henry looked up some old friends that evening and enjoyed himself enormously. Having more money to spend on more girls, especially as it was not his, added to the fun. He delighted in dispensing dozens of dollars and found that he was even more popular than he had been during his last trip when he was only a general manager. It was a pity that Wendy and Anna were both on holiday but he did know that in advance.

The following day Henry asked for a full list of staff on the US payroll. As he glanced at it casually, one name leaped out at him. He dialled the individual's number and told him to come and see him immediately, in the boardroom. The Muswell man knocked timidly on the open door and, when beckoned, sat down opposite Henry. He tried to speak but a restraining hand and fierce glare from Mr Perkins silenced him.

"I'm going to speak and I don't want you to even open your mouth. I see that you've worked here for about six months. I presume you've enjoyed working here?" The sullen victim nodded, sensing that it might be best to say as little as possible in an effort to terminate this interview rapidly. Clearly, nothing would be gained by beginning a conversation. He knew why Perkins was in town. "Well, BF, I'm going to terminate your contract, with immediate effect." As Henry enjoyed hearing himself use the phrase, he repeated it. "Just in case you don't understand what I mean, let me express it in American. I'm going to have to let you go. With immediate effect. You're fired. Goodbye and shut the door after you."

BF said that this was unfair and that he was sorry to have tried to dismiss Henry but please could he have another chance? Henry pointed to the door and shouted "did you ever give anybody a second chance? Get out". He really had enjoyed that session.

Uniting the two groups meant that there were opportunities for cost savings. New terms of employment allowed Perkins and his senior colleagues generous bonuses if profitability was improved and disposing of so many people would be a material help. It almost became a game: the more staff who were dismissed, the more money Henry earned and the more he enjoyed life.

To justify the acquisition and to please financial institutions, severe cuts in numbers were essential in the UK and US. About 60 per cent of these would be of MP personnel. One problem was how to break the news to the individuals concerned without causing a weakening in morale, as employees wondered if they were to be dismissed. There was an easy solution. Every US office and installation had a public address system and Henry arranged for the names of all those who were to be fired to be read out at each location at precisely the same time, as far as possible. The names also appeared on the company's internal web site.

Henry's metamorphosis, which had begun in the club, had taken hold. Jill, now promoted in her own company, and spending more time with Denis, was disgusted.

"Why are you like this? Are you trying to retaliate for all the frustrations that you suffered for decades? If so, you are fighting the wrong people. You're attacking the very people I thought that you'd defend! You're just like those senior managers you used to despise. What's happened to the old Henry, the one that I married? He's gone and I don't like his replacement. You're besotted by money and power."

Henry ignored what Jill had said and prattled on patronisingly about basic economics. "Quite simply, we now have two of everything and we cannot achieve the cost savings that the city and our shareholders demand unless we have a major clear-out. The industry today is all about efficiency and we cannot lag behind our competitors in what's an increasingly difficult world."

The first step in the UK for PETS, the personnel employee termination scheme, was to dismiss the hundreds who worked at the Broadoak refinery. It was uneconomic to operate two large refineries in the UK when market demand was weakening. The MP refinery, rebuilt and modernised after the fire, was sophisticated and efficient so the Broadoak plant would be closed and the site sold to a supermarket. The refinery had been the only significant employer in the area so the impact on the local community was considerable. Local shops had to close, because of the new competition and the younger refinery engineers were forced to become shelf-fillers and checkout staff if they wanted to remain in work locally. More mature staff faced permanent unemployment even although many were only in their fifties.

As Henry explained to the local people, "I've a business to run, not a charity, and we just can't afford to keep this plant open. If we do, we could undermine employment prospects elsewhere in the group." It was unfortunate that this comment coincided with a statement from the newly-appointed head of corporate communications, Jerry Kann.

The company had appointed four new non-executive directors, who would receive £100,000 annually for about 50 days' work.

An angry Jill attacked Henry again about the job losses. "Let me get this clear. You're sacking many hundreds of innocent and hard-working staff, in Broadoak and Muswell, just like the old Henry, because you've got what you and your cronies crudely call an overlap in physical and human resources. After closing offices, filling stations, depots and a refinery, you'll make massive cost savings. What else do you achieve? I'll tell you. Fewer jobs and less competition. Will motorists pay less for their petrol because you're allegedly more efficient? Ha, ha. Who benefits? Shareholders, many of whom don't need more money, and you and your colleagues. Are you happy that your income's linked to the numbers of people you condemn to permanent unemployment?

"Why did you buy Muswell? I think you bought them because they'd threatened you with a takeover, so you would have been one of those prematurely rejected by an industry that you had served all your life. It was revenge, wasn't it Henry? But, as I've said before, you're taking it out on the wrong people. These poor people are just like you a year or two back. Don't you remember how you felt? What became of your sense of injustice and promises to behave differently, when you were promoted? What on earth has changed you?

"Why are you like this? I still don't know for sure that the thief that you identified in your speech was the boss of MP but even if it was, and I don't know how you found out, don't you think that you've descended to his level by firing all these people?

"Where have all your fine morals and principles gone? Why've you changed? I'm really disappointed in you. I just don't recognise you these days. I don't like what I see at all. You're just like those people you used to hate."

Henry ignored the main charge.

"I agreed with my informant that I would never reveal either who the thief was or how I found out. As for saying that our taking them over was motivated by revenge, well, that's frankly, silly. It made good business sense and many of those that have been fired would have lost their jobs anyway, if MP had won the battle, so they can't complain. Anyway, look at our financial results, you'll see just how justified the acquisition was. Our return on capital has risen spectacularly and our shares have gone up. It's been a success."

Jill observed sardonically that it was not a success for those who would never work again. Her husband resumed.

"There are rules in business and you can't change them, even if you want to, if you want to succeed. Business is all about increased efficiency and we must listen to the financial institutions and our shareholders. They want higher profits and they want them now. It's really not just the oil industry: all industries are competing not only internally but with each other, for new people, capital and opportunities and we have to work in a society that demands higher environmental standards but which is often not prepared to pay. What can I and my senior colleagues do? We want to remain in business so we have to play according to the rules.

"We must move with the times so nobody can have job security any more and that's why we use, I mean, employ people on short-term contracts. There's a lot of rubbish talked about 'fat cats'. Companies compete for senior managers so they must be rewarded, through salaries, share options and of course bonuses for reaching targets. That's the way that this game is played and it's the only way if you want to survive."

Jill sighed. She was not sure that she wanted to live with this new, greedy, soulless corporate monster. "Do balance sheets show how people are treated? Is profit all that matters? Who are you? I don't know you any more."

Neighbours Ian and Shirley had invited the Perkins in for a drink. One of their rare but regular meetings was not due for some weeks, so the Perkins, whose relationship was becoming increasingly strained, were speculating on the reason for the invitation as they knocked on their neighbours' door. After routine pleasantries, Ian took the initiative. "It's always a pleasure to see our beautiful and successful neighbour and her famous husband but we asked you in tonight because there's something that we wanted to tell you. You remember the builders who said that they might be interested in buying our place and some land for new houses?"

The Perkins nodded in unison.

"Well, they've been back and made us an offer, that at our stage of life, we simply couldn't reject. Apparently, they already have provisional planning approval to knock down our house and to build three new houses on our land and on some that they're buying from our neighbours on the other side. They plan to start work within three months. We know that this means major disruption for you, but frankly, we really didn't have a choice. Sorry."

Henry and Jill looked stunned. They would be living next door to a building site for many months and the value of their own property would fall although that mattered rather less, following the bonus that Henry and his board colleagues were collecting each quarter when performance matched some easy targets that they had devised. Henry's income had also risen as he was now a non-executive director of several companies. Naturally, he had been happy to offer similar posts to some of his new friends.

"Obviously, Ian, we shall be very sorry to see you go and I can't pretend that we're happy at the thought of all the noise, dirt and dust that we'll have to endure for weeks but we wish you well and understand why you took the decision. I'm sure that we would have done the same in your position."

Jill nodded, thinking that this might be her prompt to leave Henry, and asked where Ian and Shirley would be going. As part of the deal, the builders would pay for their furniture to go into store for as long as necessary and would also house the couple in a luxurious flat for up to six months. This would give them plenty of time to find a new home in the same area or somewhere else. At present, they just didn't know where they would go.

The following morning, Henry phoned the builders and persuaded them to visit the Perkins' home that evening. He then told Jill what was happening.

By the end of the week, the builders, now delighted that they could extend the size of the estate and take advantage of the rise in house prices that had occurred in the previous quarter, had agreed to buy Chez Perkins. Henry secured a premium of 70 per cent over the market price and also successfully negotiated a series of other astonishingly generous concessions. The builders, in turn, were delighted at the opportunity to buy substantial land, in prime areas, from the company at very reasonable rates as depots were closed.

Henry and his colleagues also had to consider the choice of location for the new head office. Despite some swingeing costs imposed on anyone who wanted to use the capital's roads and the almost unbearable pressure of using the antiquated and potentially dangerous public transport system, companies still wanted to have major offices in London. It was, therefore, an easy decision to sell Broadoak House, which was bought by a television cook for £120 million. The MP office in the country had spare capacity as 500 of the European Union regional staff had now moved to a brand new block in central London. This gave Henry the opportunity of moving to the country, close but not too close, to head office. The journey to work only took about 15 minutes, providing the chauffeur eschewed the main roads. The new home was the very definition of pretentious but, as Henry explained to Jane, who had now replaced the retired Rose, there were problems. For example, it was difficult to find gardeners and reliable staff to assist with dinner parties were equally elusive.

Henry's contribution at her conference had made Jill the toast of her company and she had followed this success by organising an international event where the attendants "visited" through the internet. Jill, too, now worked long hours and her journey to the office was longer. Sometimes, especially when conferences were imminent, she stayed in a hotel close to the office. Fortunately, Denis was often available to take her out to dinner when she worked late. The only time that the Perkins spent together was mainly over the weekend, because of work pressure on Henry. Usually, both Perkins were too tired to indulge in much conversation and their relationship was even more negative. Jill was now actively pondering divorce. One Sunday, she made an effort to have a conversation.

"You remember Wendy, Lynda's girl? I heard from her the other day. Apparently she's working in Houston."

HP tried not to look startled.

"I told Lynda that you ought to look her up next time you go there. You'd like to see a friendly face out there, away from work, wouldn't you?" Henry nodded but didn't ask what Wendy did or where she did it.

A few weeks later, Henry and some of his new graduate colleagues, who were already provoking much innovative thinking, were disentangling some remaining UK MP assets and activities. One suggestion was that as the company had left central London, Broadoak ought to acquire a luxury three-bedroom flat with meeting rooms in the capital. Henry readily agreed.

His main interest, at this time, however, was the result of the latest and last MP well that the group had been committed to drill in Aipotu, although there was a tacit understanding that three more would be spudded. The experts' view was that there was no prospect of finding oil or gas. Later that week, Henry was dining with a very senior civil servant, Sir Augustus Knowall, who tactfully but unambiguously indicated that the government would be pleased, very pleased indeed and grateful, if Broadoak would withdraw from Aipotu. The new Henry merely looked serious and emphasised the difficulties of what he called a premature departure and how any early disengagement could undermine the company's ability to secure exploration acreage elsewhere. Somehow, it didn't seem right to say that the company had already taken that decision on purely economic grounds. The civil servant looked more pensive, leaned forward, stared meaningfully at Henry and muttered "very, very grateful".

Another six months passed and Henry Perkins, OBE, an enthusiastic member of a QANGO investigating employment opportunities in the oil sector, was thumbing through an oil magazine review of a major conference and exhibition scheduled for Houston shortly. That reminded him. He pressed a buzzer under his desk, to alert his newly-appointed PEA, personal executive assistant, that he wished to see her.

The door was pushed open and a stunningly attractive girl entered. She was wearing a black suit and white blouse and her high-heel black suede shoes glided through the carpet, collecting whiskers en route. She sat down without waiting for an invitation and looked up, leaning forward expectantly, with large, innocent blue eyes, like a hopeful child about to be asked what was wanted for a birthday present, subject, of course, to continued good behaviour. She waited until the door had closed fully, smiled a greeting, crossed her long and elegant legs, leaned forward to squeeze his hand and said "Hi Perky, what's up?"

"I was hoping that we can have dinner together today, as I want to discuss the use of the company flat with you." Anna grinned and nodded meaningfully.

ISBN 141202937-6

The Displaced
by
Sharif Gemie